Reviews for
# HIGH BRIDGE

"Great novelists can reveal more about the past than the best historian. We in the profession don't like to admit this, but writers can provide a sense of place, time, tension, sight and sound that those of us bound by the convention of footnotes cannot achieve. Michael Miller is such a writer and High Bridge a book that brings to life late-nineteenth-century America's politics of sex, race, money, and power. A most enjoyable and useful read indeed!"

—**Jeffrey A. Engel, PhD**, Director, Center for Presidential History, Southern Methodist University

"*High Bridge* by Michael Miller is a brilliantly crafted novel that blends true history and fiction to tell a story of two American icons. Miller utilizes the actual history that Grover Cleveland and Matilda Joslyn Gage both lived in the Fayetteville, NY, area at the same time in the mid-nineteenth century. With no existing historical proof available on how much a young Grover Cleveland may have known or interacted with Mrs. Gage during this time, Miller fills in the gaps with compelling fiction. He tells a wonderful story of what might have been, truly capturing the essence that history knows both Cleveland and Gage to be: honest, fair, and defenders of human rights. As a historian and a native of the Fayetteville-Manlius area, I can attest to Miller's impeccable research in writing this fascinating novel."

—**Laurence L. Cook**, Presidential Historian and Author of *Presidential Coincidences, Amazing Facts, and Collectibles*, and *Symbols of Patriotism: First Ladies and Daughters of the American Revolution*

"A highly engaging and thought-provoking journey into what might have resulted if suffragist Matilda Joslyn Gage and future president Grover Cleveland, who lived in the upstate village of Fayetteville at different times, had instead known each other and become friends. By endowing them with a twenty-first-century social justice consciousness, the author skillfully invites us to consider the issues they faced, which we still do today."

—**Sally Roesch Wagner,** Founder and Executive Director, Matilda Joslyn Gage Foundation and Museum, and Author of *The Women's Suffrage Movement, We Want Equal Rights!: The Haudenosaunee (Iroquois) Influence on the Women's Rights Movement, Matilda Joslyn Gage: She Who Holds the Sky,* and other books

"It was so exciting to see history come to life in Miller's *High Bridge: Matilda and Grover Battle Learned Ignorance.* The Fayetteville village scenes were so vivid, compelling me to read on, considering the fictional relationship between the Cleveland and Gage families. This book recreates important moments in New York history that need remembering. I can't wait to recommend this book to fellow readers."

—**Maija McLaughlin**, Local History and Special Collections Librarian, Fayetteville Free Library

"A moving and inspirational novel, beautifully rendered, with evocative themes and fascinating characters. Author Michael Miller's depiction of nineteenth-century Upstate New York leaps off the page with vibrant images, pitch-perfect language, and nuances of customs and behaviors. The book's themes are particularly relevant; the nascent perspectives of nineteenth-century progressives with respect to inclusivity and equality, which the book so vividly portrays, are still unrealized—and are in fact currently under attack in our nation."

—**Robert Steven Goldstein**, Author of *Will's Surreal Period, Cat's Whisker, Enemy Queen,* and *The Swami Deheftner,* and other novels

"Michael Miller's *High Bridge* is a cleverly written historical novel that imagines the suffragette, abolitionist, and free-thinker Matilda Gage befriending a young Grover Cleveland in the New York town where both lived. Set in the late 1800s, the story sets the stage for the type of president Cleveland would become. It's well researched and a delight to read."

—**Carter Taylor Seaton**, Author of *The Other Morgans*

"As far as records show, activist and author Matilda Joslyn Gage (1826–1898) and President Grover Cleveland (1837–1908) met only once during their lifetimes. However, in *High Bridge*, Michael Miller reimagines with a certain verve the intertwined lives of these two nineteenth-century historical figures, who have largely receded from popular historical memory but to whom we should be reintroduced. Gage was one of the era's leading feminist and abolitionist activists, as well as an early and staunch supporter of Native American rights. Grover Cleveland, the first Democrat to be elected to the presidency after the Civil War and the only one to serve two nonconsecutive terms, is known for strengthening the power of the executive branch. In this fascinating novel Miller traces both of their paths to activism from early hardships and years of political apprenticeship at local and state levels. It is an engaging novel, well worth taking the time to read, and trust me, it will make you pick up another history book to get reacquainted with this period."

—**Sharon Halevi, PhD**, Director of Women's and Gender Studies Program and Chair of Department of Multidisciplinary Studies, University of Haifa

"*High Bridge* is a wonderful story. It brings the past alive and conveys a great sense of place. Miller's research pays off with lots of fine historical details. Matilda Joslyn Gage, a little-known figure from the women's movement of that era, clearly deserves to be rescued from obscurity."

—**Eileen Heyes**, Author of *O'Dwyer and Grady Starring in Acting Innocent, O'Dwyer and Grady Starring in Tough Act to Follow, Tobacco U.S.A., Children of the Swastika*

"High Bridge by Michael Miller is an intriguing and informative read that illuminates the role of Grover Cleveland and Matilda Joslyn Gage, an early feminist and suffragist. The story unfolds in the almost forgotten heyday of upstate New York when it was the hot bed of commerce with the Erie Canal as the economic engine and the political cauldron of women's rights. Heady stuff that is not necessarily evident in the contemporary landscape.

"Miller does an admirable job of tying together bits and pieces of history to weave together an exciting and often heart-wrenching story that moves easily from fact to fiction and back again. His research is top notch and serves him well as he brings to life a time and circumstance that are easily forgotten. The book is also prescient as so many of the issues he writes about are with us today. It serves as a way of looking back at the past to see how it might serve as aids to navigate our course forward."

—**Bird Stasz Jones**, Professor Emerita, Elon University, Co-author of Blue-eyed Slave and Hold Fast

"In High Bridge, Michael Miller does what the historian must do: He convincingly transports us back to a time and a place, and introduces us to compelling characters whom we want to know better. With a light but precise touch, Miller imagines a youthful friendship between Grover Cleveland and human rights advocate Matilda Joslyn Gage. In High Bridge, you crouch in fear that an Underground Railroad rendezvous might go wrong; you can hear the noise from the docks along the Erie Canal; you tense up when Gage represents a Black man wrongly accused; and you marvel that the impish Cleveland boy somehow became the solid two-time president. The imagined Cleveland–Gage relationship, in which the activist is the mentor and the future President is the protegé, is the glue that holds the book together. High Bridge is a great history lesson, a great metaphor for the times we live in, and a great read."

—**James D. Nealon**, Author of Confederacy of Fenians

"Michael Miller has a kind of time machine. His new novel, High Bridge, transports the reader into the compelling lives of Matilda Joslyn Gage, future president Grover Cleveland, and others through a series of momentous events and developments in the tumultuous mid to late 1800s in the United States. In his hands, it all remains accessible, proximate, and keenly relevant to matters we still struggle with in our culture today. Miller has masterfully done his part in carrying out his own book's theme—that we must, each one of us, relentlessly pursue equality and opportunity for all with both creativity and energy if our future is to be better than our past. High Bridge is immersive and terrific."

—**Greg Funderburk**, Author of The Mourning Wave

*High Bridge*
*Matilda and Grover Battle Learned Ignorance*

by Michael Miller

ISBN 978-1-64663-813-0

Published by

**◤ köehlerbooks**™

3705 Shore Drive
Virginia Beach, VA 23455
800-435-4811
www.koehlerbooks.com

Cover art: The painting of *Pittsford on the Erie Canal* by George Harvey (1837) is an image in the public domain provided via the Wikimedia Commons. https://commons.wikimedia.org/wiki/File:Pittsford_on_the_ Erie_Canal.jpg

The map of Onondaga County in 1848, appearing also in the front pages, was generously made available by The Lionel Pincus and Princess Firyal Map Division, The New York Public Library. https://digitalcollections. nypl.org/items/a652d480-d35a-0133-201b-00505686a51c

Front pages: The painting of the *View of Erie Canal* by John William Hill (1829) was generously made available by The Miriam and Ira D. Wallach Division of Art, Prints and Photographs: Print Collection, The New York Public Library. https://digitalcollections.nypl.org/items/510d47d9-7ba7-a3d9-e040- e00a18064a99

The street map of Fayetteville in 1849 by Porter Tremain in the front pages was provided courtesy of the Onondaga Historical Association.

# HIGH BRIDGE

*Matilda and Grover
Battle Learned Ignorance*

## Michael Miller

VIRGINIA BEACH
CAPE CHARLES

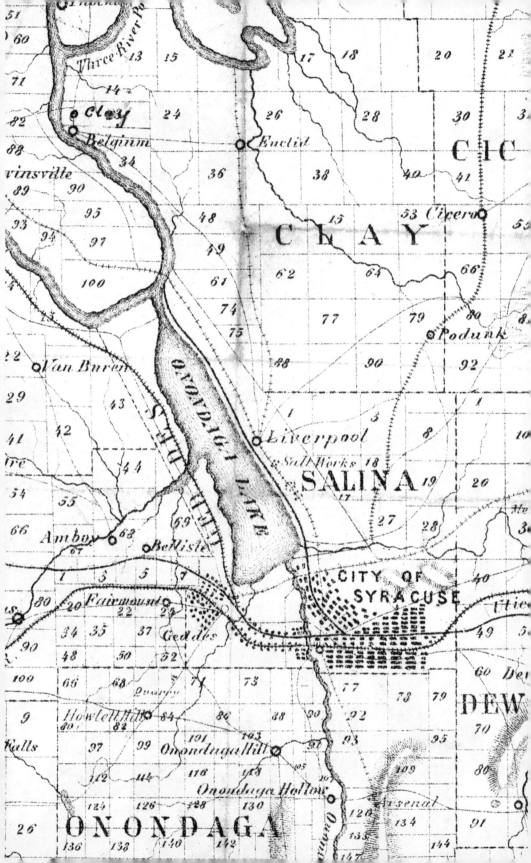

# M A P

### of the

## VILLAGE OF FAYETTEVILLE, NEW YORK.

### With the

### Adjacent Lands, and Water Powers.

Population
944

Scale. 4. Chains to an Inch

Porter Tremain

1849

*To my wife,*
*untold thanks and love.*

# TABLE OF CONTENTS

# PROLOGUE

Gage home, 210 East Genesee Street, Fayetteville, New York
Wednesday, March 14, 1888, 3:00 PM

T EMPERATURES PLUNGED TO frigid single digits. Winds howled. Bare trees bowed. Snow piled to depths of nearly five feet. The Great White Hurricane, the blizzard of blizzards, brought the Northeastern United States to its knees. Millions of people were snowbound. Hundreds died.

Sixty-two-year-old Matilda Joslyn Gage sat in her cozy, dry parlor, a virtual prisoner of the winter. As she gazed through a window half covered by drifted snow, she confided to her daughter, "Maud, in less than two weeks, the National Woman Suffrage Association is supposed to meet in Washington. I worry. Will attendees living in eastern New York and New England be able to get to Washington?"

Maud offered, "I cannot help the others, but I can clear the way from our home and get you to the train in Syracuse."

"Thank you, but that is only part of the solution. Will the NWSA be able to get notices out to people if mail and telegraph systems are paralyzed? Darn if this storm thwarts our hopes, prayers, and plans for women's rights. Will those who are not so committed not make the effort to come? Will attendance suffer? Will our movement be thwarted?"

By the time Matilda arrived in Washington on March 25, it was apparent she had little to be concerned about. Nearly two thousand driven people successfully braved the elements. The campaign for women's rights would not be denied.

## Morrison-Clark Hotel, 1011 L Street, Washington
## Sunday, March 25, 1888, 5:30 PM

A dozen past and present officers of the NWSA collected in a large meeting room of the hotel. After greeting each other and milling about, the women sat in chairs about a grand cherry table. A set of portraits hung on the walls, all European men who fought for the nascent United States and its ideal of freedom for all—Friedrich von Steuben, Casimir Pulaski, and Gilbert du Motier, the Marquis de la Fayette. It was unclear whether the piercing gazes of these icons were condemning or egging on the women. Did the painted patriots "see" that a storm was brewing?

Matilda took the floor, pleading with her colleagues sitting around the table. "We must stand together." She focused on Susan B. Anthony and Elizabeth Cady Stanton, her closest collaborators. "Since we birthed the NWSA nearly twenty years ago, we've held strongly to the goal of full rights for all women. We've fought for employment, marital, and voting rights equal to those of men. Such rights must be honored, regardless of a person's race, creed, or sex."

Miss Anthony declared, "For years, I've heard Matilda argue for rights for women—even more, for the universal rights of all people. Her support for those lofty, broad goals seems fathomless." Then, turning to Matilda, Miss Anthony added, "You've written extensively about these goals in pamphlets, editorials, and books. I've endorsed it."

"Actually, Miss Anthony, in most of our publications, you essentially affixed your name to my writings." Matilda added, "Now it seems that you are campaigning to erase my name from history."

Miss Anthony shot back, "That's of no matter. Where have the books and pamphlets gotten us? Coloreds—"

Matilda cut off her colleague. "Why do you call Black people 'coloreds'? If you are indeed a co-author, then of all people, you should appreciate the power of words. When you use that word, you presume White is the standard for comparison—that White is 'correct,' that White is supreme. All of us agree that all Americans are equal."

"It sounds like you have been talking with my Frederick Douglass," Anthony snapped.

"Your Frederick Douglass? He is anything but yours. And you, you are most certainly not his."

"I beg your pardon." Miss Anthony sneered. "Even Mr. Douglass understands that Blacks—Black *men*, that is—were granted the vote by the Fifteenth Amendment. Women, regardless of their skin color, were abandoned. We were left to continue our fight alone. We must work for one right at a time."

"Balderdash! Are you going to abandon the grand goals to which all of us dedicated ourselves? You know there are other critical rights! Are you willing to focus on just the vote? Are you prepared to marry our national assembly with the single-issue American Woman Suffrage Association?"

"Yes, to all of your questions. I am willing to accept the blurring or the erasure of the political lines between church and state to achieve women's suffrage. I am even willing to accept temperance and ally with its Christian acolytes. I am not beholden to you, or anyone in this room!" Miss Anthony's eyes bored into Matilda with a withering intensity.

Matilda rose abruptly and left the room muttering, "I must focus. We must have full rights for all people: White, Black, or indigenous, regardless of their sex. Civil rights for all. A strong separation of church and state. Anthony threatens to twist a dagger in the corpus of universal equality."

Mrs. Stanton followed Matilda out the door, called for her attention, and confided, "It is easy for Susan to abandon reworking marriage and religion, institutions that you and I well know subjugate women. Keep in mind, Susan is unmarried and calls herself a Quaker." Mrs. Stanton inhaled and then continued, "Let's discuss this further at another time. Right now, we must collect ourselves to attend the presidential reception."

## Executive Mansion, 1600 Pennsylvania Avenue, Washington Sunday, March 25, 1888, 7:00 PM

Selected dignitaries of the National Woman Suffrage Association rode carriages down frozen, rutted Pennsylvania Avenue. They dismounted at the Executive Mansion beneath the columned portico made famous in daguerreotype images and postcards. Dodging the crusty remnants of the massive snowstorm, now covered by a light powder from flurries earlier in the day, they entered the grand foyer.

Each of the four corners of the foyer boasted a bust of a Founding Father who served as president. Matilda remarked to Mrs. Stanton, who was standing nearby, "It's interesting, Liz. Three of the presidents glorified with busts were from Virginia, and each was a slave owner. What does that say about our nation's leadership?" That rhetorical question hung heavily in the atrium.

The NWSA honorees shook the hands of Grover Cleveland and the First Lady, Frances Folsom Cleveland. The president received each with a handshake, shallow bow, and the message "On behalf of our nation, we welcome you to the Executive Mansion. We appreciate your tenacious devotion to women's suffrage."

The last guest to greet the president was Matilda. On seeing her, Grover's bushy mustache rose with his broad smile, and his work-worn eyes twinkled. He gave Matilda a hearty hug, as if he did not want to let her go—as if he feared this was the last time he would see his dear, childhood friend. "As always, it's wonderful to see you, Mrs. Gage. And a happy belated birthday, yesterday!" Gesturing to his right, Grover continued, "Let me introduce you to my wife, Frances. You can call her Frankie."

As gracious as the newspapers described, Frances greeted Matilda. "It's a pleasure to meet you! Grover has told me so much about you—your work on the Underground Railroad, for abolition, and for people's rights. Come, tell me more about yourself and my Grover when he was a child."

Susan Anthony gawked as Frances linked her arm with Matilda's and the two Clevelands escorted Matilda to the residence for private conversation and to reminisce.

# PART 1.

## *MATILDA*

And yet I ask sometimes in wonder,
as I wander the meadows among,
can brother for brother feel hatred,
as he hears the lark's musical song?

*Liberté, Equalité, Fraternité*
Victor Hugo, 1830

# 1

Cicero Swamp, Cicero, New York
Monday, September 21, 1840, 11:30 PM

AN UNRELENTING WIND buffeted Father, Mother, and me, whipping tall bulrushes into a snarled, nearly impenetrable fabric. The three of us trudged through the grassy labyrinth that swallowed our every footfall. The marsh seemed larger than it did during the daytime. The moonless dark rendered it more menacing, more intimidating.

As I pushed through the grasses, my thoughts drifted. *How can we break the slavery that wraps and restrains our country? How do we keep from being mired in the muck that impedes our steps toward freedom? Is this conundrum resolvable?* I wished I could answer these questions, or at least, I wished Father would help me find the answers. What I did know was that my family was determined to help those brave and bold enough to leave everything they had behind. In my thirteen years, I had met many runaways. There had to be a better way.

As if he'd read my mind, Father broke the silence. "Matilda, attend to the present. Focus on everything. Notice anything. Be quiet." *Oh, Father. You need not remind me. I have done this so many times before. Must you repeat yourself again and again?* Even so, I did not argue with him. I abided his instructions.

Stimuli were few. Everything appeared in tones of black. The only movements I detected were ours. *Schlurpa, schlurpa*: the suction from my parents' steps carried across the night. *Can't they be quieter? Why don't they use a Haudenosaunee approach for silent tracking?* During my previous summers with the Haudenosaunee, when I lived with Edward Cornplanter and his family, all great friends of Father, I learned how to move through the marsh. I could tell from the way Father talked about Mr. Cornplanter that he cared for and respected the Seneca chief, so why hadn't he invested himself and learned from him as I had? I took care to step on exposed roots and downed branches. I timed my strides to match the chirping of peepers. It was sheer delight to navigate the night world, lithe and lyrical, like my Seneca teachers.

We reached our appointed drop point, a lone black walnut tree in the middle of the open marsh. We were scheduled to meet Mr. Loguen, a longtime conductor on the Syracuse Underground Railroad. Tonight, he was shepherding two runaway children. We were tasked to transport them safely to Fulton, New York. We must not fail.

Father raised his right hand and double-snapped a tin signal clicker.

Moments passed.

Nothing.

The lulling serenades of night fauna continued uninterrupted: the drone of thrumming crickets, the bravado of belching bullfrogs. This deceptive calm was broken by the song of an owl searching for its partner and the fleeting, distinct odor of a muskrat scampering across the marsh. But there was no sign of people.

Again, Father clicked. This time, I strained and heard a distant *click-click* on my left. Father must have heard it, too. He responded with a trio of clicks. Three quick clicks returned.

I exhaled and relaxed. I considered our situation. There were three possible sources for the clicks. It could be indigenous people. That possibility could be eliminated because they would not have clicked; instead, they would have imitated a bird call. It could be our runaways. After all, they were likely not trained in tracking. They would be noisy and clumsy as they pushed through the brush and muck. The third possibility was the one that scared me. I asked Father, "Bounty hunters?"

I detected an uncharacteristic disquiet in Father. "Time will tell."

*Does Father know something he's not telling me?*

Once again, Father clicked twice.

A double-click response returned. Then a silhouette partially blocking the starry sky passed along the horizon.

I nudged my parents and pointed.

We worked toward the sound. As I pushed through the reeds, I felt an acute, irritating twinge in my right foot. *Nah, that's nothing; we must focus on the important tasks.* Within moments, we were staring at Mr. Loguen and the runaways he was escorting: a preteen boy and a slightly younger girl.

Father whispered, "Jermain. It is always good to see you."

"'Tis a great relief to see you, too, Dr. Joslyn."

I approached the girl slowly, kindly. She cowered behind Mr. Loguen and appeared ready to scream. I abruptly reached to cover her mouth. That, in turn, alarmed the boy. He stepped forward to wrestle me, but before he had a chance, Mr. Loguen grabbed him, gagged him, and commanded, "Boy, do as dese people say."

Attempting to calm the situation, Mother knelt to look directly into the children's faces. In hushed words, she said, "We'll get you tae safety." She urged the scared runaways to crouch below the tops of the cattails.

I marveled at Mother's easy manner. She continued in her Scottish lilt: "Keep doun. Stay quiet. Hold on to this rope tae follow us." The children followed her every direction.

Gazing at the navy sky, I used autumnal stars—notably Orion, his unique belt of three stars, bright Rigel, and the distinctive red of Betelgeuse—to guide our party through the marsh. After navigating the thick reeds and spiky salt grasses, we arrived on solid ground, but we were still not in the clear. The persistent threat of hunters hung in the air. Mother ordered, "Follow ma girl and Mr. Loguen. They'll help ye onto our cart. Lie doun. We'll cover ye with blankets." The girl shot a petrified glance to the boy, who forced a smile and nodded.

Being an experienced guide, Mr. Loguen reinforced, "Dese are good people. Trust dem."

The runaways obeyed Mother and loaded onto the cart. To further settle the children, Mr. Loguen lay in the cart with them. I covered all three with blankets. As I mounted the driver's bench next to Mother, I winced at the sharp reminder of pain in my right foot.

Mother asked, "Ready, Matilda?"

I grimaced. "Yes."

As she tugged on the reins, the horses shook off their drowsiness, rolled their broad necks, and eased forward. Riding beneath the star-speckled sky, Mother and I kept Polaris on our right as we directed our horses homeward.

Father armed himself with two stout sticks and paced the cart from behind as protection against unwanted intruders. I thought I overheard him praying he would not have to use the sticks, but I, for one, was comforted by his vigilance.

Our way home was tense. Just the noise of our cart rolling on the washboard, dirt road in the otherwise silent wee hours of the morning was enough to attract the unwelcomed attention of hunters. Voles scurried across the lane. Patrolling owls hooted from perches in tree boughs outlined against the moonlit horizon like craggy arms reaching to grab us. I heard a loud scratching on trees and twigs breaking.

The scritch-scratching alarmed the boy. He jutted his head from the blanket, then scuttled turtle-like back under. "What's dat? Someone followin' us?"

"Ooh, no," I whispered. "It's just a raccoon searching for food." Even though I was certain it was only a furry, masked bandit making a familiar noise, I still had the shivers. I still had the feeling we were being followed. Cicero's sword of Damocles hung above us.

2

Joslyn Farm, 8560 Brewerton Road, Cicero, New York
Tuesday, September 22, 1840, 2:00 AM

REACHING THE SAFETY of our home did not afford me time to relax. Quite the contrary! Father, Mother, and I had urgent, well-choreographed responsibilities to perform.

As I dismounted the cart, I felt the searing pain in my right heel again. I wished it away; duty called. Limping into our farmhouse, I ensured the drapes in the road-facing rooms were drawn. I collected two pairs of candles from the cupboard in the kitchen, then lit and placed the first pair on the kitchen table. These were my favorites because they bore the carved figures of Odysseus and Penelope. I carried the second pair to the desk in the office, casting ominous shadows to dance on the walls and the bookcases.

As per our plan, I prepared the house while Mother attended to the runaways. Having removed the blankets covering the children and Mr. Loguen, she secreted the three into the office and joined me. Mother and I silently pulled a corner of a bookcase forward to reveal a four-foot-deep, windowless space. It was vented through gaps between the wood slats comprising the skin of the house. The wind whistled and slivers of moonlight filtered through these spaces.

After Mother and I ushered the children into the alcove, Mr. Loguen offered, "Mrs. Joslyn, I'll settle the boy and girl and stay with 'em tonight."

Mother nodded. "Very well. I will be back in a few moments with fresh provisions." She turned to the girl and handed her a knitted doll. "Would ye like this?"

The little girl nodded, forced a weak smile, and hugged the doll. Mother and I looked at each other as we reset the bookcase.

Meanwhile, Father arrived at the house and heaved his sticks into the cart. I knew his duties by heart, having served them before. He unhitched the horses, guided them into the barn, then stabled, fed, and watered them. Filling two buckets at the well in the front yard, Father carried them to the kitchen and decanted the water into jars. Mother met him there and collected the jars along with bread, dried fruit, and jerked meat. She returned to the office with the food.

Facing the bookcase, Mother set aside two large anatomy books to expose a passage to the hidden space. In a gentle but firm voice, she said, "Welcome tae our home. Ye are safe here. Here is some food and water. If ye need tae relieve yourselves, thare is an urn in the corner. At the other end, thare are blankets for ye tae sleep. We'll wake ye after sunrise." She smiled, replaced the books on the shelf, and set off for a short sleep.

With the runaways secured, I finally afforded myself the luxury of attending to my painful foot. I removed my shoes, peeled off my socks, and revealed a one-inch blister on the rear of my right heel. Just looking at my wound was painful, but it was refreshing to expose my burning skin to the air. *How could I let this happen? I know full well how to prevent blisters from forming.*

As usual, Father could not restrain himself. "Oh, my dear, it looks like your foot got wet and the irritation caused the blister to grow."

*Pish, I know that much.* Careful not to sound insolent or disrespectful, I asked, "Father, do you have calendula and hypericum flower extracts? Haudenosaunee rub them into irritated skin. Then they wrap the wound with a clean cloth."

"Fiddle-faddle. That won't work," Father parried. "Instead of encasing the wound, you need to rid your body of the infection. Slash the blister, drain the pus, and then expose the damaged skin to the elements."

*Why did he and Mother send me to live with the Seneca if he is so reticent to learn from them and to use their medicines?* "I appreciate your suggestion, Father, but the Seneca taught me to rely on the body and its powers of repair. Our task is to promote those inherent abilities." Rather than annoying Father, I offered a compromise. "If you have hypericum, I'll apply it after I drain my blister."

"Using your so-called medicine makes no sense at all."

Sometimes, Father so frustrated me. It seemed the only way to be correct was to follow his way.

"Father, why are you set against Seneca treatments? Aren't most of your medicines from plant extracts? You have hypericum in your cabinet, don't you?"

"Humpf," Father puffed as he pawed through bottles on his shelves. He fashioned a concoction and handed it to me. "As you wish—hypericum. I even added some calendula."

"Thank you." I accepted the medication with a smile, then hobbled to my second-floor bedroom where I lanced the blister and applied the salve to my heel. I lay down, asleep before my head touched the pillow.

# 3

Joslyn Farm, Cicero, New York
Thursday, September 24, 1840, 5:45 AM

SUNRISE CAME EARLY. I rose from my bed, blinked the morning into myself, and donned my robe. Hearing clatter in the kitchen, I limped barefoot down the stairs, holding the banister for support.

"Good morning, Matilda. How do you feel?" Father asked.

"Better, thank you. The burning is largely gone."

"A miracle cure. Who would have thought of using a flower extract for skin medicine? Humpf."

I fought to keep from being drawn into a tussle with Father.

Mother, who was preparing fried eggs and toast for Mr. Loguen and the runaways, deftly ignored our banter by asking, "Zeke, please carry the breakfast food tae the office and help me swing the bookcase aside."

"Indeed."

The three of us walked to the office, and my parents swung open the bookcase. Dim morning light poured into the hiding space. It stunned Mr. Loguen and the children, who had acclimated to the dark. Through a squint and a yawn, Mr. Loguen said, "Good morning, Mrs. Joslyn. And thank you."

"As ye well know from your years working with us on the Railroad, 'tis our honor tae help." Mother turned to the children, who were still rubbing morning sand from their eyes. "Today, we will escort ye tae Fulton. From there, you'll be taken tae Oswego where you'll board a boat for Kingston, Ontario. Once there, local Canadians will set ye up for the rest o' yer lives—yer lives as free people."

Father added, "Yes. After traveling for months without your parents, you are within reach of completing your run from the terror of the plantation and the fear of bounty hunters." The two children shyly gazed at their feet and smiled.

Mother, Mr. Loguen, the children, and I ate breakfast. Afterward, I played a card game with the boy. I wandered to the parlor where I snuggled into my favorite reading chair with a good book while Mother and Mr. Loguen prepared for the next leg of the children's journey. While I read, I fought to stay awake. It looked like Father lost his fight while he was "working" at his desk. Following a sudden commotion in the office, I looked through the window to see Father breathlessly bolting through the front door, yelling, "Helen, is the rig all set? Are the children secured in the rear?"

"Hezekiah."

*Eeks.* I braced myself. Normally Mother had the patience of Job, but when she used Father's full name, I knew to give her a wide berth.

"I hope ye enjoyed your nap," Mother snipped. "The rig and the children are set. Mr. Loguen will accompany me tae Fulton. We expect tae be home by midafternoon."

Father read the tea leaves. "Helen, I am very sorry. I just, well . . . I'm sorry. I know we all could have used more sleep."

Taking a slow breath, Mother said, "Zeke, all is well. Mr. Loguen helped me square the children and the rig."

A shame-faced Father offered his hand to help Mother onto the bench. "Helen, do have a safe trip."

Father lifted the blanket covering the children and offered them a wink of confidence. Mother nodded and smiled at Father. As best I could tell, all was forgiven. She tugged at the reins, and the horses whinnied. Mother, Mr. Loguen, and the children were off.

# 4

Joslyn Farm, Cicero, New York
Thursday, September 24, 1840, 10:30 PM

AFTER TENDING TO chores about the farm, Father retreated to his office. It was a magical place, and I enjoyed its cozy feel of hope and promise. Shelves, replete with dusty, leather-bound books, lined the office walls. The cabinets were jammed with vessels containing extracts and elixirs of different hues that could treat everything from a common cold to cancer.

I poured myself some tea in the kitchen, picked up my book, and slipped down the hall into the office. I loved watching Father fuss. What was he thinking while he arranged and rearranged things on the shelves? *Is he working through a case? Considering a strategy for how to deal with a situation should it arise? Is he trying to understand a new approach he read about in one of his books or periodicals?*

Whatever Father was thinking, he continued unaware of me and mindlessly recited a favorite of Hamlet's soliloquies. "What a piece of work is man! How noble in reason, how infinite in faculty, in form and moving how express and admirable." Suddenly, he realized I was reading in a corner chair and shifted his attention to me. Without hesitating, Father pivoted and posed a medical question about human structure and function. "Matilda, how does your body accommodate to stresses induced by running up the side of a tall mountain?"

Normally, I enjoyed Father's challenges. After all, I had learned my fundamentals—grammar, Greek, Latin, literature, mathematics, and science—from my parents, principally Father. He used what he called the Socratic method: interminable questions. I long considered Father's questions a game but now found them increasingly irritating. In a fit of indiscretion, I shot back, "Father, why do you do ask me so many questions?"

Father looked squarely at me, his face etched in confusion, maybe even hurt. I knew he wanted me to follow in his footsteps, to become a physician. If all went according to his plan, I would become the first woman physician in the United States. Such a course would make decisions about my life easy. I wouldn't have to think of what I would do as an adult nor hew a new path or develop a new business. I would just assume Father's practice. Nevertheless, I felt queasy whenever he raised this topic. Why didn't he give me the respect of asking what I was thinking?

Rather than confront him with my thoughts, questions, and ambivalence, I worked to please him. I broke the silence and returned to Father's question. "Are you asking me how pulmonary, cardiac, renal, and muscular responses dovetail?"

Father grinned, evidently relieved that I had accepted his challenge. "Yes, that's it." I wished he would leave it there, but he continued. "To be an effective physician, you must appreciate how the body works as a unit. How does each system contribute to the dynamic of the whole? How does the demand for fresh air and the purging of used air relate to heart function? Pumping frequency? Blood pressure? How do these changes support the increased needs of limb muscles?"

I pursed my lips. Before I let slip something I would regret, I excused myself and walked to the kitchen for more tea, passing Mother, who had just returned from Fulton.

Father commented, but not so quietly that I could not hear, "Helen, you know I've enjoyed teaching Matilda."

Hearing my name, I stopped in the hall to listen. *Is he as frustrated as I am?*

"Yes, dear," confirmed Mother.

Father continued, "Matilda has become the thinking, caring person we dreamed of. We discuss the classics, learn languages, work through questions of science and mathematics, but I believe that I've reached the limit of what I can teach her. She needs to develop her skills in research and self-dependence. These are things that neither we nor the Seneca can teach her. It may be time to send her to a school where instructors can teach in more depth and engage Matilda more broadly."

Mother responded, "We knew there would come a day when either we'd exhaust what we could teach Matilda or we'd find that we did not have enough time tae devote tae her education. Maybe that time has come. Maybe we should consider a seminary or college."

I was aghast. *How can they think of sending me away?* I was happy at home. *Why change things?*

Though boiling mad, I focused on the here and now. I continued to the kitchen, where I poured a cup of tea and picked up a favorite book, Virgil's *Aeneid*. Returning to the office, I sat in my usual corner chair. Still piqued by my parents' conversation and their plans for me, I rifled through the pages and read a portion aloud. "'Give up what I began? Am I defeated?'" I paused to gauge Father's expression. Seeing no change, I continued. "'Am I impotent to keep the king of Teucrians from Italy? The Fates forbid me, am I to suppose?' Father, what do you think this passage means? Each question seems to contradict the notion of free will. Weren't free will and personal responsibility central to the philosophies of Aristotle? Epicurus? Zeno?"

Father appeared stunned. He glanced pleadingly to Mother.

"That's yer girl. That's our young woman." Mother flashed a smile of gratification, nodded, and raised her left eyebrow. "She's a product of yer education."

-ᴏ⧄ᴏ-

# 5

Village of Cicero, New York
Thursday, September 24, 1840, 1:30 PM

AFTER CLEANING UP from our midday meal, Mother and
I walked the half mile to the center of the village. Shopping with Mother
was always fun. Partly, I enjoyed looking at the new things, but mostly,
the joy came from spending time with just Mother.

A bell gently tinkled as we opened the door to Gage's Dry Goods.
Standing at the center of Cicero, the shop was flanked by a Methodist church
and a two-story building with a tavern, a cobbler, and housing above.

On hearing the bell, the owner ambled from the rear of the store.
Judson Gage had a gaunt face and a small mouth that looked as though he
had just eaten a lemon. Mother knew Mr. Gage well as he and Father had
served as town supervisor off and on for much of the last fifteen years. I had
known him since I was born, but he and I had spoken infrequently, at best.

Mr. Gage stood behind a counter boasting jars filled with knickknacks
and penny candy. "Mrs. Joslyn." He nodded curtly while focusing and
fussing on merchandise displays. "What can I get for you today?"

Mother shrugged off Mr. Gage's brusque greeting. "Good afternoon,
Mr. Gage. Matilda and I are looking for fabric tae make work clothes."

Straightaway, Mr. Gage made for the back of the store, saying, "I have
just the thing for you."

After Mr. Gage disappeared, Mother pored over samples of fabric displayed on a wall bracket. She lifted a pink floral print in front of her. "Matilda, what do you think?"

"Elegant, and fun."

Mother replaced the sample and selected a blue gingham cloth. She held it in front of me. "Do you like it?"

"Maybe if you wanted to dress me in a tablecloth."

We both laughed, and I left Mother to poke about. As I explored, I stumbled upon a small table I had not previously seen, strewn with magazines. They were interesting, but what surprised me was the wooden shelf perched on top of the table and leaning against the wall. It was filled with used books! In all my times visiting this store, I had not noticed it. I was drawn to it like a moth to a candle. I read the titles as I ran my fingers over the book spines: *Frankenstein, Last of the Mohicans, Tales of Mother Goose,* and *The Sketch Book of Geoffrey Crayon, Gent.* I selected *Frankenstein* and asked, "Mother, could we buy this? It's written by a woman."

"Excellent choice. *The Modern Prometheus,* another Greek myth for ye tae read."

"You're teasing me, aren't you?" I could not read Mother's face.

She flashed the slightest trace of a mischievous grin. "Yes. How much does it cost?"

"Just twenty cents," I pleaded.

"That's fine. Let's consider it a half-birthday present."

I had forgotten what day it was. *How does Mother always remember things and times that are important to others?*

The door opened, and the bell tinkled again. Mother and I turned to see Daniel Baum, a neighbor who lived on Lakeshore Road. Mr. Baum bade, "Greetings, Helen."

"G'day, Daniel. How are Mary and yer children?"

"Everyone is well, thank you. And how is Hezekiah? I've not seen him in a while."

Before Mother and Mr. Baum got any further, Mr. Gage bounded from the back of the store empty-handed. *What was he doing back there?*

"Ah, Daniel. How are you this fine day?" Mr. Gage said.

"I'm well, Judson." The conversation unfurled from there. Mother tried to slip in a word and recollect Mr. Gage's attention, but she was unable. Fortunately, Mr. Gage's twenty-year-old son, Henry, emerged from the rear of the store. In contrast to his father, Henry had a gentle demeanor and pleasing countenance. I guessed he looked like his mother, whom I had not met.

Mother asked, "Henry, can you help me? Do ye have any rugged muslin I could use for sewing work clothes?"

"Yes, Mrs. Joslyn. I believe we do. Let me see what we have in the back. I'll return in a jiff," Henry promised.

"Thank ye, young man."

Though his father continued jabbering with Mr. Baum, Henry was true to his word. "This blue muslin is thick, pliable, and a good, dark color."

Mother accepted. "That'll do just fine. I'll take six yards."

"Very good. I'll cut it for you." Henry slipped into the back again. Moments later, he reappeared with the fabric folded and tied. "At thirteen cents per yard, that'll be seventy-eight cents for the muslin."

Henry's attentive and thorough service impressed me.

"Will there be anything else?"

I placed *Frankenstein* on the counter. "Yes. This book."

Picking up the book to read the title, Henry looked at me. I was unsure how to read his expression until he said, "Excellent choice. I've been reading it in my spare time. I'm about halfway done. Please, let me know how it finishes."

I was a bit surprised by Henry's invitation, but I was spared having to respond as Mother laid down a silver dollar.

Henry took the coin, nodded at Mother, and gave her two pennies in change. "Thank you."

"Ye as well."

Henry and I exchanged smiles, and Mother and I left the store to the tinkle of the bell.

As we walked home, Mother and I fell quiet. After a bit, I asked,

"Mother, don't you find it irritating that men tend to talk with other men and ignore women?"

Normally Mother would dodge such a question, but this time she answered, and directly. "Ay. The slights are so commonplace, I've grown accustomed tae them. That does not mean such behavior is excusable. I just don't see an opportunity tae address it."

I was unsure how to respond to Mother's obvious sense of resignation. Men's behavior was often irritating. I would have to pay more attention to see if Father acted the same way.

On arriving at our farmhouse, Mother set to work. "Matilda, I am going tae put away the fabric and work on supper. Join me if ye like."

"Thank you, but if you don't mind, I'd like to take a few minutes and look over *Frankenstein*?"

"That's fine. Enjoy yerself."

I sat on the divan in the corner of the parlor, settled into my new book, and tried to lose myself in Geneva, Switzerland.

Moments later, Father wandered into the parlor. "Ah, Matilda. How was your shopping?"

I nodded, hoping Father would leave me to myself, but he persisted. "What's that you are reading?"

I placed *Frankenstein* on the side table. Without hesitating, I picked up *The Odyssey* and announced, "I'm reading Homer. It occurs to me that most classical Greek literature that I've read was created by men. And the stories focus on the men. Is it a reflection of their patriarchal society?" I could have stopped with just firing rhetorical ordnance at Father. I probably should have. But I felt compelled to elaborate. "Unlike his male contemporaries, the stories of Homer presented the world in a different way. Despite being blind, Homer 'saw' what most Greeks did not. The women of *The Odyssey* were formidable."

"Tosh, the men drive the story," Father interrupted.

"Maybe, but without the women, there was no story. The women were some of Odysseus's ablest adversaries. Three that come to mind are Calypso, Circe, and Scylla. Odysseus was challenged by their wiles. He did not defeat them; rather, he figured ways to navigate about them. They were at least equal to the canny Odysseus. Even Penelope, Odysseus's wife, was a strong woman. She worked within the confines of her society; she pushed societal limits. At the same time, Penelope held true to her ideals and passions." As I spoke, I watched Father's eyes grow wider and wider. *Have I insulted him?* I wanted to confront him, but I did not want to offend him.

Father submitted, "Matilda, that is an amazing analysis. I am impressed by your clarity of understanding and your novel insights. It's a perspective I'd not appreciated." His eyes twinkled. "I hope that you don't see me as one of those men."

I did not respond.

# 6

Joslyn Farm, Cicero, New York
Monday, October 5, 1840, 10:30 AM

I WANDERED INTO Father's office, plucked an anatomy book from a shelf, blew off the dust, and carried it to my second-story bedroom. Leafing through the volume, I fed my fascination with the role, location, and design of discrete organs. The interdependence of the organs was particularly intriguing. I surmised that it was not by chance that the lungs flanked the heart. Breathing must affect cardiac activity. *Is the reverse also true? Context must mean something. Context may mean everything. Hmm.*

My thoughts were broken by a movement in the corner of my eye—a woman working her way down Brewerton Road toward our farm. She was wearing a simple, torn frock and carrying a heavy bag. Her gait was wobbly. *Is she intoxicated?* As she drew closer to our farm, it became clear why she was staggering. She was great with child. I rushed down the staircase to the kitchen to find Mother.

I should not have been surprised that Mother was already aware. She opened the side door and welcomed the woman.

"Is the doctor here?" the exhausted young woman huffed.

"Na, not at the moment. I expect him soon. Who shall I say is calling?" Then Mother added in her best Seneca, "*Naho:ten iesa:iats?* What is yer name?"

"Sarah Iotiwisto," the woman puffed. "Sarah Snowbird." As Mother escorted Sarah inside, the pregnant woman grimaced, paused, and breathed deeply.

Through my wonder and confusion, I asked, "Mother, why did she come here?"

Mother stated the obvious. "She is giving birth."

"Yes, I see that, but why did she come here?" I repeated, and then clarified, "Haudenosaunee have wise women and medicine men of their own." Embarrassed by my tone, I tried to eat my words.

Fortunately, Mother ignored my rudeness and acknowledged my point. "Indeed, they do. Maybe we can get answers later. Right now, we must attend tae her and ease her labor. Dear, please go tae the kitchen. Set a pot o' water on the stove. Bring it tae a boil so we can clean tools. Then, carry the pot tae the office. Also, collect clean rags and towels, and bring thaim, too."

I went about doing just as Mother asked, leaving the doors between the kitchen and the office open so I could watch Mother with Sarah.

As Sarah winced, Mother turned, held her hand, and waited for the contraction to abate. "Sarah, please, come with me tae the office. I think we have what we'll need thare." I met them at the office with the supplies. Despite all the books held therein, none addressed childbirth. That made for an extra challenge as Mother was a clinical novice. Nevertheless, she kept her calm and exuded confidence. "Sarah, make yerself as comfortable as possible. Please, tell me about yerself."

"I twenty-two years. This my first pregnancy. I am Seneca. I leave tribe when I marry White man. Husband hit me, leave me." Sarah abruptly halted as another contraction overcame her. After that wave passed, she continued. "Have no home in White world."

I stared blankly at Mother, who returned my gaze. We helped Sarah get comfortable. I cradled her hand as she worked through another contraction. Once that passed, Mother signaled for me to follow to the kitchen. There, Mother explained, "I think Sarah is right. Among White people, she'd be shunned for having a child alone. Worse, without a husband, her baby would likely be taken from her. Matilda, ye know that had Sarah stayed with her native people, e'en as a single woman, she would have been welcomed and supported. E'en if she returned tae her people after the marriage, she would be embraced. Thare must be a story behind why she's not rejoined her tribe."

"Which story is hers?"

"There are so many possibilities. Maybe her husband was not respected by the tribe. Maybe her native family disowned her, though that would surprise me, for it is not the Seneca way. We know that her native Seneca live in far Western New York. That is more than a week o' travel from here."

Nodding, I mumbled, "Context."

"Pardon?" Mother asked.

"Don't mind me. It was just an idle thought." Returning to our conversation, I suggested, "We could send a message to Edward Cornplanter, but if we did, it would take weeks before we'd get word back from them."

"You're probably right, on both counts. Even so, it would be worthwhile to send Mr. Cornplanter a note." Mother signaled for us to get back to Sarah.

I understood, but I felt compelled to ask, "Why? Why is our culture so cruel? It seems anti-woman. Who wrote these rules?"

Mother slowly shook her head, grim faced. "It pains me tae admit that the answers lie in the teachings o' the church. Maybe that should not come as a surprise. The church is directed by men." I was confused by these comments, but Mother cut off our discussion. "We should discuss this further, but not right now. What I can say is that in this house, Sarah is a valued person, as valued as anyone." Despite her evident stress, she forced a smile. "We must focus on Sarah. Comfort her. This baby's coming into the world, whether it's fair or not."

# 7

Joslyn Farm, Cicero, New York
Monday, October 19, 1840, 5:30 AM

MORNING WAS MY favorite part of the day. I loved the warmth of the golden sun, the songs of waking birds, and the wafting of the zephyr wind. This early serenity was split by the crying of Sarah's baby. As I walked into the bedroom next to mine, Sarah groggily awakened, drew her two-week-old daughter close, and nursed while humming a gentle, melodic song I recognized from my Seneca summers. The setting was serene, almost biblical. As I looked on, I asked, "Sarah, why did you name your baby Cherry?"

In an offhand manner, Sarah answered, "It is what she looks like when she cries."

I chuckled.

Within moments, Cherry settled back into a peaceful sleep. On laying Cherry in her cradle, Sarah rose to begin the breakfast routine she'd developed over the last week as I went about my own chores. I marveled at her organization, her energy, and the joy she brought to every day.

Carrying a bucket and a basket from the kitchen, Sarah came to the barn to milk a cow alongside my parents and me and collected eggs from nests in the chicken coop. I knew that after returning to the kitchen with her dairy bounty, Sarah would fry salt bacon and set a pot of water to boil for tea. Once the bacon finished, she would mix eight eggs with milk, scramble them briskly, and fry the mixture.

As Sarah finished her routine, I smelled the alluring aroma of the sizzling bacon. I finished milking and nudged my parents. "Time for breakfast." We scurried to clean up from our chores and moved to the dining room. Sarah had laid the food with bread from yesterday on the dining room table. After everyone settled in their places, Father recited the daily grace.

"O Lord, bless this food, and bless us to thy service. Keep us ever mindful of the needs of others."

Mother and I uttered in unison, "Amen."

Sarah joined in, too, even though I am quite sure she did not know what the prayer or "amen" meant. I think she just wanted us to know that she appreciated our generosity.

Mother was moved to say, "Sarah, you've been with us for two weeks. Would ye like tae stay here with us? Ye are welcome for as long as ye like."

With a broad smile, Sarah nodded enthusiastically. I was delighted.

The collective focus shifted back to eating breakfast. Morning gatherings were a simple joy. We talked about matters ranging from local farming and family sagas to activities on the Underground Railroad. I particularly enjoyed learning about the goings-on in our community, New York, and the country. Watching Father and Mother debate current events was fun, especially when they disagreed. Since including Sarah at our meals, we had a new topic of discussion—the Haudenosaunee.

As the day's conversation began, I served myself from the offerings of eggs, bacon, and bread. When it came to preferences for tea, there were varied opinions. Father and I liked ours with fresh milk, Mother liked hers without, and Sarah had not yet developed a preference. All agreed that tea was best with a touch of home-harvested honey.

Once our plates were full, the give-and-take began, but Mother made one thing clear: "Filled mouths are not for speaking."

When the meal was half over, Father said, "I have office hours this morning. Matilda or Sarah, can you assist me?"

"Yes. Happy to help," Sarah answered. "Let me check if Cherry still sleeps."

I offered to teach Sarah the ropes.

"Thank you both. I'll be setting up formulations and surgeries."

Uncertain what Father had just said, Sarah tilted her head but smiled and finished her breakfast.

After the meal, Father left for the barn to finish fixing the cart wheels. He joined Sarah in the office shortly thereafter and began preparations. "Let's review the morning protocols."

Sarah eagerly awaited instructions.

Father leaned over his desk to peruse the notebooks arranged on the shelves and selected the ones associated with the patients scheduled that morning. His thoughts were split by the wailing whistle of a train passing through Cicero Swamp. It ran on a track south of our farm that had been constructed only a few years earlier. The morning train was a pleasant interruption. In fact, its regularity provided structure to the morning rituals. The first train of the day signaled the time of Father's first appointment.

Father turned his attention to me. Looking on with pride, he said, "Matilda, I know that I've said this before, but I do hope that you become a physician."

I offered a wan, silent response.

Father continued, "You have many gifts; indeed, you have a rare combination of abilities. You communicate effectively. You develop easy rapports with people. Beyond all that, you have a clear head, an aptitude for science, and a native curiosity. Together, these abilities make you superbly qualified and eminently suited to be an outstanding physician."

"Thank you, Father." I did not know how to reply. Yes, medicine was exciting, and I liked the puzzle of the science and engagement with the people; but, well, being a doctor did not feel quite right. It could have been a desire to call my future my own and not be my father's child. I really did not know. Instead of discussing this with Father, I shifted to the pressing needs of the morning. "Are you interested in me providing support while you talk with the patients?"

"That would be a great help. And helping Sarah get oriented would be greatly appreciated."

I rose and peeked into the waiting room, spotting the ragamuffin eight-year-old girl who lived down Brewerton Road sitting with a distinguished-looking but disheveled young man, the elderly farmer and five-year-old boy who lived in the house next to the Baums', and a couple in their twenties who recently moved into the lodging above Gage's Dry Goods.

Sarah and I entered the waiting room. I stepped back to record information Sarah gleaned as she welcomed patients and prepared them to see the doctor. Her first stop was the eight-year-old girl. "*She:kon. Skennenko:wa ken? Naho:ten iesa:iats?* Oh, excuse me. I must speak English. How are you? What's your name?"

The elderly man rose and moved to the far side of the room, pulling his young charge with him. His rude actions appalled me.

A Black man in his mid-thirties and a Black woman entered the waiting room. While they brushed fluffy snow from their coats and hung them on the clothes tree in the corner of the room, I encouraged Sarah to introduce herself. As asked, Sarah greeted the Black couple, "Good morning. May I have your names?"

"Yes, of course. Hiram and Miriam Nash."

On seeing the Nashes enter the sitting room, the elderly man rose and announced, "What's dis place about? Da ya serve anyone? Injuns! Nigras! Have you got no standards?"

Father hurried to the sitting room to settle tempers. "Yes. We do have standards. We offer care to anyone who enters my office. Anyone who needs help. That includes you. That includes the Nashes. I would hope that you would have no problem with that. If you do, you may leave."

"Dr. Joslyn, you are a blasphemy, an insult to our integrity."

"Whose integrity is that?" Father responded.

"The integrity of Whites, of course." With that, the man and his grandson abruptly rose and left the sitting room.

On the heels of that exchange, the front door swung open wildly and slammed against the wall with a *BANG!* I shuddered as two rough-clad men burst into the office. The taller one was a hulking presence. He had a pocked complexion, a patch over his right eye, and he limped as he entered. In a gravelly voice, this ruffian declared, "You!" He pointed at Father. "Are you Dr. Joslyn?"

Father clenched his jaw and answered calmly. "I am. May I help you?"

"Yeah. We're lookin' fer a fam'ly of five coloreds. Seen 'em?"

The second man scoured the waiting room. He was more scruffy in his clothing and no less frightening than the first, particularly in his scowl. Pointing at the Nashes, he snarled to his partner, "Hey, Beau. Lookee what we got here."

I walked to stand with the Nashes, who rose in fear, pushing their backs against the waiting room wall. Sarah braced herself next to the eight-year-old girl. Ignoring the conversation between the intruders, Father boldly retorted, "No." Staring the man down, Father continued, "I've not seen any such family. And what is it to you? For that matter, who are you?"

The second intruder sneered, "They're runaways. We've been ordered to return 'em to Virginny."

"Excuse my impoliteness," the first bounty hunter said. "Lemme introduce mahself. Ah am George Beauregard. You can call me Beau. We bin watchin' you. Seen curious activity here. We seen Blacks comin' and goin'. Suspicious behavior for certain."

On hearing this chilling message, Father stepped between the Nashes and the hunters. I was proud of Father, yet I was scared. The hunters in the flesh terrified me as much as they did in my nightmares.

Father declared slowly, emphatically, "These. People. Are. My. Guests. They are free people. Free people! They live in Onondaga County. They have lived here for many years."

Beau growled, "A family of five coloreds been seen in these parts. If you've seen them, Ah wanna know. If you ain't seen them, keep a looksee for them, or else—"

Father interrupted, "Leave us. Now. We need to get on with our business—the good health of *all* members of our community."

The second hunter walked menacingly toward the Nashes. Looking past Father, he barked, "And you. You seen 'em?" The Nashes kept their tongues. "Answer me! If ya knows what's good for you."

Father did not wait for either Nash to answer. He commanded, "There'll be no threats here. Be gone." I was not used to seeing Father so assertive, so courageous.

The hunters were not deterred. Beau grunted at the Nashes, "How long you bin in these parts?"

Father brandished a broom and repeated, "Be gone!"

Beau scowled. For whatever reason, he decided not to respond to Father physically. "We're looking for runaways, but we ain't 'fraid o' takin' blackbirds."

I turned to Father and whispered, "What's a blackbird?"

"A free Black," he answered quietly.

"Cease yer blabbin'," Beau demanded. "Mind me. You ain't seen the last of us. And remember, we're watchin' you."

The two hunters left the office as abruptly as they had entered.

Mr. Nash broke the tense silence. "Affffh. Sets me back years—back to when I was running." He shook his head, closed his eyes, and grimaced. "I was sweating. My heart was racing. Thought them days and feelings were gone."

Father responded, "No, Hiram. So long as hate exists, the danger persists."

# 8

Joslyn Farm, Cicero, New York
Sunday, March 14, 1841, 12:30 PM

"WHAT A GLORIOUS time! The Supreme Court finally found for freedom!" Father proclaimed as he walked into the parlor when Mother and I were reading.

"How so? What happened?" Mother inquired.

"After church services, Daniel Baum told me that the justices acquitted the kidnapped captives on *La Amistad*."

I was confused. This story did not ring bells for me. Evidently, Mother was in the same boat. "I feel that I should know what yer talking about, but I don't. What is the *Amistad*? What does this court decision mean?" She spared me from having to ask the same questions.

Father explained, "As I remember the story, four years ago, the crew of a Spanish slave schooner, *La Amistad*, carried fifty-three Mende Africans abducted from Sierra Leone. They were intended to be slaves on Cuban plantations. Once the Mende realized what was happening, they revolted and wrested control of the ship from their captors. They sailed along the East Coast and landed in Montauk, at the tip of Long Island. After a chase, the Mende were arrested in Connecticut for murder and piracy. On Tuesday the ninth, after a four-year fight, they were exonerated and freed by the Supreme Court. This is cause for celebration."

"Bravo for the Supreme Court!" I exclaimed.

Mother added, "Finally. They agree it's not acceptable tae be taken from your home and carried off without yer permission. That should be a strong blow against slavery."

"Maybe this decision will be a warning to our new president," Father posited.

"How is that?" I asked.

"During his campaign, Harrison aired his noxious stance promoting slavery, even in free states. Hopefully, seeing where the Supreme Court stands will force him to moderate his position."

"We can be e'er hopeful," said Mother.

"Yes, maybe. Clearly, Harrison is a man of fortitude. At his inauguration, he spoke for two hours in the pouring rain, then paraded past throngs of cheering crowds. Let's hope he can marshal that strength and find a path to unify our country. That would be something to celebrate." In an aside that was not intended for me, I heard Father whisper to Mother, "With all this good news, maybe it's time for us to broach the subject of Matilda's education with her."

"That is not going tae be easy, but I believe ye are correct," Mother responded.

Father asked, "Matilda? Your mother and I would like to talk with you."

I braced myself for the conversation I feared. "Yes, Father," I answered with flat apathy.

"Your mother and I have been talking. You'll be fifteen years old in a dozen days. We believe we've reached the end of what we can teach you."

I pleaded, "Father, Mother. Please don't dispatch me. I can read more. There are so many more books from which I can learn."

They both looked pained, though I wasn't sure why. *What do they have to lose? What would change for them?* The idea of sending me away for school was theirs.

"No, dear. I think you misunderstand. You are not going to be—what did you say?—'dispatched.' We know you can read more, but that's not the issue. We believe you need to master your academic skills, be challenged to research and process information, and learn subjects in which your mother and I are not versed. Beyond that, you need to socialize with age-mates and others. School provides these experiences."

I thought on Father's words. They made sense, but I was not excited or even interested in the idea of being sent from home. I looked at my feet, struggling to conceal my uncertainty, fear, and anxiety of the unknown. *How can they do this to me? Don't they understand?* It appeared that Father and Mother were tormented by this decision, as if they were losing something too, but this seemed a charade for my benefit. I was the one being sent away. I was the one whose life was being threatened.

Father continued, "We want you to be accomplished and prepared. We want to make your dossier for medical school admission compelling, irrefutable. Your mother and I explored many options for your schooling."

I just stared ahead. Father prattled on. "One good choice is Oberlin College. It's an outstanding, small school in northern Ohio. We are excited about Oberlin because their curriculum looks tailor-made for you."

"Father, I don't want to go to Ohio," I shot back. "It's nearly the other side of the country."

Reading the situation, Mother attempted to soften Father's message. She had a knack for making uncomfortable options seem palatable, even preferable. I braced myself.

"Matilda, what concerns ye about going tae college?" She paused. "Why don't ye want tae attend Oberlin?"

I was dumbfounded. *Don't my parents even know me?* Except for summers, they had lived with me all my life, nearly fifteen years. *Why don't Father and Mother understand me? Aren't things fine just as they are?* I was happy at home with them. At a school, I would be among strangers who neither knew me nor cared to know me.

Mother continued, "As ye know, seats at most American colleges are restricted to men. In the spirit o' exploration, we contacted the dean at Oberlin College. Beginning four years ago, they accepted four women to their rolls. This has been a great success. The matriculated women are on target tae graduate this spring. Don't ye want tae join them?"

"No," I stated emphatically.

Father and Mother gaped at each other, apparently stymied.

Then Father spoke. "The only other option is for you to attend the Clinton Liberal Institute. Attending the Institute would formally prepare you for attendance at college, bolster your credentials for medical school, and buy us time while new programs for women develop."

*Why does he say "us"?* I felt like a mouse cornered by a cat. *Medical school, medical school, medical school.* I tried a different tack. "Is your goal to get me out of my home?"

Mother was flummoxed, but she held strong. "Absolutely not, but 'tis our responsibility tae best prepare ye fer yer life."

"Like marrying me off?"

Father and Mother shook their heads. Father collected himself. "Matilda, that is the last thought on our minds. We want you to feel free to make your own choices, to define your own life path."

"Your words sound grand, but I think they are disingenuous. You want me to be a physician. That is your dream. I am not so sure."

I watched my words hit Father. They stung of truth.

# 9

Joslyn Farm, Cicero, New York
Sunday, January 2, 1842, 7:30 AM

BLUE SKIES GAVE way to skimpy cirrus clouds scampering from
the unseasonable thunderclouds rumbling in the distance. After loading
my baggage onto our rig, Father opened the front door of the house and
bellowed, "Matilda, it's time to mount the carriage if we expect to arrive
in Syracuse and meet your coach for Clinton. Your mother and I are set.
We will be waiting outside."

In the kitchen, I offered last-minute instructions to Sarah. "Please
make sure that my horse, Elmer, gets his carrots. He loves them so. They
are stored in the root cellar. And my goat needs her hay three times a day.
Otherwise, she gets listless and starts hunting for all sorts of things to eat.
That results in trouble—trouble that is certain to irritate Father."

"I'll take good care of the animals. Go. Have good time. Learn. Make
your parents proud," Sarah said encouragingly.

Hugging Sarah, I bolted outside to the carriage. On the face of it, I
was all smiles, belying my deep trepidation and lingering resistance. My
gut had been upset for the last couple of days, but I refused to let on to my
parents. The idea of formal schooling was foreign to me, as was the idea
of living somewhere other than home, with people other than my family.
Mother argued that attendance at the institute would be an adventure.

I joined my parents on the carriage. Father roused the horses. We were off.

The plan was that I would spend two years of schooling at the Clinton Liberal Institute. I acquiesced to this arrangement after months of chilled exchanges with Father and Mother, but I did exact the compromise that I could leave Clinton if it was untenable or nonproductive. I fortified myself for the challenge with resolve. I'd read enough about the Stoics to appreciate this approach.

Though glum and resigned, I did my best to honor my pledge. I pushed myself. I focused on my studies. On the backside of two tough and lonely weeks, I was convinced that attending the Clinton Liberal Institute was not for me. After supper, I left the mess hall, went to my room, sat at the small wooden desk in my sparsely furnished room, and wrote:

**8560 Brewerton Road**
**Cicero, New York**
**Wednesday, January 19, 1842**

*Dear Dr. and Mrs. Joslyn,*

*Being here is difficult. I am trying. Truly I am. I promised to give the institute two weeks, but this is not working. I am not enjoying my classmates. I mostly sit alone during classes and at meals.*

*My age-mates are self-centered, demanding, and insensitive. I have little in common with them. The boys shun and laugh at the girls. If they do interact with the us, it is usually to let us know that education is wasted on us. They are most annoying. The girls are not much better. One complains about being shelved here by her parents. Others whine about the difficulty of the work. I do not wish to talk with them, much less live with them.*

*I find the classes interesting, but the curriculum is poorly articulated and lacks fluidity. The subjects are arbitrarily arranged into compartments. This undermines the goal of synthesizing the material and fostering thought. More than ever, I appreciate our free-ranging, open discussions.*

*Much of the content is easy. The best example is classics. We are studying the Iliad. It is child's play. You and I have studied this material so many times before, so much more deeply, and in the context of other Greek writers. On the other hand, the algebra is challenging. Determining unknowns baffles me.*

*I look forward to coming home. I miss Sarah and playing with Cherry. I miss the animals, too.*

*Your daughter,*
*Matilda*

I posted the letter in the morning and waited for a response. Impatient, a week later, I wrote a second letter. Day followed day. Schoolwork was a refuge, even though I found that much of it was based on books with which I was already familiar.

Days later, snow flurries wafted onto the sidewalks and roads, covering the village, rendering it pristine. It was beautiful. Unexpectedly, a classmate, Abigail Jones, invited me to walk about the village with her. We kicked through the snow. We made snow angels. Being with Abigail was such fun that I wanted to tell my parents.

8560 Brewerton Road
Cicero, New York
Sunday, January 30, 1842

*Dear Mother and Father,*
    *Today, I explored the town of Clinton. It is lovely. It is fun to*

be in a village and be able to shop at stores, even if it is vicariously, through front windows.

The surrounding area is beautiful. The hills and forests seem to go on forever. I would love to explore them with you and Mr. Cornplanter. Yesterday's snow silenced the usual bustle of the village. It was magical.

For the past couple of days, I studied with Abigail Jones. She is my age. Her home is in Albany where she has four younger brothers. We talk about everything—school, current events, dreams. She makes this place bearable, maybe even enjoyable. I help Abigail with Greek and Latin. She helps me limp through algebra.

I look forward to a visit from you when the opportunity arises.

Love,
Matilda

Nine days later, I received a letter postmarked Cicero, New York:

### Clinton Liberal Institute
### Clinton, New York
### Wednesday, February 9, 1842

My dearest Matilda,
Please offer my heartfelt thanks to Abigail. I thank you, too.

Love,
Father

# 10

Joslyn Farm, Cicero, New York
Wednesday, April 3, 1844, 5:30 PM

Aᴛ ʟᴇᴀsᴛ ꜰᴏʀ the moment, life was bliss. What could be better than reading a good book in the warmth of the kitchen oven? I was keeping to myself, minding my p's and q's, when Mother called, "Matilda? Can ye help me bake some savory rolls?"

"Mother, must I? I'm enjoying *Don Quixote* right now. He's tilting at windmills!" Evidently, that was not a satisfactory answer. I looked up. Mother was frowning at me. *Why is she being more insistent than usual? Is she concerned about national events? Is something going on with Father?* I was sure it had nothing to do with me. After all, I'd finished my two years at Clinton Liberal Institute before Christmas, and we had more or less restored our previous routines at home. The notable exception was that Father and Mother no longer taught me lessons—at least, academic lessons.

"Come. I'll be yer Sancho Panza." Mother met my gaze pleadingly. "I need, or shall I say *knead* with a 'k,' yer help."

"Oh, Mother." I rolled my eyes at her bad pun. Then, to let her know that I was not delighted to stop reading, I put down my book with emphasis.

Mother overlooked my reticence, my impertinence. "Please, get me some cream."

"How much?"

"A cup should do."

I snared a clean, empty bottle and walked down the rickety pine stairs to the cool basement. While the smell reminded me of a crisp April morning after a drenching rain, I shivered at the closeness of the earthen-walled space. I removed a bottle of fresh milk from the ice box in the corner, inhaling the antidote to the ambient dampness, the rich aroma of fresh cream. Decanting the cream floating at the top, I capped and returned the bottled milk to the icebox and carried the collected cream to the kitchen, determined to show a little less vinegar in my attitude. "Does this baking mean there is another train to meet tonight?"

"Yes, but it'll be just ye and yer father. I'll hang back." After fussing about, Mother tried again. "Now can we make the rolls?"

"Oh, sure. What is the next step?"

I followed along with the instructions as she gave them. "The oven is stoked and warm. I already proofed the yeast. In a separate bowl, mix in an egg with a quarter cup o' soft butter. Add the yeast tae the eggs. Now it's time tae add half o' the contents o' the bowl tae the dry ingredients. Mix."

"It looks like large grains of sand." After a few moments of vigorous stirring, I conceded, "This is fun! It feels like when I used to play in the mud."

"I'm glad you're enjoying this. Now on tae the tricky part. Slowly add a generous cup of the cream tae the yeast–flour mixture. Form a dough that is barely sticky tae the touch. The dough should just stick tae yer hands. If it's too sticky, add a little flour. Not sticky enough, add more cream. It's finicky, and not overprecise."

I playfully chimed in, "Ooh, Mother. Look at my hands." I held up both hands coated with dough mittens.

"Matilda, sometimes ye act like a seven-year-old rather than the eighteen-year-old ye are." Mother and I joined in a hearty laugh. "I hope ye always keep yer sense o' joy and play. It will make the sorrows and challenges o' life easier tae bear. I realize that I'm changing the subject, but now that you've completed yer training at Clinton Liberal Institute, do ye have thoughts on yer next steps?" Mother turned the dough onto a lightly floured table and sprinkled it with caramelized onion, a handful of grated cheese, and a bit of flour.

"I'm not sure. I think I could enjoy teaching. I admired the instructors at the institute: exploring new subjects and opening minds. I've not forgotten Father's thoughts on medical school, but that path continues to look unlikely." While Mother and I carefully cleaned, dried our hands with a towel, and coated our hands with flour, I added, "You know that I love Father, but his presumptions infuriate me. Why doesn't he just ask me? Not the Socratic academic stuff, but the simple, meaningful questions. What would I like? What do I think? How do I feel? He seems to assume that I think as he does, that there is only one way to see the world—his way."

Mother nodded while she rolled the dough into a sheet. "I understand. He wants only the best for ye." She wadded up the dough. "Matilda, should it give ye pleasure, knead the dough twice, thrice, or more."

"I do enjoy research. I find it inspiring to read old books, learn things forgotten, and use information from original writings to better understand our current world. How I can use that in the future is anyone's guess. One thing is for certain: I plan to continue serving the Underground Railroad, serving as part of the runaways' high bridge to freedom. That said, I hope the need for such work will soon come to an end."

"Dear, I fear that's wishful thinking, so long as we have ineffectual, sometimes malicious presidents." Back to their baking, Mother added, "Anyway, I like punching the dough. It feels good when I'm frustrated or angry. It helps dissipate my frustration with politicians, and more than once, it has helped me from arguing with your father."

I laughed, rarely seeing Mother's playful side. I rolled the dough a few times to play along. "It does feel good, especially when I begin to dwell on the uncertainty of next year and the few options available to me."

"It is frustrating to think that yer possibilities are limited tae being a wife, mother, teacher, or anything else that men think is beneath them." Mother pounded the dough.

"Maybe I should become a sea captain, lawyer, or military officer," I suggested.

Mother blanched. I thought that indicated my ideas were preposterous, but instead she said, "Funny that ye mention them. Those are the same notions I had when I was yer age." I thought I saw a wistful look in Mother's eyes as she punched the dough with a bit more energy.

I had not previously considered the choices Mother had to make, or the few options she had available. Maybe in another world, such as that of the Haudenosaunee where women are revered, Mother would have followed a different path.

Shaking off the frustration, she refocused. "Matilda, it's time tae roll the dough into a sheet half an inch thick." Once the dough was flattened to her satisfaction, she showed me how to cut out three-inch rounds with a cookie cutter.

"Mother, this is fun. Why have we never done this together before?"

"I don't know. Maybe ye were focused on yer studies."

We balled up the remaining dough, rolled it out again, and cut more circles. After placing the dough rounds on an ungreased baking sheet, Mother and I brushed the top of each with reserved cream and sprinkled them with crushed savory. "Let's cover the rounds with a dry cloth and let them rise for half an hour. After that, we'll bake them for twenty-five to thirty minutes, until they are slightly risen tae a light golden brown. They should smell divine and sound hollow when we rap on them."

Mother and I brought the bread-making utensils to the sink for cleaning.

"What do we know about the train coming tonight?"

"Your father has the details. He told me 'tis a family o' five."

"That's different."

"Yes, we rarely see a family running together. There is much more risk with a large group, and especially one with mixed ages. They attract more attention, are more difficult to coordinate, and present a greater challenge to hide. Anyway, I am sure the rolls will be greatly appreciated. Go find your father and get ready."

"I enjoyed pounding the dough. It seems that no matter how many deliveries I receive, the stress never goes away."

"Nor should it. That stress keeps us on our toes. It alerts us and protects us from harm." As I turned to leave, Mother added, "Matilda, thank ye for helping me with the baking. Let's continue talking about yer thoughts for yer future at another time."

It was refreshing to talk with Mother in such a relaxed manner. I wished that I could have such discussions with Father, but that was not how he and I worked.

# 11

Joslyn Farm, Cicero, New York
Wednesday, April 3, 1844, 9:30 PM

CLIMBING THE STAIRS to my room, I dressed in the overalls I'd crafted specifically for night work. They were dark to make me less detectable, pant-legged to help me move and keep me warm, and pocketed so I could carry tools for orienteering and emergencies. Wearing such legged clothing was considered unseemly for women, but I did not kowtow to convention. Father and Mother taught me function was most important. Besides, no one would see me to take offense.

On leaving the house, I collected tools in the barn: a kerosene lantern jury-rigged to direct light downward, a dozen dark blankets, and filled water jugs. I placed these items in the cart and took my place on the bench seat, waiting for Father. No matter how many times I met a train, I still got flutters.

Sarah gently guided a pair of our draft horses from their paddocks and harnessed them to the rig. When we first got our horses, they were ill-at-ease about working at night, but they grew accustomed to working in the dark after many trips. They probably came to prefer it to working in the heat of the day.

Wrapped in a heavy overcoat and laden with a dozen rolls from the kitchen, Father emerged from the house and joined me on the rig.

"Are we all set?" asked Father.

"Yes," I confirmed.

Father gently urged the horses down the drive and along the road to Cicero Swamp. It was a peaceful night. The synchronized *clip-clop* lulled me, their steps following the cadence of Mozart's *Eine kleine Nachtmusik*, one of my favorite pieces. I closed my eyes and imagined myself playing the piece on the family piano in the parlor. I fingered the keys in the air.

Eventually I broke the calm of the night by asking, "Father, I know we do not talk about this much, but how did you grow so committed to helping runaways?"

"Matilda, I've not had the misfortune of being a target of the heinous acts of Southern taskmasters nor witnessed their violation of slaves. On the other hand, I've seen the backs of former slaves in my office. They have long, deep welts. And their heads have fared no better. I can barely imagine the intensity of the whippings and beatings that caused such severe scars. It is inhumane. It is unforgivable."

I shuddered. "What can possess people to inflict such cruelty? Where does such hatred, such mistrust come from? Are people taught to be so awful to other humans?"

"I do not have the answers, but the abuse is so profound, both physically and mentally, that runaways choose to risk their own deaths, to leave their families, to live in isolation in a strange new place, and to endanger family members back home. Their pursuit of freedom is born from desperation."

Father wakened me to how fortunate I was. I was able to go where I wanted, when I wanted. I could live without the ever-present fear that I would be ripped from my bed, taken from my family. To me, the security, safety, and stability of home was a given.

"I cannot conceive of the fear and pain that must drive runaways' quests for freedom. It seems beyond bearable. All they have are the shirts on their backs and their dignity." Father added, "It's our responsibility to partner with these courageous souls in their pursuit of safety, liberty, and equality. We must respect them as full people, but we must remember, we are not their saviors." Father inhaled the brisk air. "We should never take for granted the privilege we have merely because we are White and in the majority."

Thoughtful silence enveloped us. Few stars were visible through a gauzy cover of clouds, and I pondered the "power" of the stars over people's lives. I was born under the zodiac sign Pisces. Supposedly, that meant I was a focused, dedicated person who was empathetic toward the less fortunate. What convinced me that astrology was bunkum was that my horoscope also claimed I was a daydreamer. I would have none of that. Serious tasks were at hand.

Father broke my reverie with a gentle nudge. "We're here. It's time to hitch the horses to the tree and work our way to the drop site."

# 12

Cicero Swamp, Cicero, New York
Monday, April 3, 1844, 11:15 PM

NEATH THE LIGHT of a full moon, Father and I once again worked through the bulrushes. The spongy swamp soil seeped through my shoes. Cold ran up my legs and chilled my core. Soon, I was shivering—partly from the cold, and partly from my anxiety.

Having worked with Father on scores of successful missions for the Underground Railroad, I should have been more sure-footed, more comfortable with our plans. Yet tonight I struggled with an inexplicable sense of foreboding. *Why do I feel this way? Is it uncertainty in my skills? Is it bounty hunters again?* Whatever it was, I felt queasy. *Is this what some people call intuition? If it is, I'll take logic any day.* I closed my eyes and forced myself to breathe slowly, deeply—in, out, in, out.

After finding the lone black walnut tree, Father and I scanned the swamp. Minutes passed. Nothing. More time passed, searching and searching for faces dark as the night. Then, movement.

I whispered, "I hear something." We redoubled our listening efforts. There it was again.

Father suggested, "Whoever they are, they are clunky and noisy."

"I think it's only one person."

Father opened his mouth as if to correct me, but before he spoke, a single White man appeared ten feet from us. Father spoke in hushed surprise. "Henry, you startled me!"

Henry Gage responded in a voice sure to waken sleeping swamp animals. "I learned of your plans for tonight through folk at the pub. I thought I could help. So I came."

"Shhh!" Father commanded. "Advance notice would've been appreciated. Seeing as you are here, join us." Father redirected his attention to me. Shaking his head, he exhaled his frustration.

The sky grew more overcast, blocking out the stars. The air grew colder. A brisk wind kicked up. The three of us gathered closer together. While that may have blocked some of the wind, it did not make the time pass faster. As best we could tell, the moon was high in the sky.

Father pulled on his fob and drew out his pocket watch, straining to read the time in the cloud-dimmed moonlight. "If I am seeing this correctly, it's 1:20! The rule of thumb is to give a train a half-hour leeway. We can give them until 1:30. After that, we're to presume the delivery was canceled or intercepted. We don't want to risk exposing our identities. Ten more minutes."

"But, Father, we've never missed a train." I implored, "Let's give them more time. Half an hour?"

"Very well, dear, but a clammy mist is rolling in. I'm ashamed to admit, I would not mind settling down with a hot drink by the fire before retiring to a warm, cozy bed." I was always awed by Father's strength of mind, body, and conviction. This intimated a weakness I had not previously detected.

Henry had remained quiet. Suddenly, he whispered, "I hear something to our right." That surprised me—not so much that there was noise, but rather that this rank amateur detected something before me. Regardless of my hurt pride, he was right. A distinct rustling rolled in from the rushes. My disdain for Henry would have to wait.

I squeezed Father's signal clicker twice. Almost immediately, a pair of clicks returned. It sounded as if the runaways were at most ten feet away. Before Father, Henry, and I knew it, we were face-to-face with a band of five people: a family of two adults in their twenties, a ten-year-old boy, a girl nearly that age, and a babe in arms.

The exhausted adult man puffed hard in exhaustion. "You the engineer?"

"Yes," whispered Father.

"Sorry we're late. Think we were follared. Hunters. Had to shake 'em."

# 13

Cicero Swamp, Cicero, New York
Thursday, April 4, 1844, 1:40 AM

$M$Y PREMONITIONS AND former fears returned. I felt exposed, inadequate. On one level, I knew I was trained and capable of navigating obstacles and challenges thrown my way, but the niggling unknown of what lay before us disturbed me.

"Let's play it safe," whispered Father. After mulling the options, he said, "Let's find cover. The old Vedder Farm is just half a mile up the road. It is rarely used and is chock-full of hiding places."

Our party moved silently, cautiously through the swamp, then up the road. Spring peepers sang. The night was split by a blood-curdling squeal. Everyone froze. I whispered, "That screech was from a rodent caught by an owl." The family relaxed. We continued our journey.

Arriving at the dark, hulking barn, Father tied up the horses and secreted the group through the broad doors. "Matilda, I'll take the family to the hayloft and settle them for the night. You and Henry set up on the ground floor so we can be alert to any potential problems." Keeping the lantern at its lowest setting, Father worked through the darkness of the barn with the bewildered runaways. Sequentially, each family member scurried up a ladder to the loft.

My heart raced. I had heard harrowing stories from Father and neighbors about bounty hunters, and I remembered our confrontation with the two at Father's office. To relieve my anxiety, I focused on the task before me. I instructed, "Mr. Gage. Let's prepare places for Father, you, and me to sleep."

"Miss Joslyn, please call me Henry."

"As you like, Henry," I conceded, though I did not reciprocate. Not having a second lantern, I asked, "Do you see any candles?"

Bumping into chairs and slamming his right shin into a table leg, Henry struggled to stifle himself. As he reached down to massage his shin, he knocked over a hurricane chimney with a candlestick. Fortunately, he caught it before it fell. "Miss Joslyn, I found a candlestick and holder." Rooting about, he opened a drawer under the tabletop, then added, "And a box of candle matches." Neither Henry nor I could understand why there was a table with chairs in the barn, but we did not look a gift horse in the mouth.

"Splendid." I worked toward Henry's disembodied voice and the taper he lit, my eyes drinking up the flickering light as I searched for a dry place to sleep. "Henry, there's a good spot along the far wall. Now to find some hay." We were more likely to find some on the loft. Stumbling into a harrow and horse harness, I found the wooden ladder Father and the runaways had used. I shook it. It seemed stable. Screwing up my confidence, I said, "I'll try it first." I shivered as a bracing, cool breeze passed through the barn and up my spine.

Henry declared, "I'll hold the ladder." I nodded and climbed. Higher and higher. Henry asked, "Is everything good?"

"I've gone ten rungs. Relax, Henry." Despite my outward confidence, I appreciated Henry's attentions. The climb felt endless. One laborious step followed another. The eleventh rung gave out a heartrending squeak, but the step held, and so did my resolve.

After nine more steps, my hand flattened on the loft floor. "I made it." My heart settled. "Come up, Henry. I'll steady the ladder for you."

Henry cautiously followed me. The dim light of Father's lantern shone at the far end of the loft. Having left our light on the barn floor, we relied on the hazy moonlight passing through a pair of quarter-circle windows below the crown of the western wall. After rooting around for a few minutes, Henry exclaimed, "I've found piles of loose hay!"

"Great. Can you slide some over to the opening in the floor?"

"Yeeesss." Henry picked up a wood-handled pitchfork leaning against the hay. After some work, he said, "Phew. I piled hay at the edge of the hole."

"Good. Now push it down." A moment later, I heard gentle thuds as clumps of hay landed on the barn floor.

Henry and I worked our way down the ladder, pushing away the hay stuck to the rungs. When we reached the bottom, we collected the hay, carried and wedged wads of it against a wall, and arranged it into three flat piles, each about a foot thick. Then came a stroke of luck. We found a stack of folded horse blankets next to the wall. I took three and laid them over the trio of hay piles so we would not have to wake in the morning coated in itchy stalks, then collected three more blankets for use as coverings. "My, this actually looks inviting."

While Henry and I admired our work, we heard Father bumping about the loft. He climbed down the ladder one-handed, holding the lantern. I cringed as he hit the squeaky step and heard him sigh when he reached the barn floor. Stumbling once, he worked his way to Henry and me and our makeshift beds. "The family is all settled. Am I exhausted?" he asked rhetorically. Falling into his straw bed, Father said, "Thank you for making these beds." His voice trailed off, and within moments, he was fast asleep.

Henry and I settled in, but neither of us could shut our minds off as quickly as Father. I fell quiet, at least in part because of my discomfort sleeping so close to a man whom I barely knew.

Henry broke the uneasy silence. "Miss Joslyn, how did you come to these parts?"

I thought this a curious question in the wee hours of the morning. "I came with Father to help him with the train."

"No, no. I mean, how did your family end up in Cicero?"

"Ah. Like my father, my grandfather was named Hezekiah. He was born in Connecticut and moved to Cicero when he was in his middle twenties. That was just after the first war with England. He and my grandmother moved west, to where they could buy their own land to farm."

"That's a common story."

"I guess. My grandfather bought the land where our home and farm now stand. He died before I turned ten. I remember him as a kind but aloof man. I never met my grandmother. She died four years before I was born. Whenever I think of her, I am reminded how blessed I am to have had my parents for as long as I have."

Henry interjected, "Yes, I feel the same way. As I think on my family, I realize that I too often take their continued presence in my life for granted. It's a gift. Hearing your story, Miss Joslyn, I reflect on the blessings of what I have. I know many others who are not so fortunate."

I did not know why I was so talkative. Maybe it was my difficulty winding down. Maybe it was Henry's proximity or his disarming nature. Whatever it was, I felt an urge to fill the void. "My mother's family was from northern Scotland, near Aberdeen. Her mother was from plain folk, but her father was of noble lineage. I'm told that he descended from Sir George Leslie, Earl of Rothes. My maternal grandparents moved to Albany, New York, when my mother was one year old. They were escaping the narrowness of small-town Scots. They yearned for a new life where all people were treated equally. My grandmother died five years after she arrived in America, when my mother was six. I do not believe they found what they searched for. Seems to me, they traded one kind of narrowness for another."

"How so?" Henry queried.

"What they found in the States shocked them. People were equal—so long as they were White. Blacks, Haudenosaunee, and other indigenous peoples were less, at best. Eliminating that inequality compels my family to this day." Realizing I was rambling on, I turned the conversation to Henry. "And you? From where do your families hail?"

"Miss Joslyn, I do not have a history like yours. I am not well educated, but I am driven by the injustices I see. I was in Peterboro half a year ago where I heard a speech by the great abolitionist Gerrit Smith. I left that meeting perplexed. Slavery is an offense to God. We Americans pride ourselves as Christians, yet when it comes to Blacks, we behave as heathens bereft of soul, respect, and empathy."

I was charmed by Henry. I looked directly at this good, honest man, his eyes shining even in the dim light. "Henry, please call me Matilda." And with that, we both fell silent and into well-earned sleeps.

# 14

Cicero Methodist Church, 8416 Brewerton Road,
Cicero, New York
Sunday, April 7, 1844, 10:20 AM

A DANK, CHILLY morning greeted us. It was the kind of day best suited for staying cuddled in bed. Alas, this Sunday was Resurrection Day. Regardless of the weather, the observant rejoiced in the gifts of our Lord and attended morning services. Congregants dressed to the nines. As we filed into the church, Mother and I wore layered dresses with flowered prints and bonnets. Father wore a long wool coat and silk hat.

A second reason to rejoice was the return of Reverend Moses Lyon. Father appreciated that man so. After serving as the minister at Cicero Methodist Church for ten years, he was recently assigned to a new post in Syracuse. Like Father, I found Rev. Lyon accessible. Instead of being a fire-and-brimstone minister, he wooed congregants by appealing to our intellects and to our better angels. On this holy day, Rev. Lyon's additional challenge was to be uncustomarily dynamic and counter the draining, dreary weather. Rev. Lyon delivered. He urged us to mind the meaning of the day. He led us in hymns that we sang with joy and psalms we recited with responsive gusto. Rev. Lyon's reading of the scripture and his sermon were received with rapt attention.

Following the service, all trooped out of the sanctuary—animated, interactive, and celebratory. Even the weather seemed pleased. As if by divine edict, the rain stopped, and the sun broke through the parting clouds.

Amid the throng, we bumped into Daniel and Mary Baum. Mr. Baum spoke first. "Good Easter to you, Zeke and Helen." He tipped his hat as he looked at me. "And to you, Matilda."

"Good afternoon, Daniel." Father spoke while Mother and I simply smiled and nodded to Mary. "It's a coincidence to see you today. Helen and I were just talking about your cousin Benjamin and his bride, Cynthia, a few days ago. Are they still conducting a station in Chittenango?"

"Indeed. It certainly is risky out there. Riskier in the East than in these parts. I guess there is more public suspicion, and hunters lurk."

"Yes, so we've been told. Anyway, we need to catch up. Helen and I would very much like to have you over for a meal."

Mr. Baum nodded. "That'd be lovely, but it'll have to be soon."

Cocking his head, Father asked, "Why? Is the dairy farm not working?"

"Not as well as we'd like," Mr. Baum responded. "Competition for butter and cheese is keen. Even though the farm has been productive, we've had steady losses for years. We cannot keep this up. If we lived closer to the canal, we'd be able to get our product to market better. In fact, that's why we're selling the farm and moving to Syracuse."

Father commiserated. "Canal business is compelling. We'll be sure to have you over before you move. Let's find a convenient time."

Tipping their heads, the Baums thanked Father. Father turned to Mother and me. "Lovely folks. I'll miss them."

"I'm not so sure I will," Mother replied. I nodded in agreement, but Father looked confused.

Before he could inquire further, we were interrupted by more neighbors stopping to shake our hands and offer wishes for a blessed week. In a lull, Father turned to Mother. Before he had a chance to ask, Mother volunteered, "I enjoy Mary, but Daniel only grudgingly talks wit me, and he barely acknowledges Matilda. Most men are not like ye, Zeke. They look past women and children. They see us as, well, as necessary encumbrances. They certainly dae not seek us oot or appreciate us."

"Matilda, do you feel the same way?" asked Father.

"Yes. It is rare that an adult man is genuinely interested in the thoughts and cares of women and children. If he is, it's likely in the purpose of obtaining something for himself."

Father went stone quiet while Mother and I chatted. Suddenly, Father said, "What you say disturbs me. Am I opaque to this? Is this general male behavior?"

Mother answered, "Ay."

"Am I complicit?" Father sheepishly asked.

Mother tried to soothe Father. "Ay, but it's yer opacity that makes you so dear." She smiled, and the tension fell from Father's face.

*Mother is amazing. She has an uncanny ability to walk the razor edge of simultaneously being direct and softening her message. I hope that trait is heritable.*

Changing the subject entirely, Father turned to Mother and energetically shared, "My, it was good to have Reverend Lyon with us again. I do miss him. He continues to astound me. He finds ways to challenge us, or at least me, even with the mundane."

"Yes, he does," Mother said almost reflexively, having heard such praise from Father many times.

"Take today's sermon. Reverend Lyon linked his namesake's story of the plagues to the rebirth of spring. He went on to talk about Jesus, his crucifixion, and resurrection. Then, he tied the sacrifice of Jesus to the paschal lamb. Marvelous. Simply marvelous."

"Yes, dear. I agree." Mother was distracted by the crowd and barely listening. "I often find myself wandering back tae his words during the following week."

"His words engage, energize, and sometimes haunt me," Father replied. "There are times when I wish I could turn them off."

"That is an interesting idea—silencing my mind. My mind simply won't rest while I'm awake," Mother said. "It's always running. Not always productively, but always running. I thank my stars that my mind does rest while I sleep."

Father teased, "I don't think the reverend would be happy to see you degenerating to Zoroastrianism."

My curiosity was pricked. "What? Zoro-who?"

"Zoroaster, a prophet who lived in Persia more than three thousand years ago. He thought the stars had the power to shape one's actions and destiny. He may have been the first prophet to believe in a single God."

"Zeke, where did you pluck an obscure reference like that?" asked Mother.

Before Father could reply, he was interrupted by Henry Gage. "Good morning, Dr. and Mrs. Joslyn. Matilda."

I was pleased to see Henry. His increasingly frequent appearances made me happy, though I was confused as to why.

"Good morning, Henry," bade Father and Mother.

Mother added, "How is your family?"

Her question surprised me. She had not previously shown much interest in the Gages—if anything, the opposite.

"They are well; thank you for asking." Henry raised his hat a bit in appreciation. Then, turning to me, he asked, "Matilda, may I walk you home?"

I offered Henry an eager smile. Though I could not quite figure it out, Henry made me feel comfortable, respected, safe. I nodded to Father and Mother as Henry and I left the throng. We followed a longer route through the fields. To distract myself from my confused feelings, I focused on the nearby pasture speckled with brightly colored spring flowers bursting through the drab winter beige and brown. "I love this time of year. The explosion of life is dazzling. The first spring azure butterflies flit among early cress blooms. Robins gather food for newly hatched little ones. Soon there'll be broken eggshells for me to collect. They have beautiful colors— light blue, egger green, alabaster white."

"The spring colors are splendid. I particularly enjoy bluebirds. They're beautiful, and I enjoy their lilting songs." Henry fidgeted, but he looked directly at me.

I clutched a bunch of crocuses and plucked their petals, one by one.

"Matilda, would you accompany me to the dance at church this coming Saturday? I would dearly like to attend the annual Cicero Spring Fling with you."

"Henry, I'm not much of a dancer, but I'd enjoy going to the dance with you. I cannot stay out too late. I have to prepare for my lecture."

I watched the anxiety melt from his face, replaced by relief. "That is wonderful." Then, realizing all I had said, Henry asked, "Lecture? What lecture?"

"I was asked to discuss astronomy at a meeting of the Cicero Literary Society next week. I still have much information to gather. And my father's words have reminded me I may discuss astrology, too."

"That sounds exciting, and scary. Have you spoken to an audience before?"

"Yes, it will be scary, and no, I have not spoken in public. Regardless, I can spend time with you today."

We settled down in the grass. Having time to talk with Henry was lovely. He was easy to be with. After a few moments, I asked, "Henry, how did you get involved with dry goods?"

"That's a curious question. Why do you ask?"

"Well, I am trying to sort out things for myself. Father has ideas, but I must figure out what I want to do, what I'll do after I leave home."

"Leaving home?" Henry's face fell.

"I'm just thinking of the inevitable."

Looking relieved, Henry replied, "I am expected to continue our family dry good store. Recently, my brother and I took over the day-to-day tasks. Father had an accident. At least for a while, he is unable to continue."

"I don't mean to pry, but what kind of accident?"

"He was restocking high shelves in the store, reached a bit too far, and fell off his ladder. He broke his arm."

"Oh, Henry. I am so sorry. Is he going to recover?"

Henry blushed at my sympathetic response. "Likely, but he's not easy to be around while he's on the mend. Looking at the bright side, his injuries have given me time to think and question things."

"How so?" I asked.

"I'm thinking of setting up my own store—from the start. I admire my father very much, but I want a place where I do not have to do what he wants. I want to set up the store the way I think serves my customers best and makes me proud. I want independence. In my family, my father is the unquestioned authority."

"I think I can see that in your father."

"My family is so different from yours. Your parents seem to have a balanced partnership. I am awed by how they challenge yet care for and respect each other. That does not exist in my family," Henry explained. "Anyway, I don't want my store just to sell things. I want the store to be special."

"Special? How so?" I asked.

"I want to support people not just by selling supplies but also by helping them navigate their lives. I want to become a lawyer."

"That sounds terrific. I hadn't thought of that before. It makes so much sense when you describe it like that—"

Henry was gaining steam and, in his exuberance, cut me off. "And I do not want to help just White people. I want to help Blacks, too. We all need to live together."

"That sounds great." Despite my getting swept up in Henry's enthusiasm, I was confused and a bit crestfallen by my situation. "Like you, my father has plans for me. He expects me to follow in his footsteps and become a physician."

"Matilda, you are great with people."

"Thank you. You are kind, but I am not so sure. I often feel uncomfortable with others." As I said this, I realized how relaxed I felt with Henry. He made me feel different. He saw me for who I was. "I just don't know. If I did become a physician, I am certain I could do a credible job."

"Credible. You would be more than credible. You would not settle for less, and your father wouldn't have it any other way. He wants to share his work with you. He wants to help you grow. That is enviable. Also, I've seen you with children and adults."

I was puzzled. "You've seen me with children? Where?"

Sheepishly, Henry added, "At church."

I looked at him warmly.

Henry and I rose together and walked the remaining stretch to my farm in an easy silence, a silence punctuated by glances that were furtive at first, and then met with reciprocating smiles.

# 15

Joslyn Farm, Cicero, New York
Sunday, April 7, 1844, 3:30 PM

To TAKE A break from the chaos of holiday meal preparation, I gazed out the kitchen window. All appeared peaceful in the world—fitting for Resurrection Day. I closed my eyes and recalled the lovely walk with Henry. When I opened them, my attention was drawn mindlessly down Brewerton Road, a ribbon of packed dirt leading to our farm. Far away, something was moving, approaching our farm. The movement wasn't an "it." Henry was riding his horse toward us!

Meanwhile, Mother orchestrated final meal preparations. At her direction, Father garnished the potatoes, Sarah laid out serving dishes, and I set the table. As my parents entered the dining room, ready to sit for our celebration, a knock came at the door. Father and Mother looked at each other. Knowing it was Henry, I went to greet him and found him brushing road dust off his coat. Speaking loudly enough to be heard in the dining room, I asked, "Henry, what a pleasure it is to see you again. Would you care to join us for dinner?"

Without delay, Henry accepted. "Thank you. How may I help?" While Henry removed his coat and hat and hung them on hooks by the door, I realized how different he was. I had little experience with men, but that simple question spoke volumes.

In the dining room, Mother welcomed Henry. "Hello, Henry. Good tae see ye, and so soon. Just carry a plate and utensils for yerself from the kitchen, sit down, and enjoy dinner."

Mother was an accomplished cook. We all enjoyed a fine feast of lamb, spring greens, and potatoes. Thanking Father and Mother for including him, Henry declared, "This food is *dee*-licious!"

"Henry, you are kind, but this meal was mostly prepared by Sarah. She taught me how tae spice the vegetables and how tae use a Seneca method of slow-braising meat."

"Marvelous." Turning to Sarah, Henry said, "Thank you for the great food. The meat is so tender, and I am particularly enjoying the greens. What spices did you use?"

"Wild onion, tarragon, and juniper from last fall's harvest."

Father and Henry nodded in appreciation.

"Dr. and Mrs. Joslyn, thank you for including me."

Following the delicious meal, we cleared the table, stored uneaten food, and wiped down the dining table. As Mother, Sarah, and I cleaned up and shelved the dishes, Henry gathered his resolve. "Dr. Joslyn, would you be interested in a game of chess?"

"Absolutely. I never turn down such an offer. Set 'em up. I'll be there in a few moments, after all the dinner cleanup is complete."

Henry collected the chessboard and a box from a bookcase in the parlor, then carried them to a small table, placed chairs on opposite sides, and sat. Carefully opening the box, he removed thirty-two carved wooden pieces and set them in their starting positions.

After Father finished putting the dried dishes in their appointed places, he stood over the chess table and grabbed a pawn from the white army in one hand and a black pawn in his other. Behind his back, he shuffled the pieces between his hands and presented his fists to Henry. Henry tapped Father's left. Opening that hand, Father declared, "White it is. You begin."

Henry changed chairs to sit behind the white pieces, and Father sat behind the black army. The parlor fell silent. The traditional medieval battle was joined.

A few pawns and other pieces were moved. A couple pawns were captured. Henry advanced a pawn to fork a black bishop and knight.

"What the dickens!" cried Father.

Mother, Sarah, and I watched with amusement. I leaned over to Mother and quipped, "As I look at the chess pieces, it occurs to me that there was no pretense of a separation of church and state in the medieval world. I wonder if religious leaders like Joseph Smith and William Miller play chess? If so, do they dream of the 'good old days'—when religion drove the state?"

Mother asked, "Have things really changed?" This comment caught me by surprise.

Moments later, I not so discreetly whispered to Father, "Move your knight to queen's bishop three."

"Thank you, dear," Father uttered dismissively. "I have this game well in hand." Father turned back to the board to consider his options. Moments later, he moved his knight just as I suggested.

Sarah watched in wonder. "What is all this?"

"It is a game in which one person moving the white pieces tries to capture the black king." I pointed to the tallest black piece so Sarah could understand. "The other team is trying to take the white king. Whoever gets his opponent's king first wins."

"Sounds like war," Sarah observed.

"Yes. It does."

"Not a good lesson. Why can't people learn how to get along rather than practice war?"

I pursed my lips and nodded.

Father lifted one of his pawns, prompting Henry to note, "Sir, you may not move that pawn. It's pinned. Moving it would place you in check."

"Ah, yes. Good point." Father moved his bishop forward two spaces.

A moment later, Henry raised his right hand to touch his queen.

I cleared my throat and shook my head.

Henry retracted his hand, then moved it over to a knight.

I shook my head again.

That gesture was noted by Father, who furrowed his brow. "No assistance from the *silent* audience."

Clearly, Father had conveniently forgotten my help to him earlier.

He added, "And whose side are you on anyway?"

I rolled my eyes, smiled, and turned away.

Henry craftily moved his castle to pin Father's bishop before his king.

The game proceeded. Queens were exchanged. Finally, Father studied the board and realized that he had few options, and regardless of what he did, in three moves he would be checkmated. He glanced at Mother, then graciously tipped over his king and shook Henry's hand. "Splendid game. Thank you."

I winked at Henry.

# 16

Joslyn Farm, Cicero, New York
Thursday, July 4, 1844, 7:30 PM

THE FRONT FIELD of our farm shimmered in blinking, pale-yellow lights—fireflies putting on their annual summer show. Nature celebrated its abundance and another successful tour of earth around the sun. I watched the spectacle from the window of my bedroom with awe.

Henry approached our farmhouse, wearing a pensive, drawn look, and sat on a chair set askew to Father's in the front yard. Father continued to read in the waning sunlight, apparently unaware of Henry's presence.

Even from where I sat, I could hear Henry swallow and clear his throat. I was anxious just watching him. His noises interrupted Father's reading. Looking up, Father asked, "Henry, are you alright?"

"Why, yes, Dr. Joslyn. I'm fine." Henry's pallid face revealed his anxiety. "In fact, sir, I'm more than fine. Dr. Joslyn, please know that these last four months have been among my happiest. I've had the joy of getting to know your family, particularly Matilda. As you might have guessed, I admire. . . I love Matilda. She brings joy and purpose to my life. If I may be so bold, I would like to ask you for her hand in marriage."

*What did I overhear?* I was flabbergasted! *Where did that come from?*

Henry continued, "Um, Dr. Joslyn, before you interrupt, let me—"

Father did interrupt him. "Henry, you are a fine lad. You are kind, hardworking, and evidently care for our Matilda. The difference in your ages is of little import to us. What does speak to us, however, are the great hopes and plans that her mother and I have for Matilda. Matilda has a high calling. She is destined to be the first woman physician in the United States."

I had heard Father talk about his aspirations for me before, but why was he filling Henry with all this talk?

Father continued, "Matilda's mother and I have worked hard toward gaining admittance for Matilda at Geneva Medical College. I discussed the matter with my mentor and the current dean, Thomas Spencer. Dr. Spencer assures me that enrolling Matilda at his medical school is a formidable challenge. There is great resistance by the college administration, and by society, to the idea of a woman as a physician. That said, he is willing to consider Matilda."

*Oh, how I wish I could save Henry from Father.*

"To make this possible, Matilda's record must be extraordinary—not only among women but, more importantly, among men. Having Matilda follow me in medicine would be one of my greatest joys. I do not want to see that hope frittered away by a premature marriage."

Henry girded himself. "Dr. Joslyn, I appreciate what you are saying. I, too, would like nothing more than to see Matilda achieve her dreams. If she pursues medicine, I will support her in every and any way I can. I love Matilda for who she is."

Henry was such a dear, and while Father's face showed he was moved by Henry's heartfelt entreaties, he remained unmoved in his aspirations for me. "Henry, I am sorry, but I cannot give you my blessing."

On hearing Father's proclamation, I stormed down the stairs and onto the front field where Father and Henry sat.

"Father, if marrying Henry means giving up your dreams for me, so be it. I want to marry Henry."

Normally loquacious, Father was struck dumb by my forthrightness but quickly collected himself. "Matilda, let's take our time with this. I will discuss things with your mother. Does that suit?" Father neither expected nor wanted a response. He knew full well that his decision did not please me.

As he stood to end the conversation, I did respond. "Father, why are you treating me differently than your parents did you? As I remember your story, you not only attended medical school after you married mother, but I was also born before you completed your studies. Why should my situation be any different than yours?"

Father looked pained by my words. Henry's proposal was an affront and threat to his plans. Rather than say something he might regret, Father demurred. He turned toward the front door.

I continued. "Father, do you not believe that I could balance multiple responsibilities as you did? Is that because I am a woman? Do you not act in concert with your convictions?"

Father walked into the house without a word.

A smile spread across my face as I squared to Henry and engulfed him in an exuberant embrace. "Yes. Yes. I will marry you." With that, the decision was made for Henry and me, and for Father.

# 17

Joslyn Farm, Cicero, New York
Thursday, December 26, 1844, 2:15 PM

WHILE I SHOULD have been happy, I felt blue, at sea. I was betrothed, but there were no definitive arrangements. Father's plans and hopes were thwarted by Geneva Medical School. They denied me admission, unwilling to take the courageous step of enrolling a woman. As I wandered about my home, I passed the office where Father and Mother were having a quiet conversation. Father saw me and beckoned me inside. "Matilda, your mother and I have been talking."

"Yes, sir. What is it?" I remained unable to break the remoteness between Father and me. The most frustrating aspect was that Father seemed obtuse to my feelings.

"Matilda, your mother and I have an old friend, Jermain Loguen. If memory serves, you met him years ago when he was escorting a couple of children through Cicero." Father paused. "Anyway, we think he'd be an excellent officiant for your wedding. We know Jarm as a former slave and conductor at an Underground Railroad depot in Syracuse. More to the point, he is a minister with the local African Methodist Episcopal Church."

"Whatever you would like to do is fine with me. Fine for us. We just wish to marry as soon as possible." I left the office as quickly as I arrived but overheard Father say, "Helen, I don't understand Matilda's curtness."

I paused in the hall to eavesdrop.

"Zeke, Matilda feels unsupported. Ye leaned hard tae block this union. She finds yer behavior disorienting. Whenever we've asked her tae do most anything, Matilda barely squawked. We raised her tae be a strong, independent young woman. This may be the first time in her life that she's questioned your support."

Father suddenly bellowed, "Matilda! Please come back." I dragged myself to the office. "Matilda, I've been writing notes to thank people for their holiday kindnesses." Father fumbled with a stack of notes ready to post. Next to the stack was a letter he had already shared with me, from Dean Spencer. It was deeply creased, presumably from being folded, unfolded, and refolded. I remembered the text verbatim: *Thank you for your interest in having your daughter, Matilda, attend the Geneva Medical College. We are unable to admit her to our program.* The message was painful. Its terse and impersonal manner was the acid that burned Father.

"Ah, here it is." Father picked up another letter from a corner of the desk. He handed it to me. "Please, read this note and let me know if you endorse me sending it."

320 Pine Street
Syracuse, New York
December 26, 1844

*Dear Jarm,*

*Fond greetings from Helen and me. We hope you had a peaceful holiday. We would like to ask two favors of you. You can think of this as tying the tally.*

*First, our daughter, Matilda, is marrying a Henry Hill Gage. We would be honored if you would officiate the ceremony. They are planning their nuptials for early January, tentatively the sixth. You are welcome to overnight before or after the wedding to make your round-trip journey less onerous. Please let us know if this is workable.*

*Second, having lived in quiet Cicero for most of her life, Matilda and Henry wish to set up their new lives in a vibrant locale with a promising future. I believe Syracuse or somewhere along the Erie Canal would offer such opportunity.*

*Matilda is caring, compassionate, and accomplished. We groomed her for attendance at the Geneva Medical College. Unfortunately, despite my imploring the dean of the school, the school is not yet ready to accept and educate a woman. It's our disappointment, their error, and the community's loss. Where that leaves Matilda is anyone's guess.*

*Henry is a good man. He works at his family's dry goods store. He expresses interest in starting a venture of his own. Henry seems particularly keen to become a lawyer to complement the standard offerings of a dry goods store. Please sound him out. Then, anything that you can do to help him find his path will be greatly appreciated.*

*Helen and I await your responses.*

*My sincere wishes,*
*Zeke*

I shook my head in disbelief and then burst from my chair to hug Father. "Oh, Father, how can Henry and I ever thank you? We know you do not agree with us, but we so appreciate your support."

Ever the diplomat, Mother shot me a conspiratorial glance. I returned it with a smile of acknowledgment.

## 18

Joslyn Farm, Cicero, New York
Monday, January 6, 1845, 9:30 AM

THE QUIET COMMOTION of wedding preparations proceeded. Mother and I worked together in the kitchen, lost in our individual thoughts of my wedding day. Our coordinated solitude was broken by a rap at the door that echoed through the farmhouse. While I was confused, Mother was giddy. She ran down the hall and flung open the door, barely containing her enthusiasm. I heard her from the kitchen.

"Jarm! It is so good tae see ye. Come. Put down yer bags and—"

Before she could finish, Father rushed from his office. "Welcome to Cicero." As I left the kitchen, I watched Father swing his right arm around the shoulder of a lanky, bearded Black man—Jermain Loguen, the minister from Syracuse.

"Ah, the two of you are sights for sore eyes!" our guest said in a clear, resonant voice.

"Come, let's go to the parlor," urged Father. "Jarm, would you like some tea?"

"That would be delightful. Thank you."

Father and Rev. Loguen followed Mother down the hall to the parlor while she continued to the kitchen. As I approached them, Father boomed,

"Ah, here comes the bride. Matilda, I'd like to reintroduce you to our great friend, Jermain Loguen."

"I am most pleased to see you, sir." I tipped my head. "Welcome to Cicero."

"Thank you, Matilda. The pleasure is mine." Rev. Loguen offered his hand and shook mine. "And congratulations. You certainly have grown since we last met years ago."

"Matilda, would you join us in the parlor?" requested Father. The three of us sat, and Father dominated the conversation. "Well. Where to start. Life in Cicero is good. Helen and I happily farm. We tend our small herd of dairy Brown Swiss and a dozen or so chickens. In addition, we have a Ryeland ram and three ewes. Shearing and spring lambing are just around the corner. All in all, the farm keeps us quite busy. Oh, and Mother dotes over our four workhorses. They are beauties."

Sometimes, Father's filibustering was frustrating. *Why is he prattling on about our animals? Why aren't we talking about my wedding? About Henry and me?* I did not want to look conceited, so I smiled and added my two cents in hopes of interrupting Father. "Each of us has our favorite. Mine is Elmer. He has a red star on his chest. Elmer is strong yet gentle, but he walks with a decided limp."

"Thank you, Matilda." Father reinserted himself. "Mostly, we use the horses for tilling the fields, reaping crops, and pulling the cart when marketing or working on the Railroad."

I rolled my eyes. "Father, please stop with the farm. Reverend Loguen came here to learn about the wedding. Can we talk about that?"

Father laughed nervously. Rev. Loguen tried to dissipate the obvious tension. "Zeke, caring for the farm seems overwhelming!"

Just then, Mother appeared with a pot of hot tea. Having not heard my comment, she added her thoughts on the farm. "Ay. It can be, but we do enjoy the animals. Matilda is a natural with them. When she walks into the barn, the animals look up. They seek her attention. Also, while Zeke doesn't often admit it, he enjoys the animals, too. They're like family tae him."

*It's a conspiracy!* Try as I might, I could not redirect the conversation from the farm to the day at hand.

Father continued, "As much as we enjoy the farm, I think we largely keep it to disguise our work on the Railroad."

"Many of us in Syracuse are very aware and appreciate your selfless service. I, for one, am deeply in debt of your help and support."

"Oh, I should add that Helen keeps me on task in my office."

Being self-effacing, Mother redirected the conversation. "Zeke continues tae tend tae the health o' our community. He has such a gentle way, particularly with people o' limited or no means. He's an ardent combatant for people who don't get a fair break. Last year, Zeke talked down some bounty hunters who accosted the office. He also booted patients from his office because o' their awful behavior toward Sarah, a Haudenosaunee woman who has since joined our family."

The conversation in the sitting room continued for another half hour without ever coming around to the wedding. Such deft dancing must have been the result of a conscious effort to discuss everything under the sun but the wedding. Then, Father and Rev. Loguen excused themselves and walked down the hall, disappearing behind a door to the office. Father closed the door behind him. This was uncharacteristic of Father, and I was confused and offended by being excluded.

As Mother and I retreated to the kitchen to finish dinner preparations, I asked, "What are Reverend Loguen and Father discussing?"

"Matilda, I am not quite certain. I'll ask your father this evening."

An hour later, four Gages arrived: Henry, his parents, Judson and Eleanor, and his brother, Ichabod.

Henry was dapper and serene. *How can he be so calm? It is our wedding day!* Henry navigated through the crowd to embrace me. It was just what I needed to pull me out of my mental solitude, calm me, and draw me into the joy and solemnity of the occasion.

Father, Mother, and Henry's parents exchanged greetings. Though they knew each other well, having lived in Cicero for many years, this meeting was a bit different. After today, we would be family. Father shook Judson

Gage's hand and pulled him into a brotherly hug. I do not know about everyone else, but this broke the tension I was feeling. Following that cue, all the parents forwent handshakes and embraced each other.

Mother, Eleanor, and I went upstairs to prepare for the ceremony. As I donned my full-length, beige cotton dress, Mother asked, "Dear, how are ye feeling?"

"Truth be told, I cannot say that having a wedding is a dream come true. As you well know, being married has not been my life's ambition."

Mother shook her head.

"Even so, I am marrying a wonderful man, a man whom I love, and someone with whom I'm ready to share a life together."

Mother silently beamed her blessings on me.

"Besides, I feel beautiful in this dress."

"Matilda, you look lovely," Eleanor remarked.

I responded, "Thank you. How could I not? It's the gown Mother wore when she married Father."

Mother tipped her head and added, "The embroidered yoke is one of the few things I have from my mother."

While we prepared upstairs, the men were in the parlor downstairs. Presumably, they were smoking cigars and enjoying our newest yield of cider.

Shortly after noon, the wedding began. Everyone was ready to celebrate Epiphany with the consecration of Henry's and my union.

Mother, my matron of honor, wore an unadorned, pastel-blue gown and stood to the right of Rev. Loguen. Henry and Ichabod, his groomsman, were classy in their black dress coats, pressed white shirts, and black pantaloons. They stood to Rev. Loguen's left. The reverend wore a formal, long black robe and octagonal felted beret.

At my request, Eleanor Gage played the "Wedding March" from Mendelssohn's *A Midsummer Night's Dream* on the piano. I'd recently heard the organist at our church practicing it for a wedding. She told me the piece was played nearly five years earlier at the wedding of Queen Victoria and Prince Albert.

As the processional music played, Father escorted me to the front of the parlor. Everything was perfect. We stopped before Rev. Loguen, and I took my place next to Henry. Father kissed me, and then joined Mr. Gage, Sarah, and Cherry in the audience.

Rev. Loguen opened the ceremony with a reading from Colossians 3:14. "Over all of these virtues put on love, which binds them all together in perfect unity." Looking to the groom, the reverend asked, "Henry, do you have anything to say to your bride?"

"Yes." Henry faced me. "Others, such as poets and politicians, deftly turn a phrase. I am not so endowed. I am best to turn a cheek, a page, or a profit, but they are of little consequence. I freely turn myself to you, for our lives and future."

Rev. Loguen looked to me. "Matilda, do you, in turn . . ." He coughed as he realized his inadvertent punny phrasing. The assembled tittered. The reverend began again. "Matilda, would you like to say anything to Henry?"

I offered, "Henry, you are generous and honest. I pledge my heart and mind to you, toward an equal partnership in which we celebrate mutual respect, sharing, and patience in our new life."

Father and Mother glanced at each other and nodded approvingly. Rev. Loguen smiled, opened his notes, and read from Genesis 1:27. "So God created humankind in his image, in the image of God he created them; male and female he created them." He expanded upon the passage. "Yes, God created both. He created them as equals." Then Rev. Loguen continued with Genesis 1:28. "God blessed them, and God said, 'Be fruitful and multiply.' What is a marriage if not for family?" He answered his own question with a passage from Mark 10:6–9: "But from the beginning of creation, 'God made them male and female. For this reason a man shall leave his father and mother and be joined to his wife, and the two shall become one flesh.' So they are no longer two, but one flesh. Therefore, what God has joined together, let no one separate."

Henry slipped a ring on my finger and I on his. All we could do was beam at each other. Rev. Loguen decreed, "In the name of our Lord, I pronounce you husband and wife." I closed my eyes for a moment.

When I opened them, they were locked on Henry. He leaned over and we kissed. While I was not accustomed to displays of public affection, I felt goosebumps and exhilaration.

The entire party went to the dining room to enjoy a fine celebratory meal of Great Lakes white fish, plums, boiled potatoes, and baked tomatoes. After food was passed and initial tastes were taken, Eleanor gushed, "Helen, this food is sumptuous. How did you ever get tomatoes and plums this time of year?"

Ever deferential, Mother responded, "Thank you. It was a team effort with Matilda and Sarah." Then Mother shared our secret. "We preserved summer produce by drying it with Haudenosaunee methods and reconstituting it with simmering salt water. We intended our preserved produce for Christmas, but when Matilda and Henry decided to get married, we saved it for this celebration."

As we reached the end of the meal, Father rose. That made me nervous. *What is he going to say? How embarrassing might he be? Might I feel?*

"Matilda. You have brought and continue to bring great joy to your mother and me. You are our proudest achievement. Henry, we know you are a fine young man. We pray that you, too, will cherish Matilda and the two of you will support each other. May the two of you have a life of wonder, family, and untold joy."

With tears tracking down my face, I embraced Father. "Your blather with Reverend Loguen this morning on everything but the wedding was intended to irritate me. Right?"

Father smiled and calmly said, "To distract and settle you." He winked and added, "I thought you played chess."

I nodded to Father, grinned, and turned to Henry. I held his hand, closed my eyes, and dreamed of our life together.

# 19

Joslyn Farm, Cicero, New York
Thursday, January 9, 1845, 7:30 AM

DAYS AFTER OUR wedding, I stood at the door of my native home. The idea of leaving was scary and exciting. I had gone to the Seneca nation for summers and to Clinton for two years, but this was different. This was permanent. I managed, "Mother. Father. You are so wonderful. How can I—that is, how can *we* ever thank you for what you've done?"

Mother urged, "Go. Be the best people ye can. Help others, and you'll be helped. Feed others, and you'll be fed."

Henry and I hugged my parents—long and strong. We were uncertain when, and if, we would see them again.

Once we'd set off, I turned to Henry. "My, what a whirlwind! Three days ago, we were married. Today I'm leaving my childhood home in the country and moving to the city." I wanted Henry to know how excited I was, yet I was unsure how to relay my anxiety. He seemed to understand, though. Henry rode his horse beside me while I guided Elmer, who pulled the cart carrying our worldly possessions to Syracuse.

After a two-hour ride, we arrived at Rev. Loguen's home. On opening the door, he welcomed us with an inviting smile. "Ah, it is good to see you again. Please, hitch your horses around back. That's Elmer, isn't it?"

I was wide-eyed surprised by Jarm's comment. "What a great memory!"

On entering the house, I was struck by the art on walls in the foyer and waiting room—paintings of streams, oceans, waterfalls. Each had people dowsing themselves. One painting was particularly notable, showing what I surmised was St. John baptizing a Black man and his family in a woodland creek. "Reverend Loguen—"

The minister interrupted, "Matilda, we are well past formalities. Please, call me Jarm."

"Thank you. Jarm, who painted this work? I like it very much. It is so different from anything I've seen in a church or a book."

"Yes, child. I am fascinated by people's ongoing need for repurification. The painting you note comes from a perspective you've likely not considered, a Black person's point of view. And thank you, I am the painter. But let's discuss the art later. Please, come into the dining room. Join me for tea."

After sitting down, Jarm told of his journey from slavery to freedom. "I was born a slave in Tennessee. When I reached twenty-one, I escaped and was lucky enough to ride the Railroad successfully, and one way. I was scared witless. Once, I was nearly captured. I was in the basement of a house in Baltimore. There was scuffling upstairs, which I guessed was hunters. After a notable silence, they stole downstairs. I thought it was the conductor coming to call 'All clear,' so I came out of my hiding spot beneath the floor. Fortunately, just before I walked into the light, the conductor's dog pounced on one of the hunters, and he yelped. In the commotion, I slid back into my hidey-hole and waited out the hunters."

"Oh my," blurted Henry. "That must've scared the bejabbers out of you!"

"Yes. My heart nearly stopped. Eventually, with the help of countless, nameless, and often faceless heroes, I made it to freedom. First, I lived in Canada. Then, I returned to America as a 'free' man, always living with the fear of being recaptured and returned to servitude. I attended school at the Oneida Institute and settled here in Syracuse. Now I do my best to assist as many as I can in their quests for freedom. Ah, but enough about me. What are your hopes for your new lives in Syracuse?"

Jarm's ministerial manner made it comfortable to talk about most anything. Often, I was remote with others, but Jarm was good at drawing me out, getting me to talk. "I am not sure about my direction. I labored so long with the expectation of being a physician."

"Ah, that is laudable. Someday, I hope to have a daughter who is interested in medicine. We need someone to take care of us free Blacks. But I detect there is more to your response than your words."

"Yes." I met Jarm's gentle yet insistent gaze almost defiantly. "It is disappointing to have others define your opportunities."

Jarm nodded knowingly.

I realized that I had just encapsulated the Black experience.

Sensitive not to probe too deeply, Jarm shifted the conversation. "And, Henry, what about you?"

"I aim to learn law, to help people in their day-to-day concerns and issues, to help people buy land, start and manage their businesses, write contracts, negotiate squabbles, and draft wills. My goal is to provide these services as part of a dry goods store. It would be an opportunity for me to help people build their lives."

Jarm nodded with an expression of appreciation. "Hmm. That's not a usual pairing. Fascinating."

# 20

Loguen home, 320 Pine Street, Syracuse, New York
Friday, January 10, 1845, 8:00 AM

JARM JOINED HENRY and me at breakfast and then excused
himself. "I have errands to do. I should be back by early afternoon. Till
then, walk about. Get to know the neighborhood."

After cleaning up from breakfast, Henry and I donned our coats and
tramped through snowy streets to the center of town. The sun pierced
through a light morning flurry, flanked by a pair of rainbow-colored
sundogs. It felt magical.

Syracuse was a bustling, wondrous whirl of activity. It accosted my
senses with rich sights, sounds, and smells. The center of the organized
chaos was the Erie Canal. Mules trudged along towpaths on both sides of
the waterway, pulling line boats. Beyond the towpaths were broad avenues
crowded with people hurrying to and fro. Denizens dodged horses and
carriages as they navigated streets littered with debris and animal waste.
Side streets were crowded with vendors hawking the bounty provided via
the Erie Canal: produce, grains, chickens, spices, baked foods, leather
goods, farm tools, wooden and pottery kitchen utensils, and clothes.

Henry and I ogled the buildings lining Erie Boulevard. They reached
the sky, towering four, five, or even more stories. Each building was
distinctive in its architecture. Some boasted broad, layered arches over

their entrances. Others featured carved cornices with curlicues. Many were built with mixed types of stone that highlighted windows defining each story. This splendid variety was complemented by the diversity of churches in Syracuse, each distinguished by its spire striving for the heavens.

As we gawked, I scurried to avoid being hit by a carriage. Henry was rushed across the avenue by the clanging bell of an oncoming phaeton moving at the heady speed of maybe eight miles per hour. In his effort to avoid being hit, Henry bumped into a street vendor selling roasted chestnuts. Fortunately, he caught himself before toppling the cart. The vendor yelled, "Hey, bud, watch yerself!" Despite the awkward situation, that smell was wonderfully overpowering.

Whelmed by the activity, Henry and I trudged back to the Loguen home to sit and reflect on the big city. I offered, "I'm not so sure that I could live in such a place and at such a pace. I think I prefer the calm of country life." Henry nodded and smiled in agreement.

I thumbed through some of Jarm's books until shortly after noon when Jarm returned. "Matilda, Henry, I have great news for you. You're probably unaware, but for the past two weeks, I have been searching for a place where you can live. I am happy to say, I found a place. It is a bit of a distance from Syracuse, but I think it can work. And the price is certainly right. It's a rarely used safe house for the Underground Railroad near a village called Four Corners. Ah, I should restate that. Since last year, the village renamed itself—Fayetteville. It was named after the Marquis de la Fayette. You probably know of him."

"Yes, doesn't everyone?! The Marquis was the hero of the Revolutionary War," I responded too quickly and too impudently.

Jarm nodded. "As I understand it, the Marquis rode through the village a few years back, when he was on his tour of the States. He was a staunch advocate for providing power to the people. All people. The Marquis's story continues to ring particularly true to people of Upstate New York who champion the ideals of religious freedom, abolition of slavery, and equal rights for all people." Jarm paused. "As usual, I'm going off on a tangent. A house near Fayetteville will be available in early spring. A couple months from now. You are welcome to stay here, with my wife and me, until then."

I lept and hugged Jarm. "Thank you. What a gift!"

Somewhat flustered, Jarm collected himself and straightened his clothes. "Matilda, it is my pleasure. Your father and I have been working on this plan for weeks. You may even find the next news better than the first. I found a legal apprenticeship for Henry. It's with John Wilkinson, Jr., a respected lawyer in Syracuse. In fact, I believe Mr. Wilkinson was the first lawyer in Syracuse. He practices general law at South Salina and West Washington Streets. That is not far from here, and it's accessible from your new home."

"Jarm, this is more than I could have ever hoped for," Henry enthused. "How can we ever thank you?"

"It is my honor. You can thank me by continuing to work our Railroad station at your new home and contributing to our cause of equality for all." With that, Jarm nodded and left the room.

With Henry's future falling into place, it was time for me to consider my options. "Henry, you know I am undecided about what I shall do. I could take the easy path and be a traditional wife and mother." Almost immediately upon saying that, I shook my head, knowing that option would not be wholly satisfying.

Henry nodded. "I am certain you will be a wonderful mother, but I do not see that as your only purpose."

"As I am not going to become a physician, where does that leave me? I have tossed this question about in my mind for quite some time. The questions remain: What do I want to do? What am I suited to do? I have no work experience and no thoughts."

"Matilda, you are talented, educated, and strong," Henry observed. "I'm certain you will find a way, for yourself and for the world around you."

"Maybe I could be a nurse. That's an opportunity to serve and educate people about their health." Shaking my head, I realized the flaw in that option. "Nurses only help people one by one. And after reading Dickens's *Martin Chuzzlewit*, I am not so sure I want to be associated with or work to overcome the damage caused by the Sarah Gamps of the world."

Henry rolled his eyes with that comment, and we both laughed.

I sat back and reflected. "Maybe I should think broader. Maybe I should become a teacher and help classes of children grow. That might be fun, but it might be too confining. On the other hand, I do enjoy research and working through vexing issues with others. It may be daunting to not have a direction, but it will be exciting to consider the options without the societal shackles of being a woman. Maybe we should just let time and the spirits work their magic. I am sure there is a place for me in this world."

# PART 2

## *STEVE*

Thou speak'st aright;
I am that merry wanderer of the night.
I jest to Oberon and make him smile.

*A Midsummer Night's Dream*
William Shakespeare, 1595–1596

# 21

Limestone Creek, Fayetteville, New York
Saturday, April 12, 1845, 6:30 AM

T HE CRUSTY, FROST-LADEN field sparkled with thousands of tiny jewels. My oldest brother, Will, and I ran headlong through the field, crunching the crinkly grass and shattering the morning quiet. "Wheee!" Nothing was better than running about and having a day off school.

Will and I had adopted the far end of the meadow for playing baseball, a game that only recently arrived in Fayetteville. We staked our claim to this space by hammering four short posts arrayed in a square some fifty feet per side. The farmer might not have been happy with us, but we did leave the rest of the pasture for his Guernsey cattle to graze.

On reaching the posted diamond, Will and I tossed a small, round ball to each other. The ball, a present Mother handcrafted for Will for his thirteenth birthday three days ago, was already one of his prized possessions. Fortunately, he was willing to share. After all, you cannot play baseball alone. The ball was hard, with a yarn-wrapped stone at its core. Because I was still learning how to catch a thrown ball, I had welts on my body as evidence.

Will winged it to me. A clap in my bare hands was immediately followed by my yelp of acute pain. "Blazes! Don't throw so hard! It hurts!"

I'd turned eight a month before.

Barely concealing his glee, Will chuckled. "I know, I know. Steve, I'll be gentler." Will was strong. I looked up him, if only because at nearly five and a half feet tall, he was about a foot taller than me. While we were merry co-conspirators, he always made it clear that he was in charge.

Over at the docks in the distance, I spotted Cecil running to the field. He shared his first name, Richard, with Father, so he was always called Cecil—that is, except when Father or Mother was angry with him. Then, he was called by both names. Cecil was two years older than me. Despite that, he was more than an inch shorter. Cecil was kind, but he whined often, and he carried a frowning, pouty expression. Maybe that's why he was often a target of teasing.

"Here I come!" Cecil yelled. "Will, throw it to me."

"Okay. I sure hope others get here soon. Steve and I have only an hour before we're off to work the docks."

"They'll be here. They'll be here," Cecil droned. Then, as if to himself, he muttered, "I hope they come. I hope they come."

In short order, Jacob Cartwright bounded onto the field. "Hey, guys! I got some new balls in New York!" Nine-year-old Jacob, always bubbly and generous, struggled to control the half dozen balls he was carrying as he ran. He boasted, "Last week, I saw Unca Alexander in New York. Maybe you remember me talkin' about him. He's in charge of the Knickerbockers Baseball Club. Well, he gave me these balls." Jacob dropped the balls in the middle of the diamond, or at least gave up trying to hold all of them. "Unca Alexander taught me how t' play, and he introduced me t' tha new rules he's making for the real players on Manhattan."

Moments later, three more friends joined us on the field, including Rufus, a Black classmate who attended Fayetteville Academy with me. I was happy to stop listening to Jacob. He could be such a know-it-all and sounded like someone running for mayor or something. Now there were seven of us. Each of us took a position in the field: Will stood behind the post marking home base, Cecil was at the center of the diamond, and I positioned myself between the posts for first and second bases. That was most unfortunate because the rising sun shone directly into my eyes as I looked toward home base.

Seeing me squint, Cecil offered, "Maybe Mother can sew a bill on the front of your beanie to block out the sun."

"Hey, Cecil and Beanie Boy, stop jabberin'," Will commanded. "Field some grounders."

A short time later, two more friends arrived, ten-year-old identical twins George and Sam O'Neal. Freckle-faced and fun-loving, they often switched names, and even after years, I still could barely tell them apart.

When the twins took positions in the field, Jacob declared, "Hey! We've got enough for batting around." He threw his mitt to Will, who stood behind home base as the catcher. "Take this. You'll need it more than me." Then Jacob picked up a bat—a thin oak post I'd found at the local docks that Will had shaved to a smooth, round surface. He was a skilled woodworker and, wanting to be just like him, I took up whittling as a hobby.

Cecil grabbed the ball and started pitching. When he was good, he was very good. On "off" days, however, which came all too often, he frustrated easily, wailed, and had tantrums. Cecil stared into Will, who coaxed, "C'mon, Cecil. Put the ball in my mitt." Cecil twisted his body, unwound, and released the ball. Will waited, but the ball never arrived.

Jacob swung the bat and cleanly connected with the ball. It flew over second base and bounced deep in the outfield. Jacob dropped the bat, ran to first base, touched the post, and continued running.

George chased down the ball and threw it to Sam, who had stationed himself in the shallow outfield. Despite George's strong arm, the ball bounced on the dewy ground a few times before reaching Sam. Waiting at second base, I yelled, "Throw the ball, Sam. Soak him, hit him!" Sam heaved the ball but missed hitting Jacob.

Jacob yelled, "Crikey! No soaking me. We're playing Knickerbocker rules. Only tag-outs."

By the time I collected the ball, Jacob was standing safely by the post for third base. Having batted and run, Jacob came in to pitch, and Will took his turn at bat. He slipped a cloth winter glove on his right hand to avoid splinters. After taking a few practice swings to ensure that his swing was smooth and flat, he stepped up to home base.

While Jacob stretched, Will swung his bat menacingly. Finally, Jacob let the ball fly, fast and true. Will waited for the ball to arrive and took a rip with his bat. He missed, screwing himself to the ground. Embarrassed, Will challenged, "Jacob, pitch another!"

"Okay. Here it comes." This time, Will took a sweet cut with his bat, squarely hitting the ball. It soared over my head and bounced many times till it stopped a hundred yards from home base and under cattle grazing in the far pasture. Will was fleet of foot as he circled the base paths. Indeed, Will was so fast, and so full of himself, that he ran around the bases again. George ran, dodged the cows, corralled the ball, and heaved it to me. I had run into the outfield to relay the ball to Jacob, who covered second base. In turn, Jacob threw it to Cecil standing at home base, ready to tag out Will, who fell on the ground exhausted upon completing his third time around the bases.

Now it was Cecil's time to bat. He selected a slim bat that I had carved from a birch branch. Will took a turn at pitching. He tossed the ball. Cecil swung. As he hit the ball, the bat cracked just above his grip. Splinters flew in all directions. Will disintegrated into hysterics, rolling on the ground in laughter. Cecil stood stunned. Holding the stump of the bat and watching Will, Cecil realized that the bat had been tampered with. He grew red faced and incensed. Reflexively, angrily, he bellowed, "Stephen!"

Will composed himself enough to yell, "Run, Steve. Run!"

Abandoning my position in the field, I ran. I ran for home. I ran the mile up Genesee Street, the main street of our village, as fast as I could. I dared not look back to see if Cecil was chasing.

# 22

Cleveland home, Fayetteville, New York
Saturday, April 12, 1845, 7:15 AM

UPON TURNING ON Academy Street where I lived, I afforded myself the luxury of peering back down Genesee Street. Surprised and pleased that no one was following me, I entered my house, hung up my jacket, and entered the sitting room. I worked to relax as I adjusted to the dim light. First, I sat in one of the eight high-back chairs lining the wall. Finding the chair uncomfortable and feeling anxious, I stood abruptly.

I well knew not to tease Cecil, but he was such an easy target, and, egads, it was such fun. What was a boy to do? At least, this boy. The urge to tease was irrepressible. Despite my need to needle Cecil, I paced, waiting for him to come home. It was not so much that I wanted to see him. I wanted to see my parents' reaction to him.

Nervously, I shuffled from the doorway toward the hearth and back. I sat by a fire burning in the fireplace, usually one of my favorite places in the house. Whenever I could, I would cozy up to the fire as close as possible and cover my lap and legs with a quilt. My favorite quilt was a cherished gift my parents received when they married. Their names, Richard Falley and Ann Neal Cleveland, were stitched into the back, and the words of Genesis 2:22—*And the rib, which God had taken from man, made he a woman, and brought her unto the man*—were embroidered around the border in blue and amber letters.

Shaking my head and staring at my feet, I mumbled, "Family. Why do I need to have Cecil as a brother?"

My breathing settled, I looked up as someone filled the doorway. Mother greeted me with a gentle look, an easy smile, and a warm embrace. Soon after, Father came down the hall to join her in the sitting room. He was less welcoming. As Father looked about, I saw him shake his head, close his eyes, and exhale with resignation. This was not the first time I had seen that expression on his face. Firmly, stiffly, he ordered, "Stephen, go to your room."

*Why does he act that way? Does he know something happened? How? Can he read my face?*

Obediently, I scaled the stairs to the room I shared with Will and Cecil, hanging my head in shame—mostly for Father's benefit. Wads of muddy turf fell from my shoes onto the treads. I purposely stepped on the fourth stair with emphasis, knowing that it would creak. Family tradition held that the stair sounded as if a wounded buffalo lived under it. I found that description curious; I had neither seen nor heard a wounded buffalo. But who was I to argue?

On reaching the top step, I turned right toward my room. Anna, my oldest sister and most reliable supporter, popped her head through the doorway of the girls' room on my left. She whispered, "Steve. Steve, come in here."

Confused, I slinked into her room and asked, "What?"

"I heard the commotion downstairs. Let Father simmer down. Stay here. Later, you'll get your comeuppance, but it will be less unreasonable." I knew this was sound advice, learned from hard experience. So I hid behind her door. "Steve, scoot over here. We can listen to the conversation through the heating grate." Anna and I scrunched together and listened.

In mid-argument, Father declared, "Ann, that boy must stop tormenting his brother."

I looked at Anna. "How did he know?" *Sometimes, parents are magicians.*

Father continued, "God knows Stephen enjoys a good prank, but this is too much. I am going to give that young man a piece of my mind, and quite likely, a piece of my hand as well."

The color drained from my face. My ears, nose, forehead—everything felt clammy and cold.

Anna watched me. "Steve, I know Father can be forgiving with children, particularly the children of members of our church. He just isn't forgiving with us. That's the way he is."

I nodded and grimaced because I thought I understood what Anna meant.

Anna continued, "Father has high standards for our behavior, particularly for you boys. He expects—no, he demands exemplary character, forthrightness, and honesty. Remember, Father was raised in the home of strictly observant Protestants. Mother has a different view of childhood. She was raised in a relaxed, easy home. So she is forgiving, maybe even supportive of our enthusiasms. Alas, that's of little consequence because she defers to Father. I think she often tames her tongue."

As Anna finished talking, I heard Mother try to settle Father. "Richard, please consider Stephen's spunk, his creativity. We mustn't crush that."

"Thank you, Mother," I whispered.

Anna smiled her agreement.

Father parried Mother's sympathy. "Why must Cecil always bear the brunt of Stephen's creativity? It is as if Stephen knows that Cecil is ill equipped to fend for himself. We both know that Cecil is not a robust lad. He has few friends, limited social skills, and is prone to crying. Why should Cecil have to endure Stephen's ridicule in front of age-mates? How is he ever to make friends? How is he to learn independence?"

I looked at Anna dumbfounded and said, "I'd no idea Father had favorites. I only knew his temper was short with me."

"I'm just as surprised."

Mother said, "Richard, you are not Cecil's protector. Just because he's your namesake doesn't mean you must defend him from the slings and arrows of childhood, even if they come at the hand of his brother."

Father retreated a bit. "Of course, you're right, dear. Give me a few moments to settle myself. I will discipline Stephen."

Just then, Will and Cecil burst into the house. Cecil's huffing, blubbering entrance seemed to verify Father's and Mother's fears. Mother rushed into the foyer to hug and console him. Father shooed Mother away and admonished, "Cecil, hold your head high. Do not let others shake your composure or learn you've lost yours."

Cecil reeled back from Father and stood stock still. As best as I could make out through the grate, he looked devastated, abandoned.

In a flash, Father stormed from the room and up the stairs. Once on the second floor, he paused outside my room and barged in without knocking. I heard him rip the belt from his trousers. Thanks to Anna, I was not there. Father barely raised his voice, but he was terse and scared the devil out of me. "Where are you? Stephen, where are you?" Receiving no reply, he stormed from the room and back downstairs.

The house was stone quiet. Time passed. *This is cowardly, hiding in the girls' room. I need to take my lumps.* I marched downstairs and found Father in the sitting room, reaffixing his belt. "Was that meant for me?"

Father's expression showed his surprise at seeing me. His flat visage turned stern—it brought a chill to my spine. "Sit, boy. It's brave of you to come to me. For that, I will not give you the strop." He continued to thread his belt through his pants loops. "You must know, tormenting your brother is not acceptable. It is not kind." Father's eyes drifted upward. He said nothing. His silence was devastating. Then, he spoke again. "Baseball is dear to you. It was the reason for this most recent incident. Therefore, it seems fitting that you not be allowed to play baseball for the next week. Further, during that week, you will collect, carry, and stack fire logs in the house—by yourself."

"Yes, sir." On that, Father left the sitting room.

I was relieved to dodge a beating. The last time I was punished, I could not sit for a week, even on chairs with cushions. *This room should be renamed the non-sitting room.*

I had little time to digest what had just happened because Will and Cecil reentered the sitting room. I looked Cecil in the eye. "I'm sorry I played that trick on you." Cecil neither returned my gaze nor accepted my apology. He still smarted, which was probably fair because I could not completely hide a smirk. Needling Cecil was fine sport. I could not banish my thoughts of teasing him again.

As Cecil left the sitting room, I muttered to Will, "I offered myself to Father. Why wasn't that enough to avoid being punished? I don't mind the log work. That's just another chore. But not playing baseball for a whole week—that's nasty." The more I dwelled on it, the angrier I got.

Will raised his eyebrows. He elbowed me. "Maybe it's time to poke the bear."

"What are you talking about?" I asked.

"Wanna get back at Father? I have a great idea," Will confided.

A sly smile spread across my face. As Will described his plan, I nodded faster and faster.

# 23

Cleveland home, Fayetteville, New York
Friday, April 18, 1845, 6:20 AM

"STEVE, WAKE UP." Will insistently shook me. "Your week of no baseball is done tomorrow. Time to begin our next job."

I opened my eyes slowly. Pitching away the grogginess of the night, I blinked away my eye sand and batted at the morning light. "Will. Will? Is that you?"

"Yes. C'mon, let's get going." Will continued shaking me.

"What?"

"I asked you, should we keep to our plan?" After a short pause, Will continued. "We need to make a rope. A loooong rope."

"What? What are you talking about?"

"Steve, go to the docks. Find as many scraps of rope as you can. If need be, go to the cobbler. Collect shoelaces. After that, go to the tailor. Gather all the long pieces of strong fabric that you can. Then, bring your treasures to the shed behind our house. Let's meet before school starts."

"Will do!" After dressing and going to the kitchen, I grabbed a slice of bread slathered with berry jam and a hard-boiled egg Mother made last evening. Then, I bolted for the docks on the feeder canal. My first goal was to locate a bag to carry the rope scraps. Finding a large burlap sack, I started collecting scads of rope. I combed the docks. I pored over spaces near buildings and mills where received parcels were unwrapped and outgoing packages were bundled.

"Master Cleveland. Good mornin' ta ya," a kind, bearded boat captain greeted me. "What ya been up ta? Available ta help me?"

"Morning, Cap'n. Sorry, I can't help today. I've got a church project I'm working on. Collecting rope."

"That's a shame. Rope, ya say." Stroking his beard, the captain suggested, "I saw a bunch over near the barrels leaning against the Daly Buildings."

"Much obliged. Good day." I skedaddled to the Daly Buildings and was richly rewarded. Most of the discarded pieces I found were three to five feet long. I screened each piece I found. *Hmm, this one is good, strong, and nice to have some with color. Bah, don't want that one. It's frayed in the middle.* While I had the luxury of being picky, I did not have the benefit of endless time. I needed to be back to our shed before 7:30 to get to school on time.

Before long, my bag was filled with an assortment of rope fragments. Lugging the load up Genesee Street, I reached the shed. Will was waiting. I opened the sack and dumped the load on the floor.

"Weehonk! That's spectacular, Steve," congratulated Will.

The two of us tested each piece for strength and ensured it was not frayed. "Okay, let's come back after school to finish tyin' our tether."

# 24

Cleveland home, Fayetteville, New York
Sunday, April 20, 1845, 6:30 AM

MY PARENTS TAUGHT me that Sunday was a day of thought. It was a time to pause from the busy week, think on what had happened in the preceding days, and prepare for the coming week. These normal Sunday reflections were dashed by the glorious morning I saw through my bedroom window.

The town shone crisp in the bright morning light. The bluest sky I had ever seen was punctuated by red-orange cirrus clouds rising on the eastern horizon. The flowering trees lining Academy Street smelled delicious. I could almost taste them. The serenity of the church-mouse quiet was barely interrupted by the gentle *clip-clop* of a horse cantering by our house, the bark of a feral dog in the schoolyard, and cheerful chirps of the proverbial early birds. These sounds echoed off the clapboard facades of homes lining Genesee Street. I closed my eyes; it was like I imagined heaven to be, plus a baseball field.

Father added to the gentle clatter as he quietly collected and ate his breakfast. The slap of the kitchen door when Father left the house was the cue Will and I had been waiting for. The day was ripe with anticipation.

Will and I scrambled from bed, dressed, slunk down the stairs, and ran to the shed. Splayed on the floor was the ragtag rope we had fashioned. We struggled to coil it; it seemed to have a mind of its own. Finally, we wrestled it under control, threw it over our shoulders, and ran through neighbors' yards like a pair of clowns in a horse costume. Will commanded, "Left leg, right leg. No, no. Together. Left, right." After tripping over the rope and each other a few times, we developed a rhythm, crossed Genesee Street, and slipped behind hedges in front of the Fayetteville Presbyterian Church.

My heart raced. I sat motionless. From my vantage point, I saw Father approaching the church. He seemed happy—his eyes were closed, his head tipped to the heavens. He whistled. I was stunned; he was quite good. After a few moments, I recognized the tune as "Amazing Grace." I was shocked not so much because of the tune but from just hearing Father whistle. I don't ever recall hearing him whistle and being carefree.

While Father was clearly happy, I remained petrified that he would see Will or me. Fortunately, Father's attention was drawn to Samuel Jameson, a church deacon, who waited for him on the portico next to one of the stately, two-story Ionic columns in front of the church. As Father scaled the steps from Genesee Street, he said, "Good morning, Mr. Jameson. Isn't a beautiful day?"

The taciturn deacon grunted, "Indeed."

Father fumbled for his key, and unlocked and pulled open the grand oak doors. "Mr. Jameson, it's time to call the people to prayer."

"Yes, sir." Mr. Jameson followed Father into the church.

Seeing our opportunity, Will softly encouraged, "C'mon, Steve."

"Okay, Will. I'm trying, but this rope does what it wants." I sweated: partly from fighting the rope and partly from anxiety.

After scanning our surroundings and making sure the coast was clear, Will and I slid behind one of the opened front doors. Having accompanied Father many times on his Sunday routine, I pictured what was happening. Once in the foyer, the deacon would turn right, facing a narrow wood door on the west wall at the base of the bell tower. Will and I knew that door well. We'd played in the tower many times while Father met congregants in his office. In my mind, I watched Mr. Jameson unlock the door and enter the dark core of the bell tower. He unraveled the rope tied to the east wall and tugged it three deliberate times. A resounding *clong, clong, clong* echoed from the bell tower. He paused for a moment. Then he repeated the triad. After a third time, he wound the rope, hung the coil on a hook eye-high on the wall, left the bell tower, and closed the door behind him. Deacon Jameson then walked into the nave, joined Father, and prepared the pews.

While Father and the deacon prepared the sanctuary for the Sabbath, Will and I slipped into the foyer. We passed through the open front doors and entered the church. Blessedly, Deacon Jameson had left the bell tower door unlocked, likely so he could get in to ring the bells again after services were over.

We snuck into the tower, tugged our ragtag rope inside, and closed the door behind us. The tower was dark and narrow. I slid my hand along the wall until I reached the spiral staircase in the corner. Will stood at the door. "I'll stay here and keep guard. Tie the rope around your waist and climb."

Though my rapid pulse felt like hammers pounding inside my head, I did as I was told. The stairs creaked and groaned as I climbed. "Egads, Will. It's so dark in here. I can barely see where I'm goin'. What if I miss a step or two, or trip over the rope and fall?"

"Don't be a baby, Steve. You can do it!" Will cheered. "Take one step at a time. Hold onto the banister. Keep turning left. Put on your brave beanie."

"Okay." I clenched my teeth and climbed. The tower seemed endless. I worked higher and higher. One turn of the spiral. Then another. And then another. After reaching the top of five spirals of the stairs, I banged my head on the ceiling. *Ooch.* I rubbed the pain from my forehead. Fortunately, the ceiling door did not fit snugly, so I was able to make out the outline by the outdoor light leaking into the dark tower. As I eased the door open, the bright morning sunshine poured through, temporarily blinding me.

Sweating, I clambered up the last steps to reach the floor of the belfry and tugged our rope onto the floor after me. Once it was in a serpentine pile, I slumped against the wall, regained my breath, and removed the rope from my waist. I tied one end to the clapper of the cast bronze bell. *Where is the end of the rope?* Hunting through the coils, I found the ragged free end, threw it out the east window of the tower, and paid out the slack until there was little rope left on the belfry floor. *Humpf, this rope is long and heavy.* Finally, I heard the free end hit the ground. *What a relief!* I had feared that we had not made the rope long enough.

My job done, I slipped back through the belfry floor, closed the door as my head cleared the hole, and carefully went down, down, down the stairs. I tried to go as quickly as possible, but I began to feel queasy. Finally, I landed on the floor of the tower where I was welcomed by Will. I stood still for a bit to settle my spinning head and twirling tummy. Will peered out the door to the foyer and Genesee Street. Seeing no one about, he urged me to scurry from the bell tower, out the front door, and down nearby Edwards Lane.

Once beyond the house on the corner and out of view of the folk on Genesee Street, we ducked behind some pine trees, cleaned ourselves, straightened our clothes, and headed back. Blending in with the other congregants, we soon joined the rest of our family outside the church.

Anna looked at Will and asked, "Where have the two of you been?"

Will shook his head to silence our sister. He and I entered the sanctuary with our family and sat as if everything were usual.

Father began the service with a responsive reading, the opening of Psalm 133.

> *Behold, how good and how pleasant it is*
> *for brethren to dwell together in unity!*
> *The foundation of our world comes through struggles*
> *toward completing small and grand goals.*
> *Completion of such tasks brings us satisfaction*
> *as individuals and as a community.*
> *The weakest define the limits of our strength.*

Father followed with quotes from Hebrews 10:24–25 and the First Thessalonians 5:14. After the call to worship, congregants joined Father in singing "A Mighty Fortress is Our God." Then, Father delivered a somber sermon extolling the importance of community: how it provides succor to the individual, which in turn supports the vitality of the community. Father summarized with the Golden Rule. "One should treat others as one would like others to treat oneself. That is the essence of a healthy community."

Everyone sang a second hymn, "All People that on Earth Do Dwell." Father offered a prayer of dedication, invited those in attendance to recite the Lord's Prayer, and provided a final benediction.

As usual, I was a rapt listener and eager participant during Father's services. On this Sunday, the service was more intense; Father's words bored into my soul, as if he were speaking specifically to me. *Was Father urging me, commanding me to do better for myself? For the community? Does Father know what Will and I are going to do? How could he? Should I feel guilty for just the thought of Will's and my plan?* My head throbbed.

After services, I strolled home with my family. Together, we enjoyed a festive Sabbath meal of fried bacon, brown bread, and a hearty root vegetable soup. I looked forward to these meals every week. What I did not look forward to were our after-dinner activities. I ached to run to the pasture to play baseball when the day was warm and the sun was high. But it was the Sabbath. In our home, we could not even enjoy a game of checkers or cards. Father expected us to sit, read, think.

Sometimes, being an observant Presbyterian took so much work.

# 25

Cleveland home, Fayetteville, New York
Sunday, April 20, 1845, Sunset, 6:55 PM

THE EVENING QUIET on the second floor succeeded daytime rambunctiousness. It was my favorite time of the day. My brothers and sisters holed up in the girls' room together. This was when we talked about what we'd seen and done during the day. We exchanged hopes, prayers, and secrets. Some were, well, secret and were not openly discussed.

This night, my brothers, sisters, and I huddled to share by the light of a pair of lanterns. Will played checkers with Cecil, my sisters knitted, and I read Cooper's *The Deerslayer*. It was one of my favorites because I loved the idea that everyone had worth and a place in the world. By 8:30, all of us were in bed, except Anna, who at fourteen was allowed to go downstairs to talk with Mother. Mary and Margaret, who were older and younger than me, respectively, settled down quickly. Cecil likewise fell fast asleep, unaware of what Will and I were scheming. Will and I, who shared a bed, kept ourselves awake so we could finalize our plans.

While Will eventually drifted off to sleep, I forced myself to stay awake. I was bound and determined to get back at Father. I whispered songs I'd learned in school. The tall clock downstairs chimed once. I figured, *Ah, half past the hour. But what hour?* I willed myself to stay awake, at least for another half hour. I played counting games. I tweaked my toes and pinched my face. Finally, the clock tolled the hour: *gong, gong, gong* . . .

*Was that ten times? Maybe it was eleven?* I was so groggy that I could not tell topsy from turvy.

After dozing fitfully, I awoke. This cycle repeated, and again, as I worked to stay alert. It was torture. *Did I hear the chimes?* I counted. *Yes, I think that was twelve gongs. Time to wake up Will.* I shook him and whispered with increasing insistence, "Will? Will?" Finally, he stammered something unintelligible. I clapped my hand over his mouth until he realized he was awake, who and where he was, and that all was well.

Will and I dressed quickly. With him in the lead, we crept down the stairs, one step at a time. In his mental fogginess, Will stepped on the fourth stair. *Creeeak!* We cringed. Our hearts stopped. Our eyes swelled. The quiet of the house held. Will and I exhaled.

Now more awake, Will and I collected our cloaks from the foyer. He opened the front door with care, and we slipped into the still of the night. I heard a quiet but secure click of the latch as Will ensured that the door closed.

Any remnant of sleep was shocked from me by the bracing, cold air. Under a nearly full moon, a barred owl asked, "Who cooks for you?" Another responded rhetorically, "Who cooks for you all?"

Will and I slinked down Genesee Street to the church. My heart pounded with apprehension and anticipation. I followed Will, step for step, until we reached the church. Working around the church into the moon-shadow of the bell tower, we groped about. Finally, we found the rope hugging the back wall of the fieldstone tower. Will and I grabbed it, stared at each other, smiled, and tugged. The bell made a dull clang.

I looked to Will. I felt his beaming smile.

Will whispered, "Weehonk, Steve. It works."

Will and I pulled the rope a second time, this time with extra effort. Now the bells began to resound. Triads of clangs rang through the village.

Lit candles appeared in windows here and there in the homes along Genesee Street. Front doors and windows slapped open. Bleary-eyed, robed folk peered out to assess the emergency. Will and I grinned madly at one another and drew on the rope one more time, with all the gusto we could muster. The bell rang. The rope broke! *Oh no! Now we are going to get caught!* We fell backward and tumbled on our heads. "Quick, Will. What shall we do?"

Will was dumb-frozen.

I gathered the fallen rope as quickly as possible and elbowed Will. "Hide this under your cloak. Then, let's walk down Maple Street and act as if we don't know what's happenin'."

Will obliged.

From the corner of my eye, I saw Father run into the street, presumably trying to discern whether the ringing had come from his church. With Father outside, Will and I dumped the rope into a nearby garbage bin, ran through some neighboring backyards, and slipped into our home through the kitchen door. We hung our coats on hooks in the foyer and ran up the stairs two at a time—skipping the fourth step. Being ever so careful to keep quiet and not wake up Cecil, we slid into our room, removed our shoes, and settled into bed.

Will and I degenerated into fits of giggles.

# 26

HABITS ARE HARD to break. Despite being groggy from ringing the bells late last night, I woke faithfully at dawn. I managed to dress quickly and run to the docks. *I gotta get to the boat slips first.* My goal was to find work as a runner, drudge, or light jobber. I really wanted a baseball mitt like Jacob's, and besides, Father and Mother appreciated a contribution.

I had only a short time to work before I needed to be at school. Opportunities were often limited, so finding work was keen. Being among the youngest boys working the docks, my greatest advantage was arriving and finding work before the others. To date, this strategy had worked reliably. I scanned the docks. It looked like it would be a good day; I was the first to arrive.

It was an unseasonably warm spring morning. A billowy fog wafted over the feeder canal and Limestone Creek. To the uninitiated, the docks must look chaotic, but I had learned to flow with their innate rhythms. I watched the dance of line boats being unloaded of grains from Batavia and salt from Syracuse while others were loaded with parcels from Fayetteville: lumber, wool, and paper.

In my time at the docks, I had learned that salt was a great telltale of how careful a boat handler was and which captain would be a good one with whom to work. Good captains made sure that their salt cargo was wrapped in paper and kept dry. In other boats, salt blocks might be exposed and wet. These were indications of either a bad boat or a sloppy hoggee—a canal boat captain. I used this clue to steer myself toward better jobs.

I searched for my regular captains. Not seeing any, I hawked myself to any takers, but this day, activity on the docks was nearly nonexistent. Finally, I saw movement down the east side of the dock. Running to the end, I introduced myself. "Morning, Captain. My name's Steve. Need any help?"

A slim, nattily dressed Black man responded, "Fine to meet you, young Stephen. You can call me Professor. Everyone does." After shaking hands, he asked, "This is my first time in Fayetteville. Usually, I just pass by on the main canal. What can you tell me about this place?"

I was silent, fascinated by Professor's remarkably bushy moustache. I refocused myself long enough to say, "Blazes. Pardon me. Welcome to Fayetteville."

"I've heard much about this stop. It's one of the many places that arose because of the Erie Canal. I remember years ago when the Erie Canal was ridiculed as 'Clinton's Big Ditch,' a boondoggle for builders, investors, and politicians. Since its completion twenty years ago, however, people have seen things differently. Now Clinton and his great vision are celebrated. It helped New York grow into the envy of the world and to achieve its destiny predicted by George Washington. It's sad that after such a short life, the success of the canal is already being undermined. It pains me to say it, but the railroads are coming."

"I think I know why you're called Professor. But I'm not sure what you mean—the feeder is awful busy. While it's slow today, it's usually jammed with line boats carrying freight and packet boats carrying people and cargo."

"Yes, Stephen. I'm sure it is busy. That may be true now, and maybe for the next few years, but mark my word, this is not forever."

"Huh? What does that mean?"

Professor stopped teaching for a moment, long enough to appreciate some of Fayetteville's attributes. "Hooooweee! This canal does smell."

"When the wind blows the wrong way, it does stink. I guess I've gotten used to it." By design, canal waters were flat so boats could readily travel in either direction. Hence, there was little or no flow through the canal, making the waters stale at best. Adding to this were the pervasive odors from garbage and sewage dumped into the canal by local businesses, people, and animals. "Maybe we put up with it because of all those things you said the canal brings."

"You're a pretty wise one yourself."

I blushed at Professor's compliment and could only say, "So, Professor, what can I do for you? Need some help?"

"Young Stephen, I've enjoyed getting to know you. Alas, I am sorry to say, I do not have any work for you. This was a stop of curiosity, not business. I'd heard this village has a checkered record on respect for people who aren't White."

"I don't know nothin' about that, but I sure had fun talkin' with you. Enjoy your visit to our village."

Back in the hunt, I found a job as a runner for Cap'n John Smith, as he called himself. He was a gruff hoggee from Buffalo. He commanded, "Boy, bring dis list to Beard Crouse Paper Mill. Find out how long it'll be before their d'livery is d'livered."

"Will do, Cap'n." As I ran up the hill, my buddies Rufus and Jacob arrived.

"Hey, Steve. Any work t'day? I really need it. I'm working for a new baseball mitt. I want one like the players use in New York City." Jacob smashed his right fist into the open palm of his left like a ball being caught by his mitted hand.

Rufus chimed in, "Yeah, and I need five bits to get a new pair of shoes."

I told my pals, "I didn't find much. All the regulars seem to be away. I'm working for this captain from Buffalo. He's carryin' wood and stuff to Utica and beyond."

"Okay, we'll get crackin' on finding a job. See you at school," said Rufus.

After rushing up the hill from the North Mill Street docks, I arrived at the paper mill to collect Bertrand Beard's list for Captain Smith.

Mr. Beard, known as Bertie, was a tall, jovial fellow and a good friend of Father's. "Top of the mornin' to ya, Master Cleveland. Did ya hear the church bells last night?"

"Yeah, that was funny," I responded, closing my eyes and hoping no one would glean the truth.

"Woke me from a sound sleep. Ya know anything 'bout them?" Bertie probed.

"At first, my brothers and I were confused, but then we were amused. It was funny seein' people going into the street and hangin' out their windows in their bedclothes. Good thing it didn't rain."

"That musta bin a sight for sure," Mr. Beard said with a growing guffaw. "So, what brings ya up here on such a fine morn?"

"Working for a Cap'n Smith. He says you've got a list for him."

"Indeed I do. Here's da shippin' list for yer cap'n. We got quite a bundle for 'im, but not so much as we thought. Just didn't have 'nuff pulp wood to fill his order. Please apologize to 'im for me. I'll git the order together and git it to 'im in half an hour."

I considered the delay and decided to make a detour before returning to the docks. I went a bit farther down South Mill Street, which was lined with factories and warehouses. I turned the corner on Washington Street to pay a call on Hatch and Beard Flour and Pearl Barley Mill. The mill was monstrous—a whole block long. The brick factory had two enormous waterwheels powered by the falling waters of a stream that dumped into Limestone Creek. Knocking on the office door, I called out, "Morning, Mr. Hatch. I am tryin' ta fill a boat for Cap'n Smith. Got anythin' for him to ship east?"

Robert Hatch was a partner of Bartholomew "Barti" Beard, Bertie Beard's brother. Robert was short, somewhat overweight, and gentle, though serious. "Good morning, Master Cleveland. That's right kind of you to think of us. As it happens, I do have a half dozen hundred-pound sacks of grain that need goin' to Utica. If'n your hoggee has space on his line boat, I'd be mighty obliged."

"That would be terrific. I'll talk with him and get back to you. Thanks a bunch."

I ran back to the docks and presented the two loading lists to Captain Smith. "My boy, what's your name?"

"Stephen, Steve Cleveland."

"Well, boy, I'm mighty impressed. Next time I come through these parts, I'll be sure to look for ya. Come to think of it, I got two more tasks for ya. Let the barley mill know I can take their sacks, and d'liver these med'cines to a Dr. William Taylor. After you've d'liver'd 'em, get the payment and bring it back to me. Got that?"

I nodded and was off again—first to see Mr. Hatch and then to the village physician, Doc Taylor. Doc was tall, imposing. He was looked up to. He was so highly considered for his knowledge, skills, and manner that he was elected to the state legislature six times running. I was impressed by the great stories Doc told about life in faraway places, like the raucous streets of Buffalo and the chaos of the government in Albany. I was eager to see these places someday for myself.

Unfortunately, Doc was not in, but his wife took the package and paid me. I ran back to the docks, gave the money to the captain. "Very impressive. You are fast, reliable, and honest." For all my labor, the captain gave me six shiny Liberty Head pennies. That was double what I normally got for a morning.

"Blazes! Thanks, Cap'n!! I'll be sure to be here next time you come through."

# 27

Fayetteville Academy, Fayetteville, New York
Monday, April 21, 1845, 7:30 AM

MORNING LIGHT ILLUMINATED an approaching slate-gray curtain in the west. Even I could predict that the line of thick clouds forebode an intense storm rolling into Fayetteville.

Huffing and puffing, I ran up the hill from the docks to my school in the village center. The first school bell would ring at 7:55, the late bell five minutes later. I hurried along the shortest path, which passed through an undeveloped wooded lot peppered with jack-in-the-pulpits raising their blooms over the leafy floor, like students sitting at attention at their desks. Arriving at school just before the late bell, I was greeted by the O'Neal twins in the schoolyard.

George called, "Hey, Steve. Did you hear the church bells last night? I woke with the clatter in our house. I don't know what it was about, but it was terrific. This morning, when we sat for breakfast, our parents went on and on. The bells this. The bells that."

Before I had a chance to answer, Sam interrupted. "Yeah, they were blabbin' about the bells. It was hi-lar-i-yus!"

George added, "Yeah, Father said he'd tan the hide of whoever woke him last night. Hoowee, was he grumpy! I'm so glad it wasn't me."

Not to be outdone, Sam said, "Dad said if those bells were ringin'

like that, the Redcoats better a bin comin'. Ooh, he was hoppin' mad."
George and Sam continued interrupting and one-upping each other. I was
thrilled to hear about their father's reaction, yet at the same time, I was
scared of the consequences.

All of us filed toward the one-room schoolhouse as the late bell rang.
Our teacher, Miss Rose Cole, a prim spinster of about twenty-five years
old, greeted each of us by name as we entered the large classroom decorated
with a map of the United States, the Declaration of Independence, two
blackboards, and pictures of George Washington and the Marquis de la
Fayette. The floor was filled with four rows of five desks and headed by a
single large desk for Miss Cole. On reaching my place, I sat and lifted open
my desktop. I fumbled for the first book my fingers touched, closed my
desk as quietly as possible, and buried my head in the book to avoid my
mates. Fortunately, it was a book on my favorite subject, American history.

My schoolmates sat in their seats. Quiet settled over the room. This order
was destroyed when Miss Cole entered the rear of the classroom. She hurled
a piece of chalk toward the front, where it exploded on contact with the
blackboard. Miss Cole calmly walked around the student desks, picked up
a fragment of chalk on the floor, and drew two concentric circles around the
impact site. Turning to face her stunned students, she declared, "Bullseye!"

My mates erupted in laughter. I was bewildered.

After a few moments, Miss Cole clapped her hands to snap everyone
to attention. She selected her history book and instructed us to open to
the story of the British assault on Lexington Common. "Class, let's read
about the 'shot heard round the world.' This is a timely story. That shot
rang out seventy years ago today. Are there any volunteers to start reading?"

Though I was not the most accomplished student, I worked hard
and did not goof off in class. I had learned the story of the first encounter
of the Colonials with the British through Ralph Waldo Emerson's poem
"Concord Hymn." I volunteered by standing up and reciting,

> By the rude bridge that arched the flood,
> Their flag to April's breeze unfurled,

*Here once the embattled farmers stood*
*And fired the shot heard round the world.*

Before I could proceed, Anna burst into the schoolhouse and passed a note to the teacher.

On reading the note, Miss Cole declared, "Mr. Stephen Cleveland, your mother asks you to return home. Immediately."

I was struck dumb. *Should I be anxious? Scared?* Trying not to make a fuss or draw any more attention to myself, I collected my things in my bag, left school, and crossed Academy Street to my home.

I opened the front door. The front rooms were quiet and dim. I continued to the kitchen where Mother sat at the table, head in hands. She turned, looked me in the eye, and spoke in a quiet, measured voice. "Stephen, did you have anything to do with the bells ringing in the night?"

My heart sank. I shied from her gaze. I wondered, *Should I make up a story to protect Will and me?* I realized there was no real choice. I gathered my courage and answered, "Yes."

"Why?"

After what seemed an interminable time, I blurted, "Egads, I was angry."

Aghast, Mother scolded, "Stephen. You musn't speak like that!" After a short pause, she urged, "And you must tell your father."

"I cannot," I quavered.

"Why?" Mother asked with empathy.

"Father's mean. He doesn't understand. He never understands me." There was an uncomfortable silence, like the silence that had lingered between when I once dropped a pottery mug and when it hit the floor.

I was sure Mother was going to respond, but she did not. In fact, her face held an inscrutable expression. She offered, "Do you want me to tell him?"

After a moment, I conceded. "No. I will do it."

I dragged myself down the street to Father's church. As I entered the sanctuary, I kneeled and apologized. "Dear God, I'm sorry for what I've done. I'm sorry to Father and to others who I tricked."

I rose and found Father in his rectory. He was staring at a book on his desk. Barely noticing me at the door, he asked, "Good morning, son. Why aren't you in school?"

My heart raced. "I came to apologize."

Father was still distracted and kept his attention on his work. "Apologize for what?"

"I rang the bells last night."

Father abruptly stopped what he was writing, craned his neck, and focused his full attention on me. Peering over his spectacles, he prodded, "Go on."

"When I worked the docks this morning, I heard people talking about the ringing. Then, when I got to school, my mates were talking about the ringing. They talked about how angry their parents were. I had no idea funning people would anger so many so much."

Despite turning red, Father did not rage at me. His reaction left me relieved, confused, and scared. Maybe I would get off easy with just a small, "meaningful" punishment.

"Stephen, thank you for confessing." I could tell Father was choosing his words carefully. "I need to consider what you told me. Go back to school. We will discuss this further this evening." His response was neither what I expected nor what I hoped.

<hr>

After school, I caught up with Will. I told him what had happened with Father and Mother. "Will, I didn't think about what would happen after our prank. Why didn't everyone laugh and enjoy the joke?"

Will was speechless. He did not offer to accompany me, and I did not request it.

I said to myself, *Father's response is the worst. Now I am stuck thinkin' about what'll happen all day. Why couldn't he decide? The strop. The cane. Anything! No matter how painful, it would have been better than not knowin'.*

For the rest of the day, I was withdrawn, short with my friends. I played baseball after school, but my heart was not in it. I failed to hit the ball when I batted or chase it when I fielded. I went home, sulked, and shifted uneasily in a parlor chair while I waited for Father.

# 28

Cleveland home, Fayetteville, New York
Monday, April 21, 1845, 6:55 PM

THROUGH MY BEDROOM window, I spotted Father walking home. He was followed by a blazing sunset that cast a spectacular red across the horizon and over his shoulder. I ran downstairs to meet him in our kitchen. His hands were trembling. Offering no pleasantries, he asked, "Stephen, why? Why did you ring the church bell?"

Fearing Father would misunderstand me, I spoke carefully, with brutal, confronting honesty. "I was angry about how you punished me."

Father nodded a few times. Then, replying slowly, through gritted teeth, he said, "Stephen, revenge is not a remedy. It neither makes you whole nor soothes your sense of being wronged or harmed."

Without thinking, I exclaimed, "I don't hurt anyone!" As soon as I spoke, I wished I could eat my words.

Father continued as if uninterrupted, "No, Stephen. Quite the opposite. Your revenge blinds you. It consumes you. You must learn to channel your emotions. There are so many less fortunate than you. Focus on helping them. Direct that boundless creativity of yours for good."

I grumbled, "Oh my. Am I the topic of one of Father's sermons?" *Cripes, I hope I did not mutter that loud enough for Father to hear.*

After a few moments of silence, Father chastised, "I am profoundly disappointed in you. Yet, I must admit, no real harm was done. Indeed, I believe you learned a valuable lesson—actions have consequences. You must consider the consequences of your actions."

Again, Father paused. His deliberate way of speaking was excruciating, especially when I was the target of his words. I wanted to get out of the kitchen, away from Father in the worst way.

Finally, Father lowered the boom. "I think a fitting punishment is that you ring the church bells to call congregants to prayer for the next month. Furthermore, during that month, you shall work with the deacon to prepare the sanctuary and set the pews before services."

I opened my mouth. Fear of adding to my punishment compelled me shut it.

Hezekiah Joslyn was widely respected as a physician, abolitionist, and conductor of an Underground Railroad station, undated. [courtesy of the Onondaga Historical Association]

The Joslyn homestead at 8560 Brewerton Road, Cicero, New York was the birthplace of Matilda Joslyn Gage and where she was home-schooled by her parents, undated. Is the woman near the front porch Helen Leslie Joslyn? [photograph generously provided by the Cicero Historical Society]

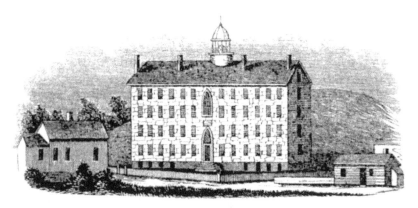

The Clinton Liberal Institute (c. 1842) was an educational home for Matilda Joslyn Gage for two years (1842-1843). Coincidentally, Grover Cleveland attended the Institute for one year (1850-1851). [generously provided by the Library of Congress]

Henry Hill Gage, undated [courtesy of the Matilda Joslyn Gage Foundation]

Matilda Joslyn Gage and her first child, Helen, when she was about four years old, c. 1849. [public domain image provided by the Wikimedia Commons]

The Steven Mallory Clement farm in Manlius was like one in High Bridge where newlywed Matilda and Henry might have lived. c. 1850 [generously provided by Chuck Lachiusa]

The Steven Mallory Clement farm in Manlius was like one in High Bridge where newlywed Matilda and Henry might have lived. c. 1850 [generously provided by Chuck Lachiusa]

As an adult, Matilda Joslyn Gage was a powerful abolitionist, warrior for women's rights, and champion of the rights of indigenous people. c. 1880 [public domain image provided via the Wikimedia Commons]

Matilda Joslyn Gage's gravestone in Fayetteville Cemetery where her cremains are buried. The epitaph is her motto and reads "There is a word sweeter than mother, home or heaven and that word is liberty." [provided by the author]

Genesee Street, Fayetteville, New York looking west toward Limestone Creek and the feeder canal, c. 1848. As noted above, the telegraph poles were installed in 1846. [courtesy of the Onondaga Historical Association]

Tolls for conveying merchandise through Syracuse on the Erie Canal were determined and assessed at the weigh lock station, c. 1873 [generously provided by the Library of Congress]

Richard Falley Cleveland, c. 1850 (left) and Ann Neal Cleveland, c. 1870 (right) [courtesy of New Jersey Department of Environmental Protection, Bruce White, Photographer]

The Clevelands lived in the parsonage of the Presbyterian Church at 109 Academy Street. c. 1870 [courtesy of the Fayetteville Free Library]

 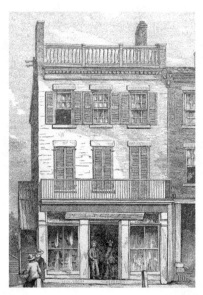

Fayetteville Presbyterian Church (left, c. 1848) and McVicar's General Store (right, undated) were located on Genesee Street. [courtesy of the Onondaga Historical Association and the New Jersey Department of Environmental Protection, respectively]

Fayetteville Academy where Grover his buddies and siblings went to school. [courtesy Fayetteville Library]

William Neal Cleveland graduated from Hamilton College in 1851 (left) and Grover Cleveland (right) was a legal apprentice at Rogers, Bowes, and Rogers in Buffalo in 1853. [generously provided by Hamilton College and the Library of Congress, respectively]

Frances Folsom Cleveland, 1886 (left) and Grover Cleveland, 1884 (right) [images courtesy of the Library of Congress]

# PART 3.

## *MATILDA AND STEVE*

Prejudice is not so much dependent upon natural antipathy
as upon education.

*The "Extinguisher" Extinguished*
David Ruggles, 1834

# 29

Cleveland home, Fayetteville, New York
Saturday, May 10, 1845, 5:45 AM

"SONS, IT'S A beautiful, warm day. Let's off to Brickyard Falls
and fish in Limestone Creek." This proposition was uncharacteristic of
the Cleveland boys' father. Reverend Richard Cleveland rarely offered to
have fun or spend special time with his children. Maybe it was guilt he felt
for any possible contribution he'd made to Stephen's most recent prank.

Will shouted, "Weehonk! I'll git the rods, worms, and meet ya
in the front hall."

"Do we have to?" whined Cecil.

Steve yelped, "Fishin'? Hooray!" He sped off to change into his
scrubby baseball clothes, notable for the holes that aligned with
scabs on his knees and legs.

Little Lewis, only four years old, looked puzzled and seemed not
to know what to say. Instead, his mother spoke for him. "Lewis, you
stay here with me. We'll play with hoops and bake some bread." She
crinkled her nose at him. "We'll have lots o' fun." Lewis giggled and
went back to playing with his balls and sticks.

The motley crew of four donned their shoes, hoisted their
gear, and trundled out of the house. As they reached the corner of
Academy and Genesee Streets, they were surprised by Bertie Beard

galloping on his horse down muddy Genesee Street. "Whoa!" Mr. Beard pulled up abruptly, barely avoiding the Cleveland party. "Well, what have we here?"

Steve enthused, "We're going fishin'!" His grin was as big as a jack-o-lantern's.

"That sounds splendid, young man." Bertie turned to Rev. Cleveland. "Mind you, Reverend, it looks like an iffy day. But you four have a fine time, for so long as yer there. And enjoy yer fish dinner, if'n there's one in yer future." Mr. Beard tipped his hat, and off he went.

Peering over Mr. Beard's shoulders, the Clevelands were treated to a striking red sky painted on the eastern horizon. Father commented, "Well, boys, Mr. Beard may be right. It may be a short day at the falls. After all, 'red sky at morning, sailor take warning.'"

Steve flashed a confused look at his oldest brother. "Why's Father talking about sailing? I thought we were going fishing?"

"We are, silly," snickered Will. "Father just meant the sky foretells the weather, and we should expect rain today."

Steve frowned. "Why can't people just say what they mean? It's like at church. There are lots of words, but I don't know what they're talkin' about most o' the time."

"Oh, brother!" All Will could do was smile. He grabbed Steve's head in the crook of his arm and rubbed his brother's slicked-back hair with his knuckles.

The foursome ambled west, down Genesee Street, like a gander and goslings. They passed the feeder canal on North Mill Street, crossed the north-flowing Limestone Creek, and turned south to walk upstream. The Clevelands' shoes were soaked from the trail—coated with morning dew and mud-encrusted from the ground saturated by the downpour yesterday. Scores of geese grazed along the creek while others took off on their migration north with peals of nasal honks.

Steve skipped down the trail, whistling and frequently turning around to walk backward to talk with his brother. He babbled so no one else could get in a word. After walking along the creek for half an hour, Steve spied an isolated cluster of houses across the meadow to the west. "Father, who lives in the houses o'er there? I don't think I e'er noticed 'em before."

"I believe that's the hamlet of High Bridge. I don't believe I know anyone from there. If memory serves, no members of our church live there. Maybe some day soon, you and I could go over and introduce ourselves. How does that suit?"

"That'd be fun! I like meetin' new people. That's part of the fun of workin' at the docks." Steve chattered on. "Have I told you about the Professor?"

After hiking for another half hour, the boys arrived at the base of Brickyard Falls. The falls and Limestone Creek were swollen from the rains. Water crashed over the sixty-foot falls, cascading over a tiered, stony escarpment to a churning pool at its base.

"Here we are, boys. I'm told these are ideal fishing conditions. Go. Try your luck!"

It did not take much urging for the boys to cast their line, draw their bait, and entice the trout. While Cecil and Will went to the pool, Steve went a bit downstream where the waters ran over a rocky bed. Within moments, he'd hooked a brook trout. "Blazes! I got one!"

"Hold on, Stephen." Father ran over to help. After a short struggle, Steve landed it.

Not being comfortable with collecting the fish, he watched as his father grabbed the fish, got it under control, unhooked its mouth, and then dropped the flapping, foot-long creature into a basket floating in the water. Father remarked, "Stephen, that's a beauty." Its shiny flanks were speckled and iridescent in the morning light. As time passed, Will, Cecil, and Steve added to the basket.

In their fishing joy, the Clevelands were unaware of the dark, storm-blue clouds ominously filling the western sky. Father blanched as he looked up. "Boys, it is looking downright diluvian. Noah should be ready for a nasty ride. It's time for us to pack up."

As they readied to go, Cecil landed his final fish. The hook caught in the gills. He worked the hook from the fish, twisting it free, but in his haste, the hook grabbed his thumb and opened a yawing gash. Cecil yowled in pain.

Removing his handkerchief, the reverend ran to his son and wound the fabric around Cecil's wound. Without hesitation, he ordered Will to take Stephen home. "I am going to rush Cecil to Doc Taylor's to look at his cut. We'll meet you at home. Do you understand?"

Will nodded as Father and Cecil sped off to visit the good doctor.

Suddenly, Will and Steve were alone in the woods. "Okay, Steve. Let's gather the gear and get home before the skies split." The boys walked apace along the stream, passing the time by singing tunes like "Ole Dan Tucker." Will piped a verse,

> Ole Dan Tucker was a fine ole man,
> washed his face in a fryin' pan,
> combed his hair with a wagon wheel,
> and died with a toothache in his heel.

Steve joined Will for the chorus,

> Get out da way, ole Dan Tucker.
> You're too late to come for supper.
> Supper's over and dinner's cookin',
> ole Dan Tucker just stand there lookin'.

In the distance, the boys saw White and scattered Black farmers tending their fields and thunderclouds climbing high in the sky. Will put out his right hand, palm up. An occasional raindrop wet his hand. "Steve, I think we're in fer it." Seconds later, the sky flashed brightly, thunder rumbled, and the heavens burst. Sheets of rain pelted them. The boys scanned the sides of the trail for anything resembling shelter. Randomly spaced beech and maple trees bordering the path provided only partial protection from the deluge.

Steve remembered, "Hey, Will. Let's cross the field and git to them houses we saw earlier. What did Father call 'em? High Bridge? We can wait out the storm there." Will agreed in hopes of finding a place to dry off and warm up. The two boys struggled with their rods, creel, and catch as they tramped across the muddy pasture. By the time they reached the middle of the field, they were so wet that more rain could not make them any soggier. The boys stepped carefully, pulling their feet from the mud.

"Let's get to that white house over there." The boys reached the first home, walked through the fence gate, and huddled together under the eaves to shelter from the driving rain. While Will shivered and drifted off to sleep, Steve stayed keen to the world.

After a bit, Steve elbowed his brother. "Hey, Will. Looks like it's clearin'." Failing to gain a response, Steve repeated in a lilting, drawn out, "Wiiiillll? C'mon, Will." With still no response from his brother, Steve asked, "Hey, Will. I got an idea. Wanna make mischief?"

Groggily, Will drawled, "Yeah. What's your *big* idea?"

"Let's introduce ourselves to High Bridge, Cleveland-style. You know, let the locals know we were here. What do you say we take the pins from the hinges of their front gates? We can use the tool we used to take the hook from the fish we caught."

"Grand idea," Will responded. "Just let me warm up a bit."

Finally, the rain ended. Raindrops caught in the gossamer webs spanning corners on the porch sparkled in the morning sun, which shone full bore from the east. With a look of awe, Will tapped Steve on the shoulder and pointed. Across to the west, the boys were treated to a splendid, rare morning rainbow. It stretched from horizon to horizon. The boys exclaimed in synchrony, "Weehonk!" Beyond the rainbow was a broad, dark region framed by a dimmer but equally spectacular secondary rainbow with reversed colors.

Steve proclaimed, "Will, those rainbows are a divine blessing of our plan if ever there was one."

The boys set off, house by house, to free the front gates of their pins.

# 30

Gage house, High Bridge, New York
Sunday, May 11, 1845, 9:15 AM

"HENRY, IT'S TIME for church," Matilda beckoned her husband with a gentle but firm tone. "Are you dressed for Whitsunday?"

"Yes, dear. Why must we go today? There is so much work to do to prepare for spring planting. After all, it's an antiquated holiday at best." Henry shuffled his tie back and forth to align it under his starched shirt collar. After three more tugs in each direction, he got it just so.

"If it is such a minor event, then why do you fuss?"

"Having everything right is important. If we must go, the opinions of others greatly matter. I must be mindful of my preparation to set up a local business."

"Yes, but that won't be until years from now," remarked a confused Matilda.

"Rome wasn't built in a day. The journey of a thousand miles begins with a single step. A penny saved is a penny earned." Henry centered on his inner Polonius.

"Very well. I'll collect the holiday breads and meet you on the carriage." Matilda slipped her plain spring coat over her shoulders. She had been taught that wearing flashy clothes was a waste of money. Furthermore, it exhibited vanity when people should warm to you because of your essence.

Despite this, Matilda honored Henry's mind for the future.

Matilda buttoned her coat front and collected a half dozen loaves in her arms. Liberating her right hand from the loaves, she managed to open the kitchen door and step outside. She closed the door with her right foot, and continued down the flagstone front entrance walk. Matilda drew in the crisp, spring air and sighed contentedly, but her sense of well-being did not last long.

Confronted by the closed gate, she assessed her options: she could put the bread on the muddy ground while she opened the gate, or she could tuck them under one arm and work to open the gate one-handed. In the end, she chose a third option—carefully arranging the loaves in a pyramid propped against her mid-section, securing them with her left arm, and raising the latch with her free right arm to ease the gate open. It was a good plan, but instead of swinging to the left, the gate fell top-first on the ground. The loaves went flying, and so did Matilda.

Another time, the situation might have been comical, but on this Sunday, Matilda was not amused. She was trying so hard to fit into her new community. And there she lay, sprawled on the ground. It was all she could do to produce a plaintive "Henry!"

Hearing the commotion, Henry dashed out the front door. "Are you all right?" He helped her stand. "Is anything bruised?"

"Just my pride." After gathering her wits, Matilda surveyed the gate, which was off its hinges. She glanced to the neighbors' house on her left. Their gate was also twisted and on the ground. *Curious.* She scanned nearby houses; their gates were catawampus, too. Realizing that this was not by happenstance, Matilda straightened up, girded herself, and declared, "I'll find out who's behind this."

Matilda and Henry rode to the Fayetteville Methodist Episcopal Church. Church was a great place to meet people—and to do detective work. Matilda introduced herself to their High Bridge neighbors. "Good day. My name is Matilda Gage. My husband, Henry, and I recently moved to High Bridge. I think we're neighbors." Without missing a beat, she pummeled them with questions. "Have you noticed anything peculiar over the last few days? Things not in their right places? Were there people snooping about who are not normally in our parts?"

The replies were consistent. "Good morning. No, can't say that I have. Again, welcome." Put off by Matilda's brusqueness, the neighbors then turned to reengage with people they already knew.

After some negative responses, Matilda spotted the Black couple who lived in the house catty-corner to hers. "Good day to you. I believe you live near us, in High Bridge. My name is Matilda Gage, and this is my husband, Henry."

"Please to meet you both. I am Hiram, and this is my wife, Miriam." After a short pause, Hiram looked more closely at Matilda and asked, "Ma'am, I don't mean to stare, but do I know you from somewhere? You look mighty familiar."

On prompting, Matilda, too, did a second take. "Is it possible you came to my father's office many years ago?"

"Possibly. Who is your father?"

"Dr. Joslyn. His office is in—"

"Cicero," completed Hiram. "Well, I'll be. You're the daughter of that kind, wonderful doctor. Yes. We know your father. In fact, we owe him our lives. Dr. Joslyn not only protected us from bounty hunters, he helped us settle into this area when we moved north on the Railroad. It was because of our deep appreciation that we rode all the way to Cicero to visit his doctor's office. We even named our youngest child after him."

"Mr. and Mrs. Nash, thank you for your kind words. It is such a pleasure to see you again. And to be living so close! We must break bread together, sometime soon." The Nashes and Gages heartily clasped each other's hands. "Right now, however, I do have an immediate question. As we were walking to church, I noticed that your gate was off its hinges. Are you having problems? Are you looking to have your gate repaired?"

"Well, interesting that you ask. Our gate worked well for years, but this morning, I pushed the gate and it fell into my hands. Quite peculiar."

"Did you notice anything or anyone different in our neighborhood during the last few days?"

"Come to think of it, I saw two Cleveland boys bouncing around yesterday. Strange to see them in High Bridge. Their father's the minister at the Presbyterian church down the road. I believe they live around the corner from the church, on Academy Street."

Matilda's first instinct was to disbelieve that children were responsible. She continued her detective work. After a couple more inquiries, Matilda learned that the Cleveland boys had a proclivity for pranks, particularly the lad named Stephen. As her pride still smarted, she resolved to teach this young man a lesson.

# 31

Gage home, High Bridge, New York
Sunday, May 11, 1845, 1:15 PM

THE SUN CRESTED in the cloudless sky as Matilda and Henry completed their Sabbath meal. Henry cleared the table and Matilda washed dishes, mindlessly gazing out the kitchen window. She broke from her daydream when she saw a carriage rolling down the road. The passengers were her parents, Hezekiah and Helen Joslyn! They wore heavy overcoats for the unseasonably chilly weather. Matilda darted from the house, not even taking the time to don her coat, and embraced her parents. "Father? Mother? It is so good to see you. But why are you here?"

"Matilda, you are a sight for sore eyes," responded Helen.

"Let's go inside, warm up, and catch up. I've got to tell you about the darnedest thing. Our neighbors are the Nashes, Hiram and Miriam. You remember them, don't you?" Matilda asked.

Smiling his awareness, Hezekiah turned back to the carriage and beckoned, "Sarah, please join us in the warm house." It was then that Matilda noticed Sarah sitting on the luggage in the rear of the carriage, holding her sleeping four-year-old daughter, Cherry. Matilda's smile broadened further as she opened her arms to hug Sarah. "It is so wonderful to see you."

"Thank you. It's good see you too, Matilda." Though her English had improved, it was still stiff. Regardless, Matilda could read the joy in Sarah's face and body language.

After everyone settled in the kitchen near the woodstove and warmed a bit, Matilda asked, "Father, Mother, it is great to see you. Do not mistake me for asking, but why are you here?"

Helen fielded the question in the most calming manner she could. "Matilda, yer father is not well. He has difficulties breathing, e'en when he is not extending himself. On the advice o' others, we sold the farm and are moving tae Wisconsin. Reports are that the air in Wisconsin is therapeutic. We hope the West is redemptive, rehabilatory, and that your father can reestablish his good health and energy."

This was one of the few times in her young life that Matilda had been struck dumb. After taking a few moments, she looked at her father and spoke directly, unvarnished, the way she knew best. "Father, how serious is this? Should I be worried? Are you dying?"

Hezekiah expected such frankness. "No, dear. It is true I am not well. I am often tired and easily winded. I need time in a good, clean environment and without the demands of farming, doctoring, and conducting an Underground station. Your mother and I believe Wisconsin affords these attributes."

Matilda gave her father the benefit of the doubt when it came to medical concerns. "If you are sure. How long can you stay with us? When do you leave?"

"We will stay for a couple days; then we best be off."

# 32

Gage home, High Bridge, New York
Monday, May 12, 1845, 1:15 PM

HELEN SETTLED INTO a spare room upstairs. Cobwebs
guarded the corners of the door casing, walls were partially covered by
patches of peeling paint, and other walls were bare wood. Helen ignored
the dilapidated state of the house, knowing that Matilda and Henry had
more important demands on their time. She walked down the stairs and
joined her daughter in the kitchen. "Matilda, what are you making?"

"A mess. Care to join me?"

Helen smiled. Recipes for peasant bread and winter vegetable soup
were strewn across the kitchen table, recipes Matilda had learned as a
child from her mother. Despite the apparent chaos, a calm came over the
kitchen as mother and daughter focused on the business of making supper.

Matilda measured and mixed the flour and other dry ingredients, then
added the dry ingredients to the proofed yeast mixture and kneaded the
dough. There was a bittersweet energy in the kneading. Helen chopped
onions, turnips, carrots, and potatoes for the soup. She put the vegetables
in a pot, covered them with water, and spiced the water with local salt,
thyme, basil, and rosemary from last year's harvest.

The consensual silence broke when Matilda said, "Mother, I am so
happy you're here, but it breaks my heart to know you're moving so far

away, and for who knows how long."

Glass-eyed Helen reached over to Matilda, smiled, and hugged her daughter. "We will be back, once yer father regains his vigor. After all, it appears that we will soon have another reason to return."

Pushing back from the embrace and looking incredulously at her mother, Matilda asked, "How did you know?"

"A mother knows" was all Helen said.

"I just told Henry last week. I'm likely three, maybe four months."

Mother and daughter smiled, hugged again, and exhaled slowly. "You've a lot tae consider."

Matilda nodded and arched her eyebrows. "I am not ready. Yet I am so excited."

A few moments later, Helen remarked, "It was generous o' Jarm tae find this house fer ye. Its condition is a bit questionable, but it has a homey feel. Are the two o' ye all right here?"

"Absolutely. As you can see, the house is a work in progress. Squirrels entertain us by running through the attic. We think they're playing tag. Sometime this summer, we plan to find and plug their access. It's entertainment we can miss. Henry and I have been working on one room at a time. Some rooms take more effort than others. In one, there was a hole clear through the wall. Henry patched it, and since then, that room has been bug-free."

"Sounds like ye have yer hands full."

"After our bedroom and the kitchen, our first project was the room in the basement we use for the Railroad. Now it is cleaned up and not too scary for people who are already terrified. Last week, Jarm stopped by to see how we're settling in. He is such a gentle soul. He was pleased with what we've done, particularly the space in the basement. Jarm told us we should expect deliveries soon."

"Thank ye for picking up the baton. Leaving our station weighed heavily on us. I am sure yer father will be particularly pleased."

"Henry and I would have it no other way. Unfortunately, we've not worked on the room where you and Father are staying. It'll be finished when you return. Speaking of that, what are your plans, your expectations?"

Helen answered as Sarah entered the kitchen. "I wish I could answer that question. Yer father's breathing difficulties grow worse. We wish we knew why. We hope the change will refresh his health." She continued, "Sarah has decided she will not go to Wisconsin."

Sarah added, "That's right. Matilda, I would be happy to stay here with you and Mr. Gage if you would like."

Matilda beamed. "That would be lovely. You know you're like a sister. You and Cherry are always welcome here."

"Very good," said a thankful Sarah.

The two-day visit passed too quickly. On Wednesday morning, Hezekiah and Helen packed their bags, loaded their carriage, and then hugged Matilda, Henry, Sarah, and Cherry.

Hezekiah looked Matilda in the eyes. "Please know how proud we are of you. You made a fine choice in a partner, one who supports you and deeply cares for you. I am humbled by the way you're carrying on family traditions such as supporting the Underground Railroad but at the same time navigating your own life path." His eyes teared as they realized he did not know when or if they would ever see each other again, much like the last time they had parted.

Helen, too, cried. "We'll send ye our address soon after we get settled. We want to hear about ye—all three of ye." Matilda and Henry smiled at that comment.

# 33

North Mill Street docks, Fayetteville, New York
Tuesday, May 20, 1845, 10:20 AM

"G DAY, DR. TAYLOR," Matilda greeted the town physician as he walked from the North Mill Street docks up Genesee Street.

"Ah, and top o' the morning to you, Mrs. Gage. How's Mr. Gage faring in his apprenticeship?"

Matilda was taken aback by the question. She had only briefly met Doc Taylor a month earlier to discuss her family situation with him. *Must be the local gossips.* Just the same, Matilda answered, "Quite well. Thank you for asking. How are Mrs. Taylor and her Italian chickens?" Matilda had learned of the prize imported poultry through chats with neighbors.

"Quite well indeed." Doc smiled warmly, acknowledging their mutual use of the small-town rumor mill. "Sometime soon, my wife and I would enjoy having you and your husband for tea."

"That would be delightful. Thank you."

"I'll have my wife contact you about a convenient time. Till then, adieu."

"Oh, Doc. Before you go, would you be so kind as to direct me to the Cleveland home?"

"Certainly. They live on Academy Street. That is up the hill. Pass the Presbyterian church on the right, and a few yards on the left you will find

Academy Street. Their house is the first one on the left."

"Thank you." Matilda ascended Genesee Street, found Academy Street, and moments later knocked on the front door of the white, two-story home at 109 Academy Street. Hearing no response, she rapped again, a tad more insistently. Finally, a rather haggard-looking, tall woman answered the door, holding a crying two-year-old on her hip. "Good morning. May I help you?"

"Well, yes. My name is Matilda Gage. We recently moved to a home in High Bridge. This may seem like a strange question, but do you have any boys—perhaps between the ages of eight and twelve years old?"

"In fact, we have three that fit that description. Will turned thirteen early last month, Cecil is nine, and Steve recently turned eight. They are all at school just now. Pray tell, why do you ask?"

"Some puzzling events occurred in our neighborhood. I thought they might be of interest to your boys. Would you please give these to them? Thank you." And with that Matilda placed a dozen metal hinge pins in Mrs. Cleveland's free hand, turned, and walked down the street.

# 34

Gage home, High Bridge, New York
Wednesday, May 21, 1845, 2:45 PM

STEVE KNOCKED TENTATIVELY on the front door of
the Gage home. In short order, the door creaked open. A tall man in a
business suit welcomed him. "Hello, young man. May I help you?"

Presuming the man to be Matilda's husband, Steve answered, "Good
afternoon, Mr. Gage. I am Stephen Cleveland."

Henry stiffened. "Ah. My wife and I have been expecting you. Please,
come in." Henry stepped aside, revealing the foyer of the house. In an
attempt to hide his anxiety, Steve eyed details of the room as he entered.
Henry closed the door, sealing Steve's exit, and led the lad down the hall
to the kitchen.

On walking into the kitchen, Steve came face-to-face with Matilda.
She was standing at the sink, plucking and cleaning a chicken.

Henry presented Steve. "Dear, we have a visit from Stephen Cleveland."

"Ah, Master Cleveland. Do have a seat."

Although Mrs. Gage made her offer politely, Steve raised his eyebrows,
detecting a menacing tone. He sat erect on a straight-back, Shaker-made
chair, much like one in his dining room. Matilda commanded his full
attention. "Do you have anything you'd like to say?"

Putting his right hand in his pants pocket, Steve grabbed the contents and laid a collection of hinge pins on the table. "My apologies," he said gravely, but he could not withhold the hint of a mischievous grin and crinkles in the corners of his eyes.

Steve's courage and honesty were disarming. Matilda covered her mouth, barely muffling her snicker. "Young man, would you like some tea?"

"Yes, that would be very kind. Thank you."

Matilda added water to a tarnished copper kettle and set it on the stove. She reached for a tin on the shelf over the stove, withdrew a couple scoops of black leaf tea, and added the leaves to an empty teapot. Looking toward the kitchen door, she asked, "Henry, would you like to join us?" He nodded, and Matilda added another generous scoop. "I trust that black tea will work for you both."

"Thank you," Henry responded.

"I guess that sounds good to me," added Steve. While he had drunk tea before, he had little knowledge of the varieties and their different tastes.

Filling the teapot and the time, Matilda prompted, "So, Master Cleveland, tell me about your family."

Steve rapid-fire rattled off a series of facts. "My father is the minister at the Fayetteville Presbyterian Church. There are seven kids in our family. Anna, that's my sister, is the oldest. She's fourteen years old. Mary is twelve. I have two older brothers—Will and Cecil. Oh, and I have two siblings younger than me, Lewis and Susan. But they barely count; they're only three and one."

The kettle shook as the water roiled to a boil. Matilda lifted the kettle and poured water into the waiting teapot. Returning to the topic of families, she responded in her deliberate fashion, "I am an only child. That's good because I had my parents' full attention. It's also bad because I had all of my parents' attention."

Steve smiled and nodded. "I'd like a little less attention from my parents sometimes, too."

Matilda added, "I did not have brothers or sisters to do things with."

Starting to slow down his speech, Steve said, "Yeah, brothers and sisters are largely good. I get along with most of them, except maybe for Cecil.

He's all right, but he whines a lot. And he never jokes."

Patiently continuing her inquiry, Matilda asked, "Have you been in Fayetteville your whole life?"

"Nah. We moved here four years ago. Fayetteville is a great place. It's got fields for playing baseball, forests for exploring, and streams for fishing. Except for Anna, who is finished with school, we all go to the Fayetteville Academy. It's an okay place. I do my work."

"Very interesting." Matilda cocked her head and asked, "Steve, what's this 'okay' mean?"

"It's something the guys say. I've heard workers use it at the docks. It means 'all right' or 'everything's fine.'"

"Well, okay then." Matilda poured three cups of tea. Henry took his and walked to the kitchen door. As he left, he winked to his wife, as if to give his approval for Matilda's interrogation.

Matilda proceeded, "I grew up in a town north of here; it's called Cicero. Mr. Gage is also from Cicero. We moved to High Bridge a few months ago and have a lot to learn." Matilda paused for a few moments and returned to her drilling of Steve. "So, all you do is go to school and play?"

"Oh, no!" Steve replied enthusiastically. "I work at the docks. It's a dandy place. Lots of things goin' on. Boats comin' in all the time. They always need help loading and unloading. I help with that stuff. I also run errands to people in Fayetteville. The hoggees always need my help."

"Hoggee? What's a hoggee?"

"Oh, they're the boat captains, the guys that guide boats along the canal. Most of them are friendly, but some are right nasty."

"They pay you for this work?"

"Sure do. Pay's pretty good, too. Why, I can get as much as a nickel a morning if I work hard and find the right hoggee. I split it with my parents—half to me, half to them. I'm saving up for a new mitt for baseball."

"What is this baseball you talk about?"

"Weehonk, you really don't know nothin', do ya?" Steve flushed, realizing his rudeness. "Ooh, pardon me." Then, with unbounded enthusiasm, he described, "It's a great game. A player tries to hit a ball with a bat. That's a stick. It's best when you hit the ball just right. The bat sings. After hitting the ball, the player runs the bases and tries to get home. If he does, he scores a run. The team with the most runs wins."

"My oh my! Bats. Balls. Going home. Doesn't make sense."

"It does if you watch it. Come sometime. Watch us play. You can even play if you like. Boys and girls play, and grown-ups join us, too."

Matilda abruptly changed the subject. "You seem mechanically inclined."

Steve cocked his head like a puppy encountering a new sound. "What do you mean? Meknick-what?"

"Me-chan-i-cal-ly inclined. That means you are good with machines and tools."

"Well, yes. I suppose so. Why do you say that?" Steve stammered.

"When you first arrived, you presented me with a bunch of hinge pins. How about you tell me about them."

"Oh, them." Steve's voice dropped and slowed, and his head dipped. "I was hoping you weren't gonna bring that up."

"I am sure you were," Matilda said flatly. "So?"

"We wuz just havin' fun." Steve paused a few moments. "Guess we never thought about the people."

"Maybe you should from now on. And who is 'we'?"

"That's no matter. I'm here, and I'm sorry."

"Are you sure?"

"Yes."

"Have it your way. So, what shall Mr. Gage, you, and I do about this? I could have Henry take you out back and tan your hide. I could tell your parents what you did, but I suppose that's already been done, as I handed your mother the pins and you passed them to me." Matilda raised her eyebrows as she gazed at the pins on the table. "I could have you go around and apologize to the Nashes and others whose gates you jacked open. Or I could have you do chores around the neighborhood. What do *you* think is appropriate?"

"Hmm. You could give me a piece of pie and send me on my way!" Steve proposed with a hopeful, winning grin.

Matilda barely concealed her amusement.

Steve continued, "Probably I should say I'm sorry to you, the mister, and the neighbors . . . and I could do some chores."

"You're a wise one, Stephen Cleveland. Honest and direct. And at such a young age." Matilda was indeed impressed. She pondered. "Why don't you come around next Wednesday after school? Check with your parents. We'll start your rehabilitation then."

"My what?" Steve did not know what rehabilitation meant, but Matilda's tone indicated it was something he would not like.

"Just come by next Wednesday," Matilda said by way of reassurance. "And now, how about a piece of nut pie?"

# 35

Gage home, High Bridge, New York
Wednesday, May 28, 1845, 2:10 PM

"STEPHEN. STEPHEN?" MATILDA rose from her rocking chair, stood on the white wraparound porch, and leaned over the rail to scan the grounds for the young lad. She heard a faint voice from the green two-story barn that stabled the Gages' stocky workhorses and stored plows, harrows, and hand tools.

"Mrs. Gage, I'm here," came a distant yell from the barn.

Matilda briskly walked across the yard, entering the barn and spotting Steve's legs extended from under the wagon. As Steve emerged, surrounded by hammers and wrenches strewn about freshly cast sawdust, he used the heel of his greasy hands to scrape away the dust from his clothes and brown hair hanging over his face.

"I see you finished cleaning the barn," chuckled Matilda. "Very good. What are you doing now?"

Steve coughed up some sawdust. "While I was cleaning the stalls, I leaned on the wagon and almost fell to the floor. The wheels were so rickety. I'm trying to snug 'em up."

"Well, thank you." Matilda smiled. "That's mighty kind of you. I'll let Henry know so he can finish the job. Meanwhile, why don't you wash up and have some tea?"

"I'd like that, thank you. You sure it's okay for me just to leave this as it is?"

"It's *okay*." Matilda winked at Steve. "Come to the kitchen when you're ready." She walked back to the house alone, quietly laughing.

Five, ten, twenty minutes passed. The tea water was now cool, and Matilda grew concerned. She walked back to the barn to find Steve had taken the two back wheels off the cart and was staring at the pieces with confusion. He could not figure out how to put things back together.

Matilda mused, "I do not think I have ever met an eight-year-old as determined, inquisitive, and courageous as you."

"Thanks. I think. You might think differently if you spoke to my school teacher. I think she thinks I am a nuisance 'cause I talk to my buddies. But I usually complete my homework and I pay attention in class."

Shaking her head, Matilda said, "Apparently, she is not seeing the true you."

Steve cracked a crooked smile, rose, and brushed off the dirt and dust. As he and Matilda left the barn, Henry crossed over from the chicken coop. He carefully looked at both: first glancing at a smiling Matilda and then studying Steve, who looked baffled at the chaos he had wrought. Assessing the situation, Henry grinned and walked to the house with them in silence.

"Let me reheat the water." Pivoting, Matilda continued, "So, Steve, tell me about your school. What are you studying?"

"Well, I like American history most. We're learning about the Seven Year War. What confuses me is why were we fighting with the British and against the French when just ten years later we were fighting the British with help from the French. Even our town is named after a French hero." Matilda read Steve's puzzled face. "I think that must have been so exciting to have soldiers all around. With fights, guns, shooting, and all. That Marquis sure was something special. I'm glad to live in his town."

"Yes, he must have been a special man. Leaving his home to fight for the rights of others. Pretty special indeed."

Henry nodded his agreement.

"I also like penmanship, especially cursive. The loop-de-loops and crossings and dottings. They're fun. It's a good thing my name is so long."

"What do you mean?"

"Well, let me show you. Do you have a pen?"

Matilda rummaged through a drawer in a roll-top desk and brought over a pen, inkwell, and blotter paper. "Here you go."

Steve carefully dipped the pen into the well and tapped off the excess ink, making sure not to splatter on the paper or table. He moved his hand up, down, and around until he'd painstakingly completed his three names. Blotting his work, he showed it off to Matilda:

*Stephen Grover Cleveland*

"Sometimes words just don't make sense. The *p-h* in my first name is pronounced 'v,' and the *v* in my middle and last names are not pronounced 'ph.' Doesn't make sense, does it?"

Matilda fought to contain herself, lest young Steve think she was laughing at him.

Covering for Matilda's amusement, Henry interjected, "That is a fine name you've got. Tell me about the Grover. Where is that from?"

"I don't rightly know. Maybe it's some old or dead family member. Anyway, I'll stick with Steve."

Henry and Matilda responded in unison, "Steve it is."

As if to prove her compliance, Matilda asked, "Steve, would you like another cup?"

"Why, yes. Thank you." Steve drained his cup.

"And a biscuit?"

"Oh, that would be sweet." Steve did not appreciate his own pun, but Matilda did, smiling warmly.

Matilda looked at her husband, placed her hand on his shoulder, and said, "Henry, would you like your tea warmed?"

Henry cocked his head and glanced up. "Thank you, dear."

Steve watched the caring interaction between Matilda and Henry, the ease and gentleness between them that any child could detect. It was reassuring. Yet it was also confusing. Such balance was foreign to him. In his family, it was clear his father was in charge, but the Gages were partners. He was not sure why, but it made him feel comfortable, and he smiled.

# 36

North Mill Street docks, Fayetteville, New York
Saturday, May 31, 1845, 8:30 AM

MATILDA AND HENRY explored the two-story red-brick shops abutting the mule trails lining the feeder canal. The shops sold all sorts of supplies: grains, spices and teas, tobacco, clothing, furs, and hardware. During mud season, shopping was a dirty activity, so Matilda was dressed in a simple, homemade, red-and-green-checkered frock and a light coat that hung open due to the unseasonably warm weather.

One of Matilda's shopping goals was to find fabric to sew clothes that accommodated her progressing pregnancy. After spending nearly an hour in the fabric store, she left with yards of solid-blue muslin and green gingham. Matilda smiled as she recalled shopping at Gage Dry Goods with her mother.

The hemming and hawing in the fabric store and the other errands left Henry bedraggled. He was eager to visit the local dry goods store, but that might have to wait for another day.

On completing most of her shopping, Matilda glanced across the canal and spotted Steve. "Steve! Good morning!"

Seeing no response, Henry said, "Maybe he didn't hear you. Let me try." Henry pivoted toward Steve and roared, "Stephen!" in his best foghorn timbre.

Steve jerked and yelled across the marketplace, "Hey, Mr. and Mrs.

Gage. Morning to you!" Dressed in scuffed, stained overalls, he danced about the mud puddles formed by days of drenching rains. Bounding over to the Gages, he cheerfully added, "Surprised to see you here."

Matilda remarked, "Today must be one of the days you work with, with . . . What did you call them? Hoggees?"

"It is! That was a couple hours ago." Steve huffed from running. "What brings you here?"

"We discovered the docks are a great place to find fresh provisions right off the boat. It's a challenge. Shopping here is almost irresistible because items are inexpensive! But everything comes in large amounts. We must buy much more than what just the two of us need. We have to either find ways to preserve our food or share our purchases with neighbors."

Steve asked, "Do you know about Mr. McVicar's General Store? It's up Genesee Street, past Father's Presbyterian church. My brother Will works there after school. Other than food, Mr. McVicar has most things you need."

"Thanks," Henry acknowledged. "I've been wanting to get over and explore. Who'd you say is the owner?"

"Mr. McVicar. He's a deacon at my father's church."

Henry looked about. "Steve, does anyone around here sell fish?"

"Absolutely. I just helped the hoggee down the end set up his stand. He's got catfish, white fish, trout, and some other stuff."

"Sounds scrumptious," said Matilda, who found herself eating more than usual these days. "I do like white fish, particularly from the Great Lakes. Henry, before we get fish, can you check to see if any boats from Syracuse have come through with blocks of salt?"

"What's the salt for?" queried a confused Stephen.

Henry responded, "Preserving the fish. Matilda learned about salting fish from the Haudenosaunee. It keeps the fish for months."

"Cripes. I must tell Mother about this. Does the fish taste salty?"

Matilda replied, "No, not at all. You wash away the salt before you cook it."

"Interesting. Anyway, most of the boats from Syracuse moor on the east side of the canal. Now that I think of it, my hoggee had blocks in his hull. Lemme go ask him if they're for sale."

"Thank you," Matilda said.

A few moments later, Steve struggled toward the Gages, burdened under the load of a salt block. "Yes. Here's one. It's nicely wrapped in the brown paper it's shipped in. He's got two more if you want them."

"One will be quite enough. Please take this money to your hoggee. It should cover the payment. And please thank him."

"Weehonk, Mrs. Gage! That hoggee said I'd get a penny just for that sale. A whole penny! That makes today a five-cent day for me! I'm on my way to my leather baseball mitt!"

Matilda and Henry smiled with Steve at his well-earned wages. Then, she turned to her husband. "Henry, can you take the packages to the cart?"

Matilda and Steve continued down the muddy mule trail. After a few steps, they happened upon Steve's parents. Ann was a slender, tall woman who complemented her imposing, broad-shouldered husband. Opening his right palm and shoving his hand toward the sky, Steve showed off his five cents. "Mother, Mother, look!"

Ann beamed at her joyful son. Rev. Cleveland looked quizzically at Steve's stroll-mate, whom he did not know. He broke the silence. "Good morning. I am Richard Cleveland, and this is my wife, Ann."

"Pleased to meet you, sir. Steve has told us so much about you. I am Matilda Gage. I had the pleasure of meeting your wife nearly two weeks ago, if I remember correctly."

"It's a pleasure to see you again, Mrs. Gage," Ann said. Handshakes were exchanged. Rev. Cleveland looked confused, until his wife clarified, "This is the woman who brought over the mysterious pins."

"Ah, yes. I do remember that story," confirmed Rev. Cleveland.

"We have yet to finish our shopping, but would you like to come over for some tea later this morning?" Ann asked.

Taken aback by her brazen friendliness, Matilda said, "That would be lovely. We'd enjoy that. Let—"

Ann cut her off. "Please. We would very much like to thank you for befriending our Stephen, particularly after the harm he caused you."

"I'll find my husband. We have a few tasks to complete, and then we will come to you. Likely, we'll be about half an hour."

# 37

Cleveland home, Fayetteville, New York
Saturday, May 31, 1845, 10:30 AM

AFTER LOADING AND securing the morning's purchases on
their cart, the Gages covered the parcels and guided their horse and cart
eastward along Genesee Street toward the village center. On their way to
the Clevelands, they passed stately, new, white clapboard homes. Each
was multistoried, boasted Doric columns, and spoke to the new wealth
of a prosperous young village. Matilda and Henry passed the Presbyterian
church, with its muscular, two-story spire, on the south side of Genesee
Street. Shortly thereafter, they turned north onto Academy Street, passed
the Fayetteville Academy on the right, and reached the Cleveland house
on the left.

Henry rapped on the partially varnished pine front door. Shortly, Rev.
Cleveland answered the knock in his usual dour, hulking manner. After
ushering the Gages into the foyer, he offered, "Welcome. May I take your
jackets?" The Gages shed their overclothes, handing them to the reverend,
who hung them on hooks in the foyer. "Please, follow me." Matilda and
Henry obliged. As they walked down the hall to the sitting room, Matilda
peered into the dining room. Spotting Steve in the mirror, she winked.
Steve responded with a short wave.

The hall was unadorned, with beige walls and spare, simple furnishings in the adjoining rooms. Matilda furtively glanced to Henry as if to communicate her surprise that an established family did not have a more fully outfitted home. Having a small stipend and a large family evidently provided neither creature comforts nor financial flexibility. Henry discreetly raised his right eyebrow. The Gages and Rev. Cleveland sat down on the high-back chairs.

Though the Gages had only been married for a short time, Henry was aware that Matilda had a pattern of coming across as strong, particularly with new acquaintances. So Henry spoke first. "Lovely home. We are pleased to be here. How long have you been in Fayetteville?"

Before the reverend could answer, Ann joined the gathering in the sitting room. In contrast to her husband, she was warm and solicitous. Disregarding any previous conversation, Ann welcomed the Gages. "Thank you so much for coming. We are delighted to get to know you better." Bending down, she poured tea for the guests and then for herself and her husband.

The Clevelands and Gages discussed everyday topics—spring plantings, where to buy certain items, and the comings and goings on the canal. Ann offered, "Fayetteville is a new village. Most everyone has been here fewer than twenty years. That includes us. We moved here just four years ago."

Matilda said, "I've lived in New York State my whole life. I grew up on a farm not too far from here, in Cicero."

"I have heard tell of Cicero. Isn't that on Oneida Lake?" Ann asked.

"Yes, it is," Matilda replied. "But Cicero is sleepy compared with Fayetteville. In Fayetteville, it seems that more people are moving here every day. Likely they're drawn by the opportunities, quest for wealth, and the promise of a better life."

Rev. Cleveland added, "We've enjoyed our time in Fayetteville. It's a quiet, family town. There are many young children. We have churches and schools in the village. People keep to the business of raising their families. The few public houses that we have are down by the docks. They keep the rowdies away from our children. But everyone is caring and willing to help others."

"Yes, I can see that Fayetteville is similar to Cicero. From what you said and what I've seen, people seem to be largely focused on themselves and their families. But I sense something missing." Unable to resist airing her causes, she continued. "I wonder how interested villagers are in others and in the needs of the broader community. Are they troubled by the plights of Blacks? Indians?"

Rev. Cleveland's face immediately reddened, but his response was tempered. "Mrs. Gage, you ask intriguing questions, but I believe most locals would rather mind their own business than think about such abstract issues."

"Isn't that disturbing?" Matilda opined. "I find it so. Many mire and content themselves in a state of learned ignorance. The people you describe, the people on which you rely, are consciously unwilling to search for the truth. For example, when people marry, they do not become equal partners. Come to think of it, inequality does not just regard marital accord and domestic contracts; it is of broader impact. It defines our acceptance of others, particularly those who differ in appearance or background. I would argue that acceptance is the essence of faith."

Matilda's spoke as if a cork had been removed from a bulging bottle. Unable to control herself and apparently oblivious of the impact her words were having on the Clevelands, she continued. "Faith. The security blanket of religion. In all other facets of life, we promote and reward curiosity, verification, and problem-solving. But when it comes to issues of who we are and why we are here, we fall back on the standard bromide: faith. Why is that? Why do we sell ourselves short? Are we inherently lazy? And when we are threatened, why do we demean, debase, or demonize those who do not align with and reinforce our beliefs?"

Henry and Ann sat dumbfounded. Rev. Cleveland's slack face reflected the offense he took Matilda's words. He was goaded to fight. "Those are the comments of a disbeliever. Jesus speaks of tolerance and acceptance. He rejoices in diversity. The Bible provides insight into God's answers to your questions of origins and destiny."

"If so, then why do we wage war in God's name against other God-fearing peoples?" Matilda retorted. "How can two opposing forces both genuinely claim to be fighting for God? Who is to say that the Presbyterians,

Lutherans, or Methodists have it 'right'? And what about Jews, Muslims, or Zoroastrians? Are they wrong, too?"

"Zoro-who?" Rev. Cleveland wanly asked.

"Never mind." Matilda chuckled, and a wry smile emerged as she reflected on a conversation with her father years ago.

Before Matilda could continue, Henry interrupted, "Rev. Cleveland, how large is your congregation?" but his effort to divert the conversation failed.

Matilda's train was gaining steam. "These religions ponder the same existential questions, grapple with the same challenges, and value family and community. They use different approaches, different words, and may find different answers. Who has the right to stake out a lofty position of unique righteousness? How do we *know* that the polytheistic religions of the Greeks, Romans, and Haudenosaunee are 'wrong'? Aren't all people searching for comfort? The comfort of having answers to the unanswerable? Comfort in manner of prayer? Comfort of knowing others who have similar aspirations and dreams?"

Henry tried again to derail Matilda. "Rev. Cleveland, have you ever taken a ride on a canal boat? I see people often use them as transports."

Ignoring Henry's efforts, Matilda barely missed a beat. "The seven sacraments. Now, there are actions by which to structure your life. Martin Luther revealed their true purposes in maintaining the church: a tether to the past, manna for its present, and assurance for its future. They codify the patriarchal order, an order that is most certainly not the only way. It may not even be the best way. Life can proceed in other manners— Haudenosaunee flourished for centuries as a matriarchal society."

Exasperated, Rev. Cleveland shed his cloak of detached, pastoral concern and countered with uncharacteristic bluntness. "Mrs. Gage, you certainly do like to talk, or shall I say, pontificate. But you know little of the workings of God and society." Scoffing, he asked, "What is your training?"

"Little formal training. Mostly from my father, a physician in Cicero, and at the feet of Plato, Rene Descartes, Jane Austen, Mary Wollstonecraft, and Marion Reid. Their teachings were complemented by reading repressive, misogynist diatribes of Aristotle, Georg Hegel, Martin Luther, and others. And you, sir?"

The minister was flabbergasted. Not only by Matilda's words, but by her impertinence. "Sounds to me like you rely on literary flibbertigibbets."

Matilda well knew that the reverend was aware of the greatness of the people she cited. While she enjoyed being provocative, she did not want to be insulting. To avoid saying something she would regret, Matilda grimaced, tipped her head to the Clevelands, and bade her hosts adieu. "Thank you for an invigorating chat. I look forward to getting to know you better."

As the Gages rose and walked toward the foyer, Matilda looked toward the dining room. She spotted a stunned Steve, who barely understood what had been said but most certainly appreciated its tone.

# 38

McVicar's General Store, Fayetteville, New York
Saturday, June 7, 1845, 11:00 AM

SATURDAY'S DRY WEATHER was the first for Fayetteville
in a week. A flock of passenger pigeons delighted in undulating waves
and obscuring a brilliant mackerel sky. Henry strutted up Genesee Street,
whistling "Open Thy Lattice Love," a catchy new song by a promising
young composer named Stephen Foster. His spirits soared with the glorious
weather. Despite his gaiety, he was on a serious mission. He was going to
introduce himself to John McVicar and his dry goods store. Henry's goal
was to assess whether Mr. McVicar would be a collaborator or competitor.

Opening the door and entering the store, Henry gawked at the large
room, overwhelmed by all the wonderful things. His eyes drifted to the
back, where a counter sat before a wall covered by shelves. On the left,
the shelves held large-mouth bottles filled with knickknacks and colorful
assorted candies (a baker's dozen for a penny). The shelves behind the
counter were arrayed with vials of medicines: extracts, tinctures, and
powders. The shelves to the right held row upon row of bottles with nails,
screws, bolts, and nuts of various sizes.

Everywhere he looked, Henry saw a spectacular range of wares: some
pedestrian, some exotic. The wall in the front right corner of the room was
lined with clusters of brooms, shovels, spades, and ladders. The middle

of the room was filled with tables. Though most boasted wares that were carefully arranged, others held items scattered higgledy-piggledy. These included hammers, screwdrivers, awls, and other tools. Neighboring tables carried sewing supplies: bolts of striped, solid, and checked shirting fabrics marked for 9–15¢/yd., sheeting at 12–15¢/yd., threads, and yarns of diverse colors. On the floor below the tables sat men's heavy work boots costing $2.75, and women's shoes for $2.25. No space was left unused.

Food staples lined the left wall. Rows of aged oak barrels supported by steel hoops and identified by painted signs held ground wheat for 2¢/lb., rye flour for 1¢/lb., corn meal at 1½¢/lb., and sugar for 7¢/lb. A shelf over the barrels held earthenware jars of Caribbean roasted coffee and teas for 24–46¢/lb., New Orleans molasses and Tupelo honey for 50–77¢/lb., and local maple syrup at 61¢/lb.

Henry gaped. Mr. McVicar's store was magical. Once Henry recovered from his awe, he hoped he would not have to compete with Mr. McVicar. He walked to the rear of the store and rang the bell on the counter. Getting no response, he rang again and called out, "Mr. McVicar."

A muffled voice came from the back. "I'm a'coming. Keep yer britches on." A moment later a stocky man wearing a tartan tam hurried out, hobbling with the help of his cane. "G'day ta you sir. How can I help you?"

"Good morning, sir. I'm Henry Gage."

"Glad ta make yer acquaintance. I'm John McVicar. 'Pologies. I was in the back, sortin' out today's d'livery of nails, screws, and tools. It arrived on today's train."

"Train? That's curious. Don't you use the boats on the canal?"

"Excellent question. Why do you ask? You sound like you have some experience in this area."

"Well, I do, of sorts. My family has a dry goods store in Cicero."

"Ah, then you must be one o' those Gage boys. I know your father, Judson. I trust he's well."

"Yes, I am one of 'those' boys. Sorry to say, Father has had it a bit rough of late, but overall, he seems to be fine."

"That's good to hear. Welcome to Fayetteville. As for your questions about using the canal boats, yes, I do, but less often. The rail's offerin' rock-bottom prices. They're tryin', cryin' to establish themselves. They're fightin' the canal. With these prices, I can turn a tidy profit. All I need to do is get my empty cart three miles north to Manlius Station by 7:30 AM to collect my shipment."

Henry shook his head. "With all due respect, I am surprised and confused. The canal delivers right to Fayetteville. It's the reason Fayetteville exists, isn't it? Why are you turning on it and the people who live by and support it?"

Mr. McVicar leaned on his cane and rolled up his lower lip. "Progress, m' boy. Supportin' the canal comes at a price to everyone."

Henry changed the subject. "No matter. I came to talk with you about your store. As I said, I grew up in this line of work and am interested in keeping on with it. I am looking for a place to hang my hat. At present, I am apprenticing with a lawyer in Syracuse with the plan of bringing legal services to my place of employ."

"Well, that's right fascinating. Years ago, I considered that, too. But I'm too old now. I think 'tis a right fine approach. Might'n say 'tis an inspired idea. People come in here with all sorts o' needs. Wish I'd followed through years ago, but as you can see, I ain't no young chick'n. In truth, I can see givin' this business up or passin' it over to someone in a few years. Maybe after we get to know each other, we should talk. Anyhoo, what can I do fer ya?"

Henry thought for the briefest moment, not wanting Mr. McVicar to think he was just coming in to discuss the future. He blurted, "Got any umbrellas?"

"Young man, you must be jokin'." Mr. McVicar guffawed. "Got no need for 'em here. Haven't ya noticed our streets when it rains? Messiest things ya ever did see. Last thing folks is concerned about is how wet their heads are. Interested in a good pair of galoshes?"

Matilda caught up with Henry as he left McVicar's. As they returned to their cart on North Mill Street, they came upon Richard, Ann, Anna, and Steve Cleveland walking in the opposite direction. Rev. Cleveland said to his wife, "There they are again, the Gages, our new neighbors with the strange ideas about, well, everything—God, people, rights.

Ann responded in an ironically pastoral manner. "We should all rejoice in each other's peculiarities. Others may not agree with you, but that does not diminish their worth, their participation, and their contributions. All should be valued."

Steve thought for a moment about his mother's words. As the Gages joined the group, he greeted Henry and Matilda, and then asked his mother, "Don't all people believe the same things?"

Ann responded, "Well, yes and no. This may be a good conversation for you to have with your father."

That piqued Steve's curiosity. Tilting his head, he asked, "Aren't all men created equal?

Steve's eldest sister, Anna, snipped, "Yes, but that is only men."

Enjoying the conversation, Matilda chimed in, "And only White men at that. According to the Constitution, a Black man counts as only three-fifths of a person. And women are wholly denied. And we must not forget the Indians. We must 'teach' them what is 'right' and that their land is ours for the taking. That's the policy President Jackson professed and pursued."

Henry smiled at Matilda. "I think Mrs. Cleveland agrees with you."

"Ah, thank you, Mr. Quixote," said Matilda as she affectionately squeezed Henry's hand. With that the Gages bid the Clevelands adieu and continued walking down Genesee Street to Mill Street.

Ann nodded and said to her husband, "They may be a queer pair, but they welcome our Stephen. I like them."

Rev. Cleveland looked unmoved, his face a mask without emotion. "I remain skeptical of how good the Gages are for our son."

# 39

Gage home, High Bridge, New York
Saturday, June 7, 1845, 2:00 PM

CLATTER AND CLACKS rang from the barn, occasionally punctuated by a sharp yelp. Each cry evinced a wince from Matilda. She yelled, "Steve, time for a break. Come in, have some tea."

"Thank you. Just let me finish moving these two boxes." After a few more outbursts, Steve emerged from the barn covered nearly head-to-toe in grease and sawdust. Watching Steve approach the house through the kitchen window, Matilda tittered and handed him a cloth and some soap the moment he entered the house. After he washed up in the basin freshly filled with water from the pump in the backyard, Matilda offered Steve a seat at the kitchen table. She poured two cups of tea.

Sipping his tea, Steve noted, "Oh, this is so good. Mint?"

Pushing a plate of cookies in Steve's direction, Matilda nodded. "Yes."

Steve chomped on a cookie. "Ooh, these are tasty! What kind are they?"

"Shortbread. I like it with fruit, like the strawberries. They're just coming in, so maybe next time you can try them together."

Steve munched and mused, "Mrs. Gage, I think that you are just a few years older than my sister Anna. I think that she's all mixed up. She is also trying to figure out what she wants to be. I think she wants to be Mrs. Somebody. What do you want to be when you grow up?"

Matilda smiled. "Steve, for many years, I was expected to become a doctor. That's what my father intended. I may have thought so because he thought so. It's hard to sort."

"I never thought about that. What's the difference between what my parents hope for me or what I want?"

Matilda continued talking almost without regard to what Steve had said. "Medical schools are not willing to have a woman in their classes."

"Why not?"

"They think a woman as a doctor is unseemly. Have you ever had a woman doctor?"

"No, I haven't. I've only had Doc Taylor," Steve said slowly as the reality dawned on him.

"Neither have I. Don't you think that strange? Women probably know more about children. They certainly know more about women." Matilda paused and then continued, "In fact, other than being a mother or a house servant, few jobs are available to women."

"Why's that? It doesn't make sense. It can't be because girls are stupid. The girls at my school are just as smart as the boys. Smarter, even. In my class, my sisters Margaret and Mary are the best pupils. They know all the answers." Steve mockingly raised his right hand like the know-it-all girls.

Matilda directed a piercing stare at Steve for his disrespectful action. Then she smiled. "People, or shall I say men, are not yet ready to have women do the jobs men do. They say the Bible makes it clear that men and women should perform different tasks. I am not so sure."

Steve cocked his head and rubbed his forehead. Matilda seemed to be describing his father, who often said such things in their home and in church.

Staring out the kitchen window, Matilda said, "I didn't go to a school like yours, but from what I can see, something happens when schoolgirls get a bit older than you. They *act* less smart. Maybe it's to appeal to boys. Whatever the reason, it's sad because they bury their thoughts, their cleverness. You may not have seen this yet, or even understand what I am saying, but in time you will. Just do me, and yourself, the favor of seeing people for who they are. Treat all people equally."

"Okay, I'll try." Steve twisted his face, not quite sure what Matilda meant.

"Inequality takes many forms. For example, consider Mr. Nash. Have you noticed how people in the village respond to him?" Barely waiting for an answer, Matilda pressed on. "He was a slave. If I remember correctly, he was a slave in North Carolina. Anyway, he ran from his master, found his way north to New York, and was protected by people in the village. Even so, many talk and act differently with him. They may not mean to, but they do. As he has different origins, different experiences, different ways he sees the world, villagers do not—cannot—think the way he does. They cannot, nor do they dare to, put themselves in his shoes."

"His shoes? What's different about his clothes? Doesn't he put on his shoes like other people, one foot at a time? They seem to fit him just like they do anyone else."

"Steve, you keep thinking like that; see things just as they are, and you'll be just fine." Matilda grinned at Steve. "I've not had experiences like Mr. Nash's, but I will fight for his right to have the freedoms everyone else has."

Matilda thought for a moment, studying Steve, and realized that with his pranking and ingenuity, he would be a dependable partner. "I know that I should not tell you this, but I believe that you are trustworthy. You have to swear that you will not tell anyone what I am about to tell you."

Steve's eyes swelled to saucers. He crossed his heart and raised his right hand. "Yeah, what?"

"Our home is a 'safe house.'"

"Huh? A what?" replied a confused Steve.

"This house is a stop for runaways on the Underground Railroad."

"Blazes! Really? I've heard people talk of them. Didn't know where they are, much less that there's one near my home. How does it work? How do you know a train's coming through? How do you—" Steve worked himself into a lather of questions.

"Whoa, whoa, young man. Slow down. Remember, this must stay between you and me, and maybe Henry. People's lives depend on it. You may not talk to anyone, including your family, about this. Understood?" Matilda met Steve's eyes kindly but firmly. Steve nodded slowly.

"There are stations all about us, even in plain sight." Matilda paused. "Even your father's church is a station."

Steve's jaw dropped. His eyes popped.

"I hope you know that your father is a great man." Then, Matilda told Steve the story of when she and Henry took their first delivery together in the Cicero Swamp. Again, Steve fired a barrage of questions at Matilda.

"How do you know to meet someone? When? Where? How many? How to move them on? Where to send them?"

"Oh, so many questions, my young lad. Let's talk about this another time. Right now, let's have some tea, and then, it'll be time for you to go back home. Remember, Steve, you are to tell no one what I have told you," Matilda emphasized.

# 40

MATILDA GUIDED HER carriage while completing her errands. Her progress was interrupted by a brace of seven wood ducks waddling across Mill Street on their way to Limestone Creek. Strutting at the lead, the father was distinguished by his striking, sharp lines and comical clash of vibrant patterns. He was followed by his mate, in subdued, dappled plumage, and five ducklings wearing downy camouflage. Horses, carriages, and passersby halted abruptly to avoid the anatine family as it traversed Mill and lower Genesee Streets. Matilda mumbled, "Even in the animal kingdom, males have a puffed-up perception of their importance."

After passing the ducks, Matilda stopped at the corner of Elm and North Mill Streets, dismounted, tied up her horse, and looked about to gain her bearings. She set off with purpose down to the docks to check the wares. On her way, she passed Seamus O'Neal, a fellow congregant at the Methodist Episcopal Church and father of Steve's friends, the twins George and Sam.

Seamus remarked, "Ah, Mrs. Gage. 'Tis a pleasure to see you on such a grand day. If'n you don't mind me sayin', you're lookin' radiant."

"Thank you, Mr. O'Neal. You're kind, but I feel rather like a radiating furnace," Matilda retorted with a smile as she rubbed her belly. "I'm seven months along now—rotund and lethargic. But thank you just the same.

And how are those fine young twins of yours?"

"Ah, George and Sam. Me pair of bear cubs. If only they'd put as much effort inta their studies as they do their games. What's a father ta do?"

Matilda simply shrugged. Having no children yet, she stayed mum.

Seamus asked, "So, Mrs. Gage, what're ya lookin' for today?"

"I'm searching for some fresh fish. I have a soft spot for white fish."

"Just so happens, I landed fresh white fish. 'Twere caught just a few days ago in Lake Erie. They're in the hull, still swimming in barrels full of Erie water. If that don't work for you, I got some trout and largemouth bass from Ontario. They're bonny, colorful, and plump. Caught yesterday in Oswego. What's yer pleasure?"

"Mr. O'Neal, that all sounds wonderful. I'll take a white fish and a lake trout. Thanks. Whole ones, ten to fifteen pounds."

"Hoowee! You do like that fish. What'll you do with so much?"

"Well, we'll have some tonight and probably tomorrow, but most of it I'll salt and preserve for wintertime."

"Seems that fish isn't being shipped by boat no more. Fishers switched to rail. Rail is more costly, but quicker, fresher, and more dependable."

"Competition," pondered Matilda. "Maybe that will lower the prices for us."

"Wouldn't hold me breath on that, ma'am. Now, anythin' else I can get for ya? I just got some fresh corn. Been a tough year for corn. But this crop looks special. Maybe even better, I got some mushrooms I'm proud of. Rainy summer been grand for local types of mushrooms—corals, boletes, oysters."

"Thanks, I'll take a dozen ears, but I'll pass on the mushrooms. They don't agree with Henry or me. Here's ten cents for the corn." Matilda partially shucked the ears of corn to determine their health. Most were clean with a layer of silk covering robust yellow kernels. But three of the ears had a dusky growth covering their top thirds. "Looks like the wet summer was not so good for the corn. Ear rot. I'll take the rest of the bunch, but please dispose of these three."

"Mrs. Gage, I'm so sorry. Here. Please take back your money."

"No, thank you, Mr. O'Neal. I'll take the nine ears. You keep the dime." Matilda put the wrapped fish and corn into her carrying bag. "I'll go down the dock a bit. Please give my best to your wife and children."

Whistling as she walked back to her rig, Matilda put the parcels into the cart and guided her horse down the docks. As she sauntered along, she was confronted by powerful smells, both foul and sweet. The foul smell was from the canal water, fetid with waste. The sweet smells came from tables of flowers, fruits, and sundries lining the mule trails, staffed by hoggees.

Matilda visited a table laden with scores of bottles boasting spices and teas. Matilda drew in a breath and felt like she had gone to heaven. Spices included anise, cicely, coriander, fennel, and tarragon from Great Lakes states. This domestic produce was matched by treasures from Asia carried by Portuguese and Dutch companies—cinnamon, ginger, nutmeg, and pepper. The smells of the spices wafted with the sweet bouquet of bergamot, chamomile, chicory, peppermint, sassafras, and spearmint teas from Michigan and Wisconsin.

Matilda declared to the spicemonger, "Your wares are extraordinary. And if the smells are not enough, the colors are exquisite: rich oranges, yellows, and reds. The spices and teas could be used as dyes for clothing and quilting projects, though the price might be too dear to be practical."

The boat captain asked, "Ma'am, anything I can get ya?" Matilda, still in her dream state, did not hear the captain. He repeated himself, a little louder and more insistent. "Excuse me, ma'am. May I help ya?"

Alone with her thoughts, Matilda blurted out, "I don't remember spices ever being so powerful and vivid. Maybe it's my condition taking over." Returning to the greater world, she turned to the captain. "I am so sorry. I was losing myself in the smells from your bottles. I'm quite sure I could not do your job. I would just sit and breathe. It is intoxicating!"

"Whatever you say," the captain parried. "My job is to sell spices and teas. Want any?"

"I want them all; they smell so fine, but I cannot afford that. Maybe just some stick cinnamon, fennel seed, and peppercorns for now." The captain laid each spice on a separate piece of paper, folded each into an envelope, weighed it, and handed them to Matilda. Turning to the hoggee, she mulled aloud, "Come to think of it, I can use the spices to flavor meat and fish when I preserve them for winter." She asked him, "When do you expect to return?"

The captain stroked his beard and thought for a moment. "Three, four weeks. I'm on m' way to Troy at the eastern end of da canal. In Troy, I'll unload most of m' stocks from da Lakes and git new ones from da Caribbean and Europe."

"Do you know what you'll pick up in Troy?"

"Not till I gits there," replied the captain. "Depends on wha's there."

"Well then, I'll wait for your return." Matilda packed up her spices and some Darjeeling tea she bought as a special treat for Henry. "Bon voyage."

"Bone wha'?" asked the captain.

"Bon voyage. That's French for 'good travels' to you."

"Thank ya, ma'am. And good day ta ya."

Matilda continued down the docks.

# 41

Gage home, High Bridge, New York
Monday, November 3, 1845, 12:30 PM

MATILDA CALLED INTO the yard in her usual, composed manner. "Henry." Hearing no response, she turned toward the barn and repeated, "Henry?"

"Yes, dear," responded Henry matter-of-factly.

"Time to fetch Doc Taylor. Tell him my waters just broke," Matilda stated.

"Your what? Did what?" Though Henry had known this day was imminent, he was now confronted by reality. Beating himself into a dither, he wondered, *What to do? Should I follow Matilda's directions? Should I attend to her comfort?* Henry felt like a chicken without its head. *Should I set out things for the birth? Collect clean cloths? Boil water? What should I do?*

Henry did not realize that Matilda had already done much advance preparation for the birth. She had already folded a pile of clean cloths, made an ointment of beeswax and oil, collected thread for ligating the umbilical cord, and cleaned a bulb syringe.

Watching Henry wind himself up and out of control, Matilda gently repeated in a measured voice, "Henry, bring Doc Taylor here."

With that, Henry dashed from the house and yelled, "Sarah!" Hearing no response, he bounded down the front walk and ran around searching for Sarah. Failing to find her, Henry flung open the gate, which swiveled smoothly on its hinges. He pounded on the neighbors' door. After what seemed an eternity, Miriam Nash finally answered. Henry babbled, "Matilda. Matilda is having our baby! Miriam, I can't find Sarah. Can you come over? Can you help Matilda while I get Doc?"

Miriam smiled and reassured Henry, "Relax, don't worry. I'll find Sarah. If I cannot find her, I'll be over."

As she turned to close the door, Mrs. Nash was surrounded by her children: Hannah, Eli, and Hezekiah—fourteen, ten, and four years old, respectively. "Children, I may need to go next door to help Mrs. Gage. Hannah, watch the boys. Eli and Hezekiah, mind your sister."

Having secured help for Matilda, Henry ran to the barn, saddled and mounted a horse, and galloped the one and a half miles to Fayetteville to collect Doc Taylor.

Meanwhile, Matilda wobbled about her bedroom. She struggled to find a comfortable position and attempted to distract herself by reading. This was episodically interrupted by deep muscle contractions. The early contractions were mild; she was able to read through them. With time, however, they became more insistent, forcing her to stop and focus. The contractions momentarily took her breath away. Fortunately, when they became more intense, Sarah reached Matilda's bedroom. She guided Matilda through contractions as they built in frequency and intensity.

Suddenly, their attention was interrupted by a knock at the kitchen door. "Good afternoon, Mrs. Gage. It's Steve." Hearing no response, Steve yelled, "Is anyone here?"

Sarah called down, "We are upstairs. Matilda is having baby."

Uncowed by the concept or act of birth, Steve scaled the stairs, declaring, "I can help." He stood outside the door and continued, "I was around when my brother Lewis and sister Susan were born."

"Yes, Steve. Get blankets and towels, and then leave them by the door. They will make Matilda comfortable."

"Sure can. I even know where the Gages keep 'em. I'll be back in a jiff." True to his word, Steve planted piles of blankets beside the doorjamb.

Sarah used the blankets to prop Matilda into a comfortable position, but before long, Matilda shifted into another position as a new contraction enveloped her.

Steve yelled through the bedroom door, "Sarah, I'll be in the kitchen. I'll wait there till you call for something else."

Within the hour, Henry and Doc Taylor arrived. Henry flung open the front door and sped into the house. "Matilda? Sarah? Miriam?" Hearing scuffling on the second floor, he bounded up the stairs, two steps at a time.

On approaching the bedroom, Henry was shooed away by Sarah. She assured Henry, "All is well here. Go downstairs. Keep Steve company in the kitchen." Henry reached the bottom of the stairs as Doc Taylor entered the foyer. Feeling useless, Henry mindlessly pointed upstairs and stumbled into the kitchen to join Steve. Steve had already begun stoking the oven with wood to boil water for cleaning cloths and tools. Henry sat anxiously, stood again, paced, and then repeated the sequence.

Meanwhile, Doc followed the voices up the stairs and found the Gages' bedroom. Seeing the stacks of cloths and other paraphernalia, he remarked, "Good afternoon, Matilda. As expected, I see that all is in good order and that you are quite well prepared. Are you sure you need me?"

"No," Matilda puffed and bluntly stated, "I'd rather have a midwife." She broke off to focus on a new cresting contraction. Without screaming or yelling, Matilda centered herself and gritted through. After the contraction passed, she breathed slowly, deliberately. Matilda continued, "But you are among the few qualified people in Manlius that we know. Henry and I thought you'd be the proper person—" Matilda's voice stopped suddenly as she pushed through yet another seizing contraction.

"I'm honored." Doc Taylor's feelings were not the least bit hurt by the faint praise. He understood that women preferred to have other women attend their births.

At that moment, Steve knocked on the door. Doc answered, and Steve presented a tray bearing the fruits of Matilda's preparations and Steve's forethought: clean cloths, boiled water, strings for ligating the umbilical cord, and a pair of scissors. "Thank you, lad. Quite complete.

Quite impressive. Please, just put the tray down and I'll take it from here." Doc turned to Matilda. "Now, let's see where we are." He determined the birth was progressing well. The hairy head of the baby was crowning. "Matilda, you can push whenever you feel the urge."

"Thanks, Doc," Matilda puffed.

Quickly thereafter, the whole head emerged. Then, with a final push, the baby was born. Sarah collected the wee girl in one of the cloths. Doc had a syringe ready, but in short order, it was quite clear that her lungs were mighty functional. Releasing a lusty wail, she took her first breath. Doc looked over the baby to ensure that she had all of her fingers and toes and good skin color. "Well, Matilda, she looks to be a fine one. Seven pounds, I'd say." Sarah swaddled the baby and passed her to her mother.

Hearing the commotion, Henry and Steve ran up the stairs to stare. Henry sidled up to his new family with a smile as broad as the horizon.

Doc asked, "Matilda, what'll be her name?"

"Helen."

"Why Helen?"

"It's Greek for 'shining light.' She will most certainly be that for Henry and me. She is the forever link that binds Henry and me together. And she's named after my dear mother."

Shifting her attention to Steve, Matilda offered, "Thank you, Stephen. Thank you for thinking of my needs and for standing by Henry." Reflecting for a moment and composing her wits, Matilda added, "Come to think of it, why are you here?"

"I got out of school early and just stopped over to finish the work on the cart."

"You are a responsible young man. If we haven't said it before, please feel free to come here whenever you like. I'm sure Henry would agree, you are always welcome."

# 42

Clinton (Five Corners) Park, Fayetteville, New York
Saturday, July 4, 1846, 9:45 AM

MATILDA AND HENRY pushed their perambulator carrying eight-month-old Helen. They wove up Genesee Street, past scores of milling Fayetteville folk. The road was so congested it was as if someone had taken the houses in the village and shaken all the residents onto the streets. Everyone was festive for the auspicious day—the seventieth anniversary of the country's birth.

Fayetteville was festooned with flags. One was the confrontational flag boasting the "Don't tread on me" snake of rebellion. Another bore the thirteen bars and circular constellation of thirteen stars representing the original states of the nascent nation. There was also the new flag with bars and four rows of seven stars each, recently unveiled to celebrate Texas joining the Union. Children waved homemade paper flags on sticks. Red, white, and blue buntings hung from Village Hall and homes on Genesee Street. Despite the overcast weather, the spirits of Fayetteville residents soared.

A rousing round of "Yankee Doodle" emerged from the raucous crowd as celebrants waited for the parade to climb Genesee Street from its start at the North Mill Street docks to the reviewing podium in Clinton Park where Manlius Street crossed Genesee Street.

Promptly at 10:00 AM, the procession began. Town elders marched at the front of the parade. Midway up Genesee Street, the leaders sang the national anthem, "Hail, Columbia." People in the crowd joined. Matilda noted that many seemed to be mechanically singing the lyrics, as if the verses were devoid of meaning. Meanwhile, she dwelled on the phrase "that truth and justice will prevail, and every scheme of bondage fail." She repeatedly added emphasis each time she sang "every."

Following the leaders of the procession was a pair of horse-drawn water pumpers from the two companies that served the village and environs. Normally, they were competitors, but for the sake of the celebration, they buried their rivalry for the day. The Mechanics Hook and Ladder Company based on High Bridge Street showed off their work-steeds, primped with braided manes. Not to be outdone, the Hose Company from Center Street boasted a burnished carriage gleaming in the daylight. Its carriage was drawn by stout, well-trained donkeys. Normally, there were four pairs, but today the team was proudly led by a single pair. The Hose Company's tank spouted water skyward, spraying gleeful celebrants lining the street.

The hook-and-ladders were followed by children from two local schools. Children from the Fayetteville Academy strode through the village, beaming and bouncing in a free-flowing formation. All the while, they yelped at the tops of their lungs. In contrast, the children from the Eaton School were arrayed in three regular rows and strutted in synchrony. Following the children were members of the Masons and groups representing the various local churches.

Pulling up the rear of the parade were Mayor Samuel Stone and Sheriff James Smith. They were dressed in their Sunday best, doffing their hats and waving to the onlookers, always soliciting future votes. As Mayor Stone strode to the front of Village Hall, a four-year-old squealed, nudged his mother, and pointed at the roof of the hall. "Look, Ma. Up there!"

"What, dear?" The mother stopped talking with her neighbor and followed her child's hand. Adjusting her eyes to the glaring sunlight, she tittered, elbowed her neighbor to her right, and indicated the roof.

"What is it?" The neighbor squinted. "Is it a donkey? A donkey decked out like a flag on top of Village Hall?!"

The two women burst into fits of giggles.

A wave of awareness spread among the crowd like a gust of wind passing through swamp grasses. As more and more villagers became aware of the donkey, arms rose and fingers pointed.

"Another Cleveland prank!" sneered an unidentified, uninformed nosy parker. "It's always one of them Cleveland boys making mischief. But I gotta give it to them. Don't know how they got the danged thing up there."

Even the normally taciturn Robert Hatch sniggered.

Hidden in a remote recess of Clinton Park, Steve watched the attention shift from the parade to the donkey, from the blithering mayor to the donkey, and from the blustering sheriff to the donkey. Steve thought the joke was well worth any punishment he might receive. Fighting to keep his composure, his face turned beet red. He plugged his ears with his index fingers to contain his hilarity. When Steve could control himself no longer, he exploded in uproarious laughter and cackled in the corner, drawing the stares of those around him.

At the other end of Clinton Park, Doc Taylor remarked, "Well, I'll be. A patriotic ass. What'll we have next?"

"Aw, it's nothing new," responded Bertie Beard. "We already got that, Doc. We call him Pres'dent Polk."

"Well, that's not right nice, nor respectful," interjected Mr. Hatch. "Polk's doing fine. Punishin' Mexico. Annexin' Texas."

Mr. Beard retorted, "Humpf. He's not solving nothing. All Polk does is light fires, fan flames, and then take credit for extinguishing the blaze he started. He's a flimflammer, a swindler."

"Robert, I'd appreciate it if'n you'd keep yer voice down and yer opines to yerself," said his wife. "You wanna git run outta town?"

Overhearing the flying comments, Matilda could not restrain herself any longer. "Polk may be a fine leader of foreign affairs, but his domestic policies and actions are abominable. Not only does he own slaves, Polk continues buying and selling slaves from the Executive Mansion. And that man has no respect for the natives whose lands the United States takes and freedoms the government denies. Polk is actively uninterested in providing equal rights to people who are not White. He conducts himself imperially and promotes federal amorality."

Doc, Mr. Hatch, and Bertie stared at Matilda, slack jawed. Despite their surprise at a woman expressing her opinions, the political baiting and banter continued among the assembled people—that is, the assembled men.

Before long, fights popped up throughout the crowd. Doc Taylor walked past the mayor and sheriff, stepped up to the podium, and rapped the gavel to settle tempers, speaking in his deep, resonant voice. "Folks, it's a fine, fine day. It's good to see all of you and hear everyone in full voice and full force. Today's a day to highlight unity and what binds us. Unity comes from celebrating diversity and mutual respect. Diversity of opinion is the strength of our democracy. Respect for each other is the bedrock of our union. So, let's stop this quibbling and make with the celebrating. Strike up the music!" With that, arguing abated, parties shook hands, the band played, and mugs were raised.

Matilda noted to Henry, "The festivities are advertised as being for all and celebrating diversity. But they highlight men's activities, men's achievements, and men's governance. The exclusion of women as equals in the fabric of village life is not reason for celebration."

# 43

Clinton Park, Fayetteville, New York
Saturday, July 4, 1846, 12:15 PM

FOLLOWING THE PARADE, townsfolk enthusiastically threw themselves into the Independence Day fete. Celebrants from Fayetteville, High Bridge, Manlius, and other nearby communities gathered for camaraderie and fellowship. For many, this event was the highlight of the annual Fayetteville calendar. It was a chance to reconnect with friends not seen in months, maybe even since last year's fete.

For Matilda and Henry, the celebration was an opportunity to make new acquaintances, though this presented each with a different challenge. Having grown up in a community where he knew virtually all the residents, Henry's skills of introduction were not well developed. Meanwhile, Matilda's response to meeting new people was a tendency to monopolize the conversation, a reflection of her father's teaching. She was working on not overwhelming new acquaintances.

The Gages recognized few of the attendees as they surveyed the crowd. Nevertheless, Matilda's eagle eye identified two scruffy men lurking on the outskirts. It might have been the way they dressed or their nervous demeanor, but either way, Matilda's awareness was heightened. "Henry, do not turn around too quickly. Look at the two men next to the right pillar in front of Village Hall. One is wearing a red-and-blue-checked shirt.

The other has an eye patch. They seem out of place." Matilda furrowed her brows. "I think I've seen at least one of them before. I think it was years ago, but I cannot be sure. Hmm, where was it? Was it in Father's office? What was his name? Yes, I remember now. Beauregard. What do you think, Henry?"

"I see them, but I wasn't at your father's office at that time. So I do not know. Shall I ask if anyone knows them?"

"Yes, that would be good." But before they could strike out in search of locals who could help, the strange men disappeared.

"Henry, I don't see them anymore. Did you see them leave?" Matilda said with unease.

"No, dear. They seem to have vanished."

Matilda's rising alarm abated, and she suggested, "Let's let Doc know next time we see them. I hope I am wrong. Until then, let's put the mystery men aside and join the festivities." And that they did. The Gages enjoyed a fine lunch of roasted pig, green beans, peas, potatoes, and a broad variety of cakes and pies.

Steve and the O'Neal twins were playing tag among the celebrants when Steve bumped into Henry. "Oh, sorry, Mr. Gage."

"That's quite all right, Steve. Join us?"

"Sorry, can't." Steve scrunched into an S-shape to avoid being tagged by Sam O'Neal. "Gotta go." As he turned to follow his mates, he was surprised and pleased to see one of his favorite hoggees. "Professor! Professor!"

"Why, Steve, m'boy! It's a delight to see you," Professor exclaimed. "As there's no business on the fourth, I moored my boat at Mill Street to stay in Fayetteville for the night and join the festivities. Been wanting, waiting to learn more about your village. I heard all the hubbub, and, well, here I am."

"Terrific, let me show you about." Steve marched through the crowd and pointed out places and people who were important to him—where he played baseball, where he went to school, his father's church, and his home.

"My, this is a mighty fine village you've got here. Got everything a right fine village should have, and friendly people, too. I can see why you're so proud of your home."

Steve beamed. "Interested in getting something to eat? I can show you what Mother made." He led Professor to the park where tables of food were arranged.

As lunch finished, a band composed of a fiddler, flutist, clarinetist, and drummer began to play. The first few pieces were toe-tapping ditties designed to get townsfolk up and dancing—"Turkey in the Straw" and "De Boatman Dance." Then, the music switched to more "sedate" Glenmary waltzes, which segued to raucous polkas. Revelers joyfully two-stepped, strutted, and spun, whether they knew the dance steps or not. Gents' hats flew and full-length dresses billowed. Women twirled under arches formed by the unions of partners' and neighbors' arms. Once the waltzes began, Henry reached out. "Matilda, 'Come, and trip it as ye go, on the light fantastic toe.'"

Matilda blushed and turned to Doc's wife standing beside her. "Mrs. Taylor, would you be so kind as to hold Helen while I dance with my husband?"

"Matilda, I'd be delighted." With that handoff, the Gages took to the dancing square.

Henry was not a confident dancer, but he was game. Despite being all limbs, there was a grace to his movements. He bounded across the dance space like a loping deer. After a few moments, he declared, "Matilda, please stop introducing the turns. I'm capable of initiating the steps."

Somewhat defensively, Matilda replied, "I am not so sure that you can see all the obstacles that I see, but very well. As you'd have it." Relinquishing control was not one of her strengths, but she also knew that the success of the union was the ultimate goal.

The reverend and Ann Cleveland danced in the corner. In contrast to Henry's grace, Rev. Cleveland was herky-jerky. He had no sense of rhythm. After one move, he bent and twisted himself. Even across the room, Matilda saw him wince and yelp. Unable to stand, he appeared stuck in an unforgiving position.

Matilda left Henry and hurried over. "Reverend Cleveland, it is I, Matilda Gage. You look to be in acute pain. I think I can help, if you will let me." Matilda exuded a sense of confidence, composure, and compassion, and Rev. Cleveland reacted in kind. He surrendered to Matilda, silently nodding through his pain, at least momentarily disregarding his prejudices against women. "All right. Brace yourself against the wall. If you are not offended, I am going to lay my hands on your back to relieve your pain. Are you ready for that?"

In a short series of labored exhalations, the reverend puffed, "Do . . . what . . . you . . . need."

"Please let me know if I identify the site of greatest pain."

Rev. Cleveland huffed and nodded again. Matilda gently but firmly moved her hands over his back, occasionally pushing an index finger into select spots, including one a few inches above his hip. When she hit a spot two inches lateral to the spine, he cried out in pain. "Ah, as I expected. You strained a muscle that raises your thigh." Rev. Cleveland, still bent over, shuffled over to the wall. "Please, turn and face me. Plant your back against the wall. Lower yourself to a squat position. Hold that for ten seconds."

"Ooh, I can't do it," he said, but having no other advice to follow, he gingerly lowered himself along the well.

"Glide your back up the wall. That's it. Good. Rest. Now let's do it again. Ten seconds." Rev. Cleveland repeated the exercise. "Now come back to the wall. Turn around and lean on it with your bent arms." Matilda positioned herself on his left side. "I am going to add some local pressure. You can expect a bit of focused pain, but after I remove my hand, the pain should be largely gone. Ready?"

"Yes, anything to rid myself of this pain," he grunted.

"Hold up against the wall." Matilda pressed two fingers into a spot above the left hip, applying the pressure despite the reverend's grimace. Then she let go. "Try to stand—slowly."

Rev. Cleveland did as Matilda advised. He rose to his full height, surprising himself by standing fully erect. In disbelief, he exclaimed, "Marvelous!"

"I learned that bone crunching by watching Father help people twisted and in pain."

He turned, stared at Ann, and then looked at Matilda. "You learned well. My dear, you have a gift for making things right. I would never have thought I'd say this, but maybe it's too bad women cannot be physicians." Then, partially limiting his thought, he added, "Well, at least, one woman."

Matilda smiled in appreciation, but internally she winced at her opportunity denied. With that, Rev. Cleveland walked away, refusing to dance anymore at the festival.

# 44

Cleveland home, Fayetteville, New York
Monday, July 13, 1846, 6:15 AM

Humming while he collected his breakfast, Steve sliced a thick piece of bread, slathered it with butter, fried an egg, and poured a glass of milk. He was about to take a large bite when his father entered the kitchen. Steve gulped.

"Good morning, Stephen. Looks like a fine summer day to play."

"Yes, Father. I'm raring to play baseball at the Limestone meadow. But first, I'm going to work at the docks for a couple of hours. I'm hoping to make a bunch this week."

The two fell into a comfortable silence punctuated only by the soft sounds of chewing. Steve broke the quiet. "Father, I understand our church is a stop on the Underground Railroad."

Astonished, Rev. Cleveland swallowed his bite of food. "Yes, Stephen. It is. Why do you mention it?"

Steve replied, "Well, I just heard something the other day. It made me curious."

"And where did you learn this?"

"I am not free to say, but it's a good source."

Rev. Cleveland stroked his chin. "Stephen. That information is secret. You must not discuss it with anyone." He looked straight at his son to ensure that he understood the gravity of his command, though the reverend realized that if Steve refused to divulge his source, he was not a risk to the Railroad.

After a few moments, Rev. Cleveland asked, "Why are you asking me about this?"

"Well, why do you do it? Isn't it dangerous?"

Rev. Cleveland nodded. "Stephen, I do my best to protect my family, but I believe it is important to help people, particularly those who are exposed and defenseless." He added, "The church provides sanctuary."

"What does sanctuary mean?"

"It is a protected place where people don't have to be afraid of being caught or harmed. It's my God-given responsibility to help those less fortunate. I do what I can to save innocents."

To Steve, this seemed like one of those few times when his father was not irritated by him. Quite the opposite, Rev. Cleveland appeared intrigued by his son's genuine interest in understanding a complicated, adult concern.

Steve followed by asking, "Why is there a need for secrecy?"

"That is an unfortunate situation. There are people who believe that all people are not created equal. More to the point, these people do not consider Blacks to be full people or even human."

Steve was perplexed. "How can that be? They look just like us, they talk, they walk, they eat, they feel. They even play baseball."

"Yes, but it is not so simple as that. Some believe that Blacks are lesser: not as intelligent, not as capable."

"Just because of their skin color? They add two plus two and still get four. And I've had conversations with many people with dark skin that are just as interesting as any I've had with someone with white skin. Maybe even more interesting."

"Everything you say is correct. Unfortunately, not all White folks feel as you do. It is distressing, but some would do harm to Blacks if they had the opportunity, including hurting the people who help them. It would not be below such people to capture Blacks and return them to slavery."

"That's awful. Why do some people feel superior to others?"

"Stephen, that is an excellent question, and one that we can discuss at another time. To return to your original question about secrecy, I hope you can understand why the Blacks, their protectors, and their accomplices need protection. They get that protection through secrecy."

"Who are we being protected from? It can't be people who go to our church. They are good people. And I guess that could be said of people who attend the other churches nearby."

"It would like to agree with you, but the answer to your question is disturbing. As you say, most people are good, but there are people among us who would cause harm. They may even be people who you like or admire. They may hide in plain sight."

Rev. Cleveland paused for a moment. "Son, I don't want you to grow up being suspicious of everyone. I genuinely believe that people are good." Steve nodded without expression. "But you do need to be careful."

"How do I know? How can I tell?"

"It is not easy. What I can say is that it is important that you protect yourself and those whom you hold dear. I hope you can see why the Underground Railroad is not discussed publicly."

"Yes, sir."

# 45

Cleveland home, Fayetteville, New York
Thursday, September 17, 1846, 8:35 AM

GENESEE STREET WAS abuzz. Fourteen-year-old Will fought through the frenetic crowd and barged into his house. Without knowing if anyone was home, he yelled, "Line boats sank! Two line boats sank!"

Will's father, who had just finished dressing, rushed down the stairs to the foyer and found his eldest son bent over as if in pain. "Slow down, boy. What's all the hubbub?"

"A pair . . . of boats . . . is down . . . in the canal," Will puffed between shallow breaths that sounded like the whistles of a steam engine.

"Is anyone hurt?" his father asked with urgency.

"Not so far as I can tell." Will tried to catch his breath. "I heard that one hoggee was caught in his boat, but he was rescued. The other was already on land."

"Well, that's a godsend. Has a hook-and-ladder truck arrived?"

"Not yet."

"Son, take a breath." Rev. Cleveland put one hand on Will's back and the other on his arm to guide him to a chair. "Do you know where your brother is? Is Stephen at the docks? Is he working?"

This was one of the few times he had no idea where his brother was. "I don't know."

Rev. Cleveland turned down the hall toward the kitchen to find his wife. Ann was coming the opposite way to see what the frenzy was about. "There's been an accident at the docks. Stay with Will. I am going to find Stephen." The reverend mumbled as he made to bolt from the house without a coat, "Dang that Stephen! I never know if he is a victim or a culprit."

"Keep your temper, Richard. He's just a boy," Ann implored.

"As far as I can tell, he's a nine-year-old hellion without a compass. This has Stephen written all over it." Rev. Cleveland ran to the North Mill Street docks with all the speed he could manage. Fortunately, the way from the Cleveland home to the docks was downhill. Even so, his poor physical conditioning slowed him to a run-walk and left him winded by the time he arrived.

While regaining his breath, the reverend surveyed the situation. People, many of whom were from his congregation, milled about, relaying the unfolding story to other townsfolk. Some were just walking aimlessly, snooping for juicy gossip. Through his pastoral training, Rev. Cleveland had become a keen observer of individuals and groups of people. He knew that hearsay news became less and less reliable with each pass. Despite this, he forgot all of his pastoral training when he overheard two dockworkers leaning against crates.

"This is one prank where that troublemaker Cleveland went too far."

The reverend struggled to restrain his rising rage as he confronted the workers. "What's going on? Who are you talking about?"

"Ooh, ooh," responded one dockhand, who immediately recognized the minister. "So sorry, sir. Ne'r you mind."

"Ah, but I do mind. Who were you talking about?"

Hesitantly, the stevedore spilled, "Well, yer boy—Steve, of course."

"Of course," Rev. Cleveland repeated. "And what might my boy have to do with these boats?"

"Ah, ya know. He's a joker, that one. Everyone knows 'bout his prankin'."

Rev. Cleveland grimaced, nodding shallowly. "Well, have you seen this joker?"

"Can't say I has. Can't say I hasn't."

Rev. Cleveland bit his tongue, barely mounting an appreciative "Thanks" as he walked past the dockworkers. Finally, he reached the crowd at the head of the docks farthest from Genesee Street. Gawkers gazed at one of the boats, barely visible beneath the murky canal waters. The reverend scanned the crowd for a sign of Stephen, one of his son's friends, or anyone who might help his search for his reprobate son.

A truck from the Mechanics Hook and Ladder Company arrived. The truck turned around but struggled to move backwards down the narrow mule trail until Rev. Cleveland stepped forward and directed it. "Thanks, mate," said one of the firefighters, a young Black man. Based on his accent, he was likely from a Caribbean isle.

"How are you planning to raise the boat?" Rev. Cleveland asked.

"We'll climb down da laddahs into da canal, wrap da boat wit rope, hook da rope to da horses, and pull da boat from da canal."

Rev. Cleveland nodded in deference. "Let me know if there is anything I can do." He did not want to distract the firefighter any further. The young man had work to do, and the reverend had a son to find.

Within half an hour, the firefighters had lifted one of the sunken boats. As it dangled in the air, water poured over its gunwales. A noticeable stream came from a spot lateral to the shallow keel. Rev. Cleveland considered this. One might expect water to sheet over the hull, collect at the middle, and drip from there, but this flow was different. After working his gaze over to the boat, he found himself gaping at a ragged-edged hole in the hull.

He shot a glance across the canal where the Hose Company was raising the other sunken boat, then refocused on his primary mission: to find Stephen. After another fifteen minutes of scouring the docks, he gave up and walked home.

Embers of anger grew inside Rev. Cleveland as he climbed Genesee Street. By the time he passed his church and arrived on Academy Street, he was livid. Without even knowing if anyone was at home, or, for that matter, caring, Rev. Cleveland flung open the door and yelled, "Where is that boy?" His patience had run dry, his anger stoked by the insinuations heard at the docks. Finding Ann in the kitchen, he said, "That boy is trouble. I'm going to punish him something awful."

"Richard, are you alright?"

"Yes, fine," he fumed.

"Please. Tell me what happened," Ann beseeched. "What did you see? What did you hear?"

Rev. Cleveland related the scene to Ann. "Dockworkers blamed Stephen for damaging the boats. I asked for details, but they just prattled on about Stephen and his proclivity for pranks."

Ann tried to settle her husband. "They said 'proclivity'?" While Ann smiled, her husband seemed neither amused nor calmed. Tacking a bit, Ann continued, "Richard, this simply does not make sense. So far as I can tell, Stephen has been at school since early this morning. Why are you believing people you've not met before? Why would he do something so destructive? He's never done anything like this before. Let's see what he has to say when he gets home. Remember, neither of us has ever known him to lie."

Ann's words managed to salve her husband's fury; he grudgingly concurred. "You make sense. But if that boy was involved, I'll tan his hide."

# 46

Cleveland home, Fayetteville, New York
Thursday, September 17, 1846, 2:30 PM

"MOTHER!" STEVE BOUNCED into the kitchen where he found his mother rummaging through kitchen implements in a white apron and smocked, gray cotton dress.

"Hello, Stephen—"

Before she had a chance to ask about the morning's commotion, Steve breathlessly interrupted. "Mother, I had such a good day! We won every game of Annie-Over before school! I traded with Jacob. I got a baseball. See?" He showed his new treasure to his mother. "And, and, I even got all o' my arithmetic problems right!"

Though tentative, Ann forced herself to enunciate clearly to present a supportive front to her son. "Steve, I am delighted for you. Before I can hear more about your day, we need to talk about something. Something serious."

"Serious" hung in the air. The smile on Steve's face faded.

"Sit down." Ann fumbled with some wooden spoons as they sat on the spindle-backed kitchen chairs and then fussed with her clothes, carefully considering how to present the situation to her young son. "There was an accident at the docks this morning."

Steve abruptly sat ramrod straight, his pallid face alarmed. "Accident? What kind of accident?"

"Two line boats sank in the canal. One hoggee was on the dock when it happened. The other captain barely escaped drowning. Might you know anything about this?"

"No, not me. Not at all." Color seeped back into Steve's face.

Steve's mother continued her inquiry. "Where were you this morning?"

"Well, I woke and ate breakfast a bit late. Then, I went directly to school where George, Sam, some others, and I played Annie-Over in the yard. When Miss Cole called us, we went inside."

"I'm glad of that." Ann nodded in belief and relief. Steve showed none of the typical signs of his pranking—notably, his struggle to withhold his laughter. She could also easily corroborate her son's story by talking with Miss Cole or one of his mates. Ann hugged her nine-year-old. "As it happens, some folk at the dock said you were involved."

"Why would they say that?"

"Well, you must admit," said Ann, cocking her head, "you have a history of hijinks."

"Yes, but I'd never hurt or risk hurting anyone," Steve said, squarely matching his mother's intense eye contact.

"That is true, but you'll need to talk with your father after dinnertime."

Retreating to his room, Steve distracted himself, bracing himself for the unavoidable. He attempted to do homework and read his history book but found himself reading the same paragraph at least a dozen times without understanding anything. He could neither escape nor calm his fears—fear of his father and fear of false accusations. All he could consider was his father's imminent berating and an unwarranted beating.

The tall clock chimed seven as the sun set. The Cleveland family collected in the dining room for supper. Steve recognized the time was nigh. *Maybe Father's settled down over the last few hours. Maybe Mother's worked her magic.* Then the fear returned. *Or maybe he's spurred up his anger. I just hope Father gives me a chance. He always seems to think the worst of me.* Steve descended the stairs deliberately. The squeaky step notified his brothers and sisters already in the dining room that he was on his way. Everyone hushed as Steve entered and plopped himself at the table.

With all in the family assembled, Rev. Cleveland led the daily grace. "Lord, thank You for the food before us, the family beside us, and the love among us."

The family recited together, "Amen."

Ann and Anna carried a filled soup tureen and a heavily scored, wood cutting board loaded with bread, cheese, and fresh butter into the dining room. Eight hungry mouths awaited. All ate their potato parsnip chowder and corn-rye bread in uncharacteristic silence.

For Steve, the silence felt worse than the afeared scolding. He was certain his mother passed on his claim of innocence, but he stared at his food. *Why doesn't Father believe me? Why doesn't he think I'm innocent? Is Father ashamed that people think the worst of me? Does that make him feel badly?*

Steve picked at his food, pushed his plate with food barely touched toward the center of the table. He sat silently. After all the family finished dinner, the boys left the table while Anna and her sisters cleared it. Steve exhaled his relief as he scaled the stairs with Will. "Maybe Father is not going to punish me after all."

Just as Steve stepped on the noisy fourth step, he heard his father call, "Stephen. Please come back to the table." Will gazed at his brother, wrinkled his forehead, and sighed. Cecil, too, grimaced but could not muster a heartfelt look of support for his brother. Silently, Steve turned, reentered the dining room, and sat along one side of the rectangular table.

Richard Cleveland stared at his son from his chair at the head of the table. Steve fumbled with his fingers. Father and son remained silent. The reverend gave no sign that he considered Steve innocent. The girls finished clearing the dishes and pots and then went to their bedroom. The only sounds in the house were the silence-splitting *tick-tock, tick-tock* from the swinging pendulum of the tall clock, the heartbeat of the house.

Steve stayed mum, refusing to offer anything without being asked. After what felt like an eternity, Rev. Cleveland silently tilted his head up and to the right to excuse his son. Steve scrunched his face in confusion and obediently left the table. As he scaled the steps, Anna poked her head from her bedroom and said, "Steve, this isn't over. Sure as the sun rises,

Father's going to explode. And when he does, none of us want to be there."

Steve shivered and nodded.

# 47

Cleveland home, Fayetteville, New York
Friday, September 18, 1846, 6:30 AM

THERE WAS NO escape. Steve and his father were the first and only ones to make their ways downstairs for an early breakfast. Evidently, both had worked to avoid the other by rising earlier than usual with plans for an early exit.

They each collected cider, bread, and butter. Sitting at opposite ends of the table, they ate their meals in silence. On completing his meal, Rev. Cleveland coughed, preparing himself for a difficult conversation. "Stephen, yesterday morning, I looked all over the docks for you. I hunted high and low, but I could not find you."

"Father, I wasn't at the docks yesterday." Steve forcibly maintained his self-control, voice, and volume. "I was where I was supposed to be. I was at school."

"Steve, you confound me. You trouble me. You know I look bad when my son acts poorly. Also, I'm scared because you are not always where you are supposed to be. Remember when—"

"I have never lied to you, Father," Steve interrupted clearly, deliberately.

After a pause, Rev. Cleveland concurred. "No, son. You have not." Steve hoped that he'd gotten through to his father, but he was sorely mistaken. Rev. Cleveland continued his interrogation using a different tack. "Tell me what you know of the calamity."

"I don't know anything."

In disbelief, Rev. Cleveland persisted. "Come now. You work at the docks. You must have heard talk among the workers or among your mates who work with you."

Steve had been trapped in such conversations with his father before. He knew that in Father's mind, he was the first to be blamed for anything that went wrong in the family. He was the lightning rod. This time was different. The damage was not a family thing. It involved the entire community. "Father, I've not been to the docks in the last few days. Before the accident happened, no one had any idea something like this was going to happen. So how would I know about something that hadn't yet happened from people who were equally unaware that something was going to happen?"

Father elongated his face and raised his brows. "You make good sense. It may well have been an accident, though to my eyes, the damage on the two boats looked remarkably similar. Are you sure you heard no word about anyone planning mischief?"

"No word," Steve huffed in frustration. No matter what he said, his father was going to hint at his involvement.

"Very well. You may be dismissed."

Steve silently left the table and climbed the stairs. After washing up, he collected his books, ran past his brothers and sisters, who were just rising from bed, and left the house. Instead of heading to the docks or school, however, Steve aimlessly wandered the streets.

Replaying the conversation with his father, Steve was pleased with how he'd defended himself. He ambled east on Genesee Street, looking at storefronts—dreaming of the pickles he relished and toys and games he enjoyed at friends' houses.

Then, suddenly, Steve found himself standing in front of Sheriff Smith. "Good morning, Master Cleveland."

"Best to you, too, sir."

Sheriff Smith said, "I've heard that you're a reliable, knowledgeable source. What can you tell me of the sunken boats in the feeder canal?"

Steve did everything in his power to stifle a scream of frustration. The assumptions were crushing him. Crestfallen, he cast his eyes downward, then found his tongue, looked up defiantly, and responded, "I wasn't there. I know nothing." Steve walked away. The sheriff could never be as intimidating as his father.

"Son, where do you think you're going? Get back here."

Steve walked back to Sheriff Smith. "Sorry, sir."

Before speaking, the sheriff realized aloud, "I keep forgetting that while you're as tall as some adults, you may not act like one. As I think it over, I can't imagine how you'd'a done this. Get on along. But be careful. Folks around here are looking for someone to blame, and you're an easy target."

Steve was not quite sure what Sheriff Smith meant, but he knew he was dismissed. He left as quickly as he could and found his way to the safety of his school. His friends would be along soon. Until then, he kept his eyes peeled for trouble.

# 48

SEPTEMBER 18 WAS anything but a normal Friday. Maybe it was the numbers of villagers walking the streets, or the buzz and chattering among townsfolk. Or maybe it was the dark, foreboding skies. Whatever it was, an ambient heaviness was palpable.

Doc Taylor had been to the Presbyterian church to talk with Rev. Cleveland about a member of the congregation who was gravely ill. As he walked down the front steps, he spotted Henry Gage ahead on Genesee Street and double-timed it down the street to catch Henry's attention. He panted, "Henry. Good morning. How are you and Matilda?"

Surprised by the abrupt greeting, Henry responded, "Well, Doc, it's a pleasure to see you, too. Though it seems you need to get a bit more exercise." Henry smiled as Doc settled himself. "All is well at our home. Thank you. Little Helen keeps us hopping. She gets into everything. Scooting and crawling all around. I am not sure we're ever going to have a day's peace again."

Knowing that Steve was a frequent visitor at the Gage home, Doc asked, "Henry, there's a rumor running about town that young Stephen Cleveland pranked some hoggees. What do you think?"

"There is no way that Steve did anything like that."

Before Henry could continue, he and Doc were joined by Bertie Beard. With Bertie there, Doc pressed his point further. "I couldn't agree more. I think that's the most preposterous thing I've ever heard. Steve's a fine young man. Yes, he's got a strong sense of Puck, but he wouldn't even consider harming someone. I am sure there must be another explanation. Whether the accidents be circumstantial or malevolent, I cannot say. But of one thing I am certain: it's not our young Mr. Cleveland."

As his brother, Barti, joined the group, Bertie responded, "Yes, Doc, I, too, am sure about Stephen. There is no way that young whippersnapper coulda or woulda done anything like this. It's them Blacks that I ain't so sure of."

Doc was aghast at the remark and glared at Bertie. "Do you mean what you just said?"

To protect his brother and salvage the conversation, Barti interjected, "I may agree with you, Doc, but if not Steve, then who?"

Trying to recover his balance, Doc parried, "Ah, Barti. That is *the* question." Stroking his chin and fanning his fingers, he directed his words to Henry. "And at this point, I am not sure where to look for the answer."

Henry glanced at Bertie with disdain and said to Doc, "You do know you are preaching to the converted? I am delighted to hear of your support for Steve. Unfortunately, unthinking villagers add two plus two and get five. And harmful gossip is built on bricks of rumor. The result is a crusade of prejudice. The challenge is to change minds after they're hardened, but it's not impossible. Keep in mind that villagers' awareness is like a house of cards; such a house can be toppled with sound facts. I suggest we find those facts. We must keep our ears to the ground."

"Somber words. Sound advice," Doc commended.

# 49

Gage home, High Bridge, New York
Saturday, September 19, 1846, 8:30 AM

SATURDAYS FOR STEVE were normally free for playing baseball, fishing, and mucking about. Despite the crisp, welcoming sky, this Saturday, Steve walked under a cloud. Head down and kicking a rounded stone, he worked his way down the dirt path on the west bank of Limestone Creek.

As expected, villagers identified Steve as the one whose prank swamped the two canal boats and nearly resulted in the loss of a hoggee's life. Steve felt shame and dejection over the suspicions. With Will, his usual co-conspirator, busy at the docks, Steve wandered. Before he knew it, he'd arrived at the Gages. Their farm was a fine distraction. He fussed about the barn to keep his mind free and unburdened.

In the kitchen, amid preparations for Sunday dinner, Matilda suddenly heard a *tink, chink, bam!* ring from the barn. Matilda asked Helen, "Do you hear that?" Donning her coat, Matilda scooped up her daughter and hurried to the barn. When they arrived, the horses whinnied softly, affectionately.

Absorbed in his own world and unaware of Matilda, Steve continued disassembling the Gages' carriage. He sat on the floor, surrounded by the wheels, axles, and suspension, holding a wrench in his right hand and cradling a screwdriver under his left arm.

Even from twenty feet away, Steve's preoccupation was obvious. Without a word, Matilda pivoted, returned to the house, and settled Helen into her crib. She arranged slices of apples picked from a tree behind the house and a small pot of fresh honey that Henry had recently harvested.

The back door banging in the gentle breeze behind her, Matilda returned to the barn to invite Steve for a snack. He was nowhere to be found. All that was left on the barn floor were abandoned pieces of the cart. Matilda walked through the barn to find Steve sitting on the fence of the backfield. He was shaving down a stick and whistling mindlessly.

"Good morning, Steve. Would you like some apples and honey?"

Steve raised his head slowly, forced a smile, and nodded. Together, they walked to the house. Steve would not meet Matilda's gaze even when they were face-to-face in the kitchen.

"It's good to see you. What brings you to us this morning?"

Talking to the floor, Steve flatly offered, "Fixin' the cart."

"That's kind of you. Why?"

"I heard a squeak." Steve yielded another perfunctory answer as he fumbled with his stick.

"Steve," Matilda implored. "Tell me what happened."

Steve grudgingly raised his head. "I'm not guilty," he proclaimed. "Why are they sayin' I am?" Steve's pause was matched by Matilda's silence. Then the dam broke. "I wasn't anywhere near the docks. I don't like being blamed for somethin' I didn't do. And I don't like the nasty stares from people in town. It's not fair. It's just not fair! People don't know anything about anything. Why do they blame me?"

Matilda nodded in understanding. The unsubstantiated accusations and looks of condemnation were rampant through town. "My sympathies are with you, Stephen." Matilda scowled, then raised a single brow as she considered the situation. "It is sad. People can be small, unthinking. They don't know how much their loose talk hurts others, particularly innocents like you."

She mulled the options aloud. "What shall we do? We could ignore the rumormongers and wait for things to settle. We could confront and expose the fopdoodles for their unfeeling, hurtful ways. Alternatively, we could turn the tables and spread rumors about them." Shaking her head, she added, "That last thought is neither practical nor honorable. Perhaps we could silence them by finding out how the boats sank?"

"Right now, I don't care who did it, or why. I just don't want to be blamed for something I didn't do."

Matilda fixed Steve with her piercing gaze. "I understand. It is painful, but I think that figuring out the cause of the accident is our best path. It will silence the gossip, vindicate you, and shift the disgrace to where it should lie, on the perpetrators and the thoughtless shamers."

Realizing that Matilda's logic was sound, Steve fell quiet, anger welling at having been wrongly fingered by the mindless minions. While Steve stewed, Matilda returned to her mincemeat pie preparations. She offered Steve a piece of the shortbread she'd made earlier. After a few moments of chewing, he blurted, "I agree."

"Let's map out a plan to determine who was responsible. If we're lucky, maybe we'll even figure out why."

Matilda collected some paper, pens, and ink to take notes and record their plans. She called Steve to the dining room. "Let's do this logically. Let's look for patterns, signs, consistencies between the two boats." After scribbling a few things down, she continued, "Maybe it will be helpful to look at the boats that were not affected. Might there be something similar about them, too? Might that tell us something?"

"Those sound like good ideas." Steve's countenance began to lighten.

"You know boats well. One morning while you are working, can you sneak over to study the sunken boats?"

"Sure can. What should I look for?"

Matilda was a fusillade of questions. "Well, look at the holes. What does the damage look like? Is it similar on the two boats? What were they carrying? Where had they docked before North Mill Street? Where were they going? Was the damage accidental or intentional?"

Steve got swept up Matilda's enthusiasm. "That's a lot of stuff to remember. Maybe we should make a list so I don't forget anything."

"That's a fine idea. By the way, is this the first boat to sink at the North Mill Street docks?"

"Seems so. At least, it's the first I'm aware of."

"Do you want me to go to the docks with you?" Matilda asked. "It might be helpful to have two sets of eyes."

"That's right nice of you, but I think it'd be best if I go alone. I'm often about the docks, so I won't look out of place. But you, well . . . your being there would look strange."

"Steve, you must realize that you are doing something dangerous. If you get caught, you'll reinforce the accusations of the townsfolk. It will not go well for you."

"I understand, Mrs. Gage, but the risk is worth it."

"I'm glad that you're on board. I'll draft a list and send you with a pencil. You can check off tasks as you complete them and take notes."

"What's a pencil?" Steve queried.

"It's a writing tool. It's a piece of lead wrapped in wood. Don't you use them at school?

"No, we use ink pens."

"Ah. A pencil is more portable and eliminates the need for carrying messy ink. You'll just need to be careful not to break it or to poke yourself." After fumbling through one of the kitchen drawers, Matilda found a pencil. "Ah, there it is. Take this."

"Thank you. Now what?"

"When you go to the docks and find the damaged boats, you need to collect samples."

"Samples? Samples of what?"

"Bits of whatever you find. Whatever looks different or interesting."

"How will I know what that is?"

"I've not done anything like this, but I think you should look for things that don't look normal. Things that look out of place or different than the usual."

"Do you mean like a bear in a boat?"

"You're an imp. Yes, something like that." Matilda glared at Steve.

"And don't get any ideas!" She continued with her instructions. "Collect the samples. We can study them later. Some samples will be dry. They include solid things and powders. As you collect them, note the context. Record where you found each sample on a piece of paper, and then fold it into the paper."

"What if they are wet samples?"

Matilda rummaged about and collected some glass vials, handing a dozen to Steve. "Collect them in one of these vials."

"Great. Then we've got a plan." Steve chuckled. "You're almost as much fun to scheme with as my brother Will."

Matilda grinned. "I'll take that as a compliment."

# 50

Cleveland home, Fayetteville, New York
Monday, September 21, 1846, 6:00 AM

THE LAST DAY of Steve's summer was a time for neither celebration nor play. As per his Monday-morning ritual, Steve rolled out of bed, dressed, ate breakfast, washed up, and headed to the docks for an hour before school. Unlike other days at the docks, his prime mission was not earning money. Instead, he focused on digging for data, probing for proof. As he turned off Genesee Street to walk up North Mill Street to the docks, Steve spied hoggees jabbering away. He beamed when he saw a familiar face. "Professor, have work for me today?"

"Hey, lad. Good to see you again." Professor grimaced and tipped his head. "I've been hearing some stories about you. Word when hoggees gather around is that you're a bad egg."

Steve was flap jawed. Was even his work at the docks spoiled by rumors?

"But I take no heed of those rummies." Then the happy hoggee raised his voice for others to overhear. "I know you, Steve. The hands are wrong. You're a good egg. Yes, I've got some work for you. There are bags of beans in the bulkhead. If you put twenty of them on the cart over there, that will get you four coppers."

Steve was stunned. "Wow! That'd be great." Not only did he appreciate the support, but with that money he would be more than halfway toward his goal of buying a new mitt. Steve boarded Professor's boat and walked down a half dozen steps to the hold. Turning to the front of the boat, he found burlap bags labeled *White Beans* and *Navy Beans* neatly piled in a corner. With some difficulty, he picked them up one by one and carried the bags to the cart until he had off-loaded nearly two dozen.

While he clomped back and forth, Steve flexed his detective skills. He searched the planks of the hull for anything unusual. All seemed normal. The hull was dry. Planks and supports were intact. At that point, he shook his head. Hunting for things that seemed out of order might be a more difficult task than he imagined. Even when the job was finished and the base of the hold was visible; everything appeared shipshape.

As Steve piled the last bag on the cart, he signaled to Professor that he was done with a curt hand salute. "Impressive. You made short work of those bags, young man. Here you go."

Professor was good to his word. One at a time, he flicked four pennies into the sky. Steve deftly caught each with his "mitt" hand and pocketed it with his throwing hand.

"Thanks. Hope to see ya next time you're around," Steve said with a smile. Heading down the docks toward the two damaged line boats, he secreted himself behind the back of the nearest one. At first, both looked normal. Their prows tipped elegantly skyward. Long, sleek planks with graceful, convex lines followed the full seventy-five-foot length and wrapped the fourteen-foot span of each boat. The water line on each hull marked its draft depth at about three and half feet.

As he approached the first boat for closer inspection, Steve stared at a gaping hole near the middle of the hull. Interestingly, this hole, which Steve measured as the width of three fingers by the length of one hand, was bordered by ragged edges. It did not look as if the boat had run aground or hit a rock. Rather, the edges were worn and blackened, and the wood was soft. Steve noted these features, made hasty sketches of the hole in his writing tablet, and removed samples of planks both intact and damaged with his trusty clasp knife.

Steve worked to view the damage from inside the boat. Fortunately, the boat was tilted, creating a three-foot space between the gunwale and the ground. This allowed Steve to climb onto the deck and move to the base of the hold. Most of the cargo had already been removed to save as much merchandise as possible, but some remnants were strewn helter-skelter, particularly in the fore and aft. Enough was cleared, however, to enable him to glean the manner and integrity of the construction.

Constantly on the alert for intruders, Steve's eyes darted about. In the area where the planks were frayed, the metal bands were rusted through as well. Steve drew this and took some fragments from the frayed edges of the wood and wiggled off samples of the rusted bands.

While collecting his last samples and finishing his drawings, Steve was startled by voices. They came from people close by—maybe even standing beside the boat or on the deck. Steve's heart raced, his breathing shallowed, and his eyes flitted about. The boat was largely empty, other than some discarded rolls of paper in the bow. There was nowhere to hide. He tried to conceal himself behind the risers of open steps. The voices got clearer, louder.

A deep, raspy voice asked, "Heard about them boats in Canastota?"

"Yeah. Just da same as here in Fayetteville. Three boats down, and a hoggee, too!" responded his partner in a high, squeaky Jamaican voice.

News of the accident in Canastota floored Steve. *Whoa, three boats down, and a cap'n dead.*

The raspy-voiced man interrupted Steve's thoughts. "I just don't understand why he'd jump back inta da boat?"

"Poor hoggee. What was he tinkin'?" squeaked his partner.

"Guess he was jus' tryin' to save money. Didn't even save his own goose. Cargo's jus' cargo. Stupid ta risk your life over tings," responded the gruff-voiced man.

"What gets me is how that Cleveland boy did this one too. And from so many miles away. That boy sure is a crafty one."

An infuriated Steve nearly popped out to defend himself, but he kept his place, bit his lip, and stayed quiet.

The voices of the dockhands waned with their footsteps, like they were walking from the boat. Steve poked his head through a cabin window, hoping to catch a glimpse, but unfortunately was unable to identify the gossipy hands.

Steve was relieved to slip out of the first boat without being caught, and with all of his samples. After ducking into the other grounded line boat, he got back down to his detective business. He quickly sketched the shape and features of the damage, collected samples of wood, and rent pieces of metal supports for later study. Bundling these specimens, Steve noticed that metal bands through much of the boat were rusted, but those near the hole were particularly thin and fragile. Running his fingers over the metal near the damage site, Steve noted the surfaces felt like the crusty chickenpox he'd had three years ago.

As he climbed from the hull, Steve spied a ragged, short-billed, blue-and-white-striped cap under the steps. *Is this a baseball beanie? Or maybe it's a railroader's hat? I'll show it to Matilda.* Steve stuffed it in his satchel with the drawings and samples, and then ran from the boat and docks as quickly as possible.

Suddenly, a dockhand reached over and grabbed Steve by the ear. "Caughtcha, boy! Whatcha up ta? No good, I'll bet."

Steve dropped his bag and froze. Unable to turn to see who grabbed him, he stammered, "Umm, umm?"

"Where's your pa?"

Steve winced and managed to say in a strained, high pitch, "He's at church."

Still with a good hold of his ear, the dockhand said, "Well, me thinks he'll be mighty interested ta know whatcha been doin'. I'm curious ta know meself. Let's git."

As they stepped toward Genesee Street and before Steve knew what had happened, his ear was suddenly released. Disoriented and smarting, Steve turned toward a familiar voice.

"Leave the boy be. He's working for me." Less than a moment later, the dockhand was laid out, with Professor standing over him. "Steve, you need to be more careful. I knew something was up when I saw you poking about the boats. I saw this character watching you. Now, you best get along. I'll deal with this lowlife."

Steve nodded, rubbed the life back to his throbbing ear, and gathered his bag. Hurrying off to the Fayetteville Academy, he bolted through the door and wended his way through his schoolmates, who were jostling and teasing each other. Instead of joining the banter, Steve isolated himself by plopping into his seat. He lifted the desktop, threw his satchel into the belly of the desk, and finished settling in just as the opening school bell rang.

The day seemed extraordinarily long. Steve passed through the daily motions of classwork, recess, lunch, and more classwork like an automaton. Finally, 2:00 PM came, and Miss Cole rang the bell.

Before his classmates even stood, Steve had collected his belongings, dropped his desktop with a sharp crack, and scooted out the door. Minutes later, he flung himself into his house. Steve scaled the stairs two at a time, the wounded buffalo under the fourth stair dutifully greeting him on his second stride. He dumped his books on his bed, turned about, and rushed back down the stairs with his satchel. Flying from his home, he hurtled toward the Gages' with his treasures.

# 51

CHORES WERE DAILY. Responsibilities were unending. While Henry apprenticed with Attorney Wilkinson in Syracuse, Matilda and Sarah developed regular routines. They had similar challenges of performing domestic tasks and minding their daughters. When little Helen was awake, Matilda sewed, quilted, and smocked clothing. These tasks became progressively more taxing as Helen gained mobility. Likely Matilda's greatest success was with planning and making meals, for then Helen could be contented by playing with kitchenware.

After nursing, Matilda settled Helen down for a nap and walked to the barn to tend to animals during the quiet.

On this end-of-summer afternoon, Matilda wandered into the barn to check on the calves but stumbled into Sarah, who was milking the cows.

"Oh, Sarah, pardon me. I didn't see you."

Sarah contributed a great deal to the farm, and particularly to animal husbandry, including more efficient ways to milk. The cows were happier and the Gages produced more milk, cheese, butter, and other dairy products.

Sarah looked up from her one-legged stool, silently greeting Matilda with a nod and smile. Six-year-old Cherry bounced about the yard and chased a chicken into the barn. As she circled both Matilda and her mother, she kicked up dirt and straw hither and yon. Sarah prophetically warned, "Watch where you're—" But it was too late. Cherry bumped into the bucket, spilling milk everywhere. Sarah stared sternly at her daughter; no harsh word needed to be uttered. Cherry stopped in her tracks and fumbled about, trying to right the bucket. But the damage was done. There would be less farmer's cheese come the next few days. So much for the success of regular chores.

Matilda sidled over to her favorite Guernsey, and in her overwhelm plaintively asked, "Sometimes I wonder how I got here. Why can't you discuss Homer with me?" Hearing nary a response, she grinned and attended to her quiet routine.

Moments later, Steve burst into the Gages' yard, yelling, "Mrs. Gage! Mrs. Gage!"

Alarmed, Matilda charged from the barn. "Steve. What's all the excitement?"

Reaching into the satchel slung around his neck, Steve exclaimed, "I have samples from the boats!"

With that announcement, Matilda's enthusiasm soared. "Let's get a look at them! No, wait. Let's do it in the house. I have tools there that may help us examine your finds."

Matilda and Steve rushed into the house and drew up stools to the kitchen working table. Steve proudly opened his satchel. He removed wads of labeled, folded papers enveloping samples of wood that appeared like spring-plowed masses of spent pasture from which last year's chaff projected.

"Ah, so the pencil worked its magic?"

"Yes, yes. It was great. But lookee at this!" Steve pointed to a packet with stained wood shavings.

As she pored over the collection, Matilda's eyes widened more and more with each new packet. "Steve, these are splendid. I am not quite sure what we have, but I see all sorts of things."

"Oh, I forgot. Here's my book showing where each sample was taken from." Steve presented Matilda with a writing tablet he used for homework assignments. He opened to pages with carefully enumerated descriptions that identified where each sample was found, the size of the object from which it was extracted, and a guess at what each sample was. Thus, despite the apparent random arrangement of the collected samples, they were well organized and documented.

"This is impressive!" Matilda carefully unfolded an envelope marked *Boat 1, bow*, picked up some fragments, and examined them through the convex base of a thick drinking glass. "The samples you collected from the fore of the hull contain fur. Based on its color and coarseness, I believe it's beaver." Peering again through the glass, she posited, "I see apple stems, peach pits, walnut shells, and sunflower seeds. Unfortunately, not knowing how often these hulls were emptied and cleaned, I cannot say whether these items were carried recently or previously." Matilda scratched her head. "Let's look at the samples from the mid-hull." Unfolding a second envelope, she noted, "I see corn kernels, beans, and salt. I also see cotton fibers. At least, I think they are."

Seeing that Sarah had reentered the house, Matilda asked, "Sarah, please come here. What do you think of this?" Matilda pointed to the unidentified strings. "Does this look peculiar to you?"

Sarah screwed up her face. "It's not cotton. It's not puffed or twisted. I think it looks like corn silk."

"Corn silk. What an interesting idea." Turning her attention to the shards of wood, Matilda looked a bit puzzled. "This is confusing. The edges of the pieces are blackened. Steve, how broad was the area of blackened wood?"

"The hole was maybe four, possibly five inches long. The black area was an inch or so wide all the way around."

"Interesting. Sarah, what do you think? Was it burned?"

"Could be, but I do not think so. Not fragile enough. I think it turned black from another cause, though I'm not sure what that is." After a closer review, Sarah suggested, "Maybe a disease."

"Disease. Hmm." Matilda rifled through the other finds. "This blackened wood seems soft. Like it is fraying. It reminds me of a tree trunk rotting on the forest floor."

A scream followed by a lusty cry came from the upstairs. "That is Cherry," Sarah said. "I'll find out what the crying is about and be back as soon as I can."

Turning to Steve, Matilda asked, "Did you collect any samples of undamaged wood?"

"Yes, I did." Shuffling though his samples and papers, he declared, "Here are some from the first boat. I had to dig and scrape the hull to collect these." While he was pawing through his finds, Steve noted, "Mrs. Gage, did you hear about the accidents in Canastota?"

"No, what happened?"

Steve elaborated, "I heard that three boats sank and one hoggee died."

"Oh, that's terrible." Stunned silent, Matilda cast her head down. "I think this makes our task more important, more immediate. Five sinkings. Are they related or isolated events?"

Steve did not know the answers to those questions but offered, "Maybe this can help. Here are some pieces from the second boat."

"Interesting. These samples look different than the pieces from the damage site. They are lighter, both in color and weight. Curious. Let's try an experiment." Matilda thought, fussed about, and then collected a set of bowls from the shelves. "Let's try to replicate the conditions in the bottom of the boat. Before we do, we need to make two assumptions. First, the breach in the hull was where the water seeped in. Second, the blackness was a consequence of the damage. Let's put a shard of wood, a nail, and water in each bowl."

Wide eyed, Steve asked, "Why the nail?"

"The nail is there to substitute for samples of the iron bands. You know, the bands that bind the staves."

Steve met Matilda's statement with a cocked head and quizzical look.

Matilda patiently said, "I know, Steve. What's a stave? Come to think of it, stave may not be the correct term for a boat. I should call it a plank. That shows how little I know about boats. From what I do know, a line boat is constructed like a barrel. In the barrel, wooden staves are bound on the outside by metal hoops. In a line boat, however, the planks of the hull are bound on the inside by metal bands."

"I saw those! They had chickenpox!"

Matilda squinted at Steve with skepticism. "What does that mean?"

"The metal bands going anywhere near the hole in the hull were rusted, broken, and bumpy. The bands in the dry parts of the boat were shiny and smooth. That is in one boat. In the other, most of the bands were rusty."

"Great Caesar's ghost! That's brilliant, Steve." Matilda's grin was broad as a Cheshire cat's. "It's just as I suspected. Our challenge now is to determine which came first: damage to the wood or rusting of the bands? Or did they both occur at the same time? Let's put different things in each bowl to see what may have caused the wood to turn black. A piece of the metal bands, nails, seeds, and whatever else you found in the hull. Then, let's see what happens. It might take days before we see any changes." Matilda paused to gather seeds, nuts, and fabrics from the kitchen and added them in the bowls.

On completing her arranging, Matilda asked, "Now, Steve, shall we have some tea and savory rolls? We might even have some baked Indian pudding."

Steve bounced and enthusiastically answered, "Yum."

# 52

Gage home, High Bridge, New York
Wednesday, September 23, 1846, 12:30 PM

T HE MIDDAY SUN shone bright with promise. On finishing his one-and-a-half-mile walk-skip-run to the Gage home, Steve panted and pounded on the flimsy kitchen door. Flecks of peeling white paint flew with each knock. Hearing no answer, Steve yelled, "Hey, Mrs. Gage! Did our experiment work?" Still no answer. Steve ran to the barn, poked his head into its darkness, and yelled again, "Did our experiment work?"

A surprised Matilda straightened from a stooped position. "My, you're here early." She had been hunting for eggs throughout the barn. Wherever clumps of straw gathered was fair game for a laying chicken. She commented half to herself, "These chickens must enjoy finding inaccessible sites to lay their eggs. They play a great game of hide-and-seek." Matilda was good at that game too, though; she'd gathered more than a dozen eggs in her wicker basket.

Talking past Matilda's remarks about egg hunting, Steve excitedly responded to her first comment. "Yes. In the fall, Wednesdays at school are short. We're released early to help with the harvest. Father has no farm, so here I am." Returning to his focus, Steve once again asked, "Did our experiment work?"

"No," replied a disappointed Matilda. "It failed. There was no change in any of the wood samples." After a few moments of reflection, she added, "Failure is not defeat. We need to rethink this. Come, let's go back to our laboratory." On walking into the house, Matilda rested her basket on the kitchen floor. She extended a curled lower lip and cradled her chin in the thumb and index finger of her right hand. After a few moments, Matilda said, "We know the metal bands are rusty, and the wood is soft. If the water was the cause of the damage, did the hull damage begin on the inside or from the outside? Either way, with fresh water, it takes a long time for iron to rust. How about with salt water? Would it happen faster?"

"But, Mrs. Gage, the canal is filled with fresh water," said Steve.

"Quite so." Matilda nodded and pursed her lips. "Let's figure this out, step by step. Suppose there was salt water in the hull; where would the salt come from?"

Knowing the comings and goings at the Mill Street docks, Steve confidently stated, "Based on where they are docked, these two boats must have come from the west."

"Excellent. That's a start. What is west of here? Rochester? Syracuse?"

Steve said, "Yes. I've heard them called Flour City and Salt City. I don't know why they have those names."

Matilda stared at him. A smile grew on her face, and her eyebrows rose.

Steve fidgeted under Matilda's intense gaze. Then, he got excited. "That's it! I found salt crystals in the hulls of the boats."

"Steve, you're a genius! Maybe the boats were loaded with samples from the salt farms in Syracuse."

"Thanks. What's a salt farm?"

Matilda described the process of filling pools with salt water from the salt springs and brine pump houses sprinkled around Onondaga Lake, evaporating the water, and collecting the residual salt. Satisfying Steve's curiosity, she declared, "Let's repeat our experiments."

"Yes!" replied an eager Steve.

The two "scientists" arranged their samples. The setup was the same as before, but this time, they added salt to each dish. "Now we wait," directed Matilda.

"I'll wait right here."

"No, silly. It'll be days before we see anything. What do you say we go back to the village? Sarah and I will walk you home, and then we can do some shopping. We need some flour, salt, and maybe produce—beans, greens, and corn."

# 53

Limestone Creek, Manlius, New York
Wednesday, September 23, 1846, 4:00 PM

AFTERNOON SUNBATHED THE tall, browned hay in the lea in a golden cast. A kaleidoscope of monarch butterflies danced among clover and wild carrot flowers. Tall swamp grasses beside the path reached for the sky and undulated with the wind like waves on the sea.

Cherry skipped to and fro as Matilda, Helen, Steve, and Sarah walked along Limestone Creek toward Fayetteville. Cherry picked recently burst milkweed pods and joyfully blew the silky seeds skyward. As she danced, she sang:

> O'o:wa:' hayá'döje',
> Yesgä:wa:s gëöyade,
> Hadíöyá'ge:onö'.

> Owls fly,
> They sweep the sky.
> The sky dwellers!

Steve tried to join Cherry, but all he could manage was the English verse. After turning up Genesee Street, the party passed the Presbyterian church and arrived at Academy Street. "Ah, this is my street. Thanks for walking me home." Steve peeled off.

"Be well, young man," bade Matilda. Sarah waved, and Cherry continued to flit about.

Mindful of the late hour, Matilda led the shoppers further up Genesee Street to McVicar's General Store and Reed's Food Market. Matilda and Sarah quickly purchased what they needed, strapped their purchases to their backs in Haudenosaunee carriers, collected their children, and began their return home. Soon after leaving Reed's, Matilda bumped into Rev. Cleveland, who had just descended the steps of his church. After brushing the street dirt from her clothes, Matilda tipped her head.

"Pardon me, Reverend Cleveland. 'Tis a pleasure to see you on such a glorious afternoon."

"Good day to you, ma'am. One might even call it fortuitous. I have been hoping for an opportunity to talk with you. Is this time right?"

"Delighted. Is there something in particular?"

"Yes. My wife and I noted that of late, our son Stephen is spending a great deal of time at your home. Seems that when he is not playing baseball, attending school, or working on the docks, he is at your home. Can you enlighten us?"

"Stephen is always welcome at our home. He plays with farm animals, tinkers with our farm equipment, and is a fine conversationalist. We enjoy his company, his honesty, and his good humor."

Incredulous, Rev. Cleveland screwed his face and asked, "Are you talking about my Stephen?"

"Indeed, you might be surprised to hear that Steve is enthusiastic, self-driven, and spirited."

"Well, that does not surprise me," responded Rev. Cleveland, still a bit defensive but now reassured that he did recognize his son.

Not knowing the minister well, Matilda interpreted his comment as sarcasm but disregarded it. "I believe he feels accepted, safe, and comfortable at our home. At the risk of being disrespectful, does he get that sense at home? Is he appreciated and understood?"

Though Rev. Cleveland was thrown off balance by Matilda's temerity, he managed to say, "Mrs. Gage, you are indeed impudent." After a pause to recover his wits and to reflect on Matilda's comments, he added, "We believe that children must learn responsibilities, respect others, and know their place."

"Well then, I think you have solved your mystery. Good day." Matilda bobbed her head, turned, and rejoined Sarah and the children.

Flustered by the interaction, Rev. Cleveland muttered to himself on his walk home. On walking into his house, he called, "Ann. Ann?"

"In the kitchen, dear."

A dispirited Rev. Cleveland walked down the hall and opened the swinging door to the kitchen. "Ann, I just had a strange, troubling meeting with Mrs. Gage." His voice was halting, tentative. "She criticized our parenting by implying that we do not care for our children, at least Stephen."

Ann knit her brows. "Why ever would she do that?"

"Because I simply asked her why Stephen spends so much time at her house."

Ann gave her husband a direct look. "That was a silly thing to say to that woman. Whatever possessed you to do that?"

Rev. Cleveland shook his head. "At this point, I cannot say."

# 54

Doc Taylor's office, Fayetteville, New York
Saturday, September 26, 1846, 10:30 AM

Doc TOOK PATIENTS from the village on Saturday mornings. Relaxing for a moment between appointments, he gazed around his office at bottles of medicines, straps of bandages, and shelves filled with leather-bound reference books—much like Matilda's father's former office in Cicero.

A thirty-seven-year-old man rushed in bleeding profusely from his left arm. He cradled the injured limb, compressed with his right hand.

"So, what have we here?" With composure built on years of medical practice, Doc sat the man in a seat fitted with expandable armrests. The chair was nestled in a corner of his office next to a hutch laden with burnished surgical tools and copious brown glass vials filled with medications.

"Thanks, Doc. The head of another worker's scythe flew off and hit my arm."

Ripping the shirt sleeve and cleaning the wound with a dampened cloth, Doc declared, "Well, I've good news and bad. The good is that your wound is superficial. The bad is that the lesion will have to be sewn back together. Two stitches should do it."

"That's better than I'd'a thought."

"Sit back and relax," Doc Taylor reassured his patient. Fussing with the tools on the hutch, he collected a needle, thread, and ripped squares of fabric to mop up the blood.

The man blanched at the sight of the sharp tools and distracted himself by starting a conversation. "Doc, I just heard three boats sank in Canastota yesterday. Worse, I heard a captain died trying to bail out his boat."

"You don't say? First here, now in Canastota. What is going on?" Doc cleaned the wound with an alcohol-soaked cloth.

"Ooh, that stings. I don't know, Doc. Even more, I don't know how that scamp Cleveland arranged this."

"Really!" exclaimed an incredulous Doc as he threaded the needle and placed two stitches bridging the gash in his skin.

"Yeah. How could that Cleveland boy drown boats miles from here?" the man said through gritted teeth, trying to battle the searing pain.

"No, I meant 'really!'" Doc was furious. "How can you possibly suspect Stephen Cleveland? Are you daft? Let me rephrase that. How daft can you be?" Doc did not wait for an answer. He placed a gratuitous third stitch to seal the wound. The man predictably winced and screeched. Doc was not proud of his action; he knew the extra stitch was unnecessary. Nevertheless, he smiled to himself. He figured the man was not the only one who could be petty at a time like this.

After bandaging the sutured wound, Doc dispatched his charge as quickly as he could. He hurried to don his coat, found his wife, told her of the calamity, and then searched about in hopes of finding the Gages. Pushing through the streets, docks, and pedestrians, Doc finally found Matilda and Henry in the marketplace. "Good morning. I just heard distressing news. Three boats sank. This time in Canastota."

Matilda grimaced, having already learned of this tragedy from Steve. She looked at Henry, who declared, "Our world is going to hell in a wheelbarrow."

# 55

Gage home, High Bridge, New York
Saturday, September 26, 1846, 2:00 PM

STEVE WHISTLED AND blithely bounded down the lane along Limestone Creek. Had his and Matilda's experiment determined the cause of the Fayetteville boat accident? If so, he would be cleared. *Maybe people will stop looking daggers at me.* All would be well in the world.

On arriving at the Gage home, Steve ran to the kitchen door and knocked. No answer. Confused, he ran around to the front door. No answer, again. The Gages were always about the farm this time of day. Then his thoughts wandered. *Did they find somethin' that "proves" I'm guilty? Is Mrs. Gage talking to Sheriff Smith 'bout me?* Steve shook his head; he was innocent, and he knew deep down that Mrs. Gage would never betray him. He continued searching. Venturing into the yard between the house and barn, Steve yelled, "Mrs. Gage? Mrs. Gage!"

From the herb garden on the far side of the barn came a muffled response.

"Steve, is that you?"

"Yes. Where are you?"

"I'll be over in just a moment. Hold your horses!"

Steve mulled, *Why is she tellin' me that? I don't have any horses. And why should I hold 'em, anyway?* Before Steve could reason through the command, he saw Matilda walking down the corridor between the horse stalls.

Impatient, Steve pleaded, "What happened with our experiment? Did the salt do anything?"

"Let's go see." Together they walked into the kitchen where they found their bowls. "Looks like not much has happened. The water is the same color, and the wood looks the same, too."

"But look at the nail. It looks reddish-brown." Picking up the nail, Steve noted, "It's not all red. It's colored in patches."

"Good observations. That looks like the beginning of rust. This may explain the rusty bands, but I am not so sure it tells us anything about the wood. Maybe as time goes on, the reddish brown will get more intense. Black, even. If this is right, it would suggest the damage was an accident."

"And if it's an accident, then it proves I did nothing!" Steve's voice rang with hope. "Oh, oh, before I forget, look what I've got!" Fumbling about his satchel, Steve pawed through his schoolbooks. "I forgot to show this to you. It's been buried at the bottom of my bag since I got samples from the boats a few days ago. I don't know if it means anything."

"Let's see. What have you got?"

"I found this jammed under the stairs of the second boat." Steve dug deep into his satchel. Books and papers went flying. He yelled, "Aha!" as he removed the striped beanie with a short bill.

"Interesting. Is this something a hoggee would wear?"

"No cap'n would ever be caught wearing a cap like this. I think this is the cap of a railroad worker. Some men wear them when they play baseball."

"So then, why would it be in a boat? Was somebody just playing baseball?"

"Hmm. I don't know. Maybe it was won from a railroader in a game of poker or bezique. I don't know."

"Could be." Matilda paused to think. "But you said a boatman would never wear one of these. Hmm . . . Where did you say you found this?"

"'Twas half hiding under the steps below the deck of the second boat. Might have been kicked under there. I don't know."

Matilda pursed her lips. "Interesting. Interesting indeed. I think these are strong steps in the right direction. Salt and railroad caps. Doesn't much make sense, but I'm confident it's progress."

Puzzling with the new thoughts, Steve said, "Progress. We were just talkin' about that in school. Our teacher says progress means getting ahead, possibly at the expense of putting someone down."

Matilda responded, "I cannot agree with your Miss Cole. In fact, I would argue that the definition of progress is quite the contrary. Progress comes from putting others ahead of yourself, selflessly aspiring to respect all—including those who would undo you."

Steve wondered, *How can I understand you? Too often you speak in riddles. I just hope that whatever progress you make, it'll become clear to me—and soon.*

# 56

Fayetteville Presbyterian Church, Fayetteville, New York
Sunday, September 27, 1846, 10:25 AM

MURMURS FILLING THE sanctuary of Fayetteville
Presbyterian Church abruptly stopped when Rev. Cleveland entered.
Wearing his usual somber, black robe, the minister sat in one of the four
tall, straight-backed chairs behind the pulpit. The Sabbath choir sang
"A Charge to Keep I Have" about an individual's loyalty to Jesus. Rev.
Cleveland then led the congregation in Psalm 85, extolling people's fealty
to the Lord. The reverend left the sanctuary through a door at the rear of
the apse, leaving Deacon McVicar to lead the service in a psalm on civility,
humility, and respect.

During a short break, congregants shared fellowship with others.
Thereafter, Rev. Cleveland reappeared wearing uncharacteristic multicolored
vestments. He slowly, deliberately ascended the four steps to the pulpit. Fully
extending his limbs, he stood upright, commanding the attention of his
congregants. After clearing his throat, he began his sermon in a robust voice.

"The youngest of twelve, Joseph was the target of his brothers' jealousy.
The brothers believed that Joseph was the favorite of their father, Jacob.
Unaware of these feelings, Joseph related a dream he had one night to his
brothers. In this vision, Joseph saw twelve bundles of wheat in a field. His
bundle rose, and the other bundles bowed to it. The brothers interpreted

the dream to mean that Joseph would be their leader. This fed the brothers' hatred.

"Later, Joseph had another dream in which the sun, moon, and eleven stars bowed to him. On telling this to his brothers, they became further infuriated. The dream even angered his father. Incensed, the brothers tricked Joseph, threw him into a pit, and sold him into slavery. During his time as a slave to Potiphar, Joseph progressively earned himself a position of power."

Steve elbowed Will. "See, our teacher was right about progress."

Will shot a condemning glance at Steve. "Shhh. Father's talking."

The reverend continued, "Eventually, Joseph became the head of Potiphar's household. So established, Joseph became appealing to Potiphar's wife. She attempted to seduce him, but Joseph rebuffed her advances. Spurned and angry, she declared to Potiphar that Joseph defiled her. Joseph was thrown into prison." With resignation, Rev. Cleveland intoned, "Thus saith the Lord."

The congregation dutifully responded, "Thus saith the Lord." Then, they sighed, as if it were time to return to psalms and hymns. Alas, this was not the case.

Rev. Cleveland continued, "This story of Joseph raises many questions. Did the brothers have evidence that Joseph intended to harm them? Should they have served as his judge and executioner? Was Potiphar justified in punishing Joseph? Could such events transpire here in New York? Do we not stand by American democracy wherein one is innocent until proven guilty and where evidence is required to prove allegations beyond a reasonable doubt?"

Church members rustled in discomfort. A disquieting silence filled the sanctuary as the congregation realized the reverend had yet more to say. "Even though my sermons come from my heart, I avoid making them personal or self-serving. This is consistent with my constitution, with my training, with my agreement with God. Yet, these are extraordinary times. I am compelled to break these traditions: I must stop false accusations from festering. I must halt their noxious impact on the innocent and confront the pernicious presumption of guilt until proven innocent. I must speak out against the groundless allegations targeting my son. Stephen has been falsely accused of crimes against property and persons."

Rev. Cleveland paused, lifted his head, and scanned the assemblage. "All evidence compels a singular conclusion that Stephen had no role in the sinking of any canal boats or the tragic death of a hoggee in Canastota. While I believe these events were not accidents, I also firmly believe my son has nothing to do with them. We are obliged to find the real culprits. We must rely on evidence, logic, and clear thought. We are also obliged to presume that all are innocent. Further, we must ask forgiveness of those we have wronged."

Steve was dumbfounded, his eyes like saucers and his mouth forming an enormous *O*. Rev. Cleveland looked directly at Steve, who squirmed beneath his father's focused attention.

"To my son, know that 'no weapon that is formed against thee shall prosper; and every tongue that shall rise against thee in judgment thou shall condemn. This is the heritage of the servants of the Lord, and their righteousness is of me.' Isaiah 54:17. As it is said in Matthew 7:12, 'Whatever you wish that others would do to you, do also to them.' Stephen, please accept my most humble apology for any part I played in supporting unfounded conclusions. To everyone else, I implore you to atone for your parts in furthering baseless accusations and for the damage you caused wittingly, and unwittingly."

By the time Rev. Cleveland had finished his sermon, his head was bowed. He descended the pulpit steps to a floor-level lectern—looking like a spent man. Gathering sufficient energy, he guided the congregation in a responsive recitation of Psalm 27. On completion, Rev. Cleveland repeated verses 12 through 14, alone.

> *Do not turn me over to the desire of my foes,*
> *for false witnesses rise up against me, spouting malicious accusations.*
> *I remain confident of this:*
> *I will see the goodness of the Lord in the land of the living.*
> *Wait for the Lord;*
> *be strong and take heart and wait for the Lord.*

The congregation sang a portion of "Love Divine, All Loves Excelling." Then, the reverend gathered the energy to lead the congregation in a final passage from Proverbs 3:3–13.

With services over, a diminished Rev. Cleveland retired to his office without his usual engagement of his flock. Ann, who sat at the front of the sanctuary, stood, as did her children. Ann embraced and kissed Steve's head, lovingly smiling at him.

Steve implored, "Mother, may I see Father?"

"Not right now, Stephen. When we are at home." Ann directed her eldest, "Anna, please take your brothers and sisters home. Your father and I will join you soon." Ann then approached her husband's office and gently rapped on the door.

Richard Cleveland plaintively uttered, "Come in."

Ann opened the door wide, entered the office, and walked to her husband seated at his desk, writing in his diary. In view of anyone lingering in the sanctuary, Ann bent down and hugged him. "Richard, I know that you are a private person. Today, you did a courageous thing. You gave your son an irreplaceable gift: the gift of fatherly trust and unconditional support. To do so in public was a wonderful expression of love."

Ann's words brought Rev. Cleveland to tears. He buried his head in her left shoulder. "I could no longer be angry at a child whose honesty endorsed his innocence."

"Yes, Richard. He has a kind heart. But why and how did you come to this epiphany?"

"For too long, I've reflexively blamed Stephen. He was just being a boy. If I hadn't appreciated it before, I was confronted by my pigheadedness by that inscrutable, insightful woman, Mrs. Gage."

Meanwhile, on the front steps of the church, churchgoers chattered. Barti Beard exclaimed, "Whoa, Doc, that was something! I never heard nothing like that before."

Doc exhaled, "Ah, vindication. I realize it was a father talking about his son, but I'm gratified Steve has been publicly declared innocent."

In the eyes of the community, Steve seemed to be off the hook. But despite the reverend's call for caution, the villagers still needed someone to accuse. One whispered, "I always thought that boy Cleveland wasn't to blame."

Another villager responded, "Yeah. I was sure it wasn't him all along. I knew it was one of them Blacks in Manlius. Probably Nash."

"Nash? Who's that?"

"Aw, he's a Black living in High Bridge. You know, in that cluster of houses a mile or so up Limestone Creek."

"I know the houses, not the man. But I'm sure you're right. Makes sense."

Before long, outbursts of "String him up!" popped up amid the crowd.

George Beauregard the bounty hunter was skulking about. He perked up on hearing the villagers' scuttlebutt. A smile spread across his craggy face—a new target, a blackbird. Beau operated without the need for evidence or corroboration of the allegations. Facts were an impediment. So long as there were suspicions among the locals, accusations were sufficient. Beau slunk away to find this Mr. Nash.

On Monday, during her routine marketing, Matilda got wind of the Sunday events. Whisperings first ground through the rumor mill were sculpted into malevolent gossip so that by the time the story got to her, three salient rumors were repeated as facts.

(1) There was a crime.

(2) Stephen Cleveland was innocent.

(3) Mr. Nash was responsible for the hoggee's death.

After Henry returned from his office in Syracuse, Matilda fumed as she told him of the rumors. She muttered through gritted teeth, "Not only is there no evidence of a crime, but nothing links the events at the docks to Mr. Nash. This blather of bigots is profoundly dangerous."

# 57

Genesee Street, Fayetteville, New York
Wednesday, September 30, 1846, 4:30 PM

FOLLOWING CONSECUTIVE DAYS of misty rain, the sun finally burst through. Retreating clouds revealed a horizon-to-horizon rainbow. The evening light richly illuminated the red, orange, and yellow leaves still clinging to scarlet oak, sugar maple, and birch trees. Fallen ochre leaves matted the street. On seeing Matilda walking up Genesee Street, Steve ran to her, all smiles and bubbles.

"Afternoon, young man," said Matilda in a slow, somber voice.

"Hello! Glorious day, eh?" Steve enthused with boyish joy.

Matilda deeply inhaled the crisp, chill autumnal air in silence. She could not shake the allegations against Hiram Nash, fatuous though they may be. It was not only the accusations themselves that saddened her, but also what that gossip said about the people of Fayetteville. Matilda and Steve quietly walked past Academy Street, down the hill of Genesee Street to the west. At nine years old, Steve was already tall enough to match Matilda's pace, step for step. Walking past the feeder canal, Matilda asked, "Steve, let me tell you the story of the Erie Canal."

Confused, Steve asked, "I do not mean to be disrespectful, but why are you tellin' this to me? And why now? You must know that I've heard this story many times before."

"Steve, I need to tell you this story. It may give you some insight into what is happening. And if not for you, it may help me sort out some things about the accidents if I hear it aloud." Matilda gazed vacantly toward the falling sun. In a flat, pedantic voice, she began. "From its inception, the experiment called the United States of America was propelled by the vision, ambition, cooperation, and competition of its citizens. These qualities amalgamated in the building of the Erie Canal."

"A-whatcha-mated?"

"Amalgamated." Matilda nodded. "That means mixed, melded together."

"Oh, I get it. I've watched Anna and Will play bezique. It's a card game where players meld cards and turn 'em over in combinations to get points."

"Yes, I think." Shaking her head, Matilda elaborated, "I do not know that game, but I think you have the idea." Matilda rolled her eyes toward the sky and continued her monologue. "Anyway, most everything about the making of the canal was slow and ugly. Political fights were epic. The engineering challenges were monumental. Even more, you should know that the canal was built on the backs of Blacks: both enslaved and free.

"After decades of negotiation and construction, DeWitt Clinton's vision for New York was finally realized some twenty years ago. The Erie Canal established the cities of New York, Brooklyn, and Buffalo as key gateways to the American West. It permitted our young, muscular country to tap its natural resources and develop its economic power."

Steve focused intently. "I've heard everything you've said, Mrs. Gage, but I am still confused by many of your words. People have told me about ditches, ducts, and bridges before, but your story is different than any other I've heard. You must be makin' this stuff up!"

Matilda disregarded Steve's disbelief. "Steve, what I am telling you is true. And the story does not end there. To stay up to date, the country pushed to incorporate new technologies. Over the past twenty-five years, railroads popped up throughout the Mohawk Valley. That includes the Syracuse to Utica Railroad completed seven years ago. The railroads parallel the Erie Canal. Now there are efforts to sew them together into a single system from Albany to Buffalo."

"I don't fully understand. How does this affect our everyday life?"

"Steve, as with so many things, the answer to your question is money. Money and control."

Steve cocked his head, puppy-like. "What do you mean?"

"Let me try, but from a different tack. Like the canal, the growth of the rail system met with obstacles. One obstacle was the people who relied on and relished the status quo—that is, keeping things the same. Some people wanted the canal to succeed and make money for them. As a result, people controlling the canal blocked progress on the rail. Railroaders compensated operators of the Erie Canal for 'lost' income and to maintain preeminence of the canal."

"If I understand what you are sayin', railroaders must pay for most everything: to build the railroads, to carry cargo, and even when they don't carry cargo. They just pay, pay, pay."

"Yes, Stephen, that is it. At least for now, that's true. However, the canal will not be able to hold on forever. Progress cannot be stopped."

"What do you mean?"

"I believe the rail will win. After all, rail provides more reliable and faster transport. Trains can be used all year 'round. Canal traffic halts for one third of the year when winter waters freeze. Rail has no locks, whereas the canal is replete with these obstacles, which are time consuming."

"How so?"

"Let me give you an example." Matilda thought for a moment. "The easternmost dozen miles of the Erie Canal between Albany and Watervliet has nineteen locks. These allow boats to climb roughly one hundred seventy feet, but navigating these locks slows progress, produces time delays, and imposes considerable financial costs."

Steve realized that there were no locks near Fayetteville. "That makes traffic through the feeder canal a breeze!"

"Well, yes and no. The region near us in Fayetteville is just a short part of the canal. You must know that even though rail has its advantages, the transition from boat transport on the canal to train transport on the rail has been messy. The stakes for the shift are high. Schemes have been devised, either to block or accelerate the transition. People looking to make fast money are more than happy to take advantage of the tumult and turbulence."

Steve wondered, "What does any of that mean?"

"Well, that still mystifies me, too. I'm guessing that as with so many things, the sinkings of the boats in Fayetteville and Canastota were intentional. They had to do with money. Money and control."

Steve looked befuddled.

Unaware of Steve's confusion, Matilda continued. "Also, whatever happens, we can be certain that Blacks will be blamed." She sneered. "It's what people always do." Matilda shook her head. "Let's keep looking. Let's keep thinking."

# 58

Gage home, High Bridge, New York
Thursday, October 1, 1846, 5:45 AM

Henry BURST THROUGH the front door of his home. "Matilda, I need a club. A wooden club. Now!"

Initially confused, Matilda rose from the sitting room desk where she was writing a letter in the waxing light of a blood-red sunrise. Then, it dawned on her why Henry needed a weapon. She had to help battle the single focus of the self-appointed. Matilda hurried into the kitchen, fumbled through cabinet drawers, and offered, "Henry, take this."

Looking askance at the rolling pin Matilda handed him, Henry grabbed it and breathlessly said, "A posse of a dozen hooded townsfolk with lit torches just marched up the road from Fayetteville. It can only mean one thing." By the time Henry had run down the hall and flown through the front door, the rowdies had breached the Nashes' front door.

The normal peace and quiet of High Bridge exploded into chaos, clamor, and commotion. Henry threw himself into the Nashes' home while brandishing his rolling pin. "Out of my way! Leave Hiram alone!" Before he knew it, members of the mob had pinned his limbs to the floor, the rolling pin flew against the wall, and a thug sat on him. Others searched the house for Hiram. They looked through the living spaces downstairs, the bedrooms and closets upstairs.

The Nashes quivered in a corner of the kitchen. Miriam yelled, "Children, stay here!" and leaped toward the intruders. She pounded on them, yelling, "Out of our house!" before being summarily swatted away like a bug.

As Matilda arrived, a familiar voice emerged from the throng. "Mrs. Gage, you best stays outta this!"

"Bertie? Bertie Beard? Is that—" Matilda was shoved against the wall as rabid rabble-rousers rumbled from the house, disappointed with their unsuccessful search. Almost as suddenly as the melee began, all was quiet except for the heavy breathing of the discarded Henry, Matilda, and Miriam, and the whimpering of the scared children.

Once she'd collected her wits and checked on her children, Miriam asked, "Mrs. Gage? What have they done? Where's my Hiram?"

"Miriam, I do not know." Matilda was perplexed. "I don't know where Hiram is." Taking a deep breath, she continued, "What I do know is that those hellions believe they are chosen to run the world."

Henry concurred. "I'd never have thought people in New York could behave so deplorably, and certainly not people in Fayetteville."

Matilda added, "I, too, like to think well of our community, but evil certainly lurks in the souls of men, all too many men. I'm sure one of them was Bertie Beard. His voice was clear. I'd never have believed him capable . . ."

After composing herself and her thoughts, Miriam said, "Yesterday, Henry and I spoke with Doc about finding a protected place for Hiram. We afeared the worst and prepared for the possibilities. Before the sun rose this morn, Doc and Sheriff Smith took Hiram away. I think they took him to jail. At least he should be safe from ruffians."

"To jail! Very well," responded Matilda. "I will visit Hiram later this morning."

Sarah volunteered to stay with Cherry and Helen and keep Miriam company.

"Bless you" was all Miriam could muster.

# 59

Village Hall, Fayetteville, New York
Thursday, October 1, 1846, 9:55 AM

MATILDA STRUCK OFF for the sheriff's office in Village Hall with purpose. She mused, *The irony of it all. I am walking by two-story "palaces" on both sides of Genesee Street, owned by White businessmen, making my way to visit a falsely accused Black day worker who can barely afford the rent for his home.* Matilda shook her head. *What a world. This new wealth is a cancer in our community. Likely, it will keep us from reaching a true democracy.*

Reaching the crest of Genesee Street, Matilda arrived at Village Hall and entered a sunbathed room replete with solvents, used cleaning cloths, and gunpowder. Matilda was reflexively welcomed by Sheriff Smith, who was rocked back on his chair, his hat tilted upward as if to greet visitors. Evidently, this pose was for show, as the sheriff ignored Matilda to fix on a tall man whose back was to the door. The unidentified man abruptly turned and revealed himself; it was Doc.

Matilda impertinently asked, "Doc, what brings you here?"

"The pleasure is mine, Mrs. Gage," Doc answered, evidently trying to evade the question.

Matilda redirected herself and declared, "Good morning, Sheriff. I'd like to see Hiram Nash."

Without hesitation, Sheriff Smith rose from his chair, unhooked a ring holding a dozen keys with his right index finger, and led Matilda to a door at the rear of the building. After turning the key, the sheriff eased a massive door open to reveal a dark, dank anteroom for four jail cells.

Matilda had not been to the Fayetteville Jail—or any jail, for that matter—before. She was struck by its forbidding, featureless sterility. The white wooden walls and doors of the anteroom appeared dingy gray in the poor lighting. Each thick cell door had a small metal grate fitted to a one-square-foot window about four feet above the floor.

Stopping before the last door, Sheriff Smith rifled through his keys and opened the door. The cell at first appeared empty but for a high, metal-barred window on the outside wall and a slat bench in the rear. As her eyes accommodated to the dim conditions, Matilda saw Hiram sitting on the bench, hunched over, head in hands.

Matilda spoke gently yet defiantly. "Hiram, we will free you from these preposterous charges."

"Thank you, Mrs. Gage. Please know that I'm fine. The sheriff's takin' good care o' me," Hiram said as he looked toward the sheriff.

"Fine? How can you be fine in a fetid place like this?" Matilda shook her head and did not wait for an answer. She left the anteroom to reenter the front office. Blinking excessively in the bright light, Matilda craned and rolled her neck, breathing slowly. Nothing settled her racing heart. She accosted Doc. "How could you let this happen?"

"Matilda—" Doc attempted to explain.

"You must know Hiram could not have been involved in any crime, especially in Canastota."

"Matilda—" Doc was cut off again.

"Canastota is fifteen miles away."

Doc held his hands up as if to shield himself from the barrage. "Mrs. Gage. Stop. Mr. Nash was not arrested. He's in jail for his protection."

"Protection? You call being in jail, in that dungeon, protection?"

Sheriff Smith sliced into the conversation. "Yes. Doc and Henry suggested we get Mr. Nash from his house before any trouble began. We knew the temperature of the mob was rising. We thought it wise to get him somewhere safe. Somewhere no one would look."

"Oh." Matilda considered the situation. Then, indignantly, and somewhat imperiously, she narrowed her eyes on Doc. "Why didn't you tell me? And my husband was part of this scheme?"

"Y-yes. The decision came late yesterday. The time for planning was short." Doc squirmed, twiddled his thumbs, and looked everywhere but at Matilda. The sheriff fussed with a knife he was using to whittle the end of a stick into the shape of a line boat.

Matilda took stock of the thick walls of the office and reinforced jail door. Fighting to maintain her civility, she said, "Gentlemen, next time, do me the respect of letting me know what's happening. I did *not* enjoy getting pushed into a wall, and I'm quite certain Mrs. Nash didn't take a shine to it either."

"About that, ma'am, I am sorry," apologized Doc. "But we had to ensure that the rabble-rousers didn't smell anything fishy."

Still simmering, Matilda asked, "How did you do that? Seems to me, the wild ones were out of control. Miriam, her children, and I certainly thought so."

"They were indeed. Henry and I told them that Hiram Nash was hiding on North Mill Street where the damaged line boats are stored," Doc responded. "They went there, found no one, and then ran to the Nashes'. We expected that. After their unsuccessful searches, we hope that now they are exhausted and disheartened by failure." Doc added, "I must say, Henry did a marvelous job misdirecting them. At least, that's what he tells us."

"I suppose he would." The absurdity of the situation was obvious, and Matilda's resolve cracked. She laughed in relief, and the others joined her. After the laughter abated, Matilda considered the impending problems and the pragmatics of planning for Hiram's safety. "So, what have you thought about next steps?"

"Seems to me we have two choices," opined Sheriff Smith, leaning back on his chair, still whittling and dropping shavings. "Hiram could stay here in the jail with me, or he could return home to his family. In jail,

Hiram will be safe, but at some point, the brutes will learn he is here. Then they'll make all of our lives miserable. Another option is Hiram could go home. He should be safe there because the rabble already visited his home. If he goes home, he must stay out of sight. His safety relies on secrecy."

"Sheriff, I agree with your options, but I'm not sure what you mean by 'we,'" Doc stated. "I think Hiram should decide. What do you think? Shall all of us vote on that first?"

The sheriff, Doc, and Matilda nodded.

Doc polled, "All those in favor of asking Hiram?"

Three hands rose.

The unanimous vote was followed by an uneasy silence. All knew that more planning was needed, but they were unsure how to proceed. Matilda suggested, "Let's get Hiram."

# 60

Fayetteville Jail, Fayetteville, New York
Thursday, October 1, 1846, 10:30 AM

DOC STOOD. HE paced. Grabbing his lapels, he stared at his shoes. Then, raising his head and jutting his jaw, he asked, "Sheriff, can you bring the mayor here? I'd like to discuss some things with him." Doc commanded broad respect because of his ability to serve the broader community while selflessly attending to the needs of individuals.

"Of course, Doc. What are you thinking?"

"Not quite sure. Just bring him and we'll work on it."

Sheriff James Smith reflected, "Doc, only twice before have I seen such a determined look on your face. First was when you created a plan to construct the Ledyard Dyke on Limestone Creek. You provided a reliable source of waterpower for Fayetteville, and you've been reelected to the New York Assembly because of that forethought and persistence."

Doc grinned and nodded shallowly.

The sheriff continued, "More recently, I saw that expression of resolve when you saved a child's leg." Donning his coat, the sheriff bolted through the front door of his office.

Matilda suggested, "Hiram, when the sheriff returns with the mayor, let's discuss our next steps."

But Hiram could not wait. "Hey, Doc. I've an idea. Put me on trial."

"Trial?! Why in blazes would we do that?" After a few moments of silence, Doc offered, "That's a bold plan. It's certainly better than mine. But a trial for what? You didn't do anything."

Matilda added, "Hiram, if I understand you correctly, the path you are suggesting is risky, even dangerous."

The conversation was cut short as Sheriff Smith entered with Mayor Samuel Stone in tow. The mayor greeted everyone: "Morning, Doc, Mrs. Gage. And who is this?"

"Sam, thanks for coming." Swiveling and putting his arm around Hiram, Doc said, "This is Mr. Hiram Nash. He lives down the road in High Bridge. I believe you've heard of the commotion roused at his expense."

"Yes, I've heard talk. Pleasure to meet you, sir." After giving Hiram a firm handshake, the mayor turned to Doc. "James tells me you've something you'd like to discuss."

"Let's talk about the ugliness going on in our otherwise blessed corner of the world," Doc said.

"Indeed, the violence is disturbing. What have you got on your mind?"

Doc asked, "Do we all agree that we want our village to be a peaceful, accepting place?"

"Yes," the others responded in synchrony.

Doc continued, "This innocent man is being unfairly targeted. There aren't even charges against him. My concerns are legion, not the least of which is what will happen should the newspapers get wind of what's going on. It will not look good. The reputation of our village as a welcoming, progressive place is at risk. Our reputation determines our ability to attract new people, new businesses."

"I hear ya, Doc," the mayor said.

"Hiram has an audacious plan. Some villagers are demanding quick 'justice.' That is unacceptable. What would you think about using established processes?"

"Established processes? Doc, if you are planning what I think you are, then I must excuse myself. If you're planning to entrap someone, it's danged inappropriate for me to be here," responded the mayor.

Doc respected the mayor's discretion. "Sam, I understand."

Sheriff Smith was unsure how this would unroll, but like everyone in town, he trusted Doc implicitly. "Mayor, I'll take responsibility for this." With that, Mayor Stone left the building. The sheriff turned to Doc. "This better be good. What is it that we are planning?"

"That depends on Hiram."

Hiram said, "Yes. We need a trial."

"A trial? A trial for what?" Matilda interjected. "There was no crime. Hiram, you're only in jail for your protection. You're not being held for a crime or misdeed."

"Of course, but a trial would be a decoy," Hiram said.

"It would mislead the miscreants," Doc said thoughtfully. "And it would clear the air in the minds of the misguided many. I think the idea is inspired. If our lucky stars are out, a trial will expose the real perpetrators."

"It's a risky game of cat and mouse," Matilda protested. "Yes, we have the cheese and the mouse, but who is the cat? Even more, what happens if a jury finds Hiram guilty of whatever he is charged with? This plan is lunacy. You could even argue that what we are doing is a breach of public trust. The use of the system to find a guilty party is a miscarriage of justice. That is not what it's designed for."

"Matilda, those are excellent points. But this is Hiram's life. It's Hiram's choice." Doc turned to Hiram.

"Mrs. Gage. Everyone. I appreciate your concerns and support. Let's go to trial," Hiram firmly stated.

Doc said, "For this plan to work, we must maintain the strictest secrecy. Will everyone abide?"

While Sheriff Smith and Hiram agreed to the pledge, Matilda bucked. "Though I have my concerns, I'll support your wishes for a trial, Hiram. However, I cannot abide by the pledge to secrecy. I will have to discuss this with Henry as he will likely be the attorney for the defense."

"So be it. Henry and no one else."

A MATTE MIDDAY SUN dominated the early autumn sky. There were no shadows, no places to hide.

Henry was home early to attend to fall chores, including fixing the fence bordering the front yard and Highbridge Street. Matilda rode her horse up the lane and greeted Henry with a stern scowl. "Hiram is coming home tonight."

"Is that wise?" replied Henry as he ground the hatchet he was using to fashion replacement rails.

Dismounting without her husband's usual assistance, Matilda informed him, "Doc will escort him. They'll steal their way here to High Bridge in the light of day. That way, they should elude the mob. Members of the mob are weak and scared. They are emboldened when operating under the cover of darkness. They do not even have the 'courage of conviction' to let the law follow its course."

"Scared of what? Hurting a man for something he didn't do?" Henry asked.

"Questions, questions!" Dried leaves danced and skittered around Matilda as she turned the interrogation on Henry. "Perhaps you can answer the question of why my husband didn't talk with me about his plans. What about that?"

Henry's face immediately fell from ebullience to regret. He mumbled, "Talk about scared and sorry." An uneasy quiet settled over them like a chill morning fog. "I wish I had a better answer than 'I thought it best at the time.'"

"Hmm" was all Matilda could muster.

"Matilda, I was concerned about Hiram's safety. I know you don't lie, don't deceive. I was unsure how you would carry out the plan for hiding Hiram. Maybe I misjudged the situation. I am sorry I did not confide in you."

"Well, Henry. It was a fine idea. Even more, it seems to have worked." A sly smile spread across her face, reassuring Henry that she forgave his secrecy. "Now that we've addressed that, I must tell you about the decision that was made."

"Very well. But first, let's agree to stop making decisions for each other and without each other."

Matilda assented.

With their partnership mended, she related the conversation she'd had with Doc, the sheriff, and Hiram at Village Hall. "Oh, and we must keep this plan from our little friend Steve."

Henry nodded. "I understand. No Steve, and I will talk with Hiram as soon as possible."

As Matilda and Henry walked into the barn arm in arm, Matilda suggested, "It looks like it's time for us to collect hay into the barn for winter. Let's work on that—together."

# 62

Nash home, High Bridge, New York
Friday, October 2, 1846, 3:45 PM

MATILDA SPUN HER head to the right as the sun highlighted spidery cracks radiating from a ragged, three-inch hole in the kitchen window. It had been three days since the mob ransacked the Nashes' home. "Hiram and Miriam, please, come stay at our home for the next few days, or for as long as you need."

Hugging her husband, Miriam quietly but firmly stated, "Let's go to the Gages. I'd feel safer at their home." Hiram expressed that he was more than happy to acquiesce. They joined their children upstairs in a bedroom and described the situation. The children collected clothes and dear toys for their stay at the Gages, then carried their bundles down the stairs, where Matilda guided the five Nashes to her house.

Henry had been unsure they would accept and was pleased to welcome them, ushering the Nashes inside. As the guests entered the kitchen, Helen padded over, sat back, and extended her arms upward. Hiram hoisted little Helen to his right shoulder, where she threw her arms around his neck.

"Our little Helen certainly loves you, Hiram," observed Matilda.

"And I her. She always makes me feel special." Hiram returned Helen's hug before noticing a boy he did not know. "Mrs. Gage, who is this?"

"Hiram, I'm pleased to introduce you to Stephen Cleveland."

"Cleveland," Hiram reflected. Then, an expression of awareness crossed his face. "Ah, you're the youngin who broke my gate two summers ago!" He squinted and moved catlike across the room toward Steve. Steve retreated, but Hiram shifted Helen to his left shoulder and extended his right hand in friendship. "After what you did with that donkey on the Fourth o' July, I consider myself lucky. I've only lost a few gate pins. Young man, you've got a streak of the devil in ya."

"You know 'bout that?"

"Mr. Cleveland, you're famous in these parts. Maybe if you can direct that creativity and enthusiasm to helpin' me, then I'll be just fine."

Red faced, Steve bowed his head as he shook Hiram's hand. He was not used to being confronted by a target of his pranks, nor was he comfortable with the idea of being famous.

"A firm shake from such a young lad. I like that." Hiram smiled and nodded.

# 63

Gage home, High Bridge, New York
Saturday, October 10, 1846, 9:15 AM

ON SATURDAYS, HENRY did not go to Mr. Wilkinson's law office in Syracuse. Instead, he worked on the farm where chores were always plentiful. This Saturday was particularly busy, it being the fall harvest. Time was precious. There were so many things to do to prepare for the change in seasons: reap crops, including squash, pumpkins, and kale; collect winter wheat, hay, and corn for the animals; and bolster the barn and house for winter weather. Further, Henry needed to prepare the carriage for the winter by removing the wheels and affixing sleigh runners. The first snow could arrive any day.

As the morning sun poured through the kitchen window, Matilda navigated her world with Helen in tow. Helen, who was just learning to walk, was already proficient at getting into trouble. She still relished playing in the kitchen—sprinkling cookware around the floor, banging on pans to make "music," and wearing pots as hats. As it was a busy day, Matilda wrapped Helen in a carrier like a Haudenosaunee papoose. Not only did this contain the mess, but it also freed Matilda's hands for pickling duties.

While Matilda fussed about, Sarah and Cherry came into the kitchen to help. In her effort to teach Cherry the Senecan language, Sarah mixed Senecan and English in her speech. "Cherry, *yeögwas* dill and *o'ge:go'* garlic *gayë:thöh*."

Wanting to be sure she understood her mother, Cherry responded, "Yes, *Aknó'ëh*—I mean, Mother. Did I hear you right? You want me to harvest dill and dig up garlic in the garden?"

Listening in the corner, Matilda chimed in and confirmed, "Yes, Cherry. Thank you. Please bring the herbs to the kitchen so that I can put them in the pot to boil with the vegetables."

Moments later, Cherry bounded into the kitchen with her arms coated armpits to fingertips in mud. She handed the herbs she'd gathered to her mother. "*Aknó'ëh*, is that enough? I can get more."

"That is good for now. Thank you." Sarah smiled, taking the dill and garlic from her daughter and pointing to the kitchen basin filled with water from the pump outside. Cherry washed the mud from her arms while Sarah cleaned the herbs. Once the herbs were cleaned, Sarah and Cherry removed the flowers from the dill and smashed garlic to unhusk it. The prepared herbs were dropped into a pot of boiling water along with a healthy helping of salt.

Cherry loved the smell of the cooking herbs. She inhaled with a lusty, "Ahh."

After the herbs boiled for fifteen minutes, Sarah added cauliflower curds, wheels of carrots, and squash spears into the pot for ten minutes. Meanwhile, Matilda boiled water in jars in one pot on the Franklin stove and melted sealing wax in another pot for the preservation.

As the pickling was nearly finished, Sarah told Cherry, "Go to Henry. Help *hadí'nisdé:es*."

"Yes, *Aknó'ëh*. I will help Henry gather the corn."

# 64

Gage home, High Bridge, New York
Saturday, October 10, 1846, 12:15 PM

STEVE AMBLED DOWN the trail and, mindlessly whistling, pushed open the Gages' front gate; it swiveled smoothly. He chuckled, "The gate works!"

After knocking on the front door and poking his head into the foyer, Steve declared, "Hello! Anyone here?"

Cherry ran from the kitchen, yelling, "*Nëkoh*! Steve, we're here!"

Steve nodded.

"Come, cook with us. *I:' ye'ho:tših! ogä'äh.* Oops, I forgot to speak English. We're shucking corn." Cherry grabbed Steve's hand and yanked him into the kitchen where piles of husks were strewn on the floor. On releasing his hand, she snatched husks in each hand and threw the corn silk into the air with giggling glee.

"*Nya:wëh sgë:nö',*" Matilda welcomed Steve.

"Huh? You, too!"

Matilda smiled, "Hello, Steve."

"Oh. *Nya:wëh sgë:nö'* to you, Mrs. Gage." Steve laughed, joining in the linguistic fun.

Matilda smiled. "Steve, you arrived at the perfect time. Join us. Sarah and I were just reviewing the line boat situations in Canastota and

Fayetteville. I cannot help but think there is still a riddle to be solved. Grab an ear. Let's work this out."

As Matilda, Sarah, Cherry, and Steve pulled back the husks, they were disappointed to see that many were diseased—some with rust, others with smut. Kernels at the tips of many ears were black, covered with a powder, or easily exploded into oozy messes. These would not be good for drying, or even for animals' winter feed.

Sarah abruptly asked, "Steve, tell me about the holes in the boats. What were the boats carrying?"

"What are you thinking?" Matilda queried.

They were suddenly interrupted as Henry rushed into the kitchen, yelling, "Fire! Fire! Help! Grab a bucket. Follow me." Just as quickly, he ran from the house.

Calmly, Matilda ordered, "Steve, stay here with Cherry and Helen. We'll be back soon." Matilda and Sarah rooted about, collecting basins, and dashed out the front door. Their attention was immediately drawn to the Nashes' home where they saw licks of flames enveloping the side yard shed. Matilda and Sarah joined the Nashes in the front yard, facing the heat of the fire.

Henry directed, "Everyone, take a bucket. Run to Limestone Creek. Get some water. We'll douse the fire."

"I think we should get in a line from the creek to the fire," Sarah suggested. "We can pass filled buckets to the person near the fire to dump. Also, we should dump water on the grass between the shed and house."

Panting, Matilda turned to Sarah. "Why aren't we trying to put out the fire?"

Sarah shook her head. "The shed is lost. We need to keep the fire from spreading to the house. Maybe some water on the side of the house. Don't want sparks to catch."

Recognizing Sarah's wisdom, Henry and Matilda joined the Nashes in soaking the yard between the burning shed and the house. The firefighters did as Sarah advised, and the front yard began to feel like a soggy mess.

Matilda encouraged, "Keep it up. You are doing wonderfully!"

After Henry's tenth dump, all were beginning to flag. "Sarah, what do you think? Have we done enough?"

The flames on the shed were noticeably shrinking. Sarah said, "I think we did it."

The others concurred. "I also think we beat it," Henry panted. "Let's just watch for a bit to see what happens."

Over the next quarter hour, the fire died. Hiram and Miriam turned to the water brigade with grimaces of appreciation. Together, they all stumbled back to the comfort and safety of the intact Gage home.

Matilda picked up Helen, who was playing with Cherry and kitchen cookware, and hugged her tightly. After a full minute, she asked the obvious question. "Was that an accident?"

Henry suggested, "After the embers are cold, we can sift through the ashes to see what we can find."

"Well, it is getting late. I've got to go home," Steve said, although he was brimming with curiosity about the alarming events of the afternoon. "Tomorrow, I'll go to the docks and talk with some hoggees, try to find out if something connects the sinkings here and in Canastota."

"That's terrific, Steve. Be sure not to raise any suspicions," warned Matilda. "People would be happy to go back to blaming you."

"Yeah, I bet they would. I'll be careful. What do you think about the fire? Do you have any suspicions?"

"I do. I do indeed."

# 65

North Mill Street docks, Fayetteville, New York
Monday, October 12, 1846, 7:15 AM

THE USUAL BUSTLE of weekday business buzzed at the docks. Steve's mission was to discover a pattern that explained why the five line boats sank.

Walking along the North Mill Street docks, Steve studied his surroundings carefully. He noted that boats going east were moored on the west side of the feeder canal and boats going west docked on the east side. Both damaged boats were racked on the west side of the canal. Did this mean that the sunken boats were traveling east, toward Albany? Though these observations were suggestive, Steve needed to be sure. He saw a couple of dockworkers leaning against pilings.

Puffing up his chest and screwing up some of his usual boundless courage, Steve sidled over to ask some questions. "Good morning."

"And a fine mornin' 'tis, laddie," responded one of the hands.

"I'm just wondering. Were you working on one of the boats that sank here?"

"No, mate," answered the second dockhand. "But if memory serves, the chap at the end o' the dock was one o' the hoggees."

"Thanks. Any chance you know where those boats were going? Toward Syracuse? To Rome?"

"Methinks they were comin' from Syracuse," responded the first hand.

"Any thoughts on the boats that sank in Canastota?" Steve asked.

"I has no idea 'bout them. Coulda been goin' east or west. I dunno."

"Thanks. Do you know what any of the sunk boats were carrying?"

The second dockworker shot back, "Hey, scamp, why all the questions?"

"Aw, just curious. Part of a project. For school. See you." Steve abruptly ran off to find other dockhands to question, and hopefully the hoggee of a sunken boat.

As the time approached 8:00 AM, Steve had to get to school. He was unsure whether he had interviewed enough people, but before he left, he shot a quick look at the damaged boats. Not wanting to attract attention, he casually sauntered around them, trying to remind himself about the appearance of the holes.

The two boats were tipped on their sides against the Bangs & Gaynor Building on the west side of the feeder canal near Limestone Creek, making a quick scan of the damaged hulls an easy task. Steve had not noticed it before, but the damage on the two boats was remarkably similar. Each boat boasted a single hole. Even more compelling was the size and place of the damage: a long, three-by-five-inch gap that split a seam between two planks and was just a couple inches from the keel. That was near the lowest point of the hull. There was no other apparent damage on the shell.

Suddenly, a hand clapped Steve's shoulder. A deep voice bellowed, "Quite interesting, eh?"

Steve froze. Then he placed the voice and his heart settled. "Morning, Professor."

"Morning, lad. You do seem to have a fascination with these boats. You must know that of all people, your scouting about is likely to raise questions. Do you appreciate the forces you are confronting?"

"Huh? Oh yes, I am aware. But I must know what happened. An innocent man's life is at stake."

"Ay, you're a good lad. Someday, let's sit down and you can tell me all about it. Till then, I think you'd best be off to school."

"I guess I shouldn't be surprised that a professor would say that.

Thanks, and see you soon!" Steve skedaddled up Genesee Street to the academy, but he was confused. The coincidence of the damage on the two boats was too compelling, too confounding.

# 66

"MRS. GAGE, I'M here!" Steve yelled as he walked through the front gate. "What's for lunch?"

Matilda shooed away the chickens in the front garden while she collected herbs. "Hello, Steve. Tell me what you learned, and then we can talk about lunch."

"I talked with dockhands, but not with hoggees," Steve reported. "All of them had the same message. Both sunken boats apparently traveled from the west." His face contorted. "It doesn't make sense. After all, not all boats comin' from Syracuse sink. It kind of reminds me of my math lessons. All squares are rectangles, but not all rectangles are squares. Very confusing."

Steve continued his line of thought as he followed Matilda into the house. "So, how were the two boats that sank different than other eastbound boats that are still floating?"

Once in the kitchen, Matilda cut off a piece of bread and a wedge of farmer's cheese for Steve. "Steve, tell me again. How are canal boats constructed?"

"Line boats are long, maybe sixty or more feet. They're 'bout ten to twelve feet wide. That way a boat can pass another in the canal. The hull is quite flat. It's less than five feet from keel to waterline. Hoggees tell me that keeps them stable and allows them not to drag through the shallow canal."

"Interesting. What materials are they made of?"

"Wood planks and steel bands. Remember, as you said, it's kind of like a barrel with staves and hoops."

"Hmm. What kind of wood?"

"Hoggees boast about their boats. They say oak and cedar are used for the long planks, from trees in Vermont or New York." Saying that out loud made Steve think. "It seems to me the damaged boats weren't made of oak or cedar. I'm not sure, but I think the planks were pine." Steve stared into blank space. "The wood had many knots. What might that mean?"

"Not sure, but that's fascinating. Steve, you look at things like a Haudenosaunee. You observe details, collect facts, and appreciate truths that bind the natural world. With that in mind, let's look at what we know, but a bit differently. The sinkings happened in Fayetteville and Canastota, and the boats were traveling toward Albany. Have you heard of any other recent sinkings in Rome, Utica, or other parts east?"

"No. I haven't."

"All right then. The clustering of where the sinkings occurred suggests that the damage was not accidental. We must conclude that whatever happened to these boats happened west of here. So, if they were damaged intentionally, it could be that the sabotage occurred there. Either way, we can guess that it took a set amount of time for the damage to occur. Now, if it was freight, what might be loaded onto a line boat in the west that is corrosive and whose damage would require a certain amount of time to occur?"

Steve was reminded. "We talked about salt comin' from Syracuse."

"Yes, the steel rusted in salt water. That was an ingenious thought." Matilda then considered it a bit more. "But the salt had no effect on the wood. It did not cause it to get punky or black. Though appealing, maybe the idea of salt is misleading us. After all, the salt is loaded in Syracuse."

As Steve chomped on his bread, he recalled, "Mrs. Gage, I forgot to mention some dockworkers said the trial for Mr. Nash is less than two weeks from t'day, on the twenty-third."

"Yes, 'tis. That doesn't leave much time. We have our work cut out for us."

# 67

Village Hall, Fayetteville, New York
Friday, October 23, 1846, 9:45 AM

THE DRAMA AND fanfare of the murder trial were dizzying. Villagers dressed in their Sunday best to attend, arguably the biggest event in Fayetteville's young history. People jockeying for entrance extended from every door. The orderliness of the queued people and the crowd degenerated with distance from Village Hall.

Inside, the courthouse was a hive of activity. Villagers scurried, arranging furniture for the trial. Barti Beard directed Deacons Samuel Jameson and John McVicar, "Put the judge's desk front and center. Then, set two rows of six chairs to the left of the judge's desk for the jury and two tables before the judge's desk."

As might be expected, Mr. Jameson silently did what he was told. Mr. McVicar, who was used to displaying and rearranging merchandise in his store, asked, "Barti, what're the tables fer?"

"Well, John, the table on the left is for the defense team, and the one on the right is for the prosecutors. After that furniture is set, arrange the remaining chairs in rows behind the lawyers' tables for the audience."

As scores of citizens funneled into the courtroom, it became clear that the number of chairs was woefully inadequate. There were barely enough for a few dozen of residents, at best accommodating half the audience.

Mr. McVicar turned to some audience members and suggested, "Stake out a bit o' floorspace. Send one o' yer group home to git some additional chairs." Before long, many other groups of vicarious thrill-seekers followed Mr. McVicar's advice.

Matilda and Sarah entered the rear of the courtroom, followed by Cherry, who held Helen's hand. The two mothers picked up their children as they worked their way through the throng and took places in the first row of the audience, behind the defense table and next to Miriam and her children.

With the court furniture set, Barti took a place near the back door, directing folk, families, and nosy neighbors. Barti ushered his brother, Bertie, to a standing area at the rear of the room. In due course, Bertie directed a handful of burly bumpkins to join him. Curiously, like Bertie, each wore black slacks, a white shirt, and a black string tie. Barti cocked his head with a raised eyebrow and grimaced as this group joined his brother.

Primary players passed through the chaos, clatter, and chatter at the rear of the court. Henry Gage slipped through the crowd as he approached the defense table. Having one and a half years of experience as an apprentice with Attorney Wilkinson, and with his boss's blessing, Henry had assumed the role of defense attorney. Taking a seat, he closed his eyes and breathed slowly. While he shuffled his files and notes, the village bailiff escorted Hiram Nash to join Henry and, in something akin to a growl, ordered Hiram, "You. Sit here."

Helen lunged toward Hiram in order to hug her special person, but she was restrained by Matilda. "Dear, stay with me. Mr. Nash needs to focus and talk with Father." Helen pouted, and Matilda pivoted to supervise the bailiff removing Hiram's handcuffs.

Hiram rubbed the pain from his wrists and reached over to shake Henry's hand. Preoccupied by the weight of the case, Henry barely mustered a distracted smile for Hiram and extended his hand reflexively. It was anybody's guess whose palm was moister. This trial was Henry's first without his mentor supervising.

Steve worked his way through the crowd and found a place next to

Matilda. Surprised and confused, she asked, "Steve, why are you here? Don't you have school today?"

"Class was canceled because of the trial. Miss Cole thought this would be a good lesson in civics." As Steve spoke, Matilda realized children were dispersed throughout the crowd, and their teacher was there, too.

Tension and ambient energy in the courtroom continued to rise until an abrupt and solemn hush descended. The bailiff announced Judge Samuel Stone—the one and the same Samuel Stone who served as mayor of Fayetteville. Everyone in the room stood as he entered. Judge Stone was dressed in a ceremonial black robe and starched white cravat. After he sat on the tall, ladder-back chair behind his desk, members of the audience took their seats. The only ones who did not sit were the townsfolk without chairs. They were relegated to stand at the rear.

Judge Stone gaveled the proceedings into session. Scanning the assembled, he turned to the jury, tipped his head, and then returned his attention to the general audience. "We are here to determine the innocence or guilt of Hiram Nash in the murder of a hoggee in Canastota and in the destruction of property in Fayetteville and Canastota. I expect—no, I demand fairness and civility in this courtroom." After instructing the jury on their responsibilities, the judge asked, "Would the prosecution like to make opening remarks?"

The attorney for the prosecution began. "Gentlemen of the jury, we will show that this crime was an escalating situation—dare I say, an inevitable situation. There was history between Mr. Nash and many hoggees. They'd had previous run-ins where more than words were exchanged. We will provide evidence that Mr. Nash knew and had issues with the hoggees of four of the sunken boats. The defense will endeavor to misdirect the proceedings from the substance of the trial. That is, this Black man has lived among us for two dozen years." The prosecutor's upper lip curled as if he'd just sucked a lemon. He hissed, "The accused has a history of illegal activity. It began when he stole his freedom. He lied and cheated to run from his master. He could not be trusted then. He cannot be trusted now."

With the conclusion of the prosecutor's remarks, one of the burly bumpkins in the back of the room yelled, "String 'im up!"

Judge Stone quickly quashed the outbursts and admonished, "Such behavior will not be tolerated. If I hear any disturbances again, disruptors will be removed *immediately* and jailed." Judge Stone turned to Henry. "Would the defense like to make an opening statement?"

Henry rose from his chair, still looking at his papers while cradling and stroking his chin. Lifting his head, he faced the judge. "Thank you, Your Honor." Then, looking at the jury, Henry began, "Gentlemen of the jury. I represent Mr. Hiram Nash. A kinder, more mild-mannered man you will never meet. He has lived in High Bridge for more than twenty-five years. Neighbors respect Mr. Nash. They solicit him for his well-considered opinions. Hiram contributes to his community. He generously and selflessly helps others. Why? Simply because it is the right thing to do. Mr. Nash is guilty of nothing more than caring for his wife and children, tending to his chickens, and working his small farm.

"There is no substance to the charges. Mr. Nash is a victim of circumstance, a victim of bold, unfettered hate. The prosecuting attorney will offer conspiratorial flights of fancy founded in prejudice. He will tell you that Mr. Nash sank the boats in Fayetteville and in Canastota. There is no evidence or explanation for these accusations—for example, he cannot explain how Mr. Nash got to Canastota. Even more compelling is that Hiram has had no interactions with anyone related to the canal. He is a day worker who occasionally works on local farms and in the Hatch and Beard Flour and Pearl Barley Mill.

"I encourage you: listen carefully to my adversary. A discerning juror will hear inconsistencies about people's interactions and their antipathies. The story he tells you is generated specifically for your ears. He will argue that Mr. Nash had it out for these hoggees. We will show that not only did he not know the hoggees, Mr. Nash rarely visited the Mill Street docks. Our opponents will weave stories of whole cloth with no facts and no foundation."

Henry drew a slow, deep breath of contemplation. "Hate is an outcome of ignorance. Hate blinds people from finding the facts, from seeing the truth. I implore you, focus on sound information, not spurious statements solely intended to play on your emotions."

A smattering of applause arose from the audience as Henry sat.

Judge Stone offered, "Thank you, for the defense." Returning to the prosecution, Judge Stone invited the lawyer to present arguments.

The prosecuting attorney stood and surprised everyone by declaring, "My esteemed colleague has deftly besmirched me and the kind, generous people of this fine village. Judge Stone, we believe that the case speaks for itself. The evidence is undeniable. This man, if I can even dignify him with that description, must be the perpetrator. There is no other plausible explanation. To support this, we call two hoggees, one at a time."

A brawny man in tattered clothes stinking of the docks was escorted from a side room to the witness stand. Steve gestured to Henry, shrugging. "I've never seen this man in Fayetteville at the docks or anywhere else."

"Interesting. Thank you, Steve." Henry nodded. "Let's see what happens. Let's hear what he has to say."

After the hoggee was sworn in, the prosecuting attorney asked, "How often are canal boats damaged?"

The hoggee thought for a moment. "Not often. Sometimes boats get dinged. They could run into damaged banks of the canal. That damage could be caused by muskrats, tree roots, and the like."

"How often does such damage cause a boat to sink?"

"I never saw a boat sink."

"Does that imply that the damage was intentional?"

Henry objected, "Your Honor, that question is inappropriate. The prosecuting attorney is asking the witness to draw an opinion on a subject for which he is not an expert."

Judge Stone ruled, "Objection sustained. Mr. Prosecutor, pursue a different line of questions."

Henry smiled at his first successful objection. Matilda and Steve patted him on his back.

The prosecuting attorney's head dipped. After pausing for a moment, he informed the judge, "We have no further questions for this witness."

As the prosecuting attorney sat, Henry asked, "Your Honor, may I ask some questions of this witness?"

"As you wish," permitted the judge.

Henry approached the stand. "Have you ever been to the Village of Fayetteville?"

"No, I have not. This is my first time. Nice place, though."

"How about Syracuse or Canastota? Have you stayed in either of them?"

"Just passed through. We were paid by the prosecution to serve as a witness."

Henry was perplexed. "How can you bear witness to something when you don't know these towns?"

"I don't rightly know. It was good pay for easy work." Titters ran through the audience.

"Very well. Have you ever seen the accused before?"

"No."

"Thank you. The defense has no more questions for this witness at this time." The first witness stepped from the stand.

A scrappy, lean fellow, the second hoggee, was escorted from a waiting room into the courtroom. He provided the same answers as the first. Through the questioning, the first hoggee, who stood at the back of the courtroom, nodded vigorously as his buddy answered questions. Henry was baffled by the witnesses and even more so by the prosecuting attorney when he rose to declare, "Your Honor, the prosecution rests."

Following a short conference with his bailiff, Judge Stone recessed the court for fifteen minutes. Henry rifled through his papers and used every minute of the break to review his notes and to prepare his defense.

# 68

Village Hall, Fayetteville, New York
Friday, October 23, 1846, 11:15 AM

"HIRAM. IT'S TIME to make your decision. Are you certain you want to testify?" Henry asked with a tinge of caution and hope that Hiram would see the wisdom of declining.

"Absolutely. I am innocent. I want to speak clearly and publicly."

"As you wish," said a resigned Henry.

Moments later, Judge Stone returned the courtroom and the trial reconvened. "Would the defense like to call its first witness?"

"Yes, Your Honor." Henry rose. "We would like to call Mr. Hiram Nash to the witness stand."

Hiram approached the stand where the bailiff swore him in.

Henry proceeded. "Where were you on September 17, the day the line boats sank in the feeder canal here in Fayetteville?"

"At home! I was cleaning the chicken coop—"

Henry cut off Hiram to keep his answers crisp and to the point. "Was anyone with you?"

"Why, yes. My wife, Miriam. We were—"

This time the prosecuting attorney interrupted the proceedings. "Judge, what does this have to do with anything?"

Henry spoke to the judge. "Your Honor, I am trying to establish where

Mr. Nash was at the time of the sinkings, to show that he could not have damaged the boats in Fayetteville or Canastota."

"Point well taken," offered the judge. "Please proceed."

"Thank you, Your Honor." Henry continued his line of questions. "How about the day before—that is, on September 16?"

"I was home."

"And the day before that?"

"Home."

"And the day before that?"

"Home."

"Mr. Nash, how can you be so sure?"

"Because I was preparing for my wife's birthday on September 19."

Henry returned to the questioning. "And how about on September 26, the day the boats in Canastota sank, and the twenty-fifth, the day before?"

"I was working on all of those days."

"Mr. Nash, where do you work?"

"During harvest time, during September and October, I only work on our farm. In the summer and winter, I also do day work for some neighboring farms."

"Do you ever work at the docks of the feeder canal?"

"No. I do not."

"Do you shop in the village?"

"No, my wife does our shopping in Fayetteville."

"Thank you, Mr. Nash." Turning to the judge, Henry added, "We are finished for now with this witness, but we may ask for him to return to the stand."

Judge Stone nodded and then asked the prosecuting attorney, "Sir, do you have any questions of the witness?"

"Just a few, Your Honor." The attorney approached the witness stand. "Mr. Nash, what was your response when you saw the donkey on this building on Independence Day?"

"I thought it was hilarious. I laughed and laughed."

"Ah, so you do go into town."

"Well, yes. Rarely. For special events." Hiram gulped and tensed.

"Do the Nashes eat fish for supper?" asked the attorney.

"Yes, sir."

"Who picks out the fish and where is your preferred market?"

"My wife picks our fish. I believe that she gets it directly from the boats at the canal." After thinking for a moment, Hiram added, "Also, you should know that we have fish two, maybe three times a year. It's right dear, and we can only afford it for special events."

"Sir, thank you. I have no further questions."

With that, Judge Stone excused Hiram from the witness stand.

Matilda whispered to Henry, "I think we have addressed the testimony of the hoggees. Now it is time to call Miriam and some dockworkers. Maybe we'll include some people in Canastota and Syracuse."

"Sounds right, Matilda, but I think I have this in hand." Looking a bit confused, Henry asked, "Syracuse? What do you have in mind?"

"Not sure. Let's talk later."

Henry requested of the court, "We would like to call Miriam Nash to the stand."

Miriam was dressed in a pressed, blue-striped dress—her Sunday church outfit. She stepped in front of the witness chair, the bailiff swore her in, and she sat primly, almost haughtily.

Henry began, "Mrs. Nash, please tell us: how long have you lived in High Bridge?"

"About two dozen years."

"In all that time, have you ever been treated disrespectfully?"

"Not by folk in High Bridge. Many in Fayetteville have been good, too. But some kick dirt on me, sneer, cuss, and occasionally spit."

"Are these actions provoked?"

"No, sir. I minds me own business."

Someone from the back of the crowd yelled, "Go home!" which was immediately met by loud shushing from nearby members of the audience.

Miriam defended herself. "See!"

Henry nodded and then refocused his questions. "Mrs. Nash, your husband said that he rarely, if ever, works or shops in Fayetteville. Is this true?"

"Yes. He is more than busy working on our farm and neighbors' farms. The Goodfellows and the Wordens, who have farms down the road, have always been good to us. They hire Hiram in the summer when work on our farm slows.

"When Hiram has spare time, he spends it with our children. Though he's not learned in books, he teaches 'em stuff. Teaches about farming and handcrafts. But to your question, so far as shoppin' goes, Hiram is a dear man, but I don't trust him to shop for the right things. I do the shopping."

"What you are saying is that Hiram does not go into Fayetteville, and certainly not to the docks. Is that correct?"

"Yes. He only goes to Fayetteville for special events, for celebrations," Miriam added.

"Now, on the days of the accidents at the North Mill Street and Canastota docks, did you detect a change in Hiram's behavior?"

"No, sir."

"Did he say anything about the accidents?"

"No, sir. If I remember correctly, I told him about the accidents."

Henry momentarily closed his eyes, tightened his lips, walked from the witness stand, and then turned back to face Miriam. "What was his response to the news?"

"Hiram wanted to go to the docks to see if he could help in any way."

"Did he go?"

"No, I asked him to stay home. Anytime there's a problem in the village, my feeling is that we best stay away and not get mixed up in any messes."

"That seems wise. Thank you." Henry turned to the prosecuting attorney. "Your witness."

The prosecuting attorney approached the witness stand. "Mrs. Nash, how do you celebrate your birthday?"

"Pardon me, sir?"

"Let me repeat, how do you and your family celebrate your birthday?"

Henry objected, "Your Honor, what relevance does this have to the alleged crime?"

"Mr. Prosecuting Attorney, I do not see a connection here to the substance of the crime." Judge Stone furrowed his brows.

"If Your Honor gives me a moment, he will see the connection very soon."

"Very well, proceed, but get to the point."

"Yes, sir. Mrs. Nash, how do you celebrate your birthday?"

Miriam sheepishly responded, "It is a special day. Hiram wakes up early. He feeds the children. That's a gift in itself. He even tries to make breakfast for me. It's always fried eggs and grits. He's a terrible cook, but it always tastes good 'cause he made 'em. Later in the day, Hiram gives me a small present."

"Does Mr. Nash keep his plans and gifts secret from you?

"Well, yes." Miriam paused. "And no. Soon after we were married, he did make me surprises. But he quickly learned that I don't like 'em. We learned to discuss how we'll celebrate together."

"Hmm. So, what are some of these gifts? Items from McVicar's General Store?"

"No, sir. They are wood figures: people, children, animals that he whittled from downed branches on our farm. I have a wonderful collection. I use 'em as decorations on Christmas."

The head of the prosecuting attorney dropped to his chest. Air was escaping from the trial balloon he was furiously trying to fill. To minimize his losses, he finished, "No further questions, Your Honor."

Judge Stone asked Henry, "Does the defense have any other witnesses?"

"Yes, Your Honor. We would like to call some dockworkers."

"Very well," replied Judge Stone. "We will recess for lunch and reconvene this afternoon at 1:30."

# 69

Village Hall, Fayetteville, New York
Friday, October 23, 1846, 1:40 PM

VILLAGERS PUSHED AND shoved back into the courtroom. Once again, chaos ruled. The jury filed into their seats. Judge Stone reentered, and as protocol demanded, the bailiff commanded, "All rise for Judge Stone." Dutifully, the defendant, the attorneys, and the audience rose. The judge sat, followed by most of the audience, and the proceedings recommenced.

Ambient unruliness persisted in the audience. An outburst of "String 'im up!" erupted from the rear of the courtroom. It was followed by echoes throughout the audience. "It's the Cleveland boy!"

Judge Stone gaveled. "Order!" He pointed to the inciting rabble-rouser and directed the officers flanking the doors. "Arrest that man!"

During the melee, Matilda hissed, "Henry, I have an idea. Ask Judge Stone to direct the bailiff to bring that man to the witness stand."

"I hope you know what you're doing," Henry responded. Then, turning to the judge, he asked, "Your Honor, please hold that man for a moment. The defense wishes to ask him some questions."

Raising one eyebrow, the judge asked, "Sir, are you certain?"

Henry nodded.

Turning to his left, Judge Stone raised his voice over the ambient noise. "Officers, bring that man to the stand."

The man struggled to escape, but before he could pass through the door, he was forcibly escorted through the crowd by the officer and a spontaneously generated posse. Despite his large size, his feet barely skimmed the floor.

After order in the courtroom was reestablished, Judge Stone asked, "Does the prosecuting attorney have any objection to an examination of this witness?"

Bewildered by the rapid turn of events, the prosecuting attorney replied, "No, Your Honor."

The disruptor was unceremoniously dropped in the witness chair by the officer. The bailiff worked his way to the stand and bound one of the man's wrists to an arm of the chair with a pair of handcuffs. Amid the surrounding commotion, Matilda stared into the eyes of the man. She was right. The voice she had heard in the back of the courtroom was that of George Beauregard.

Matilda whispered to Henry, "If you don't mind, I'd like to pose a few questions to Mr. Beauregard. Ask the judge if you could just take a moment."

In a distracted state, Henry requested, "Judge Stone, would you please give us time to collect our thoughts?"

"Yes, but just a few." The audience was stone quiet.

Meanwhile, Matilda, Henry, and Hiram convened. "Henry, I know this man, and I have some information that may be key. Let me play my hunch."

"This is unorthodox, Matilda, but I trust you," replied Henry.

Hiram concurred with a nod. Members of the defense team sat back in their seats.

Henry signaled to the judge that he would like Matilda to ask some questions. A collective gasp rose from the audience as she stood to assume the reins of the defense. Whispers ran through the audience.

"Mrs. Gage, this is highly irregular!" Judge Stone asked, "Are you trying to trick us?"

Matilda shook her head, quietly and succinctly stating, "No. No, Your Honor."

Turning to the defendant, the judge added, "Mr. Nash, are you comfortable with this? With this . . . this woman representing you?"

Assured by his defense attorney, who nodded slightly, Hiram declared, "I am, Your Honor."

The prosecuting attorney sniggered, and Judge Stone mumbled, "Well, I'll be." Then the judge stilled the audience's rising clamor by raising his right hand and commanding, "Everyone, settle down."

After the commotion abated, the bailiff read the witness his oath to provide truthful testimony.

Judge Stone cleared his throat, rolled his head, and directed, "Representation for the defense may examine this witness."

Matilda rose. "Please, state your name."

Combatively, the witness gruffed, "You know ma name. It's Beau."

"Your full name, please."

The witness snorted, "George Beauregard."

Trying to learn more about Beau, Matilda probed, "Your accent indicates that you are not a local. When did you arrive in Upstate New York?"

"Ah've been in Onondaga County off and on for six years."

Matilda pressed further. "Ah, so you arrived here in 1840. When you did, is it correct to say that you were hired to capture runaway slaves and return them to their owners?"

"Fugitives, you mean. Yes, that's correct."

"Hmm. You have been in New York for six years. How have you been able to stay employed?"

"Hunting. Odd jobs. Some at the docks. Some on the trains."

"Curious." Matilda matter-of-factly continued her interrogation. "Where do you live?"

"Ah lives in Syracuse. In a boarding house next to the train station and round the corner from the canal weighlock station."

"How long have you been there?"

"Most recently, Ah arrived from Georgia 'bout two, three months ago. Ah returned to New York in August, after Ah de-livered a fugitive family to their mastahs."

"Very good. Well, not very good, but thank you." After pausing for a moment, Matilda sweetly asked, "So you had ample access to sabotage the line boats when they were docked in Syracuse?"

"Yeah, they was easy pickins." Then, realizing he had been hoodwinked, Beau exclaimed, "Wait. What do you mean sabotage?"

The audience inhaled in unison. Without missing a beat, Matilda pushed, "How did you figure out which boats to target?"

After sitting quietly for a moment, Beau answered, "Ah'm not sure Ah'm going ta answer that question."

"Mr. Beauregard, you are under oath."

Beau looked at Judge Stone, whose neck was craned forward and eyes popped. Then he said defiantly, "Ah looked for boats with hulls o' pine. Do you think Ah'm stupid, just because Ah speaks with a Southern accent?"

Ignoring that bait, Matilda asked, "Was that 'I' or 'we'? Did you act alone?"

"Yes."

"Are you certain?" Matilda asked. "Do you want to reconsider your answer?" Following a protracted pause, she added, "Remember, you swore to tell the truth."

Beau capitulated. "Yes, there was someone else, but Ah won't identify him."

"So, there is honor among thieves." Matilda pivoted. "Your actions are disturbing. Why did you do this?"

"Ah was hired by the Great Syracuse and Utica Railroad." Beau puffed himself up and smiled. "The railroad told us to scare people. The idee was, if we scared 'em, then they'd choose the railroad instead of the canal."

"Why? Do you know why railroaders wanted you to do this?"

"Well, like Ah said, the trains was losing money. Ah'm told, when the railroad was built eight years ago, it cost a pretty penny—some million dollars. Now it's losing money. The bosses tell that last year, it only earned 'bout $50,000. The year before it was barely twice that. Ah'm not so good with numbers, but even Ah can tell that if'n it don't go out of business, it'll take some time just to pay back its original costs. Ah don't think the bosses are that patient."

"So, what actions did they take to improve profits?"

"They saw the only way to speed the payback time was ta mess wit the confidence people have in their competition: the canal."

"Yes, go on. What was the plan?"

"I was to damage a couple o' boats. Tear the hulls. Sink a couple or three. Make it look like an accee-dent." Surprisingly, maybe even miraculously, Beau began to break down. He shook his head and exclaimed, "But Ah didn't wanna hurt no one! That's why we worked on boats from Syracuse—they would be line boats waiting to be loaded with freight. We avoided boats going from Albany to Buffalo. They usually carried passengers." Beau repeated as the volume of his voice trailed off, "Didn't want ta hurt no one."

"By that you mean White folks? Is that right?" Matilda confronted Beau.

The prosecuting attorney immediately objected to that comment. "Your Honor, it's not acceptable for the defense attorney to badger the witness."

"I agree. The defense should tamp down its condemnation of the witness." Both attorneys stared at the judge. Silence strangled the courtroom.

After regaining her wits, Matilda apologized, "I am sorry for offending the court." She returned to questioning Beau. "Mr. Beauregard, please continue."

"We searched for boats moored in the Syracuse boatyards that were made o' pine. You'd be surprised how few there are. Most boats are made o' cedar and hardwoods. But pine, pine is vulnerable to water, 'specially salt water. After we picked our targets, we ripped open the paper wrapping the salt blocks, spread the salt, wiped the hull with diseased ears of corn, added water, and let nature do its work."

"That is impressive. How did you come up with this recipe?"

"Easy peasy. Dis is what causes wood rot in the bayous of Louisiana and lowlands of the Carolinas. That's why cypress is so precious. It don't rot so easy." Beau beamed as he showed off to Matilda and the crowd.

Matilda pressed, "What was your hope from causing this damage?"

"Ta disrupt the flow of cargo and scare people about using the canal." Beau paused and his head fell. "I never meant for any innocents to get hurt. You gotta believe me." By this time in the questioning, Beau was whimpering.

"I believe you." Matilda coaxed, "But how about Mr. Nash?"

Beau's demeanor immediately changed. He steeled himself. "Ah, blamin' a Black was easy. Baggin' a blackbird was all the sweeter. All Ah had to do was spark the kindling. There are kindred spirits in all parts o' dis country."

Matilda was mortified. "That's ugly, but I fear it's true. So, you caused the death of an innocent man and framed an innocent free citizen?"

"Yes," Beau shamefully sputtered.

"The only difference between these two acts, and your justification for the accidental death of one man and the intended death of another, is the color of these men's skins. Is that correct?"

"Yes, but—"

Matilda cut off Beau. "For that, Mr. Beauregard, you should get the punishment that you and your supporters deemed appropriate for Mr. Nash."

Shouts from the stunned audience erupted: "String 'im up!"

Judge Stone settled the unruly crowd. He directed, "The defense may continue."

Matilda looked at the judge, the jury, and Hiram. She turned to Henry, who nodded and rose. "Your Honor, the defense rests its case."

# 70

Gage home, High Bridge, New York
Saturday, October 24, 1846, 10:45 AM

After his saturday morning baseball, Steve rushed to the Gages and knocked on the kitchen door. There was no answer. He knocked again. Finally, Matilda answered. "Come in, dear boy."

Steve entered, sat at the table, and just stared at Matilda with veneration. She poured him a fresh cup of tea and handed him a piece of warm shortbread.

"Mrs. Gage, that was terrific! You bamboozled Beau into telling the truth. My, that is such a fun word—bamboozle." Steve mouthed the word, silently drew out the *oo* sound, and then bit into his biscuit. "Anyways, Mrs. Gage, you might be a better trickster than me. How'd you figure it out?"

"Well, Steve, context and circumstance. As it happens, on the Wednesday before the trial, Helen and I went to Syracuse to visit Henry at Attorney Wilkinson's office. While I walked near the canal, I poked about the market, staring at the merchandise and looking for deals. Then, I saw something peculiar. Two scruffy men were skulking about the yard where line boats were tethered. They paced about nervously, behaving as if they did not belong. Each man carried two parcels rolled in paper."

"What were they carryin'?" Steve asked.

"I wasn't sure, but based on what you've taught me, I thought each person carried a package of wrapped salt. It didn't quite make sense, but neither did what I thought I could see popping from the top of the other bundle. Corn silk."

"Corn?" Steve scrunched his face in puzzlement and hung on Matilda's every word. "What were they doin'?"

"Well, the two of them looked anxious. Their heads were jerking like chickens on the lookout for a fox, and suddenly, they both scurried onto a boat and disappeared into the cargo hold. Moments later, they reappeared and left the boat, but only with one package each. Then, they ducked into a second docked boat. When they bobbed out of that boat, both men were empty handed, and they bolted from the dock. They went in opposite directions on Water Street."

"Very curious. Was there anything peculiar about either of them?"

"Let me think. One was less distinctive. He was tall, rough clad, and wore a striped railroad cap." Matilda glanced knowingly toward Steve. "Yes, the cap was like one you found in the boat. The second man had a patch over his left eye, a gimpy left leg, and reeled a bit when he walked. I thought I'd seen him before, but I was not sure where. Then, I realized it was George Beauregard. When I saw him at the back of the courtroom yesterday, I played a hunch."

"That's inspired!" exclaimed Steve.

His smile withered and he winced when he recalled outbursts of "It's the Cleveland boy!" from the audience during the trial. "After everything, why do people still accuse me? Can't they see the facts in front of their faces? It's like nothin' changed."

Matilda looked directly at Steve. "What do small people do when they have nowhere else to look?"

Steve gazed wide eyed.

"They depend on their lack of imagination. They act on what they were taught by their parents, friends, or communities. They ignore the truth standing before them." Matilda was not finished. "If that wasn't enough, they fall into what is comfortable, what is easy. Small people just don't think. It disappoints me to say, I don't think they *can* think. They certainly do not grow. It is our responsibility to fight such narrow behavior."

Matilda reflected, "I remember the endless parade of runaways my parents, Henry, and I assisted on the Underground Railroad. We trundled through Cicero Swamp and hid runaways behind a bookcase. And now High Bridge, we hide runaways in our basement. Why? Because we believe in our fight for freedom—personal freedoms for all." Matilda shivered as she recalled the fear and apprehension of those days. Then she smiled with the joy of recalled successes.

"Steve, I'm sorry if I sound like I'm preaching. You probably get enough of that at home. But you must know that blaming you was easy for many townsfolk with your reputation as a prankster. Dare I say, it was reflex for them. It's most disturbing. I am truly sorry. Possibly more troubling is that if they don't have you to blame, they'll accuse another favorite target, a Black man. They cannot shake their prejudices."

"That is quite sad when you put it that way," said Steve.

Matilda elaborated, "Yes, 'tis, but I believe it's even more complicated, more distressing than that. Some people are comfortable, maybe even driven by their prejudice. Let me try to describe it in a different way. As you well know, all abolitionists who support the Underground Railroad work toward a common goal: the freedom of enslaved Blacks."

"Yes," Steve agreed.

"Well, not all abolitionists have the same intent. And intent is critical."

"How so?"

"Intent defines the society they foresee," Matilda stated. "There are those who aspire to a country in which all people are truly equal. This is one in which all people live together. I consider myself one such warrior for universal rights."

"I understand." Steve nodded.

Matilda added, "Other abolitionists believe that everyone should be free but that Whites are implicitly superior. They work toward a country in which Whites and Blacks live parallel existences."

"Are you saying that such people hold a prejudice?"

"Yes, Steve. In fact, they embrace it. They depend upon it."

Trying to understand Matilda's words, Steve offered, "Is that what is meant by 'A zebra can't change its stripes'?"

Laughing, Matilda corrected Steve, "Yes, but I think the biblical reference is 'A leopard can't change its spots.'"

"Oh, Father would be disappointed in me."

"Quite the contrary," Matilda said. "I think your father would be proud of you, your contributions to finding the truth, and your role in saving the life of an innocent man. I believe he sees the worth of Blacks as equal to Whites."

# 71

Gage home, High Bridge, New York
Saturday, October 24, 1846, 8:45 PM

MATILDA SET HELEN in bed for the night and went downstairs to collect her cloak from the foyer before joining Henry on the porch. Both sat on the bare wooden bench in silence. The crisp, cool night sky was studded with stars and crossed by the dusty Milky Way. The northern sky shimmered with vivid red and green curtains. This celebratory aurora was pierced by the crescent of a waxing moon. The night was magical. Matilda and Henry were awed.

Gazing at Henry, Matilda reflected, "This grand celestial dance puts our smallness into perspective."

"Matilda, you were miraculous."

"Henry, thank you, but I don't think you have it right."

"What do you mean?"

Matilda elaborated, "I think this victory was the result of teamwork. Hiram brought his faith in people. Sarah used the ways of the Haudenosaunee to understand the role of diseased corn in this crime. Steve brought his skills of careful observation and honesty. You applied what you learned during your legal training. I relied on my experience and the power of logic. Our victory came from a team of overlooked people—a Black man, a Haudenosaunee woman, a child, an apprentice, and a woman."

Henry gazed at Matilda with the same awe with which he'd regarded the sky. "Whether it was you or we, the victory was great. Hiram has his life back. His family is reunited. The ugliness of local prejudice is exposed. None of those achievements is a small feat."

"No. They aren't." Matilda paused. "I'm just not sure that the outcome of the trial will stick. Will people become aware of their prejudices? Will they change their behavior?" Matilda and Henry sat in silence. Suddenly, Matilda exclaimed, "That's it!"

"That's what?"

"Remember when we were at Jarm's house, after we left Cicero? When we were talking about future plans, personal futures?"

"Mmm, yes," Henry agreed.

"I asked, 'What do I want to do? What am I suited to do?' I wasn't sure how to answer those questions then. I know now. I will work toward a community that accepts everyone, values everyone."

"How so?" asked Henry.

Matilda spoke as if to an audience greater than Henry. "I will work for equality for all: Blacks, Haudenosaunee, and Whites. Women and men. Equality, opportunity, and respect for all—as Jefferson said, rights endowed by our Creator."

# PART 4.

## *GROVER AND MATILDA*

Do justly, now.
Walk humbly, now.
You are not obligated to complete the work,
but neither are you free to abandon it.

*Pirkei Avot* 2:16, Third Century

△▽✡△▽

# 72

Gage home, 210 Genesee Street, Fayetteville, New York
Saturday, June 5, 1886, 7:30 PM

BARN SWALLOWS SWOOPED across a pastel evening sky. They dove, climbed, and dove again, dancing as if collectively embroidering an invisible cloth. Firmly on the ground, Matilda knitted a sweater for the fall while she gazed in wonder at the birds' dance. She absentmindedly supervised her two-year-old grandson, Frank. He bounded about the front yard bordered by a white picket fence. It was one of those rare moments over the past few months when Matilda was able to relax, rocking in a chair on the porch of her Fayetteville home.

Through ricochets of daydreams, Matilda reviewed her recent writings on the lack of support of women by the church. She mused, "Christian principles and teachings underpin the patriarchal American political system. What would our country have been if Americans adopted Haudenosaunee traditions wherein elder women led and were sought for counsel? And what if America were based on the nonhierarchical, egalitarian Zoroastrianism rather than idealizing the patriarchy of Greece and Rome? Maybe Father was pricking my life's ambition those many years ago when he introduced me to Zoroaster."

Matilda smiled, snapped out of her reverie, and jumped to the present situation of the picket fence and her grandson. Suddenly, she smiled.

"Frank, I remember years ago when a rambunctious lad disassembled my front gate." It was one of the most propitious events of her life. It was the occasion of her meeting Stephen Grover Cleveland, the child who grew to be the twenty-second president of the United States.

Matilda urged, "Come, Frank. Let's go inside and prepare for bed."

Having the selective hearing of childhood, Frank continued to dig holes in the yard.

Matilda added, "I have a great story to read to you tonight: *Alice's Adventures in Wonderland*."

"Oh boy!" Frank dropped his toys, took his grandmother's hand, and bounded up the stairs.

After settling Frank into bed, Matilda boiled some water, set up a pot of tea, sat at her desk, and wrote a letter to Steve. She shuffled through the drawers for a clean piece of paper and discovered an old letter from him.

210 Genesee Street
Fayetteville, New York
February 8, 1882

*Dearest Mrs. Gage,*

*I trust you are in good health.*

*After 27 years of stability, I find myself in a peculiar situation. Most of my life was in service to my adopted home of Buffalo, where I realize I lived longer than anywhere else. I gained a profession and apparently the support of my fellow citizens. I achieved this through working and funning local folk. Then, I moved across the state to work on behalf of the people who elected me as their governor, as well as for those who did not vote for me. I carry the hopes and dreams of people throughout the state. Yet, I feel unconnected to many. I am reliant on people who I do not know from places I have not lived or even seen. Now I am living in a city that is foreign both in its geography and culture. Very peculiar, indeed.*

*I understand that your youngest, Maud, is betrothed to a Mr.*

*Frank Baum. I am told he is an upstanding gentleman, an actor, and much like Henry in his earnestness. I could not be more pleased for Maud and your family. I am certain that your large heart will more than have room for Mr. Baum and their new family when that comes. I will be most pleased to congratulate Maud and this Mr. Baum personally at my earliest opportunity.*

*Ever yours,*
*Steve*

Reflecting on the humility and consideration of her friend, Matilda dipped the nib of her pen in the inkwell and wrote.

### Executive Mansion
### 1600 Pennsylvania Avenue
### Washington
### June 5, 1886

*Dear Steve,*

*As I write this note, I admit finding it difficult to address you as Grover, much less Mr. President. It is amazing that within five years, you rose from sheriff to mayor to governor, and now to president. Regardless, to me, you are, and always will be, Steve.*

*Congratulations on your marriage to Frances Folsom. I know you have known Mrs. Cleveland and her family for many years. If I remember correctly, you worked as a law partner with her father, Oscar Folsom.*

*As I remember, during the 1882 campaign for the presidency, rivals condemned you for fathering a child out of wedlock. Those accusations were unfounded. It was clear to me that you were protecting your friend and law partner, Oscar Folsom, and his family, including your future wife, from public ridicule. For that, you took political shrapnel and risked the end of your political career. Your actions may have appeared foolhardy to many, but I admire you for taking the road of integrity and remaining silent.*

*Your response to the Folsom situation is consistent with how you behaved as a child; you absorbed the slings and arrows resulting from your pranks. You did not let on that your oldest brother was your accomplice in your many antics. A vein of steadfast loyalty runs strong and deep within you. I continue to be impressed by you. I am confident that your loyalty, honesty, and courage in the face of absurd falsehoods will be the underpinning of a meritorious and moral presidency.*

*As for Maud, her husband, Frank, is a fine young man. He enthralls Henry and me with his fanciful stories. Interestingly, he is the son of Benjamin and Cynthia Baum, cousins of our neighbors in Cicero. Life's coincidences amaze me.*

*I wish you well in your new life as a married man.*

*Your friend, as always,*
*Matilda*

△▽✡△▽

# 73

Executive Mansion, 1600 Pennsylvania Avenue, Washington
Friday, June 25, 1886, 9:30 PM

GROVER ENJOYED THE political trenches. A current debate was unfolding over a bill penned by Illinois Senator William Morrison for low or no tariffs on domestic products. President Cleveland strongly argued that such a bill would promote American competitiveness in domestic and world markets and would help the average man on the street to succeed, not just eke out a living. As might be expected, members of Congress postured on this and other acts in preparation for the 1886 midterm elections.

Battles over legislation overlaid Grover's persistent fights with members of his own party who lobbied for pet appointments by patronage. Such requests reliably irritated Grover, who fought for a meritocracy in which qualified civil servants would be people who worked on behalf of Americans, rather than lackeys hired to improve a congressman's chances of reelection.

To relax and remove himself from the pressures of daily politics, Grover sat at his desk in the residence to write some personal letters. After writing to his brother Will, now a reverend in Cleveland, Ohio, and to his sister Anna, who remained in the village of Holland Patent, New York, Grover reread the letter from Matilda written on June 5, 1886. He wrote:

210 Genesee Street
Fayetteville, New York
June 25, 1886

*Dear Mrs. Gage,*

*It was a complete joy to read your recent letter. I appreciate the insight, support, and kind words. Please recognize that you are the pot calling the kettle black. If I learned anything from you during our precious conversations over tea and your delicious bakes, it was that we are all charged with making the world a better place than it was when it was passed on to us. It is not our responsibility to complete the task. Our task is to improve and work on things to pass them onto others who will continue the good work.*

*Your Haudenosaunee mentors taught you well to focus on the present. Why devote yourself to the future when we have the gift of now? Unfortunately, such an approach for a president is a luxury. He must divine and consider the consequences of any actionable decision.*

*Missing our chats,*
*Steve*

△▽✡△▽

# 74

## Executive Mansion, Washington
## Wednesday, February 10, 1887, 1:30 PM

NORMALLY, POLITICAL CONTESTS with Congress did not affect Grover's disposition. He had an uncanny ability to put aspects of his life into inviolable, discrete compartments. Regardless of whether his pet bill was defeated in Congress or if he was cornered into vetoing a bill that benefitted rich industrialists and hurt people, the president remained friendly with his family and staff of the Executive Mansion.

Passage of the Dawes Act greatly confounded President Cleveland. The act was designed to break up tribal lands and promote private land ownership by Native Americans. Its reception by the press was radically divergent: some were laudatory, others critical. What confused him was that the journalists who complimented Grover's political skills in passing the act were those who usually condemned him, and vice versa.

Grover fumed to Frances, "I do not understand. Two days ago, I signed the Dawes Act into law. It will help Indians by making lands available for them to purchase and extending laws to protect them. The press is raking me over the coals. Don't they understand that it will raise Indians from poverty? Provide them security? Do the Indians oppose it?" He paced. He had tried to settle down with a restorative afternoon nap. Instead, he restively tossed and woke haggard.

Frances was unaccustomed to seeing her husband distracted and despondent. "Grover, I am going to have the chef make one of your favorite foods." She grabbed a recipe box, rifled through the cards, and identified just what she wanted: Matilda's old-time baked Indian pudding. Frances giggled as she read Matilda's requisite commentary and notes of admonition. She handed the card to Grover. Reading it, Steve closed his eyes. A look of contentment overtook his face.

Summoning the chef, Frances requested, "Please make this pudding for the president. Follow the recipe *religiously*."

Grover chuckled, knowing Frances's instructions to the chef undoubtedly would have piqued the spiritual but anti-religious Matilda.

Hours later, the butler knocked at the president's bedroom door and presented him with warm pudding. Grover's spirits soared. He recognized the treat immediately, not so much by its appearance but by its distinctive nutty smell. He was immediately transported to High Bridge.

"Ah, this is just what I need." He welcomed the servant and asked, "Would you like to join me?" Without waiting for an answer, he continued, "This is one of the most delicious confections you've ever had. Please, sit."

One did not turn down a presidential request, particularly such a heartfelt one. So the butler sat and joined in on the treat. After taking a bite, a grin came to his face. "Sir, this is right delicious!"

As Grover took his first bite, a sense of serenity enveloped him. "It is like eating a joyous piece of childhood. Hmm."

△▽✡△▽

# 75

Executive Mansion, Washington
Wednesday, February 24, 1887, 10:30 AM

A N AIDE KNOCKED to deliver a letter to the president from Matilda. Such news reliably put him in a good mood. Grover sat to savor the letter.

Executive Mansion
1600 Pennsylvania Avenue,
Washington
February 13, 1887

Dear Steve,
    This is a difficult letter to write. I know you as a champion of honesty, a voice for fairness and good. This is not just a personal perception. During the 1884 election, Joseph Pulitzer of The New York World promoted your candidacy for four reasons. "1. He is an honest man. 2. He is an honest man. 3. He is an honest man. 4. He is an honest man." You are known and celebrated for your rectitude, as a fair guardian of the oppressed and abused.
    As I remember, one of the first actions that you took on becoming president was an executive proclamation rescinding

President Arthur's order and providing Indians their rights to four million acres west of the Mississippi River. It is with this understanding that I ask: how could you sign the Dawes Act? This legislation amounts to the Democrats trying to reset politics and return the South to pre-war glory. It undermines twenty years of Reconstruction, renders senseless the loss of countless lives during the War Between the States, and damages virtually every family throughout the nation.

I am certain that your intentions were honorable, but I fear that in passing this act, the Southern Democrats got the better of you. All they care about is harming their rivals and living by the credo "If you cannot do good, make your enemies look bad." Politics is a choice—the timidity of lying for expediency versus temerity of loyalty to integrity. I implore you to continue to fight the good fight.

Steve, the Dawes Act reminds me of our discussions about abolition and intent. In this case, despite your intent, a conscionable action may have negative consequences. It will remove indigenous peoples from their lands, weaken their rights, and promote the loss of their cultures. Are these decisions the re-emergence of your father's divine-inspired aspirations to be a savior?

It appears that when the injustice is directed against Hiram or is personal, you are engaged. You are supportive to the end. On the other hand, when it is impersonal and systemic, then the hidden, presumed privilege of your White father emerges. I wonder how a child gains the courage and insight to surmount parental teachings. Your challenge is to hew your own path.

Would it be possible that you could undo the damage that you have wrought?

Your friend, always,
Matilda

Grover was shattered. He paced nervously. He was proud of his reputation for setting a robust standard for fully considering the outcomes of every law he was presented. He prided himself on his thorough, fair analyses, and a willingness to wield a veto when it was the right thing to do. What fully flummoxed Grover was Matilda's disappointment and disapproval. He sat at his desk to draft a response. Raising and inking his fountain pen, he furiously wrote, as if possessed by a demon.

210 Genesee Street<br>
Fayetteville, New York<br>
February 20, 1887

*Dear Mrs. Gage,*

*I received your letter of February 15. Know that I am not here to please you. I am not here to support your frivolous causes of universal freedom and separation of church and state. I am here to do the will of the people and to protect them, sometimes from themselves.*

Grover paused from writing, closed his eyes, and consciously slowed his breathing. Abruptly crumpling the letter, he threw it into the bin and stormed off to the sitting room where Frances was knitting. Grover spilled his thoughts. "Is Matilda right? Have I blundered? Did I fail to consider the consequences of the law? Was I hornswoggled by devious Southern Democrats who supported my election?" Grover paced in silence.

Frances did not answer.

△ ▽ ✡ △ ▽

# 76

Upstate New York
Tuesday, July 19, 1887, 11:15 AM

PRESIDENT CLEVELAND TOOK a tour through bountiful, prosperous Upstate New York. Passing the beautiful, rolling hills of James Fenimore Cooper's Leatherstocking Region, Grover closed his eyes in sleep where Natty "Hawkeye" Bumppo and Chingachgook had once navigated the dense forest. The background music, the rhythmic *clickety-clack, clickety-clack*, played as the train rolled down the tracks. When Grover opened his eyes, he saw the Mohawk River meandering below the gentle foothills of the Adirondacks, full of corn and wheat fields, fecund orchards, and forests replete with every conceivable shade of green. The train stopped in Utica so Grover could take a detour to Holland Patent and pay respects at the graves of his mother and father.

On arriving in Syracuse, Grover was greeted by Willis Burns, the self-important mayor. Burns led Grover to his lodgings at the John Bedford Block Hotel at the intersection of Washington and State Streets, steps from the Erie Canal. As the afternoon waned, Grover walked to downtown Syracuse where he gave a stirring speech.

"The vitality of central New York is a model for growth throughout the United States. New Yorkers are the envy of all Americans. It is no surprise that George Washington nicknamed New York the Empire State. Our success is founded on the ingenuity and hard work of honest New Yorkers."

The next day, Grover mounted a carriage and rode along Genesee Street to Fayetteville. On his arrival, he dismounted at Mill Street. Grover walked up the main street and saluted the crowd of people lining both sides. He could make out some old townsfolk, including Miriam Nash, doddering Bertie Beard, and his brother, Barti.

Old baseball buddies George and Sam O'Neal ran up to Grover. One yelled, "Hey, Steve. It's Sam!" and the other bade, "Morning, Beanie Boy. It's George!" Grover grinned and vigorously shook their hands.

Despite the joy of seeing familiar faces, there was a conspicuous absence of many kind folk who had been important in his life—notably, Doc Taylor, Mr. McVicar, Robert Hatch, and Hiram Nash.

Villagers young and old, known and new, swelled the throng and followed Grover to Clinton Square. He was escorted to a seat beside the podium. Surveying the scene, Grover looked to the right where he saw Village Hall, which had supported the painted donkey on July 4, and to the left he saw his father's church where he and Will had rung the bells that midnight long ago.

Grover was ushered to a seat by the mayor. "Steve, please sit for a moment."

Shaking his head, Grover looked the mayor in the eyes. "Jacob! Blazes, Jacob Cartwright!"

"Yes. Welcome back, Steve."

"What a pleasure to see you, Mayor Cartwright." The two old pals clasped arms.

Glancing to his left, Grover picked out one of the prime reasons for his visit. At the back of the audience was Matilda Joslyn Gage. She was grayer and fuller figured than when they'd last seem each other some thirty-five years ago, but Matilda was unmistakable. She stood alone. Henry had died two years earlier, but that diminished neither her pride nor her fiery spirit. Matilda was still the brightest light in any crowd.

Grover shifted his attention to the proceedings as a band enthusiastically started the national anthem. Mayor Cartwright stepped up to the podium and made a few opening comments. "Welcome, President Cleveland. It is a great honor to have one of our own return, a person I am honored to call a dear friend. We are so proud of you, so proud of the job you are doing on our behalf. Please, take a few moments."

Applause rang from the assembled as Grover stood and approached the podium. After the crowd settled, he began. "What a wonderful sight. I cannot express the thrill it is for me to be back in Fayetteville with all of you. I have the fondest of memories of this village, its people. Fayetteville is the place where I spent my formative years. It is where I was schooled in the benefits and satisfaction of good, hard work. Where I learned the joy of having fun." With that last phrase, titters erupted from older members sprinkled throughout the crowd.

"As I rode the train here, through the lush, verdant landscape of Upstate New York, I was reminded of the visionaries who made Fayetteville possible. They included Dewitt Clinton, who conceived the Erie Canal, and the entrepreneurs who used that footprint to lay railroads crisscrossing the area. These transport systems connect Fayetteville with the world. I have worked to build on those advances. I unified the railroads and integrated them nationally through the Interstate Commerce Act. It should ensure that places like Fayetteville and Manlius continue to flourish well into the future.

"Please know, Fayetteville lives in the warmest part of my heart. It is the home of my oldest and best friends. I continue to infuse the lessons I learned here—honesty, integrity, respect, and equality—into my governance. You are with me, always."

On finishing his speech, Grover stepped from the dais. He shook eager hands thrust at him from all directions. Villagers slapped his broad back. Grover returned admiring smiles and kissed babies. Working through the crowd, he finally arrived at the back to meet the one he cared for most: Matilda. "Steve, it is so delightful to see you." As they hugged, he kissed her on each cheek. Matilda turned to her left. "Let me introduce you to my youngest daughter, Maud, and her husband, Frank Baum."

"It's a great pleasure to meet both of you. I have heard much about you. I feel that I already know you."

Maud replied, "It's an honor to meet you, sir." Grover gave Maud a warm bear hug and introduced himself to Frank with a hearty handshake. The latter greeting was so enthusiastic that Frank gaped at his released hand as if it had been flattened by a clothes wringer.

Matilda said, "Come, Steve. Would you like a cup of tea?"

On hearing this cherished offer, a tear came to Grover's eye. "Yes, I would like that very much." He held out his arm, Matilda linked hers in his, and the two strolled down Genesee Street. They passed the Fayetteville Academy and his former house on Academy Street on the right, and then the Presbyterian church on the left. Finally, they arrived at 210 Genesee Street.

Though Matilda's home was new to Grover, the kitchen was arranged and equipped like the house in High Bridge. "Mrs. Gage, this house feels so familiar. I know I've not been here before, but it feels as comfortable as wearing a pair of old slippers. Before we talk any further, let me offer my condolences on Mr. Gage's passing."

"Thank you, Steve. He was a dear man. I was blessed to have had such a fine life partner. Henry was a great father and a great spouse. Without his unqualified support in daily activities, such as feeding, raising, and schooling our children, I would not have been able to travel and advocate for women's and universal rights as I have these past thirty-five years."

Grover added, "Yes. It seems to me that while you fought for feminism, Mr. Gage did as well. Feminism is not solely for empowering women, promoting their civil rights. It is also for liberating men—to enable men to pursue their own paths and to build a cooperative society. Mr. Gage's thoughts and actions were wholly consistent with the Haudenosaunee ideal you hold so dear."

"I could not agree with you more."

"Also, while you speak to the humanity of the man, I'd like to note the respect Mr. Gage commanded for his tireless work on abolition and advocacy for others in this community. What you may not appreciate, however, is that he was always kind and welcoming to me. From the first time I met him, he made me feel like part of the family. Mr. Gage was funny as well, and you know how important a good sense of humor is to me." Matilda smiled as Grover continued. "All that said, possibly most meaningful is that Mr. Gage was a model for me on how a man should enter and participate in a marriage of equals. If I ever have children, I hope to be just like him. Henry Gage continues to live on in my heart."

Tears sprang to Matilda's eyes as she squeezed Grover's hand. "Steve, you are dear. Thank you. Thank you very much."

"Now, please. Tell me about everyone," Grover solicited. They talked about the comings and goings of their families and Fayetteville folk. Matilda related stories of the few who'd moved away, and the all-too-many who had died. Grover was a rapt listener, interjecting questions when the memory of a resident popped into his mind.

The conversation drifted toward the serious situation of current events. They discussed the emerging concept of strict interpretation of the Constitution. Matilda stated, "This is when people lose creativity and sensitivity, when people get lazy, and ideas become concretized. Such ideas are inconsistent with other facets of people's lives. It is remarkable that a person who relies on the strict construction of the Constitution, whether they know it or not, does not believe that the Constitution should grow and adapt just as we must. It makes me wonder whether people with such beliefs also continue the practice of sacrifice as specified in the Old Testament.

"In the mid-1780s, the Founders acknowledged the weaknesses of the Articles of Confederation and the need to replace them with the Constitution. In the drafting of the Constitution, the writers recognized that the document must be modified. They provided a mechanism for adding amendments as needed. In fact, almost immediately after the Constitution was finalized, the Bill of Rights was added. So why then should we consider the Constitution to be a static, rigid entity? Should we not have freed the slaves? If, as Thomas Dew wrote, slavery was our national original sin, should we try to protect the system and continue to work toward a more imperfect union?"

Grover assented, but asked, "At what point do we essentially modify, or even discard, constructs of the Constitution? Would this not be an opening for chaos and anarchy?"

Maud and Frank stepped into the kitchen and quietly sat to enjoy the conversation. As talk shifted to the economy, Frank timidly asked, "Doesn't the gold standard hurt farmers?"

In the mode of her mother, Maud forcefully added, "How do we control the greed of heartless bankers in the cities that squeeze as much as they can from those who have little? How do we prevail among politicians who did not have the courage of their convictions? And how do we protect against thoughtless people who unquestioningly believe whatever they are told? I must admit, I am impressed by your consistent support for the vulnerable."

Grover patiently responded to each comment.

Then, changing the subject to foreign affairs, Maud commented, "Congratulations on your handling of the Samoa problem by confronting German bellicosity. I believe you strengthened American might while respecting domestic self-determination. It would be appropriate that Native Americans also receive such governmental support. I am guessing that you did not have the endorsement of your foreign affairs team in the matter."

Grover winced a bit at this reminder of Matilda's pointed criticism of his handling of the Dawes Act. "Thank you, and you are quite right, Maud. The advice of many in my cabinet did differ with my actions."

After the exchanges, Grover made an aside to Matilda. "The candor and clear thought of your children are refreshing."

Matilda replied, "I expect nothing less."

Readdressing Maud, Grover expanded, "Through it all, I must maintain my awareness that politics is messy. The stakes are high. Many machines wield power solely to enrich themselves. I have little patience or tolerance for the seamy side of running for office or maintaining an office, but I am not naïve."

The conversation on contemporary issues meandered amiably for another half hour, and then Matilda asked, "Steve, how do you want to be remembered?"

"Ah, the legacy question. I believe the idea of legacy is a delusion and salve for the living. How many individuals from one, two, or three hundred years ago are remembered today? That is not very far back in our history, yet I can assure you that the lives of most everyone from that long ago are essentially lost to our collective memories. Let me give you an example. None of the details of those who fought in skirmishes and victories of yore are remembered, nor are their names or their contributions. We can recall the battle leaders such as George Washington at the crossing the Delaware River before the Battle of Trenton. But I'm confident that you know nothing of the identities or accomplishments of the individual rowers who silently moved the boats across the river. That battle turned on the bravery of these nameless crew members. Even more, there was the thankless sacrifice of the wives and family the soldiers left at home. I am sure you do not know who they are. So, what is legacy?"

Grover recited Psalm 90:

> *Our years may number three score and ten;*
> *If we be granted special vigor, then eighty.*
> *But their boasting is only trouble and travail;*
> *Fore soon they are gone and we vanish.*

"I suppose we are intended to forget," added Grover.

"Forget? What do you mean?" queried Matilda.

"People cannot be burdened with knowing and remembering the details of the travails, successes, and failures of previous generations. We must be able to move on, to build on foundations left for us but not be encumbered by an ever-increasing crush of information. This need, however, conflicts with how we live our lives as individuals. We presume that each of us is exceptional; we primp our self-importance. Yet because our memories and records are limited, it is imperative that our personal achievements become forever lost to the mists of nameless, formless time." Grover pursed his lips. "Matilda, please excuse my mindless musings."

△▽✡△▽

# 77

Gage home, Fayetteville, New York
Tuesday, July 20, 1887, 8:15 AM

MATILDA WAS STILL reveling in the fading aura of Grover's
visit to Fayetteville. The banter, the values, the love were all still there. She
sat down to let him know.

Executive Mansion
1600 Pennsylvania Avenue,
Washington
July 20, 1887

*My Dear Stephen,*

*It was pure joy to see you yesterday. I cannot help but reflect
on that thoughtful yet Puckish lad when I look at you or a picture
of you. I was particularly pleased that both Maud and Frank, who
had not yet met you, remarked on how affable and approachable
you are. It is remarkable that you have not lost your soul with your
time in Albany and Washington.*

*After our chat, I consulted my family Bible, which I must admit
has lain unopened for years. It seems to me that you have not fully
considered your psalm. You cut short your quote. It continues:*

*So teach us to number our days,*
*That we may attain a heart of wisdom.*
*Satisfy us each morning with Your love,*
*That we may live joyously all of our days.*

I agree with you. If you are in life for your legacy, then you are misoriented. All you can do is to present the unfinished canvas of our world to the next generation so that they may add their paint to the unfolding masterpiece of God's creation.

Thank you for humoring the ramblings of an old woman.

My best wishes to you and Frances,
Matilda

△▽✡△▽

# 78

Baum home, Main Street, Aberdeen, Dakota Territory
Friday, January 4, 1889, 3:40 PM

Executive Mansion
1600 Pennsylvania Avenue
Washington
January 4, 1889

*Stephen,*

*While I watch my grandchildren play, I realize how fortunate I am. Many of my children and their families found their way to a common place, the Dakota Territory. It is a joy for me, and I hope to them, that everyone is collected in one spot.*

*Yet despite all of us being here in the Dakota, I must admit mixed feelings. This land was not obtained fairly. Treaties were broken, indigenous peoples starved, and blood was spilled. Sometimes, I just close my eyes and breathe deeply. Is my response something that August von Rochau described in his book Realpolitik? Was I too idealistic when I criticized you after you signed the Dawes Act?*

*Anyway, my eldest is Helen. You must remember her as you were present when she was born. She and her husband, Charles, her brother, Thomas, and his wife, Sophie, their sister Julia, and her husband, James, as well as Maud and Frank have settled here. I am spending the winter with them. My thought was to trade the challenges of living a snowy winter in Fayetteville alone for a frigid winter in the Dakota with my loved ones. Though I am a bit travel weary after all these years, I know I made the correct choice. Family is always the correct choice.*

*Please accept my sympathy on your loss in the recent election. Disappointingly, the vote in the electoral college did not concur with the popular vote. You should be proud of your support of those without a voice. Your fights to make American-made products more competitive and to keep people employed were evidently appreciated by the people. Most voters rewarded you and tried to keep you in office.*

*As you well know, the current system is untenable. It drives untold numbers of people into poverty. I am disheartened by the actions and dirty tricks of the protectionists and their efforts to ensure that their supporters' businesses are maintained. Your campaigns to battle the self-serving and fight for honesty and accountability in the federal government were refreshing—dare I say, revolutionary.*

*I recently read "Das Kapital" by the German economist Karl Marx. He rightfully criticizes self-perpetuating capitalist organizations. While I do not abide by his arguments for overthrowing capitalism, his support of equality among peoples and sexes is laudatory. I believe implementation of Marx's system would fail because it eliminates an individual's drive for improvement and achievement, and it minimizes society's drive for innovation and advancement. Regardless, it is instructive about the interplay between contributions to the body politic and personal need.*

*Right now, our country is passing through a time of great innovation. I dare say that no time in human history has witnessed such profound change. Many of these changes reduce the worth of people or even replace them outright. The result is that increasing numbers of people are out of work. This cannot be the goal of a more advanced society. Finding the best use of each person and respecting each person's contribution must be our consensual aspiration.*

*I await your thoughts.*

*Best wishes to you and Frankie,*
*Matilda*

Delighted to receive mail from Matilda, Grover wasted no time in returning a letter to her.

Main Street
Aberdeen, Dakota Territory
January 16, 1889

*Dear Mrs. Gage,*

*Thank you for your recent letter. I encourage you to hold true to your ideals. It is a challenge, as I well know. I am sarcastically referred to as the "veto president" for denying the status quo of political patronage. I do not regret my vetoes.*

*From what I have learned, you were sold out by single-song Susan Anthony, and by her plagiarism. Blatant disloyalty! You even defended her in court after she attempted to vote in the '72 election. I have wondered, when you represented her, did you draw on your experience from examining George Beauregard during Hiram Nash's trial? Regardless, rest assured, Miss Anthony will get her comeuppance. Time will show that it was she who turned on her colleagues and the movement. She was the unprincipled person who did not hold to the ideals of equal freedom for all and the full spectrum of women's equality that you champion so ardently.*

*Many of our citizens are still oppressed. While the work of the abolitionists was achieved, at least insofar as slavery was eliminated and the right for Blacks to vote was established, virtual slavery persists through the economic and political subjugation of Blacks. You so accurately point out that the oppression of women comes at* the hands of the government and church. Though I have concerns about women's suffrage, it is only one step toward remedying those inequities.

True progress will not be achieved by focusing on one group or by pitting one group against another. Please, keep up your fight.

Fond regards,
Steve

△▽✡△▽

# 79

Executive Mansion, Washington
Monday, March 20, 1893, 5:00 PM

AFTER WINNING THE hard-fought election of 1892, Grover returned to Washington and reintroduced himself and Frances to the Executive Mansion staff. The Clevelands were pleased that most of the same people were there to greet them.

The fun of having a one-year-old exploring the halls was a new experience for everyone in the Executive Mansion. Ruth toddled about and secreted herself into places not previously considered. "Ruth, where are you? Mommy's looking for you" was commonly heard. A giggle would emerge from behind wall-length draperies in the drawing room or beneath a chaise in the bedroom in which Abraham Lincoln slept. Grover let out a hearty guffaw as Frances sneaked about, captured a squirmy bundle, and whisked her off to bed.

Finally, after a long day of pomp and getting the machinery of his new administration functional, Grover took a few minutes before dinner to read and respond to mail. There were three stacks of letters to address.

The tallest stack comprised letters from politicians all over the country. Most senders had ulterior motives, trying to position themselves for future political contests and negotiations. Writers included Henry Markham and Roswell Flower, governors of California and New York, respectively, the devious "Honest" John Kelly of Tammany Hall, and Charles Frederick Crisp, a Georgia Democrat who was Speaker of the House of Representatives.

The second stack contained congratulations from world leaders. Grover rifled through them, reading letters from Robert Gascoyne-Cecil and John Thompson, prime ministers of the United Kingdom and Canada, respectively, as well as Queen Victoria and King Rama V of Siam. These leaders were in office during his previous administration. Their notes gave Grover a sense of consistency across much of the world. He knew on whom he could rely for support or opposition. The letter at the bottom of this second stack was from Franz Joseph I, emperor of Austria and king of Hungary, Croatia, and Bohemia. Grover fumbled and mumbled while opening that letter. "Wonder what the ol' fuddy-duddy Who-I-Am has to say?"

The third stack contained personal correspondence. Well-wishers included Anna Cleveland, his oldest sister, who lived in Hartford, Connecticut, and Jacob Cartwright, his childhood friend. These congratulations brought sequential smiles to Grover's tired face. Toward the bottom of this stack was a letter from Matilda Gage, postmarked Chicago. After reading that note, Grover took the time to answer it.

### 1667 North Humboldt Boulevard
### Chicago, Illinois
### March 20, 1893

*Dearest Mrs. Gage,*

*Thank you for your hearty congratulations on my return to the president's house. It is remarkably comfortable, particularly since I am returning with Frankie, and now Ruth. Though Chaucer said, "Familiarity breeds contempt," I believe that familiarity begets calm and builds confidence.*

*Now it is my turn to congratulate you. Your new book, Woman, Church, and State, is a masterpiece. It is thought-provoking. If my father had any idea how antagonistic to the organized church you* would be, I am certain that my visits with you would have been censured. He certainly would have nipped the proverbial flower in the bud. You lay out cogent arguments, but I am certain that my father would have described them as heretical.

I find myself at war with myself. It is the conflict of what I was taught as a child versus what I have learned through experience as an adult. As you state in your summary,

> The most important struggle in the history of the church is that of woman for liberty of thought and the right to give that thought to the world. As a spiritual force the church appealed to barbaric conception when it declared woman to have been made for man, first in sin and commanded to be under obedience. [Woman, Church, and State, page 238]

The second sentence in this quote means a great deal to me. It refers to the line from Genesis that my parents had embroidered onto a quilt they received on their wedding day. It was the central principle of their relationship and my native family. Yet, your words separate the concepts of spirituality from the construct of the church. I appreciate your clarity.

> During the ages, no rebellion has been of like importance with that of Woman against the tyranny of Church and State; none has had its far-reaching effects. We note its beginning; its progress will overthrow every existing form of these institutions; its end will be a regenerated world. [Woman, Church, and State, page 247]

As the head of state, I should be offended and provoked on reading passages such as these. Contrariwise, in our country, the church and state are separate. Further, I must admit that as husband of a wonderful, independent woman and father of a rambunctious daughter, I can only wish a life full of unbound opportunity for them. It is from these perspectives that I endorse your sentiments. Nevertheless, truth be told, I must admit that I am not wholly in support of your goals.

In my limited understanding of the movement for women's rights, it appears that you are at direct odds with your former collaborators, Mrs. Stanton and Miss Anthony. I hope that you can mend those relations while maintaining your integrity and aspirations. Your objectives of universal rights are wholly in concert with those of Mr. Frederick Douglass, for whom I have great respect, despite his campaigning for my opponents.

I just left a meeting of my new Cabinet where we discussed if and how to broach the ideals of universal rights. Know that there is the recalcitrance and intransigence among congressmen, and many members of my Cabinet. Despite the obstacles, I endorse a frank airing of the issues. I am not sure if it would be any easier if the Senate was under Democratic control. Democrats are anything but monolithic, but we should all work toward solutions that are informed and consistent with our Christian values.

I would so enjoy sitting, having tea, and talking with you about these and other vexing issues. Maybe Frankie and I can have you down to Washington for a visit soon.

My warmest regards to you, Maud, and Frank,
Steve

△▽✡△▽

# 80

Gage home, 210 East Genesee Street, Fayetteville, New York
Monday, March 27, 1893, 4:30 PM

O**N READING HER** recent letter from Grover, Matilda paced, squared to her desk, sat as abruptly as an infirm, sixty-seven-year-old woman could, and dashed off a pithy response.

Executive Mansion
1600 Pennsylvania Avenue
Washington
March 27, 1893

*Dear Steve,*

*I appreciate your candor. I expect no less from you.*

*I have long suspected that you and I disagreed on women's suffrage. I realize it is tough to shake the shackles of parental teachings such as how religious principles, precepts, and practices frame your thoughts. Despite this, I admire your objectivity, your openness to the opinions and considerations of others, and your desire to do well by those without a voice.*

*Given that, I implore you to remove your personal thoughts. Think of what is best for the nation and each citizen; not just*

*White men, but women, Blacks, and people with different beliefs from yours. Remember the Sarahs, the Hirams, and Miriams. As a father, think of how your decisions affect our children, our future, regardless of their ancestry. The Cherrys, Hannahs, and Elis should have the same rights as the Ruths of our country.*

*I am sure I do not have to tell you that as the nation's chief executive, your solemn responsibility must be to lead the entire nation. You are obliged to abide by the Constitution, which defines the separation of church and state, keeping in mind that the church includes Christians and the many others—theosophists like me, Jews, indigenous peoples, and others who do not abide by Christian teachings. Thus, you must fight the principles foundational to the current church practice that establish and maintain inequality of the sexes.*

*My best regards,*
*Matilda*

Matilda folded the letter, slid it into an envelope which she addressed like many others she had posted to the Executive Mansion. After applying wax, imprinting her seal, and pushing her letter to the corner of her desk, she picked up a sheet of paper, dabbed her pen in the inkwell, and drafted an article for her periodical, *The Liberal Thinker*.

△▽✡△▽

# 81

Baum home, 1667 North Humboldt Boulevard, Chicago, Illinois
Wednesday, March 30, 1898, 10:30 AM

ROCKING IN HER favorite chair, Maud knitted a cable sweater
for her husband while blankly staring at the piano pushed against the far
wall of the sitting room. The somber morning was interrupted by a rap
at the door. Maud rose, crossed the room, and placed her knitting on a
table before opening the door.

A postal carrier greeted her with a cheery "Top o' tha mornin' to ya!"
as he passed a sheaf of letters to her. His cheer was met with Maud's dour
silence. Maud shuffled through the letters. The return addresses revealed
senders from all over the country. Some of the senders' names caught
Maud's attention:

Susan B. Anthony, 17 Madison Street, Rochester, New York

Elizabeth Cady Stanton, 250 West Ninety-Fourth Street, New York,
New York

Belva Lockwood, 619 F Street, Washington

Elizabeth Smith Miller, 5304 Oxbow Road, Peterboro, New York

One letter at the bottom of the stack was distinctive. It was an envelope
from Westland Mansion, 15 Hodge Street, Princeton, New Jersey, that
was embellished with a crimped seal of the president of the United States.
Maud fell back into her rocking chair, nodded, and slipped open that letter.

### 1667 North Humboldt Boulevard
### Chicago, Illinois
### March 24, 1898

*Dearest Maud,*

*It is with profound sadness that I learned of your mother's death. I note that today, your mother would have been 72 years old.*

*The nation mourns the loss of a unique voice, a champion of all people, and a warrior for liberty. Matilda was passionate, persuasive, and persistent. She had bottomless wells of empathy and respect for everyone. She viewed each person as an individual with value, appreciated the strength and support that comes from community, and had the tenacity and conviction to fight for our country.*

*Your mother was historian, driver, and clarion for the cause of universal equality. She identified and took responsibility for telling everyone of societies' failings. Instead of being a naysayer, she devised strategies to right wrongs and worked toward building a country that promotes the rights of all humans.*

*Unlike her fellow soldiers for equality, Matilda did not compromise her aspirations. She refused to settle for part of her vision. She ardently and ceaselessly fought for the rights of individuals, believing that all people must be treated fairly and with dignity regardless of sex, race, religious observance, or heritage. The only way she saw to achieve these goals was to support a diverse community, to advocate for the rights of minorities, and to maintain the separation of church and state. The country owes her an inestimable debt.*

*Your mother had a disarming charm that arose from her respect for the backgrounds, needs, and gifts of every citizen. She marshaled her lucid logic and power of persuasion in support of her national vision for our country. Through her work, she earned the admiration of many. Matilda worked ceaselessly toward convincing people that honoring individual dignity and the collective of community was paramount for our synergistic best interest.*

Though Matilda identified social needs and showed the way for people to attain common goals, she was denied seeing the promised land. I believe that your mother was a Moses of our time. We did not realize her vision in her lifetime, but I am confident that we will yet achieve it.

Your mother was a pillar of my personal growth and development. I often reflect on the many times I sat in her kitchen, enjoying tea, conversation, and philosophy. Those conversations were never dull. I came from them with my legs a bit wobbly, struggling to appreciate the new knowledge, insights, and perspectives she had passed on to me. Part of her genius was her direct, masterful manner. While she coddled me with cookies and confections, I did not realize that she was challenging my core beliefs. At first it seemed that she was agreeing with me, but with time, I realized that through deft conversation, she was encouraging me to confront my own beliefs.

The greatest lesson she taught me was that while timing provides opportunity and context defines actions, persistence supports success. Not only were her teachings key for clearing Hiram Nash, but they served as guidance during my political career.

Matilda was an extraordinary, devoted, loving mother. Watching her parent was a joy. There was no doubt where her heart lay—with her family. I just hope that Frankie and I are as effective raising our children. There will be none other like your mother.

I bless my stars that I had the chance to know Matilda, to learn from her, and to include myself in her army, working toward decency and a common truth. I mourn the loss of a mentor and dear friend, but I am immensely fortunate to have known and learned from her. I will miss her greatly.

May your mother continue to live on in your thoughts and your actions. May her life reveal the path for our nation's progress toward universal rights, mutual respect, and cultural civility.

Ever yours,
Grover

Maud nodded and spoke to the letter. "Grover, isn't each of us Moses, connecting the past with the future? The job is never complete. The baton has been passed so the fight can go on. We may never personally reach the promised land, but our responsibility is to navigate the labyrinths of our lives, to forge a path so others may get there." She refolded the letter and fell quiet.

# EPILOGUE

PEOPLE OFTEN SAY history is written by the victors. In Matilda Joslyn Gage's case, the victor would be Susan B. Anthony and, to a lesser degree, Elizabeth Cady Stanton. Some evidence is a monument in Central Park, New York, that celebrates Anthony and Stanton but ignores Gage. This is a travesty as Gage's contribution to women's rights was at least equal to those of Anthony and Stanton. Gage even served as Anthony's lawyer after Anthony was arrested for voting in the presidential election of 1872.

Anthony's singular goal was women's suffrage. She was angry that Black men received the vote before women. Consequently, Miss Anthony discarded some of the ideas for which Matilda fought: (a) broad, equal rights for women, (b) full freedom for Blacks, (c) liberties, rights, and recognition of Native Americans, and (d) the separation of church and state. Anthony embraced followers of the temperance movement in the process of writing Matilda out of history and amplifying her own role.

While women achieved the vote, Anthony's "victory" was incomplete. Equality for women and control of their own bodies remains elusive. The feminist movements of the 1960s, 1970s, and the 2010s have been condemned to repeat Matilda's work as the fight to attain true, complete equality in the home and workplace continues. Further, Native Americans continue to struggle for their ancestral lands and for the federal government to honor treaties it signed and then ignored.

Matilda would likely counter the adage that victors write history by saying that the light of day belongs to the truth-seekers. Appreciating one's place in the world was critically important to Matilda. She was a freethinker, searching to celebrate a spirituality that was not burdened by the trappings of organized (patriarchal) Christianity, which was structured for its self-perpetuation and female subjugation rather than feeding the souls of the people it purported to serve. Matilda valued each person's ability to prioritize his/her goals as that person's greatest expression of free will. Matilda's slogan is engraved on her gravestone in Fayetteville Cemetery:

THERE IS A WORD
SWEETER THAN MOTHER
HOME OR HEAVEN
THAT WORD IS LIBERTY

Matilda's epitaph notwithstanding, family was of utmost importance to her. She doted on her children and grandchildren, welcomed spouses-in-law and their kin, and treated friends like family. As a result, despite Anthony's and Stanton's attempts to assume credit for Matilda's work and to write Matilda out of history, Matilda's dear son-in-law, L. Frank Baum, ensured that she and her husband would live on in contemporary culture. They are the loving couple Auntie Em and Uncle Henry in Baum's *The Wonderful Wizard of Oz*. Like their eponyms, these two characters believed in hard work, mutual support, and respect for all.

Like Matilda, Stephen Grover Cleveland was also a great reformer. One of his professional legacies is the great popularity he earned through his honest and selfless governance. His acumen and moral compass steered him to eschew patronage and to make decisions that, though politically fraught, were the right thing to do. This sharply contrasted to preceding and subsequent presidents, who promoted self-interest and cronyism.

President Cleveland preached fiscal responsibility, practiced personal, national, and international self-reliance, and minimized party politics. For example, he was an ardent supporter of the gold standard as the foundation for a sound national economy and worked to unify the country through the Interstate Commerce Commission. Based on his ideals, Grover was rewarded by being one of only three presidential candidates to win the national popular vote three (consecutive) times. (Incidentally, the other two are Andrew Jackson and Franklin Delano Roosevelt.)

Legacy comes in different forms. Aside from his many accomplishments as an elected official, Grover is probably remembered for five things:

1. In his first term, Grover was the first president to marry while in office. He married Frances Folsom on June 2, 1886.

2. Grover and Frances had a daughter, Ruth, between his two administrations. When Grover returned to the presidency and the Executive Mansion, Ruth was the darling of the nation and the press. Ruth tragically died from diphtheria as a twelve-year-old. Allegedly, her memory persists in the namesake Baby Ruth candy bar.

3. Grover and Frances Cleveland were the first and, to date, only couple to have a child born at the Executive Mansion. Esther Cleveland was born on September 9, 1893.

4. During his presidency, the Clevelands purchased a home, Oak View, in the semirural section of Washington, between Wisconsin Avenue and Rock Creek. The address was 3542 Newark Street (between Thirty-Fifth and Thirty-Sixth Streets), in an area of Washington now called Cleveland Park. Oak View provided the Clevelands an escape to a more normal life and afforded Grover the opportunity to fish, one of his great passions.

5. Grover Cleveland lived out his days knowing that he'd served the American people to the best of his ability, with honor and integrity. He maintained international and national peace, labored on behalf of all people, fought for a clean government that served the people, not the pols, and executed his duties without guile or scheming for a future election.

Grover's overarching goal was being a steadfast warrior for the people and for providing equal opportunities for all. In 1933, Henry L. Mencken, editor of the periodical *The American Mercury*, commented, "[President Cleveland] was not averse to popularity, but he put it far below the approval of conscience. It is not likely that we shall see his like again, at least in the present age. The presidency is now closed to the kind of character that he had so abundantly."

In his later years, Grover often reflected on his halcyon youth in Fayetteville where he learned his bedrock values of honesty, loyalty, family, hard work, and how to have fun.

# APPENDICES

# I.

## AUTHOR'S NOTE: FACT VS. FICTION

GETTING TO KNOW these two special people was an absolute pleasure. Presenting them to you was my great honor. It was not only the people but also the time in which they lived and how they navigated their worlds that I found so compelling.

The core of my story about Matilda and Steve/Grover is based on fact. The framework of *High Bridge* is defined by the timelines of Matilda's and Grover's lives (appendices III and VII, respectively) and by their genealogies (appendices IV and VIII, respectively). Though the lives of Matilda and Grover as adults are well documented, details of their childhoods and adolescence are less certain. I took advantage of these ambiguities when I imagined this story.

Matilda and Steve may have been contemporaries in the Town of Manlius, including Fayetteville and High Bridge, in the late 1840s and early 1850s, but there is no evidence that they knew each other. That said, it is known that Matilda and Grover met in the Executive Mansion on March 25, 1888. Despite the uncertainty of when Matilda and Steve first met, the depictions of Fayetteville and the surroundings in *High Bridge* are accurate. This includes the locations, geographic relationships within Onondaga County (e.g., Cicero, Syracuse, Manlius, and Fayetteville), and features both natural and man-made.

I chose to place the newlywed Gages in the hamlet of High Bridge for three reasons. First, High Bridge was within commuting distance of

Syracuse where Henry gained his legal training. Second, High Bridge was a logical place from which I could integrate the Gages into the fabric of life in Fayetteville. Third, it provided opportunities for Matilda to meet and befriend Steve.

As for the two protagonists, let me first talk about Matilda. Destined to be a leader, Matilda was a headstrong visionary with clear, evolving ideas of what was wrong with American society, including the negative role the church played in America. She did not carp and complain. Instead, she dreamed of how to change the world and worked to achieve those aspirations. Her mentors were her parents. Her model was the Haudenosaunee. It is important to note that while Matilda was honorifically adopted into the Wolf Clan of the Mohawk, she neither lived with the Seneca or any of the Six Nations of the Haudenosaunee nor learned any Haudenosaunee language as depicted in the novel. That said, there was a real person named Edward Cornplanter, known as So-son-do-wa (meaning "deep night"), who became a Senecan chief.

As the historian, author, and soul of the fight for universal rights, Matilda was a person of action, not a fame-seeker. Matilda focused on her writings, including speeches delivered at women's rights conventions, contributions to *The National Citizen and Ballot Box* and *The Liberal Thinker* (periodicals she edited), many pamphlets, and books, including *Declaration of Rights for Women*, *History of Woman Suffrage, Volumes 1–3*, and her masterpiece: *Woman, Church, and State*. Collectively, these documents attest to Matilda's lifelong battle against learned ignorance.

Within days of getting married, on January 6, 1845, Matilda and her husband, Henry, left Cicero. In December 1854, the Gages moved to 210 East Genesee Street, Fayetteville, Matilda's primary residence for the rest of her life. Where the Gages lived between 1845 and 1854 is unclear. There is a consensus that they lived in Syracuse for a short time, but multiple sources state that the Gages lived in the greater Manlius community when their first four children were born. The challenge to understanding what "Manlius" means is that this name can refer to the town, the village of Manlius, or the portions of the Town of Manlius that were part of neither a village nor a hamlet, such as High Bridge.

Relative to the Gages, the history of Steve and his family is better documented. The Clevelands arrived in Fayetteville in 1841 when his father, Richard Falley Cleveland, was appointed as minister of the Fayetteville Presbyterian Church. At the time, Steve was merely four years old. Interviews of former teachers and students at the Fayetteville Academy attest to Steve's skills and reputation as a prankster. For example, the stories about ringing the church bells and putting a donkey atop Village Hall are true. There is, however, no explanation for how Steve got the beast up there—or, for that matter, how he got it down.

The Cleveland family remained in Fayetteville until 1850 when Reverend Cleveland took a new position in Clinton, New York. For a year, Steve attended the Clinton Liberal Institute. Coincidently, this was the same school that Matilda attended for two years (1842–1843). As money was tight for the Clevelands, fifteen-year-old Steve left the Institute and returned to Fayetteville to work at McVicar's Dry Goods Store for a small salary, room, and board. He was committed to contributing to his family's needs.

Steve's life pivoted in 1853. In March, he left Mr. McVicar's employ to help his oldest sister, Anna, prepare for her wedding and hopefully set himself on the path to attend Hamilton College. During the summer, Rev. Cleveland, who was overextended through his travel for work, was advised to take a less demanding job. In September, the Clevelands moved to Holland Patent, New York, where a frail Richard took a pulpit position. At the end of the month, he suddenly took ill and he died on October 1. After his father's death, Steve's hopes to attend college were dashed.

Having no prospects for work near Holland Patent, Steve joined his brother Will at the New York Institution for the Blind in New York City. In less than a year, he found that situation untenable and returned to Holland Patent in the summer of 1854. Again, finding no work opportunities in a small town, he set off west. This permanently ended his residence in central New York. Thus, Steve left Fayetteville before the Gages moved to 210 Genesee Street in December 1854, the address Matilda called home until she died in 1898.

While all members of the Joslyn, Gage, and Cleveland families and some of the villagers, (e.g., Doc Taylor and Mr. John McVicar [FYI, this name is sometimes written as MacViccar, McViccar, or McVicker]) were real people, the names and personalities of other villagers are fictionalized, though I did base their names on those of families that lived and owned businesses in Fayetteville. Most of these names were gleaned through documents (contemporary maps and newspapers) and graves in the Fayetteville Cemetery. Fictionalized folk include Sarah, Cherry, the Nashes, Barti, and Bertie.

Jermain Loguen, the officiant at Matilda and Henry's marriage, was a real and important person in mid-century Syracuse. Jarm was indeed a close friend of Matilda's father, Hezekiah. Both were active abolitionists and conductors on the Underground Railroad. Interestingly, Jarm's daughter, Sarah Loguen (m. Fraser), was one of the first women physicians in the United States and the fourth female African American physician in the United States. She attended the Syracuse University School of Medicine in 1873. Note that this school, established in Syracuse in 1871, traces its roots to the Geneva Medical College. This is yet one more of the ironic coincidences of life in that Hezekiah hoped that Matilda would attend the Geneva Medical College more than twenty years earlier. Incidentally, Geneva Medical College relented on its policy against enrolling a woman in 1847 (two years after the Joslyns lobbied for Matilda to attend). The college enrolled Elizabeth Blackwell, the first woman to receive a medical degree from an American medical school. Thus, it can be argued that Matilda and her father paved the way for the first woman to become a physician.

I would like to comment on the four borders at the tops of the pages. Each represents a different aspect of the story. Part 1 is headed by the symbol for the Haudenosaunee Confederacy that was so fundamental to the growth of Matilda Joslyn Gage. The band signifies the unity of the five original nations comprising the confederation. Atop the pages in part 2 is a line boat moving along the Erie Canal. The canal was an essential facet through Grover Cleveland's youth. As the preeminence of the railroad emerged, reliance on the canal tapered. Thus, the steam locomotive moves along the tracks at the top of pages in part 3. The last part of the book is headed by symbols for the four traditional elements: in order from left to right—fire, earth, air, and water. The star in the middle traditionally symbolizes the unity of these elements. Attaining the star here represents when great people like Matilda and Grover put the elements of their lives together.

Finally, I would like to address my introduction to and fascination with the lives of Matilda and Grover. As with many things in life, a chance coincidence became a life-changing event. Some twenty years ago, while walking through Fayetteville, I saw a historic marker identifying 210 West Genesee Street as the home of Matilda Joslyn Gage. Moments later, I walked by another sign pointing down a side street to the boyhood home of Grover Cleveland. I was intrigued. *Wow, Grover Cleveland lived here. What early, fundamental experiences shaped the life of a president? Who was this Gage woman? Did she know young Cleveland?* It was time to dig.

Soon after my walk, I became acquainted with Matilda the woman, dreamer, and worker for universal rights in a one-woman play presented by Sally Roesch Wagner. The more I learned, the more amazed I became. I felt compelled to (re)introduce Matilda and Grover to the world. If my novel has at least pricked your curiosity to learn more about these people and their times, then I am immensely pleased. Both Gage and Cleveland remind me of Michelle Obama's credo: "When they go low, we go high." Each of us needs to seek the high bridge.

# II.

## ACKNOWLEDGMENTS

TWENTY YEARS AGO, I was introduced to two remarkable yet largely forgotten people, Matilda and Grover, who once lived in the village near my home. They have been whirring in my head ever since. It is my honor to return them to our collective consciousness. Carrying this novel through the processes of ideation, writing, recrafting, more recrafting, and finally publication resulted from the support of many.

In grade school, I was taught the importance of grammar and syntax. While diagramming sentences was a chore, I learned the roles and powers of words and of sentence and paragraph structure. Writing remained a largely mechanical activity, until my senior year in high school when I took English with Rex Miller, who also served as my tennis coach. He pushed me to understand the written word, an author's intent, and impact beyond the words. Coach Miller planted the seed that I could communicate through my writing, whether I was accurately relating facts in nonfiction or weaving compelling stories in poetry or prose. I took those lessons and applied them for decades in copious scientific reports and now in my first effort at fiction.

While writing and editing are largely solitary processes, these arts are not one-way propositions. An audience is a necessity. A cogent final product depends upon readers and their thoughts. That is, drafting a piece is like the proverbial tree falling in the woods that needs an ear to be heard. I received invaluable feedback from members of critique groups in East Greenbush, New York, and Sunderland, MA. They pored over my rough manuscript, offered unvarnished, helpful comments, and sent me back to my desk to create, recreate, and refashion. The camaraderie and support of these groups were foundational. Further, I cannot say enough for the support of the Eastern Up! Chapter of the Society for Children's Book Writers and Illustrators. It is the model of an informative, supportive writers' group.

When I thought my story was fully sequenced and my prose was properly polished, maybe even finished, I sent it off to editors for their stamps of approval. Little did I know. These editors (John Briggs, Eileen Heyes, and Robert Waters) returned my manuscript with innumerable comments, corrections, and suggestions. (So much for diagramming sentences and relying on Strunk and White's *Elements of Style*. I was amazed that what was in my head was not what was written on the page.) Ideas needed to be added and fleshed out, prose needed to be edited, voice clarified, and passages added. Despite the manuscript growing nearly 25 percent, the story is paradoxically tighter. I am grateful for their insight, input, and guidance.

As the creative part of the project sunset, the production and dissemination of the book was taken over by John Koehler and Mary Bisbee-Beek, respectively. My previous life as an educator neither demanded, tapped, nor developed my abilities at self-promotion. Indeed, such skills were disparaged. These two people helped me get out of my own way in an effort to get *High Bridge* into your hands.

Likewise, I thank you, the reader. Without you, there is no story. A book sitting on a shelf is silent. It has no impact. This story must be read to appreciate the gifts, insights, and lessons that Matilda and Grover left us as we continue our work toward a more perfect union.

A final thought: I grew up in a small town like Cicero and Fayetteville. Most who lived there were White families. When I was not in school or doing chores, I filled my days playing baseball and board games. I was raised by a strong, single mother who was interested in others, was guided by her curiosity, and coped with the hand she was dealt. She was a teacher who devoted herself to her young Black students in Washington Heights, New York, championing opportunities for those who had few, and imbuing in me an aspiration for equity, fairness, and justice. I dedicate this book in her memory.

# III.

## TIMELINE OF
## MATILDA JOSLYN GAGE'S LIFE

**1826** Matilda Electa Joslyn born to Hezekiah Joslyn and Helen Leslie Joslyn, 8560 Brewerton Road, Cicero, New York, March 24, 1826

**1842–1843** Studied at the Clinton Liberal Institute, beginning January 3, 1842; completed two-year course, December 20, 1843

**1845** Married Henry Hill Gage, Cicero, New York, January 6, 1845

**1845** Matilda and Henry moved to Syracuse, New York, January 8, 1845, and then to Manlius, New York, August 1845

**1845** Helen Leslie Gage born in Manlius, New York, November 3, 1845; died, Winona, MN, May 18, 1933

**1848** Thomas Clarkson Gage born in Manlius, New York, July 18, 1848; died, Aberdeen, SD, October 19, 1938

**1849** Charles Henry Gage born in Manlius, New York, October 7, 1849; died, Manlius, New York, January 8, 1850

**1850** Risked serving six months in prison and a fine of $1,000 under Fugitive Slave Law (passed September 18, 1850) for offering her home to assist runaway slaves

**1851** Julia Louise Gage born in Manlius, New York, April 21, 1851; died, Fargo, North Dakota, March 6, 1931

| 1852 | First public address on women's rights delivered at the third National Woman's Rights Convention, Syracuse, New York, September 8–10, 1852 |

**1852** First public address on women's rights delivered at the third National Woman's Rights Convention, Syracuse, New York, September 8–10, 1852

**1854** Moved to 210 East Genesee Street, Fayetteville, New York, December 30, 1854

**1861** Maud Gage born in Fayetteville, New York, March 27, 1861; died, Los Angeles, CA, March 6, 1953

**1869** Co-founded the National Woman Suffrage Association

**1870** Adopted into Mohawk nation, given the honorary name Ka-ron-ien-ha-wi ("She-who-holds-the-sky")

**1870–1890** Wrote pamphlets: *Woman as Inventor* (1870), *Woman's Rights Catechism* (1871), *Who Planned the Tennessee Campaign of 1862* (1880), and *The Dangers of the Hour* (1890)

**1873** Defended Susan B. Anthony when she was tried for voting in the national election of 1872

**1875** Testified before US Congress in favor of a women's suffrage bill

**1875–1876** Elected president, National Woman Suffrage Association, decades holding positions as vice president and member of the executive committee

**1875–1879** President, New York Suffrage Association

**1876** Drafted *Declaration of Rights for Women* with Elizabeth Cady Stanton; presented on July 4 at Philadelphia Centennial Exposition

**1878–1881** Edited *The National Citizen and Ballot Box*

**1881–1886** Published *History of Woman Suffrage* (Vol. 1, 1881; Vol. 2, 1882; and Vol. 3, 1886) co-written and co-edited with Susan B. Anthony and Elizabeth Cady Stanton

**1884** Henry Hill Gage died, Fayetteville, New York, September 16, 1884

| | |
|---|---|
| **1887–1888** | Maud Gage Baum and L. Frank Baum moved into 210 East Genesee Street, Fayetteville, New York |
| **1888** | Honored at the Executive Mansion by President Grover Cleveland and First Lady Frances Folsom Cleveland, March 25, 1888 |
| **1890–1898** | Founder and president, Woman's National Liberal Union |
| **1890–1898** | Editor, *The Liberal Thinker* |
| **1893** | Published *Woman, Church, and State*, January 1, 1893 |
| **1893–1898** | Moved to Chicago, IL, semiannually to live with Maud and Frank |
| **1898** | Died, 1667 North Humboldt Boulevard, Chicago, IL (cremains buried in Fayetteville Cemetery), March 18, 1898 (on Grover Cleveland's sixty-first birthday) |

# IV.

## GAGE FAMILY TREE

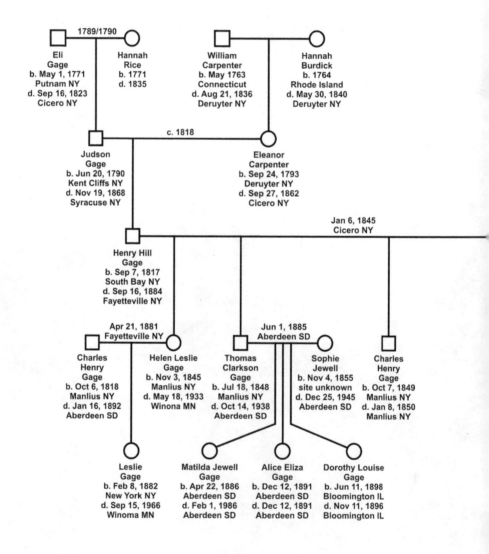

**Eli Gage**
b. May 1, 1771
Putnam NY
d. Sep 16, 1823
Cicero NY

1789/1790

**Hannah Rice**
b. 1771
d. 1835

**William Carpenter**
b. May 1763
Connecticut
d. Aug 21, 1836
Deruyter NY

**Hannah Burdick**
b. 1764
Rhode Island
d. May 30, 1840
Deruyter NY

c. 1818

**Judson Gage**
b. Jun 20, 1790
Kent Cliffs NY
d. Nov 19, 1868
Syracuse NY

**Eleanor Carpenter**
b. Sep 24, 1793
Deruyter NY
d. Sep 27, 1862
Cicero NY

Jan 6, 1845
Cicero NY

**Henry Hill Gage**
b. Sep 7, 1817
South Bay NY
d. Sep 16, 1884
Fayetteville NY

Apr 21, 1881
Fayetteville NY

Jun 1, 1885
Aberdeen SD

**Charles Henry Gage**
b. Oct 6, 1818
Manlius NY
d. Jan 16, 1892
Aberdeen SD

**Helen Leslie Gage**
b. Nov 3, 1845
Manlius NY
d. May 18, 1933
Winona MN

**Thomas Clarkson Gage**
b. Jul 18, 1848
Manlius NY
d. Oct 14, 1938
Aberdeen SD

**Sophie Jewell**
b. Nov 4, 1855
site unknown
d. Dec 25, 1945
Aberdeen SD

**Charles Henry Gage**
b. Oct 7, 1849
Manlius NY
d. Jan 8, 1850
Manlius NY

**Leslie Gage**
b. Feb 8, 1882
New York NY
d. Sep 15, 1966
Winoma MN

**Matilda Jewell Gage**
b. Apr 22, 1886
Aberdeen SD
d. Feb 1, 1986
Aberdeen SD

**Alice Eliza Gage**
b. Dec 12, 1891
Aberdeen SD
d. Dec 12, 1891
Aberdeen SD

**Dorothy Louise Gage**
b. Jun 11, 1898
Bloomington IL
d. Nov 11, 1896
Bloomington IL

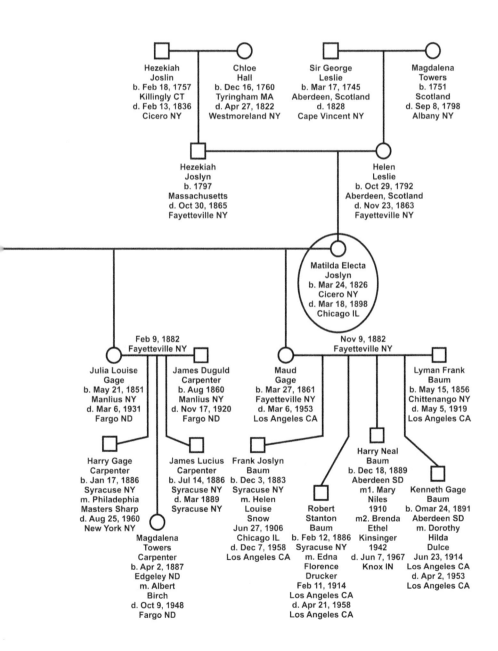

# V.

## MATILDA'S RECIPES

TEXTS AND PAGE citations are from *The Woman Suffrage Cook Book*, compiled by Hattie A. Burr (1886) Mudge, Boston
[Measurements and directions are described as in the 1886 book, but they are presented in a more contemporary style.]

### To Broil White Fish [page 29]

Among the fish of our great lakes, the white fish hold the highest rank with epicures. Those of Superior, where the water is never warmer than 40°, are the best, because of the hardness and firmness of their flesh. Upon the shores of this great inland sea I learned—a Chippewa Indian's receipt—that, to have this fish in perfection, it must be covered while broiling.

**Directions:**

1. Having prepared your fish, salting it somewhat, place it on the gridiron over the fire (of course flesh side down), and cover it with the dripping-pan.

2. When cooked upon this side and turned for the slight finish requisite, with a round-ended knife (to avoid breaking the flesh)

press down a bit of nice butter here and there over the fish.

3. It is then ready for the table, and should be eaten at once.

A white fish thus cooked tastes quite unlike one prepared by ordinary methods.

## Baked Tomatoes [page 44]

**Ingredients:**

Select enough medium-sized, perfectly ripe tomatoes to fill a deep baking tin.

**Directions:**

1. Peel them, scoop out the stem end—placing them in the tin this side up.

2. Fill the place with a small piece of nice butter, and cover so thickly with sugar their color is hidden.

3. Bake in a good oven two and a half or three hours, being careful not to burn; when half cooked turn them over.

**Notes:**

a. If rightly baked, the tomatoes, when done, will be imbedded in a rich, luscious jelly.

b. If you do not succeed the first time, try again; they are worth the trouble.

c. Remember not to be sparing of sugar.

# Old-Time Baked Indian Pudding [pages 61-62]

## Ingredients:
   3 pints sweet milk
   2 T yellow cornmeal
   1 small egg
   1 T molasses
   ¾ c sugar
   1½ tsp grated ginger
   1 tsp cinnamon
   ⅓ small nutmeg
   ½ c thick, sour cream

## Directions:

4. Put half the milk over the fire with a sprinkling of salt; as soon as it comes to a boil scatter the meal quickly and evenly in by hand.

5. Remove immediately from the fire to a dish, stir in the cold milk, the egg well-beaten, the spices, sweetening, and sour cream.

6. Bake three hours, having a hot oven the first half hour, a moderate one the remainder of the time.

7. Eat with sweet cream. Use no sauce, but sweet cream or butter.

## Notes:

If rightly made and rightly baked, this pudding is delicious, but four things must be remembered as requisite.

a. The pudding must be thin enough to run when put in the oven.

b. The egg must be small, or if large, but two-thirds used for a pudding of the above size.

c. The sour cream must not be omitted (but in case one has no cream, the same quantity of sour milk with a piece of butter the size of a small butternut can be substituted).

d. The baking must be especially attended to. Many a good receipt is ruined in the cooking, but if the directions are carefully followed, this pudding will be quavery when done, and if any is left, a jelly when cold.

## Plums to Eat with Meats [pages 110-111]

**Ingredients:**

½ lb. sugar

1 lb. common small blue plums

**Directions:**

1. Place plums and sugar alternatively in a two-quart stone jar until full, plums at the bottom, a layer of sugar on top.

2. Set the jar in an oven of bread heat, leaving the door open.

3. Bake for several days, keeping watch they do not burn.

4. When of a preserve-like consistency, take from the oven, cover them well and keep in your sweetmeat closet.

**Notes:**

a. Plums thus prepared have a peculiar flavor of their own, and are especially nice with roasts. It is best to start about three jars at once, removing all to one jar as they bake away.

b.  The oven need not be kept at bread heat after the plums have begun to cook thoroughly; the time of baking is usually a week, but largely depends upon the heat and care given them.

c.  The plums to be used are not the damsons, but the common blue variety, ripening early in September.

# VI.

## QUOTES OF MATILDA JOSLYN GAGE

M ATILDA JOSLYN GAGE wrote and lectured extensively. Thus, there is a trove of Gage quotes. Here are but a few that still ring true.

### on Women's Rights

"Enforced motherhood is a crime against the body of the mother and the soul of the child."

"Fear not any attempt to frown down the revolution already commenced; nothing is a more fertile aid of reform, than an attempt to check it; work on!"

"The law of motherhood should be entirely under woman's control."

"Down through the Christian centuries to this nineteenth, nowhere has the marital union of the sexes been one in which the woman has had control over her own body."

## on Women's Roles

"While so much is said of the inferior intellect of woman, it is by a strange absurdity conceded that very many eminent men owe their station in life to their mothers."

"A rebel! How glorious the name sounds when applied to woman. Oh, rebellious woman, to you the world looks in hope. Upon you has fallen the glorious task of bringing liberty to the earth and all the inhabitants thereof."

"My blood always boils at advice from a man in regard to a family. That, at least, should be the province of woman alone. To say when and how often she chooses to go down into the valley of the shadow of death, to give the world another child, should be hers alone to say."

"History is full of wrongs done the wife by legal robbery on the part of the husband. I hesitate not to assert that most of this crime of child murder, abortion, infanticide, lies at the door of the male sex."

"Woman is learning for herself that not self-sacrifice, but self development, is her first duty in life; and this, not primarily for the sake of others but that she may become fully herself."

"It is sometimes better to be a dead man than a live woman."

## on Democracy

"Unless the American people rouse to instant action we shall soon find our government turned into a monarchy, church, and State united and the people no better than serfs."

"Non-use of rights does not destroy them."

"When all humanity works for humanity, when the life-business of men and women becomes one united partnership in all matters which concern each, when neither sex, race, color, or previous condition is held as a bar to the exercise of human faculties, the world will hold in its hands the promise of a millennium which will work out its own fulfillment."

"There is a word sweeter than mother, home or heaven. That word is liberty."

"For one hundred and fourteen years we have seen our country gradually advancing in recognition of broader freedom, fewer restrictions upon personal liberty, and the peoples of all nations looking towards us as the great exemplar of political and religious freedom. But of late a rapidly increasing tendency has been shown towards the destruction of our civil liberties."

"We are confronted by the fact that our form of government is undergoing a radical change, with a well organized body greedy for power pressing to that end so that centralization instead of diffused power has overcome the aim and intent of a large body of people."

"The danger menacing our country does not lie with the foreigners, nor the Anarchists, nor in municipal mismanagement. Free institutions are jeopardized because the country is false to its principles in the case of one-half of its citizens."

## on Christianity

"The careful student of history will discover that Christianity has been of very little value in advancing civilization, but has done a great deal toward retarding it."

"The Christian theory of the sacredness of the Bible has been at the cost of the world's civilization."

"Both church and state claiming to be of divine origin have assumed divine right of man over woman; while church and state have thought for man, man has assumed the right to think for woman."

"It has not been without bitter resistance by the clergy that woman's property and educational rights have advanced. Woman's anti-slavery work, her temperance work, her demand for personal rights, for political equality, for religious freedom and every step of kindred character has met with opposition from the church as a body and from the clergy as exponents of its views."

"The most stupendous system of organized robbery known has been that of the church towards woman, a robbery that has not only taken her self-respect but all rights of person; the fruits of her own industry; her opportunities of education; the exercise of her judgment, her own conscience, her own will."

"The soul must support its own supremacy or die."

"Women should unite upon a platform of opposition to the teaching and aim of that ever most unscrupulous enemy of freedom—the Church."

"Do not allow the Church or State to govern your thought or dictate your judgment."

# VII.

## TIMELINE OF STEPHEN GROVER CLEVELAND'S LIFE

**1837**   Stephen Grover Cleveland born to Richard Falley Cleveland and Ann Neal Cleveland, 207 Bloomfield Avenue, Caldwell, New Jersey, March 18, 1837

**1841**   Cleveland family moved to Fayetteville, New York; Richard Cleveland appointed minister at Fayetteville Presbyterian Church, summer 1841

**1850**   Cleveland family moved to Clinton, New York

**1850**   Visited uncle, Lewis W. Allen, in Buffalo, New York, early fall 1850

**1850**   Returned to Clinton and attended Clinton Liberal Institute, Hamilton, New York, winter 1850

**1851**   Dropped out of school to support family, returned to Fayetteville, New York, worked as apprentice at John McVicar's General Store, fall 1851

**1853**   Moved with his family to Holland Patent, New York; about September 10, 1853

**1853**   Richard Cleveland died, Holland Patent, New York, October 1, 1853

| | |
|---|---|
| **1853** | With the help of his older brother, William, Stephen moved to New York, New York, to work as an assistant teacher at the New York Institution for the Blind, fall 1853 |
| **1854** | Quit teaching post, summer 1854 |
| **1854** | Stayed in Holland Patent, New York through winter 1854–1855 |
| **1855** | Left for Cleveland, Ohio; stopped in Buffalo to visit uncle and decided to stay in Buffalo, New York, May 21, 1855 |
| **1855** | Accepted apprenticeship with uncle and began study of law in the office of Rogers, Bowes, and Rogers, Buffalo New York. Apparently, this is when he began to be referred to by his middle name, Grover. |
| **1859** | Admitted to New York Bar and joined law practice of Rogers, Bowes, and Rogers, May 1859 |
| **1862** | Started law practice with Oscar Folsom |
| **1863** | Served as democratic supervisor of ward in Buffalo, New York |
| **1863–1865** | Served as assistant district attorney of Erie County, New York |
| **1871–1873** | Served as sheriff of Buffalo, New York |
| **1882–1883** | Served as mayor of Buffalo, New York |
| **1883–1885** | Served as governor of New York |
| **1885–1889** | Served as twenty-second president of the United States, inauguration March 4, 1885 |
| **1886** | Signed the Presidential Succession Act, January 19, 1886 |
| **1886** | Married Frances Clara Folsom, the first marriage in the Executive Mansion, June 2, 1886 |

**1886** Statue of Liberty gifted to the United States by France and dedicated by President Cleveland in New York, New York, October 28, 1886

**1887** Signed Interstate Commerce Act, the first federal law to regulate railroads and other transportation, February 4, 1887

**1887** Signed the Dawes Act, which divvied Native American tribal lands into separate allotments, February 8, 1887

**1888** Established the Department of Labor, June 13, 1888

**1888** Renewed the Chinese Exclusion Act restricting Chinese immigration to the US, October 8, 1888

**1888** Despite winning popular vote, lost re-election for president to Benjamin Harrison, November 6, 1888

**1891** Ruth Cleveland (i.e., "Baby Ruth") born in New York, New York, October 3, 1891; died, Princeton, New Jersey, January 7, 1904

**1893–1897** Panic of 1893, January 1893 to June 1897, i.e., a time spanning from before Grover Cleveland took office and ending shortly after he finished his term

**1893–1897** Served as twenty-fourth president of the United States, inauguration March 4, 1893

**1893** Esther Cleveland born in Washington , first birth in the Executive Mansion, September 9, 1893; died, Tamworth, New Hampshire, June 25, 1980

**1894** The Pullman Strike; used the first federal injunction to end a strike, May 11, 1894 to July 20, 1894

**1894** Established Labor Day as federal holiday, June 28, 1894

**1894** Recognized Republic of Hawaii, July 4, 1894

**1895**   Marion Cleveland born in Buzzards Bay, Massachusetts, July 7, 1895; died, Baltimore, Maryland, March 10, 1960

**1896**   Utah joined the Union as the forty-fifth state, January 4, 1896

**1897**   Richard Folsom Cleveland born in Princeton, NJ, October 28, 1897; died, Baltimore, Maryland, January 10, 1974

**1903**   Francis Grover Cleveland born in Buzzards Bay, Massachusetts, July 18, 1903; died, Wolfeboro, New Hampshire, November 8, 1995

**1908**   Died, 15 Hodge Road, Princeton, New Jersey, buried in Princeton Cemetery, June 24, 1908

# VIII.

## CLEVELAND FAMILY TREE

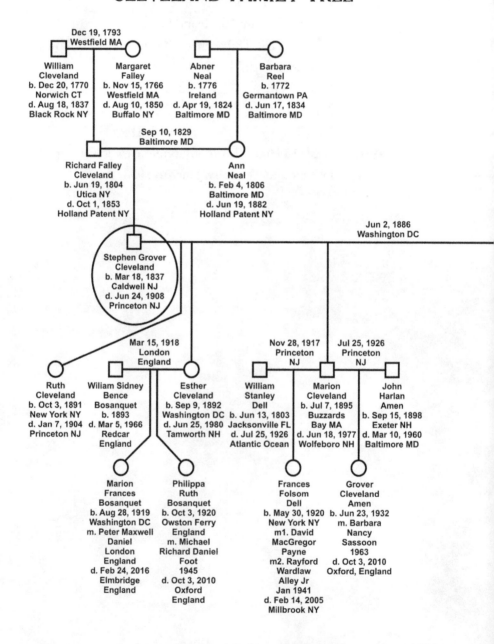

Dec 19, 1793
Westfield MA

William
Cleveland
b. Dec 20, 1770
Norwich CT
d. Aug 18, 1837
Black Rock NY

Margaret
Falley
b. Nov 15, 1766
Westfield MA
d. Aug 10, 1850
Buffalo NY

Abner
Neal
b. 1776
Ireland
d. Apr 19, 1824
Baltimore MD

Barbara
Reel
b. 1772
Germantown PA
d. Jun 17, 1834
Baltimore MD

Sep 10, 1829
Baltimore MD

Richard Falley
Cleveland
b. Jun 19, 1804
Utica NY
d. Oct 1, 1853
Holland Patent NY

Ann
Neal
b. Feb 4, 1806
Baltimore MD
d. Jun 19, 1882
Holland Patent NY

Jun 2, 1886
Washington DC

Stephen Grover
Cleveland
b. Mar 18, 1837
Caldwell NJ
d. Jun 24, 1908
Princeton NJ

Mar 15, 1918
London
England

Nov 28, 1917
Princeton
NJ

Jul 25, 1926
Princeton
NJ

Ruth
Cleveland
b. Oct 3, 1891
New York NY
d. Jan 7, 1904
Princeton NJ

Wiliam Sidney
Bence
Bosanquet
b. 1893
d. Mar 5, 1966
Redcar
England

Esther
Cleveland
b. Sep 9, 1892
Washington DC
d. Jun 25, 1980
Tamworth NH

William
Stanley
Dell
b. Jun 13, 1803
Jacksonville FL
d. Jul 25, 1926
Atlantic Ocean

Marion
Cleveland
b. Jul 7, 1895
Buzzards
Bay MA
d. Jun 18, 1977
Wolfeboro NH

John
Harlan
Amen
b. Sep 15, 1898
Exeter NH
d. Mar 10, 1960
Baltimore MD

Marion
Frances
Bosanquet
b. Aug 28, 1919
Washington DC
m. Peter Maxwell
Daniel
London
England
d. Feb 24, 2016
Elmbridge
England

Philippa
Ruth
Bosanquet
b. Oct 3, 1920
Owston Ferry
England
m. Michael
Richard Daniel
Foot
1945
d. Oct 3, 2010
Oxford
England

Frances
Folsom
Dell
b. May 30, 1920
New York NY
m1. David
MacGregor
Payne
m2. Rayford
Wardlaw
Alley Jr
Jan 1941
d. Feb 14, 2005
Millbrook NY

Grover
Cleveland
Amen
b. Jun 23, 1932
m. Barbara
Nancy
Sassoon
1963
d. Oct 3, 2010
Oxford, England

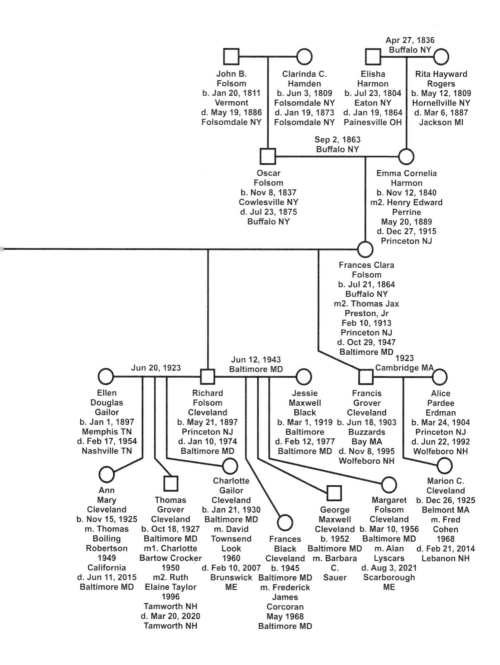

# IX.

## QUOTES OF GROVER CLEVELAND

As a politician, Grover Cleveland gave many speeches, and he was an inveterate letter writer. Below are some of the many quotes attributed to him.

### Inspirational Quotes

"Above all, tell the truth."

"A government for the people must depend for its success on the intelligence, the morality, the justice, and the interest of the people themselves."

"Unswerving loyalty to duty, constant devotion to truth, and a clear conscience will overcome every discouragement and surely lead the way to usefulness and high achievement."

"A truly American sentiment recognizes the dignity of labor and the fact that honor lies in honest toil."

"I would rather the man who presents something for my consideration subject me to a zephyr of truth and a gentle breeze of responsibility rather than blow me down with a curtain of hot wind."

## on Peace

"It is a condition which confronts us—not a theory."

"Communism is a hateful thing, and a menace to peace and organized government."

"After an existence of nearly twenty years of almost innocuous desuetude, these laws are brought forth."

"No man has ever yet been hanged for breaking the spirit of a law."

## on Government

"He mocks the people who propose that the government shall protect the rich and that they, in turn, will care for the laboring poor."

"I have considered the pension list of the republic a roll of honor."

"Loyalty to the principles upon which our Government rests positively demands that the equality before the law which it guarantees to every citizen should be justly and in good faith conceded in all parts of the land."

"I have tried so hard to do right."

"What is the use of being elected or re-elected, unless you stand for something?"

"The friendliness and charity of our countrymen can always be relied upon to relieve their fellow citizens in misfortune. This has been repeatedly and quite lately demonstrated. Federal aid in such cases encourages the expectation of paternal care on the part of the Government and weakens the sturdiness of our national character, while it prevents the indulgence among our people of that kindly sentiment and conduct which strengthens the bonds of a common brotherhood."

"Public officers are the servants and agents of the people, to execute the laws which the people have made."

"Officeholders are the agents of the people, not their masters."

"Your every voter, as surely as your chief magistrate, exercises a public trust."

"It is better to be defeated standing for a high principle than to run by committing subterfuge."

"The lessons of paternalism ought to be unlearned and the better lesson taught that while the people should patriotically and cheerfully support their government, its functions do not include the support of the people."

## on Politics

"Party honesty is party expediency."

"Minds do not act together in public; they simply stick together; and when their private activities are resumed, they fly apart again."

"The ship of democracy, which has weathered all storms, may sink through the mutiny of those on board."

"A cause worth fighting for is worth fighting for to the end."

"The United States is not a nation to which peace is a necessity."

"Sometimes I wake at night in the White House and rub my eyes and wonder if it is not all a dream."

## on People

"The laboring classes constitute the main part of our population. They should be protected in their efforts peaceably to assert their rights when endangered by aggregated capital and all statutes on this subject should recognize the care of the State for honest toil and be framed with a view of improving the condition of the workingman."

"Patriotism is no substitute for a sound currency."

"Let us look for guidance to the principles of true democracy, which are enduring because they are right, and invincible because they are just."

"Government resting upon the will and universal suffrage of the people has no anchorage except in the people's intelligence."

"Someday I will be better remembered."

"Sensible and responsible women do not want to vote. The relative positions to be assumed by man and woman in the working out of our civilization were assigned long ago by a higher intelligence than ours."

## on the Presidency

"In the scheme of our national government, the presidency is preeminently the people's office."

"I have a Congress on my hands."

"In calm water every ship has a good captain."

"I am President of all the people, good, bad, or indifferent, and as long as my opinions are known, ought perhaps to keep myself out of their squabbles."

## on Religion

"All must admit that the reception of the teachings of Christ results in the purest patriotism, in the most scrupulous fidelity to public trust, and in the best type of citizenship."

"And let us not trust to human effort alone, but humbly acknowledging the power and goodness of Almighty God, who presides over the destiny of nations, and who has at all times been revealed in our country's history, let us invoke His aid and His blessings upon our labors."

"I know there is a Supreme Being who rules the affairs of men and whose goodness and mercy have always followed the American people, and I know He will not turn from us now if we humbly and reverently seek His powerful aid."